Motorized sampans ful[...]**es overhanging the banks!**

With a puff of dirty bl[...] anti-tank rocket slammed into the tail patrol boat's wheelhouse, detonating against the steering box. The PBR stopped dead in the water. The enemy soldiers shouted victoriously and closed on the stricken boat.

In the stern, Corky laid down on the trigger of the M-60. His rounds tore into the sampans, but it didn't slow them. There were too many, packed with gooks, their AKs blazing. Return fire hit all around him, splintering the fiberglass hull.

"Behind you!" Farmer screamed, swinging his M-16 around. A quick burst sent an NVA soldier over backward. More gooks swarmed up from a sampan that had snuck up on their far side. "Sonofabitch!" he screamed.

On the lead boat, Treat Brody raced for the bridge. "Captain Powers, we got to go back and help them!" he yelled, pointing down the river.

Powers hesitated. Brody started into the wheelhouse. He was going after Corky and Farmer if he had to drive the PBR himself!

Other books in the **Chopper 1** series:

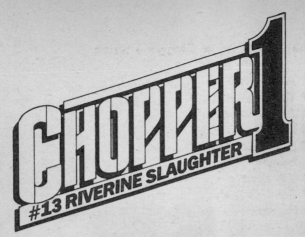

CHOPPER 1
#13 RIVERINE SLAUGHTER

Jack Hawkins

IVY BOOKS • NEW YORK

Ivy Books
Published by Ballantine Books

Produced by Butterfield Press, Inc.
133 Fifth Avenue
New York, New York 10003

Library of Congress Catalog Card Number: 88-62397

ISBN: 0-8041-0317-8

Manufactured in the United States of America

First Edition: March 1989

To Patric and all the other Swabbies who went far from blue water to fight in Vietnam.

And, as always, to Claudia.

AUTHOR'S NOTE:

In Vietnam the waterways were one of the country's major highway networks and it was necessary to control the traffic along hundreds of miles of rivers, streams, and canals leading deep into the interior of the country. Not since the American Civil War had the United States Navy been required to operate in a riverine combat environment.

In 1966, this need was met with what became known as Task Force 116 of the Brown Water Navy, code-named Game Warden. Miles from the blue waters of the Pacific Ocean, sailors in small fiberglass-hulled patrol boats battled the VC and NVA for control of the more than 2,500 miles of in-country waterways.

Early in the deployment of the Riverine force, the Army joined up with the Navy to run combined operations in the Mekong Delta region in IV Corps. Army grunts provided extra firepower for the patrol boats and the ability to pursue the communists on the land. Army artillery and gunship units supported the operations with their firepower.

While most of the Riverine force was stationed in the Delta, there were rivers in other parts of the country, and the concept had proved so successful that the Riverine forces were expanded. In late 1967, Task Force Clearwater was established to control the Perfume and Cau Viet rivers in northern I Corps around the cities of Hue and Da Nang. Again Army troops as well as Marines teamed up with the Brown Water sailors to clear the rivers of VC and insure free civilian and military traffic.

In early January 1968, the First Air Cav Division headquarters and two of its brigades moved out of their old An Khe basecamp and relocated in southern I Corps in what was known as Operation Jeb Stuart. The purpose of the move was to free U.S. Marine forces which were needed to counter increased enemy activity in northern I Corps along the DMZ and in the vicinity of the Khe San basecamp.

Division Headquarters moved to Camp Evans, north of Hue, and 3rd-Brigade temporarily occupied the basecamp at Chu Lai. The First of the 7th Cav moved to Chu Lai as part of the Brigade move.

This book is a work of fiction about the Cav's activities during this time and the Riverine forces of Operation Clearwater. Other than well-known public and historical figures, all characters in this book are fictional. Any resemblance to actual persons living or dead is unintended and purely coincidental.

Jack Hawkins
Portland, Oregon
September 1988

CHAPTER 1

The Ho Chi Minh Trail in Laos

Green Beret Sergeant Jack Wilburn dropped to the ground, fighting to catch his breath. He scrambled into the heavy brush along the side of the faint trail and brought his CAR-15 up, sighting back the way he had come. Pulling two more loaded magazines from the bandolier around his neck, he laid them on the ground close at hand. He took his last hand grenade from his ammo pouch. Holding the spoon securely against the palm of his left hand, he pulled the pin.

The faint sounds of a man running down the path came to him. Wilburn held his fire. It was Bao, the Nung mercenary, the last of the other five men of Recon Team Sleeper. Bao came into view, looking over his shoulder. He ran bent over, his hand pressed against his side. He had taken a round.

The Green Beret sergeant waved the Nung off to the other side of the trail. The NVA tracking team were right on his heels. If they were going to get out of this alive, they had to take all of them out in one ambush. They were both too exhausted to run any further.

The American's finger tightened around the trigger of his CAR-15, the submachine-gun version of the M-16 rifle, which he held in his right hand. The grenade felt heavy in his left. He forced himself to slow his breathing. He had been running on adrenaline for so long that he felt light-headed, and the blood sang through his veins. He glanced across the trail. The Nung was completely hidden in the foliage.

When he looked back down the trail, a North Vietnamese point man had appeared. He crouched down to look for their footprints in the dirt. He got to his feet and slowly scanned the jungle before waving his comrades forward.

The soldiers who were tracking them were good, Wilburn had to admit. From the dark olive uniforms and equipment they wore, they had to be NVA regulars, fresh troops just down from North Vietnam. Troops who were new to jungle fighting tended to bunch up in the woods so they could keep their comrades in sight. As soon as the NVA point man found their foot prints ending, he would know they had moved off of the trail. But by that time, the rest of the gooks would have gotten into range. Wilburn was counting on all of them being close enough to be in the killing zone when he opened up.

He let the point man get closer and closer, and still he held his fire. Bao wouldn't shoot until he did, so he didn't have to worry. Back down the trail, four more NVA came into view. They were alert, but close together. One of them carried a radio on his back. That gook had to die first.

The point man had moved to a position only ten meters away, and approached the place where Wilburn and Bao had turned off. With a snap of his arm, the American lobbed the grenade. At the same instant, he ripped off a long burst from his CAR-15, aiming for the man with the radio.

The sudden shock of adrenaline racing through his veins made everything seem to appear in slow motion. His body went into overdrive to stay alive. From the corner of his eye, the Green Beret saw the point man bear down on him with his AK, bringing it up to fire. He didn't react. It was Bao's job to take out the point man.

The grenade was still hurtling through in the air when Bao's M-16 opened up on the point man. The NVA radio man took the burst of 5.56mm in his chest. He spun around and went down on his face just as the grenade exploded. Sergeant Wilburn burned through the remainder of the ammunition in his CAR, wiping out the other three NVA.

When the bolt of his CAR locked to the rear on an empty magazine, he punched the mag release, dropped the empty out, and slammed a fresh one in its place in one smooth movement. Hitting the bolt release, he came up on one knee and emptied it down the trail.

One of the NVA dove off the trail to return fire. Accurate fire. AK rounds tore through the brush around him. Wilburn went flat on his face and reloaded his sub-machine gun. He rolled over and came up again, the CAR blazing.

He was right on target. The AK fire stopped.

A sudden silence rang through the jungle. Sergeant Wilburn slowly got to his feet and looked down the trail. There was no movement. Motioning for the Nung to stay where he was, Wilburn cautiously walked into the open.

Four of the NVA were dead, their bodies sprawled on the trail. The fifth was still alive, gasping for breath, his hands clamped over a gaping belly wound. Wilburn calmly put a bullet in his head. After searching the bodies for documents, he picked up the fallen AK-47s, their magazine carriers, and the shot-up radio, then threw them into the brush.

Motioning for the Nung to cover him, the sergeant ran back down the trail for a hundred meters and ducked into the brush on one side again. He waited for several minutes to see if the tracking team had a backup, but the jungle was quiet. Wilburn finally got up and went back to the ambush site. It looked like they had finally shaken off the pursuing North Vietnamese.

He motioned for the Nung to move out again. They both desperately needed a couple of hours' rest, but if they were going to make it out of this mess, they had to get going while they still could. Bao parted the leaves in front of him and looked up with dark, pain-filled eyes. "No, *Trung Si* Jack," the Chinese hissed. "You go. I stay."

Wilburn looked into the weathered face of the old Nung jungle fighter. Tran Van Bao was in his forties and he had been killing communists longer than the young American had even been alive.

Bao was a veteran of the Kuomintans, and had fought both the Japanese and Mao's communists in World War II. After that, he had joined up with the French in North Vietnam to fight against Ho Chi Minh's communists. Now, at an age when most soldiers were retired, the wiry old Nung Chinese was in a U.S. Special Forces Roadrunner long-range recon team, keeping track of North Vietnamese activity along the Ho Chi Minh Trail in Laos.

Their mission had only been two days old when the six-man Recon Team had stumbled into something that they were not supposed to have seen — a new branch of the Ho Chi Minh Trail leading directly into the heart of South Vietnam. The newly built supply route was extensively guarded and Recon Team Sleeper had been caught in an ambush when they tried to get in closer to take a better look. The other American on the team and two of the four Nungs had died in the initial contact. The third Nung was killed fighting a rear-guard action when the North Vietnamese started after them.

Now, only Wilburn and Bao were left, and one of them had to make it back to Special Forces Command and Control North at Kontum to report what they had found. Their radio had been on the back of the other American, Don Gurney, when he had been gunned down in the first burst of fire. Wilburn had hated to leave Gurney and the other Nungs behind, but he'd had no choice. They had been so badly outgunned that their only chance had been to run for it.

He was not, however, going to leave Bao behind to die in the jungle and rot beside the trail. Not if there was any way at all that he could carry him out. The old warrior deserved a better fate than that.

"Let me see that wound," Wilburn said firmly.

The Nung took his hand from his side. Dark blood seeped from a jagged hole under his rib cage and stained the jacket of his black and green tiger stripe suit.

Bao had been hit by a ricochet and there was no exit hole. The deformed round was still lodged in his body. That could be good or bad. There was no way to know how much internal damage it had done until Wilburn could get back to a medic.

"You're not staying behind, old man," Wilburn replied softly. "You're coming back with me. You owe me too much money."

The Nung smiled and shook his head. Poker was one of the few passions that he had left, but he was not very good at it. "No, you tell *dai uy* to pay you from my funeral money. It is time that Bao goes to join the Great-Grandfather General."

Wilburn didn't like to hear the old warrior talk about the Great-Grandfather General. The Nung Chinese had first come into Vietnam well over a thousand years ago with the army of a Chinese general who had conquered the country for his emperor. When the war was over, they stayed in Vietnam and became farmers.

As the generations passed, the Nungs grew rice and raised pigs, but remained warriors at heart. Each time a new enemy appeared, the Nungs raised their black flags, took up their arms, and quickly regained their reputation as the fiercest warriors in all of Indochina. They paid homage to the spirit of the Chinese general who had brought them to this land, and they prayed to him for success in battle as well as luck in their lives. They also believed that when they died, they would go to join his heavenly army.

The Green Beret cursed under his breath and ripped open a field dressing packet. Bao raised his tiger suit jacket and

Wilburn tied the bandage around the smaller man's waist. Dark blood slowly seeped around the edge of the dressing.

"Can you walk?"

The Nung drew his M-16 to him. "Bao can walk, *Trung si.*" Stubborn pride shone through the pain in his eyes. He was wounded, but he was a warrior and he had been wounded before.

Wilburn shrugged his rucksack off. "Give me your pack." He quickly went through both of their packs, taking only the extra ammunition, a few freeze-dried LRRP ration packs and their grenades. He slung two bandoliers of M-16 magazines around Bao's neck and clipped an extra canteen to his field belt. He pushed the rucks back into the brush, but not far enough that they were hidden.

He took two M-26 hand grenades from the side loops on Bao's rucksack. He stuffed under the first pack, making sure that the spoon was securely held down by the weight of the pack. Then he carefully worked the pin loose. The grenade was armed. Whoever found the pack was in for a nasty surprise. When the ruck was moved, the spoon would fly off the grenade fuse. Five seconds later, it would detonate. He quickly booby-trapped the other pack the same way.

He took a quick drink from his canteen and got to his feet. "Okay, old man." He held his hand out to Bao. "Let's go."

The old Nung looked up at the young American Special Forces sergeant standing in front of him. Wilburn was short and stocky, not as tall as many of the Americans were. His light brown hair was cropped short, Airborne style, and he was young. At twenty-one years old, Wilburn was the youngest Green Beret in the army. At first, Bao had had a difficult time taking Wilburn seriously because of his age. Once he saw what lay behind his smiling, faded blue eyes, he knew that this young long-nose was a warrior. He had the bright, glittering eyes of a demon god.

Bao painfully rose to his feet. "I will go as far as I can, *Trung si*. Then I will stay behind and kill *cong* so you can get away."

"We are going to fly home, old man, so you don't have to walk so far."

"How are we going to talk to the flying machine? We have no radio."

Wilburn smiled. "I know of an airstrip to the west. We will go there."

"But that is where the *cong* are."

"Yes, but they will not be expecting us in Laos. They will expect us to try to go back into Vietnam."

"Ah, so." The Nung nodded. "You are wise for one so young, *Trung si* Jack."

"If I'm so fucking wise," Wilburn snorted, "what the fuck am I doing here?"

The Nung smiled knowingly. "Ah, but you like it here, *Trung si*."

Wilburn shuddered to think that the old man might be right. "Come on," he said gruffly, "We've got a good four-day hump ahead of us."

CHAPTER 2

Firebase Lasher, Outside Chu Lai

"This place sucks heavily!" PFC Ralph Burns cursed, looking around the small, dusty firebase straddling QL1, the Vietnamese national highway that ran along the coastline. Lasher was a company-sized firebase protecting the road leading north to Da Nang, barely big enough to hold the section of three 105mm howitzers and tents for the artillerymen and grunts who manned it. There was no shower, no mess hall, and only one latrine. Even the perimeter bunkers were primitive.

"Happy fucking New Year, Farmer." Spec-4 Juan Cordova, who shared bunker guard duty with Burns, laughed and leaned against his M-60 machine gun. "This is a great place to spend 1968."

"Fuck you, Corky."

Ralph Burns didn't like his new home at all. His unit, the Aero Rifle Platoon of Echo Company, First Battalion of the 7th Cav, General Custer's old regiment, had recently been displaced from their old home base, Camp Radcliff at An Khe. Most of the First Air Cavalry Division was transferred north to take over the southern part of I Corps, freeing the marines to move against NVA units that were streaming across the DMZ into South Vietnam. Basing Echo Company in Chu Lai and sticking the Aero Rifles out on a remote firebase was part of that scheme.

PFC Burns was a kid from a backwoods potato farm outside of Pocatello, Idaho. A skinny redhead, he looked like he should have been in a Boy Scout troop, not an ass-kicking grunt outfit like the Aero Rifle Platoon. Back in Idaho, Burns had had an intense curiosity about the world beyond his family's plowed fields. He had spent much of his time in the city library looking at photographs of exotic places in *National Geographic* magazines. That curiosity had driven him to the Army recruiter's office in Boise the day after he turned eighteen. The way he had figured it, there was no sense in spending the rest of his life looking at pictures in magazines when he could see the world and get paid for it at the same time. He was sick and tired of looking at nothing but potato fields stretching as far as the eye could see.

Except for greatly expanding his vocabulary, Farmer's first six months in Vietnam hadn't changed him very much. He still had his insatiable curiosity intact and he still looked like he should have been in the Boy Scouts. He had also seen enough of Vietnam to know a shithole when he saw one.

Corky Cordova, on the other hand, didn't really care where he was. One place was just about as good as any other. In the year and a half that he had been in the 'Nam, he had learned to take things as they came. He looked at the world with a seasoned grunt's philosophy. Whenever he got the short end of the stick, he'd just shrug his shoulders and say, "Fuck it, it don't mean nothin'."

Cordova was a product of the Los Angeles barrios, the son of illegal immigrants, wetbacks, and he had a real chip on his shoulder about that. As far as he was concerned, he was every inch an American, as much as any Anglo he had ever met, and he went out of his way to prove it. Corky had already been an experienced street fighter when he enlisted in the Army. He volunteered for infantry duty in the Nam to emphasize his point about being a good American.

The Chicano machine gunner had more than proved his case. He had done almost a year and a half in the Blues humping his pig, as the M-60 was called, and killing gooks. He'd been awarded the CIB, a couple of Bronze Stars, a Purple Heart, and enough Air Medals to fill a canteen cup. He had decided it was time to *fini* fuckin' Nam. He was just waiting out the time until DEROS and his return to the States.

"Hey, what's happenin', man?" a tall burly grunt in a spanking new camo suit called out, walking up to the sandbagged bunker on the berm line.

"Check it out!" Farmer said. "Jungle Jim's got himself a tiger suit. Where'd you get that, man?"

"I picked it up in Chu Lai," PFC Jim Gardner answered. "I traded some REMF an NVA helmet and a belt buckle for them."

"You're looking real STRAC there."

"We're supposed to look that way," Gardner grinned. "We're grunts, not fucking REMFs."

While camouflage uniforms were not issued to infantry units in Vietnam, the grunts loved them and wore them whenever they could get their hands on a set. Ridiculously, more camouflage uniforms were worn by Basecamp Warriors, Saigon Commandos, and other REMFS, rear-echelon motherfuckers, than by infantrymen in the field. The best way for a grunt to get his hands on a set of camies was to trade captured enemy equipment for them.

In the Blues, Gardner was known as Jungle Jim because of his size. He had developed a muscular build logging the fir forests of Washington State's rugged coastal mountain range before enlisting in the Army. He had come incountry at the same time that Farmer had and was as comfortable in the jungles as he had been in the peaceful mountains of his home state. In the field, Gardner carried an M-79 grenade launcher. In his big hands, the thumper looked like a child's plastic toy. But the big man could put the weapon's deadly little 40mm grenades wherever he wanted with pinpoint accuracy.

"Corky," Gardner said. "Brody sent me out here to take your guard. He's got a couple of FNGs he wants you to get squared away."

"Oh boy, fuckin' new guys. Just what I need today." Corky picked up his steel pot and headed back for the platoon area.

Gardner settled into Corky's spot behind the machine gun.

"What d'you think of this fucking place, JJ?" Farmer asked.

"It's okay."

"Well, I think it sucks."

Farmer tried to keep a conversation going, but Gardner was staring past the concertina wire perimeter and didn't reply. He didn't have much to say to anyone since he had gotten the divorce papers from his wife a week earlier. He had been expecting them for a couple of months, but it had still been a shock to finally see the words in print.

Sandra, his old high school sweetheart and the mother of his young son had decided that she wasn't going to wait for him to come home to work out their differences. He thought he knew her better than that, but he had been wrong. Completely wrong.

He stared at the Vietnamese traffic moving slowly along QL1. His finger curled around the trigger of the machine gun. He wanted some local VC to stick his AK-47 out of one of the overcrowded buses and shoot at them so he could shoot back. He wanted to take his mounting anger out on someone.

In the middle of the firebase, Corky strolled up to the GP small tent that was serving as the Blues' quarters. He poked his head inside and looked over at his squad leader's cot. "You wanted to see me, Treat?"

"Yeah." Sergeant Treat Brody, the 2nd Squad Leader, looked up from a well-read copy of a month-old *Playboy* magazine. "I need you to do some baby-sitting for us."

Brody was a sun-bronzed Californian with a wild shock of blond hair and a bushy mustache. Once he had stalked the beaches of Malibu with a surfboard on his shoulders instead of the jungles of Vietnam. In the two long years since then, he had found a new sport as a door gunner with the Blues.

On the shoulder of his faded jungle fatigue jacket, Brody wore the big o.d.-and-black "Horse Blanket" patch of the First Air Cavalry Division, the Pony Soldiers. Above his left breast pocket was sewn the wreathed musket of the CIB, the coveted Combat Infantryman's Badge. All Brody lived for was to fly and fight with the Air Cav. The war had become his entire life.

"Zack's got two new guys for us. The ell tee's giving them his usual lecture, and as soon as he's done, I want you to help them get their shit squared away."

"Why me, man?"

"It beats the shit outta berm guard, doesn't it?"

"Okay, okay." Corky threw up his hands.

"Treat 'em nice now, Corky," another grunt called out from where he sat on his bunk at the end of the tent. "One of them might be your replacement."

"Fuck you, Two-Step."

The dark-haired grunt laughed and went back to loading shotgun shells. Spec-4 Chance Broken Arrow was a modern-day Comanche warrior from Montana. He took great pride in his Plains Indian ancestry and took the war seriously. To him, crawling around in the jungle was like playing Cowboys and Indians with real guns. But the way this Indian played it, the North Vietnamese were the Cowboys.

Broken Arrow carried a sawed-off Remington twelve-gauge pump riot gun in the field instead of an issue M-16 rifle, and wore a black-and-green striped tiger suit camouflage uniform. A razor-sharp K-Bar knife strapped to his right boot top completed his armament.

The Indian's buddies all called him "Two-Step." He had earned the nickname when he had been bitten by a krait

12

snake. Of the thirty-three species of snakes that could be found in Vietnam, thirty-one of them were poisonous. The most deadly of all was the krait. When a man was bitten by the small light green snake, he had time to take two more steps before he fell flat on his face, stone-cold dead.

Somehow, though, the Indian had survived the snake's venom. There had been a dustoff medevac chopper nearby, and they had rushed him to the hospital in An Khe. While he was recuperating, their platoon sergeant, Leo Zack, had hung the nickname on him and it had stuck. Some of the new grunts even thought Two-Step was some kind of Indian name.

A better name for the sun-bronzed grunt would have been "the Tiger." He moved through the jungle with the same swift grace of the big striped cats. And when he struck, he was just as deadly. He hand-loaded the ammunition for his sawed-off Remington pump gun, replacing the lead balls in the shotgun shells with steel ball bearings. Whipping the slide back and forth so fast that the shotgun sounded like it was firing on full automatic, the Indian could clear a path in front of him half the size of a football field.

At the firebase, Two-Step was putting together a new batch of his tailor-made ammunition. The army-issue twelve-gauge shotgun round held only nine .36-caliber lead balls. They were fine for hunting but as far as the Indian was concerned, they didn't pack enough punch. Not for hunting in the Nam.

Two-Step opened a dozen of the shotgun shells at a time and took out both the lead balls and the gunpowder. First he measured out 10 percent more powder than the standard and poured it back into the empty hulls, creating his own magnum loads. Then he counted out twelve .25-caliber stainless-steel ball bearings for each shell. That gave them 25-percent greater killing power than the issue rounds. Since the ball bearings were much lighter than standard lead balls, they traveled farther and hit harder. And unlike lead balls which deformed when they hit something, the steel balls kept their shape. They plowed through the target and kept going.

Once the Indian had killed two NVA with a single blast. The steel balls had torn through the first man's chest and gone on to kill the man standing behind him. Two-Step had been real proud of that kill.

Two-Step's people back home had just sent him another twenty-five-pound keg of ball bearings so he had plenty of makings on hand. Usually, he only carried a hundred rounds of shotgun ammunition in the field, but today he was making up an additional hundred rounds to stash away. With the Air Cav division on the move, he wasn't sure when he'd get another chance.

"When are they going to give us something to do?" the Indian asked Brody.

"What's the matter, man, tired of sitting around on your ass?"

"There's nothing to do here, man. No Sin City, no Red Cross Club, no nothin'. Shit, if I'm going to lay dead, at least I want something to keep me occupied."

"Zack can always use another hand filling sandbags or burning shit."

"Fuck that. I was thinking about something more exciting. Like maybe making a run into Chu Lai. Maybe getting a little shot of leg or something."

Brody looked up from his bunk. "Hey, Two-Step, what's this, my man, looking for boom-boom? You must be about ready for a vacation. You usually don't get into that stuff unless you're on R and R."

The Indian grinned. "I guess it has been a little while."

"I'll tell you what." Brody sat up and swung his legs over the side of his bunk. "As soon as I get our cherries settled down, I'll talk to Zack and see if we can catch a hop back to An Khe to pick up something. We can always tell him that we missed the return flight and had to stay there overnight."

Two-Step finished hand-loading the shotgun shells and started putting his loading equipment back into his duffel bag. "That sounds like a plan. We could take a run down to The Pink Butterfly and see who Mama San's got hanging around."

Brody was rummaging around in his duffel bag, looking for a clean set of jungle fatigues to wear in An Khe when a muscular black sergeant with a shaved head walked into the tent.

Master Sergeant Leo Zack was the platoon sergeant of the Blues. To his men he was known as Leo the Lionhearted, but the Vietnamese called him the Black Buddha because of his shaved head. By either name, a veteran of the Korean War as well as two years with the Air Cav, Zack was a force to be reckoned with.

"Brody," he barked out. "Get your people together, we got a mission briefing in thirty minutes."

"Aw shit, Leo."

"Move it, troop!"

"Okay, okay."

Two-Step watched their platoon sergeant walk away. "Well, at least we have something to do now."

Brody stuffed his last pair of clean jungle fatigues back into his duffel bag. "Fuck! I was looking forward to a little boom-boom myself."

Two-Step laughed. "You're always looking forward to a little tail."

Brody grinned. "You got that shit right." He stowed the duffel bag back under his cot. "I wonder what they've dreamed up for us this time?"

Two-Step shrugged. "Just as long as it ain't some goddamned walk in the woods."

CHAPTER 3

Chu Lai

"You wanted to see me, sir?" The voice came from the open door of a small office in the makeshift operations shack next to the chopper pad. Captain Roger "Rat" Gaines, the Echo Company commander and Python Flight leader, looked up from behind his field desk to see First Lieutenant Mike Alexander, the platoon leader of the Aero Rifles Platoon, standing in front of him.

"Yeah, Mike, come on in."

The tall lieutenant grabbed a folding metal chair next to his CO's desk. "What's up, sir?"

Gaines leaned back in his chair with a disgusted look on his face. "The flying fickle finger of fate has been shoved up our asses again, Mike. They've given us a real winner this time."

Alexander didn't even bother to ask what it was. If Rat Gaines didn't like the sound of the mission, it had to be a real gold-plated bitch.

"You and your boys are going to play Marines on a bunch of riverboats while I fly top cover with Python Flight."

"Marines, sir?" Alexander didn't understand a word the stocky southern officer was saying.

"Yeah, fucking jarheads." Gaines fished into the breast pocket of his jungle fatigue jacket and came up with a thin cigar. Snapping open his Zippo lighter with a practiced flick of his fingers, he thumbed it to life and held the flame against the end of the cigar. He sucked in a deep lungful of pungent smoke and coughed. For the hundredth time he reminded himself to stop inhaling.

"Somebody convinced the general that we should provide an escort for a river-assault-boat unit that is being brought up the Song Boung River."

"That's right in the middle of the Marine AO, isn't it, sir?" Alexander seemed confused.

"I know. But apparently the Gyrenes are all tied up along the DMZ. And since we're sitting on our asses down here in Chu Lai doing nothing, we've been elected to cover for 'em."

"When do we do this, sir, and how?"

Gaines spread a map on top of the papers littering his desk. "Well, first we've got to get the boats up the river from Hoi An and then escort them to their new base somewhere around here." His finger jabbed at the map. "I figured I'd put some of your men on the boats at Hoi An and keep the rest of them in the slicks overhead. After the Navy's settled into their new home, we're going to act as their ready reaction force, infantry, and air support."

"What about the Sea Wolves?" Alexander was referring to HAL-3, the navy Huey gunship squadron that usually provided gunship support for the riverboats of the Brown Water Navy.

"It seems that they're a little overextended as well. So for the time being, we're working with the Swabbies."

"How much time do I have to get everybody ready, sir?"

"We start tomorrow."

"Nice of them to have given us a little lead time."

"Wasn't it, though?" Gaines blew out a perfect smoke ring. "You going to have any problems with that?"

"No, sir, I'll get back to the firebase and get Zack moving on it right away." He thought for a moment. "I think I'll send Brody and the Second Squad with the boats and leave First and Third with Zack on the slicks."

"Sounds good to me." Gaines folded up the map. "Get back to me this afternoon and let me know how it's going."

Alexander got to his feet. "Yes, sir."

Gaines watched the platoon leader head out the door to the chopper pad. For an ex-Mech Infantry type from Germany, young Alexander wasn't doing that badly at playing the airmobile game in the Cav. He had certainly gotten the Blues well under control in the last few months and he shouldn't have any trouble with this mission. Now all Gaines had to do was get his pilots and aircrew ready.

"Sarge?" he called out into the next room.

The operations sergeant appeared at the door. "Yes, sir?"

"I want a pilot and aircrew meeting in an hour, and tell Warlokk that I need to see him."

"Yes, sir, I'll get the word out. 'Rat' now."

Gaines grinned at the sergeant's use of his nickname. Gaines was a man of the South, born and raised in Atlanta, Georgia. Although he had learned to talk like the man on the six-o'clock news, his speech still had traces of a southern accent. When he got excited, it became even more pronounced. His nickname Rat had come from the fact that when Gaines wanted his people to do something, he wanted it done "rat" now, and not a second later.

The son of a World War II Air Force bomber pilot, Gaines had always dreamed of flying fighters since his boyhood days. When he was a boy, he had read every story he could get his hands on about World War II fighter pilots and built dozens of models of his favorite airplanes. On graduating from high school, he had signed up for Air Force ROTC in college and started pilot training. Things were going very well for the young Gaines until his sophomore year. To his com-

18

plete disbelief, he flunked his P-1 category physical examination. The flight surgeon said that he had a slight heart murmur and he was disqualified.

Faced with a non-flying job in the Air Force, Gaines quickly switched over to the Army ROTC infantry program. If he couldn't fight in the air, at least he could fight on the ground.

Three years into his army career as an infantry officer in Germany, First Lieutenant Gaines read an article in the *Army Times* that said the Army was looking for chopper pilots. The war in Nam was eating them up at a rapid rate and they were taking anyone who wanted to fly "whop-whops." Gaines applied for flight training, passed the physical, and went to Fort Wolters, Texas to learn how. He graduated at the top of his class and requested a gunship assignment in Nam.

Gaines's assignment as the CO of Echo company suited him very well. It was an Air Cavalry Company, and he had the Aero Rifle Platoon, the Huey slicks, and the gunships of Python Flight under his command. They were a quick-moving, hard-hitting recon and ready reaction force. At a moment's notice, Gaines could get the grunts of the Blues in the air, supported by gunships, and he could put them on the ground anywhere they were needed.

It was that kind of shooting from the hip, the "quick in and quick out" action that Gaines craved. From one day to the next he didn't know what his company was going to be asked to do, but whatever it was, they were right on top of it.

"You wanted to see me, sir?"

Gaines looked up from his desk. "Yeah, Lance, come on in."

A tall, thin, scar-faced warrant officer, Lance "Lawless" Warlokk, slumped down in the chair Alexander had just vacated and tipped his hat back on his head. "What's this about our having to work with a bunch of fucking Swabbies?"

"Rumor Control must be working overtime today," Gaines laughed. "I just got our orders less than an hour ago."

19

"You know how it is, sir. Bad news travels fast."

"Don't be such a pessimist, Lance. This is going to be a piece of cake."

In a small bamboo hut hidden deep in the jungle just inside the Vietnamese border from Laos, Lieutenant Colonel Nguyen Van Tran of the North Vietnamese Army looked up from the ammunition-supply report he was reading and rubbed his eyes. With the long-awaited general offensive scheduled for the *Tet Nguyen Dan,* the Asian lunar new-year festival, less than a month away, he was swamped with paper work.

As the operations officer for the NVA 325C Division, Tran did not think that the planned surprise offensive against the cities and Yankee installations in the south was a very good idea. He did not like having to give up the guerilla hit-and-run tactics that had proved so effective against both the French and the Americans, and sending his troops into conventional battles. Particularly in the cities.

Tran had fought most of his life to free his country from foreign domination and he would continue the struggle for as long as it took to achieve the final victory. But he feared coming head to head with the vastly superior firepower of the American army. He had grave misgivings about the offensive, but long ago he had learned to keep his personal opinions to himself. General Giap and the army high command in Hanoi had made their decision. It was his duty to obey their orders.

At least the weather was good for such a heroic undertaking. But the clear skies also favored the Americans and their massive air fleet. Over the last two years of fighting against the First Air Cavalry Division in the Binh Dinh Province, Colonel Tran had learned to fear the swarms of yankee helicopters. With good reason.

It had been different when the Americans had first come to Vietnam. As an infantry battalion commander in the NVA, Tran had enjoyed battling Yankees in places like the

20

Ia Drang Valley, teaching them the harsh realities of jungle combat, just as he had taught the French army before.

For all their wealth of arms and equipment, in the beginning the Americans had been like children. But that had changed quickly. Even Tran had to admit that the yankees were brave and they learned fast.

Within months, the American army had become a first-rate fighting force, supported by a seemingly endless swarm of helicopters. Tran feared helicopters and was more than a little paranoid about them. More times than he liked to recall, he had been forced to break contact and flee deep into the jungle to escape them. Today, the mere sound of their whop-whopping rotors in the distance was enough to make him break out in a cold sweat.

Tran had been born to a small shopkeeper and his wife on the outskirts of Hanoi in 1923. When his family died during a typhus epidemic, he had been taken in by a French Catholic orphanage and raised under the stern discipline of priests. He soon learned to hate the French fathers passionately, but he had received a good education in their school. After his graduation, he went to work in Hanoi's publishing industry.

The Imperial Japanese Army swarmed into French Indochina at the start of World War II. Tran, then eighteen years old, ran into the countryside to join the Vietnamese resistance movements. He fought well, and shortly before the end of the war, he heard another resistance fighter, Ho Chi Minh, speak at a political rally. Tran had been entranced with Ho's fiery nationalistic message: Vietnam for the Vietnamese. This policy matched Tran's strong anti-foreign feelings perfectly. Though he had not been politically active before, Tran immediately joined Ho's communist Viet Minh party.

At the end of the war, Tran put down his rifle and went back to his presses, printing revolutionary pamphlets for the party. The Viet Minh, however, needed his military skills more than they did his printer's ink. Tran soon found himself back in the expanding Viet Minh guerilla army. This time, however, the enemy were the French, who had returned to Indochina to take control of their former colony.

Toward the end of that long, bitter struggle, Tran had the honor of leading an infantry assault group in the night attack that took the stronghold "Beatrice" from the French Foreign Legion during the critical battle of Dien Bien Phu. When dawn broke over the smoke-filled valley, he found that he was one of only a mere handful of Viet Minh who had survived the fierce hand-to-hand battle with the bearded, foreign savages of the Legion Paras. With the surrender of the French garrison at Dien Bien Phu, a victorious General Giap had personally promoted Tran to the rank of sergeant for his bravery during the three-month battle.

A peace treaty was signed and the French evacuated North Vietnam. Tran was sent to Peking and Moscow for intensive military training. After two years of grueling instruction under Russian and Chinese veterans of World War II and the Korean War, he returned to his homeland and was commissioned a lieutenant in the new Vietnamese People's Liberation Army.

In the years that followed, Tran served as an infantry officer in both staff and command positions. Much of his time was spent in the Republic of South Vietnam, working with Viet Cong units that were fighting the U.S.-supported puppet regime. When the American army sent combat units into the south to prevent the collapse of the southern government, Tran was posted to the North Vietnamese Army, where he commanded an infantry battalion in the struggle against the new enemy of the people, the Yankees.

After over a year of field duty, suffering one stunning defeat after another, Tran lost all interest in commanding combat units. He secured a staff position at a basecamp in Cambodia, far from the fighting. When the 201st Division needed an operations officer, he had been called back to the south. His new job had come with a promotion, but Tran felt it was scant compensation for being back in the middle of the war.

Particularly right now. The planned Tet offensive was wrong, the old, experienced jungle fighter could feel it in his bones. The only thing that would come of it would be the death of many of his best troops.

The Viet Cong in the south had been ordered to launch a general uprising to take place in conjunction with the attack. The plan called for the VC to take over the cities that the army conquered. Tran had severe doubts about that ever happening. For one thing, the South Vietnamese wanted no part of an austere communist government. Not when they could get rich living off of the Americans.

The veteran jungle fighter shook his head. As far as he was concerned, the offensive had been planned primarily to add General Giap's name to the list of history's great generals like Zhukov and Patton. In the eyes of the Western world, Giap's guerilla war victories didn't count toward military greatness. To be considered a great general, he had to fight and win a conventional land battle. Unfortunately, Giap's acclaim would be bought with the blood of thousands of North Vietnamese infantrymen.

Tran went back to his reports. There was so much to do and very little time to do it. The main problem he had was keeping his preparations a secret from the American recon teams that kept watch along the NVA border sanctuaries and the Ho Chi Minh Trail. The increased supply traffic and movement of troop units was bound to attract unwelcome attention. And that attention could bring the high-flying Yankee B-52s to rain bombs down upon them.

Every man he could spare was guarding the new supply and ammunition dumps and the road networks leading from the north. He just hoped that they were up to the enormous task that lay ahead.

CHAPTER 4

Chu Lai

Rat Gaines stood at the front of a small, run-down hut that served as his makeshift ready room at Chu Lai. The operations shack at Camp Radcliff hadn't been any great shakes, either, but it had been Python Flight's home for almost two years and had acquired a comfortable, lived-in feeling. The men brought their battered lawn furniture with them, and most of their faded *Playboy* pinups decorated the walls of their new home. But they had been forced to leave behind the heavy, old pool table.

"Okay, boys, let's listen up here," Gaines started.

The pilots quieted down quickly. If something was going down that was important enough for the captain to have called a meeting, they wanted to hear about it.

"I've got several things to go over with you today. First off, several crews are going to be moving out of here tomorrow."

That got cheers. Chu Lai was no one's favorite place.

"That's the good news," Gaines continued. "The bad news is that those of you who are leaving will be going to a place

24

on the Song Boung River and operating out of a Brown Water Navy firebase."

That got loud groans. The pilots suddenly remembered that there were worse places in Vietnam than Chu Lai.

"I need five crews, two slicks and three guns. Any volunteers?"

A few hands went up.

"Gabe, I want you."

The veteran slick pilot nodded affirmatively.

"Hitchcock," Gaines continued, "and Cross." The CO turned to Warlokk, who was standing at the open door. "Lance, you're signed up for this, too, but I want you to see me after this meeting. I've got a little surprise for you." He looked around the crowded room. "Where's Alphabet?" he asked.

"I saw him down on the flight line earlier, working on your Snake," someone called out.

"Go get him."

"Okay, here's what we're going to do." Gaines turned to the big map pinned on the wall behind him. "Tomorrow, we're taking two slicks and a light fire team out to Hoi An to escort a bunch of riverboats from the mouth of the river to their new base." He pointed at the map. "Here."

He faced his pilots again. "Then, we're going to rotate crews between here and there. One slick and two guns will stay with the Navy at all times, and the other two birds will be back here on ramp alert. That'll give you a chance to pull maintenance and get cleaned up every other day. Any questions?"

There were several, mostly about coordinating the mission and the daily changeover. "Okay," Gaines said when they were done. "Get out there and get your choppers ready."

He turned to Lance Warlokk with a big grin on his face:"Lance, I've got a couple of things I want you to do for me. First, give Alphabet an AC check ride. I think it's about time that he was an aircraft commander. Then I want the two of you to go back to An Khe and pick up your Cobra."

"You're shitting me!" Warlokk couldn't believe his ears. "You got me a Cobra?"

Gaines enjoyed the look of astonishment on Warlokk's face. Any gunship jockey with even half a pair of balls lusted after a chance to fly the new Bell AH-1G Cobra. Unlike the UH-1C Huey Hogs, slicks with a lot of armament hung all over them, the Cobra was the world's first dedicated attack helicopter. Designed from the beginning to be the deadliest machine ever to swing a rotor blade, the Cobra was a real gunship.

There were still only a handful of them in Vietnam, where they were being tested under combat conditions. Six months ago, Warlokk had been one of the first two Air Cav pilots to fly one. The first week he had it, he had been shot down. The machine had been recovered and repaired, but Warlokk had not been allowed even to get near one since then. In fact, the two Air Cav test Cobras had been off limits to all of Python Flight until Gaines had been able to talk the test unit into letting him fly one.

"A bunch of new Cobras have just come in-country," Gaines continued. "We'll be getting two of them, yours and one more. If you give Alphabet an up-check to AC, I'm going to put him in the other one and the three of us will fly together as a light-gun team."

"Outta sight!" Warlokk's face lit up. "It's about time they got us some more of those birds."

"You looking for me, sir?"

Gaines looked up to see Warrant Officer Joe Schmuchatelli, his gunner copilot. For obvious reasons, Schmuchatelli went by the nickname of Alphabet.

"Yeah, come on in, Joe."

"Sorry I missed the meeting, Captain," Alphabet said, wiping his greasy hands on a rag. "I was working on the firing circuits for the port stub wing. I think I finally got 'em fixed."

It was hard to imagine two people more different than Joe Schmuchatelli and Rat Gaines, his aircraft commander. They

26

came from different backgrounds and their personalities were always at odds. But the tall, thin gunner from New Jersey practically worshiped the stocky southern pilot. There was a good reason for it, though. Captain Rat Gaines was the best helicopter gunship pilot that Schmuchatelli had ever met, bar none.

Alphabet had flown with quite a few pilots since he arrived in Vietnam. Some of them had been good, some only fair, and some of them should never have been allowed to step into a Huey cockpit. But before meeting Rat Gaines, even the good ones had lacked the one quality that made Gaines stand out — complete single-mindedness about his work.

Gaines lived only to fly his gunship and kill the enemy. He allowed nothing to get in the way of that mission. Not women, not booze, not letters from home, nor some CO's ranting and raving about nickel-and-dime bullshit. Gaines lived to fly and fight, and since Schmuchatelli had started flying with Gaines, that attitude had rubbed off on him as well.

"Joe, I want you and Warlokk to take a little flight back to An Khe and pick up a new bird for us. On the way, Warlokk's going to check you out for an AC rating."

"But, Rat," the gunner protested. "I don't need a chopper of my own. I'm your gunner."

"Even a Cobra of your own?"

That stopped the protests. Alphabet's mouth fell open. "You're shitting me!"

"Nope, we're getting two more."

"Well, I'll be dipped in shit."

"Jesus, I sure hope not," Warlokk laughed. "Not if you're flying with me."

Alphabet's grin suddenly disappeared from his face. "But, Captain, who's going to gun for you?"

"Well, I guess that you're just going to have to find me a new gunner."

Alphabet got serious. "Let me see," he thought out loud. "Who do we have around here who's good enough to fly the front seat for you?"

"We'll worry about that later, Joe," Gaines cut in. "Right now I want to get that new bird back here as soon as we can."

"Okay, Captain. But I'll get somebody lined up for you right away."

When Lieutenant Mike Alexander briefed the men of the Blues on their new mission, they calmly took their orders to play Marines.

"You've got to be shitting me, sir!" Spec-4 Bernie Rabdo squeaked. He was in a state of complete panic. "I can't fucking swim!"

Rabdo was the platoon's artillery FO, the forward observer. He was the man who called for the big guns to shoot when the Blues had their asses caught in a crack and needed to be bailed out. Somewhere along the line the short, curly-haired New Yorker had picked up the name Bunny Rabbit, but there was nothing comical about his ability to put his high-explosive Easter eggs exactly where they were needed. Like any good FO, he was cool under fire. Nothing shook him up. Except water.

"Oh, Christ, Bunny." Alexander shook his head wearily. There was always something. "Okay, I'll tell you what I'll do. I'll let you fly with the squads in the slicks overhead."

"Oh, no," Bunny quickly replied. "I'm not flying with those weenies, sir. Also, if we get hit on the river, we'll need artillery." He thought for a moment. "How big are those boats, sir?"

"Twenty, thirty feet long."

"And they've got motors, sir?"

"Yes, Rabdo," Alexander was beginning to lose patience with the FO. "They've all got motors and life jackets on board."

"Okay, sir, I guess it's okay."

"I'm glad that you approve of my plan," the lieutenant said sarcastically.

"Oh, yes, sir." Bunny nodded absentmindedly, "The plan's fine."

"Any other problems?" the platoon leader asked the rest of the men. There were none. "Okay, start getting your gear squared away."

Alexander went to his shelter, a little pup tent, to get ready. Some officers had their radio operators keep track of their weapons and ruck. Alexander believed that his life depended on his weapon being clean and his equipment squared away, so he always took care of it himself. The soothing, familiar work was part of the officer's mental preparation for combat and helped him get over pre-mission jitters. The more apprehensive he was about a mission, the more time he spent getting ready for it.

As he worked, Alexander realized that he was very uneasy this time. He found himself disassembling his M-16 magazines and checking the spring tension on each and every one. He didn't know why he felt this way. More than likely it was because they were going to be working on riverboats instead of choppers. He forced his mind back to his preparations and reassembled his magazines. Then he carefully wiped the dirt and sand off every round of ammunition before reloading them. He was also careful to count out the cartridges as he fed them back into the magazines, loading only seventeen rounds into each one.

The so-called twenty-round magazine for the M-16 rifle was bad news. With nineteen or twenty rounds loaded in it, it almost always jammed on the second shot. The Army was not unaware of the problems with the M-16 magazines, and a new thirty-round magazine was currently being tested by some elite units in-country. The initial reports indicated that the new magazine worked well, but none of them had been issued to the grunts down in the infantry line units yet. Consequently, veteran grunts loaded their magazines with seventeen rounds.

When each magazine was reloaded, Alexander tapped the backside against the top of his footlocker to seat the base of the rounds against the back wall of the magazine. Then he put them in his pouches and bandoliers.

Next, the lieutenant stripped his Colt .45-caliber pistol, thoroughly cleaned it, and checked all its magazines as well. When he was finished, he sharpened the blade of his Air Force survival knife. A couple of years ago, someone in the army had decided that infantrymen didn't need knives anymore and deleted them from the inventory.

But, as any grunt found out, a knife was one of the most useful things a man could have on a battlefield. For one thing, a knife never needed to be reloaded. Grunts in Nam went to great lengths to scrounge knives. Some brought them from the States, but many found a way to get their hands on the Air Force survival knife or the bigger Marine K-Bar fighting knife of World War II fame.

Finally, Alexander went over his four hand grenades, checking the pins and fuses to make sure they were tightly screwed into the body. Then he taped the spoons down with black electrician's tape. If the pin snagged on something and pulled out, the spoon wouldn't fly off. It was extremely unhealthy to have a grenade spoon fly off when it was still in an ammo pouch.

With his weapons ready, he turned to the rest of his gear.

First he chose the C-ration meals he would take. Often he went short on rations in the field to avoid having to hump the extra weight, but this time he wouldn't have to worry about that. His ruck would be traveling by boat instead of on his back. And even though meals would be flown into the PBR base, he took enough food to keep him going for a couple of days, as well as all the extra coffee he could scrounge up. He also packed several small rolls of C-ration toilet paper in a plastic bag along with two pairs of extra socks.

All of this went into his ruck with his poncho liner, two sticks of C-4 plastic explosive, a Prick-25 battery, and the two extra bandoliers of M-16 magazines. His compass, penlight, grease pencils, C-4 stove, malaria pills, and salt tablets were already in pouches on his field belt, but he checked them over as well.

Finally, he went over to the Lister bag hanging outside the artillery mess tent and put fresh water in both of his two-quart canteens. Now he was ready for anything that came up. Brown water or green jungle.

CHAPTER 5

Firebase Lasher

In the Blues' tent, Treat Brody was cleaning his weapons. His disassembled M-16 rifle lay across his cot.

The Colt M-16 was a good weapon. Fired on full automatic, its small-caliber, high-velocity rounds could cut a man in half. But the M-16 had not been designed for use in the Nam. The smallest speck of dirt, sand, or hard carbon in the wrong place could leave a soldier with an inert chunk of metal and plastic in his hands when he least expected it. To remedy this, Brody had his folks back home send him a case of the civilian WD-40 spray lubricant to keep his rifle clean. When the cleaning ritual was done and every last part of the weapon was sparkling, he reassembled it and sprayed a short burst of it on the bolt.

Then he turned to loading his magazines. Like platoon leader Mike Alexander, Brody was careful to count out the 5.56mm ammunition, using seventeen rounds instead of twenty.

When he had loaded enough magazines to fill five bandoliers, he took out his secret weapon, a special magazine that was going to be in his M-16 when he ran down the river in the PBRs — a modified Russian AK-47 assault rifle magazine. The AK mag had been extensively reworked so that it would fit into the M-16 rifle. First, its throat had been ground down so that it would fit the narrower magazine well. Then the original AK magazine catch had been ground off, and a square hole was cut into the sight side so it would clip into the magazine catch of the American rifle.

This modification worked because the 7.62mm AK-47 and the 5.56mm M-16 cartridges were almost the same length, the AK being just a little longer and much fatter. When filled with AK rounds, the Russian magazine held thirty rounds, but thirty-eight of the skinnier M-16 rounds fit into it — over twice the capacity of the regular issue magazines.

It took well over an hour in a machine shop to modify the AK magazine, but it gave additional firepower on initial contact when it was most needed. On the upcoming mission, Brody wanted as much firepower with him as he could carry.

"Treat?"

Brody looked up and saw Corky standing in front of him with two guys holding duffel bags, obviously the two cherries who had been assigned to his squad. Their skin wasn't tanned, they wore brand-new fatigues, and the leather of their jungle boots was still black instead of a worked-in, scuffed-up, nasty shade of reddish brown. Their faces also had the stunned, "What the hell am I doing here?" look common to FNGs on arrival in the Nam.

Brody got to his feet. "I'm Treat Brody," he said, looking them up and down. "Your squad leader."

The two men were nothing to look at, just more bodies for the meat grinder, and there was no way to tell if either of them had what it took to become a good grunt. Not until he got them into the brush and saw how they reacted under fire. At the moment they were just extra baggage, and he really didn't want them on this upcoming mission.

"First off," he said, "we're moving out in the morning, so me and the guys don't have time to learn your names.

I'm going to give you a nickname and I want you to remember it."

The first man had blondish red hair, worn short in a bootcamp crew cut. "What's your name?" Brody asked.

"Lindberry, Larry Lindberry."

"You're Strawberry for now."

The man nodded.

Before Brody could turn to the other man, he spoke up. "My name's Richard York. I think that should be easy enough for you to remember."

Brody locked eyes with York for a moment. The man's voice had a slight accent, — like JFK's — the sound of East Coast money. "Where're you from?" Brody asked.

"Newport, Rhode Island."

"You got drafted, right?"

York flushed slightly under Brody's gaze. "Yes, I was in business school."

"Where?"

"Harvard," York answered with undisguised superiority.

"Okay, you're Harvard."

"What's wrong with 'York'?"

"It rhymes with dork." Brody stared the man down, a slight smile on his face. This was as good a time as any to see if the FNG had any balls:"And I don't like it. You might have been a big man on campus, troop, but around here, you're just another fucking FNG and you're anything I feel like calling you. You got a problem with that?"

York clenched his fists, but shook his head. "No, Sergeant."

"Good."

Brody turned to the machine gunner. "Cork, you and Two-Step see that these guys get their shit together tonight. We're moving out at zero seven hundred."

"You got it, Treat."

"And, Harvard . . ." Brody turned back to York. "Don't take this personally. None of you FNGs are worth a shit to me until you get your cherries busted."

34

York didn't reply, but he vowed that he would take care of Brody's loud mouth as soon as he learned what was going on around there.

Richard York was an angry young man. He was pissed at the dean at Harvard who had thrown him out of school and had turned his name over to the draft board, and pissed at the draft board for selecting him for service. He was pissed at the Army for ignoring his superior education and putting him in the infantry. He was really pissed at being sent to Vietnam. And now he was pissed at that smart-mouthed punk Brody. In Vietnam, no one knew that his family's name stood for power and privilege. It was bad enough that he had to waste two years of his life in the Army, but it was intolerable that he had to spend it in Vietnam living like an animal with people like those morons he had just met today. For the first time in his life, his family's wealth and position had not been able to protect him. Richard York was pissed because no one seemed to care.

Jack Wilburn and the wounded Nung were ten klicks from the airstrip at Chavane in western Laos when they were picked up by a patrol of Meo tribesmen mercenaries working for the CIA. The patrol leader, a small, wizened man whose skin was so dark and weathered that it looked like old leather, spoke enough English that Jack was able to keep the Meo from killing them. It took a little longer for him to talk them into rigging a litter to carry Bao. Wilburn had packed the wounded Nung on his back for most of the last day and he couldn't carry him another step.

The Meo and the Nungs were often neighbors in the inaccessible, high mountain areas of Indochina, but they were seldom friends. Jack had had to resort to the traditional bribery, the promise of a small gold payment, to get them to agree to carry a tribal enemy to the mountaintop CIA camp.

The Company ran several camps in neutral Laos and had their own 40,000-man army of hired mountain tribesmen fighting for them. Their primary mission was to keep an eye on NVA and Pathet Lao activities in northern Laos, as well as traffic coming down the Ho Chi Minh Trail.

The packed-earth airstrip at Chavane didn't look long enough for a Bird Dog to have landed on, but when Wilburn got a little closer, he saw the familiar hulking shape of an old World War II C-46 Curtiss Commando twin-engined transport plane sitting down at one end.

Less well known than its DC-3/C-47 stable mate of the same vintage, the larger C-46 still saw quite a bit of use by the Company's private air force, Air America. The Commando had more powerful engines than the more familiar C-47 Gooney Bird. It could carry more cargo and was better suited for bringing supplies into remote airstrips at CIA camps.

The Meo carried Bao into the dispensary, a bunker dug halfway into the ground. In the sweltering, almost airless bunker, an American civilian medic pumped the Nung full of antibiotics, a little blood plasma, and changed his bandages.

"I can't really do anything more for him here," he told Wilburn, wiping the sweat from his forehead. "You're going to have to get him to a hospital as soon as you can."

"When's that plane leaving?" Wilburn asked, pointing to the airstrip.

"Check at the hut next door. You want to talk to a guy called 'Shower Sandals'. He's the pilot."

"Shower Sandals?"

"Yeah, that's all he ever wears on his feet."

Wilburn went back outside and walked over to the hut. Sprawled out in a battered folding lawn chair by the door was a man in his early forties drinking a bottle of Tiger beer. He was dressed in a dirty baseball cap, a sweat-stained khaki shirt, and faded blue jeans. On his feet were a pair of rundown shower sandals, the kind made in Japan or Korea and sold in the PX. Above the left-hand pocket of his shirt, he wore a pair of tarnished USAF pilot's wings. This had to be Shower Sandals.

"Say, are you the pilot of that thing?" Wilburn jerked his thumb over in the direction of the Commando.

The man pulled his shades down low on his nose and peered over the tops of the rims. "Yeah," he answered, taking another drink. "Who are you?"

"Jack Wilburn, RT Sleeper working out of Dong Pek. I've got one of my team in there," he said, pointing to the dispensary bunker. "And I've got to get him to a hospital real quick."

Shower Sandals pushed his sunglasses back up his nose. "Where d'you wanta go?"

"Kontum would be fine."

The pilot glanced down at his Rolex. "Load 'em on board and we'll roll."

"Thanks a lot."

"No sweat." He tossed the empty bottle around the side of the building. "I was running out anyway."

Wilburn and the medic carried Bao's litter to the airstrip and loaded the wounded man into the cavernous fuselage of the old plane. He had just gotten Bao strapped down when Shower Sandals climbed inside and headed to the cockpit. He energized the starter on the starboard engine. With a loud bang and a puff of black smoke, the 2,000-horsepower Pratt and Whitney radial engine fired up, and the big four-bladed prop started turning over.

Wilburn made his way forward and stood between the pilot's and copilot's seats. "Don't you have a copilot?" he asked.

"Nope." Shower Sandals ran the throttle back down to idle and started up the portside engine. When it was turning over, he looked back at Wilburn. "You wanna sit up here?"

"Sure." Jack quickly slid into the copilot's seat and buckled the shoulder harness.

Without saying a word, Shower Sandals pushed forward on the throttles, and the big plane taxied out to the end of the dirt strip. He advanced one throttle and kicked down on the rudder pedal to swing the tail around, lining up on

37

the other end of the runway. Standing on top of the rudder pedals to lock the brakes, he pushed forward on both of the throttles, running the powerful engines up until the airframe shuddered and shook. When he came off of the brakes, the Commando shot forward, her big props clawing the air.

As they roared down the dusty airstrip, the pilot hauled back on the control wheel, sucking it into his stomach to keep the tail on the ground. At the last moment, he eased it forward. The tail snapped up just as they ran out of runway. The big cargo plane was airborne.

Shower Sandals quickly pulled up the gear and flaps, set his throttles, and banked away to the west. The plane climbed into a clear blue sky over rugged mountains. He set his course, trimmed the aircraft, and leaned back in his seat. Fishing in his pocket, he brought out a plastic cigarette case, opened it, and offered one to Jack. The two men lit up and watched the jungle pass by far below them. Within a few minutes, they were flying over the Ho Chi Minh Trail.

"Don't they ever shoot at you?" Wilburn asked, looking down.

"Nah, not too often," the pilot said, his gaze passing over the densely forested mountains below. "Most of the time, they just leave me the fuck alone. They know that if they shoot at me, I'll get the United States Air Force down on their scrawny asses."

Wilburn looked down at the pilot's unusual footwear. "What are you going to do if you ever get shot down in the jungle? How're you going to walk out in thongs?"

The pilot looked surprised. "Oh, you mean like the last time? I made it out in twenty-three days."

Wilburn shook his head. One thing about the pilots who worked for the Company — they were always characters.

CHAPTER 6

Dong Pek Special Forces Camp

Exhausted, Jack Wilburn walked into the team house bunker at the Special Forces camp at Dong Pek. He'd had a chance to get cleaned up at the CCC headquarters in Kontum and had changed into a clean uniform, but he was still bone tired. A hand-lettered sign over the door read, Mike Force Company A-248. Welcome to Camp Bumfuck. Home of the Mushroom Detachment.

The medics at the hospital at Kontum had assured him that Bao would recover from his wound. They weren't quite as sure that the old Nung would go back into the field again, but he would live.

"You look like you could use a cold one," came a voice from the radio room.

Wilburn sat down at the wooden table in the middle of the small room. "I could use a shitload of cold ones, sir."

Captain Larry Ringer, CO of the Mike Force Company, laughed. He got up from a bank of radios and walked over to the small Japanese refrigerator parked against the wall.

"Here's a start," he said, taking a cold beer from the cooler and punching two holes in the top with the church key tied to the refrigerator door handle. "Now, why don't you tell your old Uncle Larry all about it."

Larry Ringer was a living legend in the Special Forces. He had won every medal for valor that his country could award except the Medal of Honor. And there were many Green Berets who believed he deserved one of those as well.

Wilburn took a long, hard drink of the cold beer. "Here's to the Mushroom Detachment," he said, raising the can. "May they continue to keep us in the dark and feed us bullshit."

Ringer chuckled. At least the young sergeant hadn't lost his perspective on things. "I've got some news for you. Some good and some bad."

"I already know what it is," Wilburn said wearily. "The bad news is that our rations have been cut and all we have to eat is water buffalo shit. The good news is that there are a lot of buffalo around here and they all have diarrhea."

"Actually, PJ," Ringer said, ignoring Jack's comment, "there's going to be some big changes around here."

Wilburn looked up.

"First, your Roadrunner team has been disbanded and you've been assigned to work with me. Second, we are no longer assigned to support the RT operations."

That got Wilburn's undivided attention. For the last year, Mike Force Company A-248 had been working in support of Project Delta, the super-secret MAC-SOG cross-border recon operation. A-248 was a reaction force, a hatchet force, as they were called. If one of the six man Delta Roadrunner teams got in trouble in Laos or Cambodia, Ringer and his men went across the border and bailed them out. They were always hairy missions with very few dull moments.

"Since they've closed us down, when are they going to send us back to Nha Trang?" Jack asked, referring to the Special Forces headquarters that was situated in a resort town on the South China Sea. "I could use a little fun in the sun right now."

"Funny you should mention Nha Trang, PJ. You're flying out tomorrow to sign for a load of equipment."

"What kind of stuff, sir?"

Ringer got a big grin on his face. "Oh, stuff like black pajamas, AKs, RPGs, Chi-Com grenades. That sort of thing."

"What the fuck are we doing? Joining the VC?"

"Funny you should mention that. In a way we are."

Wilburn got up and helped himself to another beer. "Captain, if you don't mind, I'm a bit worn out today and I'm not really in the mood to listen to one of your crazy schemes."

"Panama Jack!" Ringer feigned shock. "I'm surprised at you. I can remember a time when you would have jumped at the chance to play the part of a VC."

"Well, sir, that was right before the Oscar nominations, when I was looking for a role as a leading man in a war flick. Right now, I've been shot at and missed, shit on and hit. All I want to do is to rest up for a couple of days and then try to figure out what I'm going to do next to serve my grateful country."

"I'm serious, Wilburn."

Jack looked up at Ringer's sharp tone. When the short, wiry captain got serious, it was time to listen.

"SOG is switching things around again. They've decided that they want to expand the Mobile Guerrilla Force units and we've been selected to undergo conversion. I want you to honcho the combat reconnaissance platoon I'll be putting together."

Wilburn looked at the half-full beer can in his hands. He held it up to his forehead and rolled it back and forth to cool his feverish brow.

"You've got to be shitting me, sir."

Ringer sat down on the other side of the table. "Jack, look, I need you. I need someone out there who knows how to find his ass without using a fucking radar set."

"But a recon platoon! Captain, you know I don't work well with large groups."

"But this is different, PJ. For one thing, the troops will all be Nungs. And secondly, they'll be under your direct command. I'm not going to send a butter-bar out there with you."

"Thank God for small favors," Wilburn said dryly.

The recent rapid expansion of the Army's Special Forces had seen a large number of newly commissioned 2nd lieutenants fresh out of the JFK Special Warfare School at Fort Bragg, assigned to the CIDG program. The old Green Berets saw this invasion of inexperienced junior officers as a great way to get killed. Back in the good old days, a man had to be a captain or an E-7 master sergeant to wear the Green Beret.

"You'll be going in sterile with complete control of your AO. Everything: air support, artillery, reaction forces, the whole nine yards."

Wilburn looked up from his beer. "Tell me another story, Daddy."

"Knock that shit off, Wilburn," the officer's voice rang out. "I'm offering you the chance of a lifetime, and all you can do is wise-ass me."

"Look, Captain," Wilburn backed down. "I'm sorry. That was uncalled for. I just had a damned good team shot out from underneath me because someone sent us into a fucking hornet's nest without adequate cover or support, and I guess I'm just a little gun shy right now."

"I understand that, PJ. That's why I'm offering you this job. I don't want to see you go back to Delta, find yourself stuck with a green team, and get your ass zeroed." Ringer got up from the table and walked over to the acetate-covered operations map tacked on the bunker wall. "This is going to be different than anything you've done before. You'll be pissing in high cotton this time."

Wilburn grinned at Ringer's southernism. The captain's native North Carolina accent was all but gone after his years in the army, but sometimes a folksy, down-home expression or two crept into his conversation.

"You'll be taking your platoon into Indian country and scouting around for something for the rest of us to do later on." He pointed to an area along the Laotian border. "You'll establish our resupply points and a patrol base for a month-long operation. You'll be equipped with NVA weapons and uniforms for a low profile, but you'll have U.S. radios, so there won't be any commo fuckups."

Ringer turned back and leaned over the table. "CCC has guaranteed that you'll have priority on all air strikes and resupply, both Army and Air Force assets. That, along with the backup I can give you, means that you'll be covered better than you've ever been before."

Wilburn looked at his empty beer can and sighed. He had to take the assignment. He owed it to Ringer. And there was always the off chance that somebody had gotten their act together on this one. He knew better, however, than to be too hopeful about that.

"Also," Ringer continued, "a battalion of the Air Cav will be on standby for you, as well."

Wilburn didn't know whether to laugh or cry. As a professional Sneaky Pete used to working on his own, the promise of Air Cav support was a mixed blessing. They could bring a lot of smoke down on Charlie if he needed them, but swarms of choppers drew fire like fresh shit drew flies.

He shrugged his shoulders in a gesture of resignation. "Where do I volunteer?"

Ringer beamed. "Good man," he said. "I knew I could count on you."

"Fuck you, sir!" Wilburn sang out. "And the pig you rode in on."

Ringer laughed.

NVA Lieutenant Nguyen Van Tran glared at the five officers standing at attention in front of him. "You fools!" he hissed. "You have only one mission before the New Year offensive starts, and that is to keep the yankees from learning of our preparations." He shook a fist full of papers at them. "You have more than enough men for the task, yet it appears that a small American recon team was not only able to penetrate your security, but even after being spotted, some of them escaped alive."

He rocked back on his heels and glared at the company commanders. "Well? Can any of you tell me why this happened?"

"Comrade Colonel," an older man stepped forward. Captain Binh and the colonel had been together back in the days of the Ia Drang Valley. If anyone could placate Tran, Binh could. "Those yankees were Green Berets."

"I saw only one American body," Tran replied. "The other three were Han." He spat when he used the Vietnamese name for the Nung Chinese. "Surely your fighters are capable of overcoming a couple of Americans, even Green Berets and a handful of Han mercenaries."

"Comrade Colonel," the old captain tried again, "you yourself have fought against the Green Devils, and you know that they are fierce and cunning. Worse than even the Lizards." Binh referred to the French Foreign Legion Paras from their Viet Minh days. Their nickname had come from the green, brown and purple camouflage uniforms that they had worn.

"That may be true, Binh, but the Yankees are only men. And men can be killed."

Tran walked over to the map he had propped up on an easel. "There is less than a month to go now. Carelessness on your part can bring all this work and preparation to nothing. There is always danger from the yankee recon teams, but if we are discovered, they will bomb us, and the offensive will be doomed even before it is started. You must not fail again, comrades, we have worked too long and too hard for this moment. The fate of the People's Liberation depends on you and each of your fighters." Tran's voice rang out. "Go now. Talk to your men. Tell them to carry out their duties faithfully."

The five company commanders saluted and left the small room. Tran went back to his desk and sat down. The packs that had been taken from the American recon team's dead were leaning against the wall. He had gone through the contents of each one, but there was little useful information in them.

A small radio code book had been recovered, but as Tran well knew, once the team did not check in with their home base, the code would be automatically changed. There was a plastic laminated map as well, but it gave little information. Nothing was written on it except the coordinates of the supply complex. Judging from the amount of food the men had been carrying, Tran accurately guessed that the recon team had not been in the field very long. They were at the beginning of their mission, not the end.

If that was so, then it was good news. The recon teams used their radios as little as possible to avoid detection. It was possible that this team had just stumbled into the supply area when they were ambushed and had not had a chance to radio back to their headquarters what they had found.

Blood had also been found at the ambush site. Maybe the yankees had been hit hard enough that they had not been able to make it back to their base. Maybe, just maybe, the secret of the giant supply dump in the jungle was still safe.

Tran had been in the profession of war long enough to be prepared for the worst possible case, though. The officer studied his map again. He decided to bring another infantry company in to provide more security. Particularly around that river, the Song Boung, that intruded into the area they were guarding.

He hated to cut his strength on the ground, but he felt that it was necessary. The Americans might send in more recon teams to learn why the NVA had reacted so strongly. He had to be ready for them.

He had to stop them cold.

CHAPTER 7

Camp Radcliff, An Khe

First Lieutenant Lisa Maddox took a drink of her coffee and tried one more time to figure out a timetable for moving a medical team from Camp Radcliff to the new Cav base at Chu Lai. With the relocation of two brigades of the division, the overworked 15th Medical Battalion was having a hard time covering the Cav's operations.

Several months ago, the 2d Mobile Surgical Hospital had relocated to Chu Lai, leaving the 15th, the division's own medical battalion, behind to run the hospital in An Khe all by themselves. Lisa had requested to stay with the 15th. The nurse had been with the Air Cav since she had arrived in-country, and it just wouldn't have felt right not to be around the Pony Soldiers.

However, the Cav was moving north, and she was going to follow them. She rechecked her movement schedule and placed it in the out-box on her desk. Tomorrow, the first of the advance party would get on the choppers for the move to Chu Lai. She was anxious to leave An Khe. The last several weeks had been hectic and she had seen very little of her lover, Captain Rat Gaines. Since Echo Company was also at Chu Lai, she was hoping that she would see him more often.

Her relationship with Gaines had been blowing hot and cold recently. Much of that, she knew, was simply because both of them had very little time to see one another. There was more to it than that, however. Her feelings toward the pilot were changing, and she sensed that he was having second thoughts about her as well.

Trying to maintain a romance in a war zone was never easy, but in Vietnam it was even more difficult. Lisa had never intended to fall for Rat Gaines or for any other man, for that matter. But in a dramatic rescue he had saved her life at the risk of his own, and a thank-you dinner with him had sparked her interest.

Gaines was the kind of man that she had always been attracted to — urbane, witty, sensitive, and intelligent. At first, Gaines had been like a breath of fresh air. When she was with him, he always managed to take her far from the war. Unlike other officers she had dated, Gaines always talked about something other than his job and the war. Their dinners and dates were a welcome respite from the reality of their lives.

Of course, the war had intruded into their relationship more than once. The first time they had tried to go to bed together, they had been rudely interrupted by an emergency mission he had to fly out on. Later they laughed about it. It was only to be expected since they were both in the army. Now, however, the last few times that they had been together, it seemed as if all they ever talked about was the war. Her war or his, but always the war.

But there was another side to Rat Gaines that she had been seeing more of and liking less. He seemed to have lost some of the gentleness and sensitivity that attracted her. More and more, he was being consumed by the war, and it bothered her. She was beginning to wonder if she really wanted to continue seeing him.

The next day, she was going to see him, and see how she felt about him — that was, if he wasn't out flying around somewhere in his Cobra, looking for Viet Cong to kill.

She drank the rest of the lukewarm coffee in her brown plastic mess-hall cup and got up to take the movement schedule down the hall to the medical battalion commander. She needed his signature on it before she posted it on the board.

She looked out the window over the almost-deserted Camp Radcliff and thought back to the unofficial three-day vacation she had taken at the beautiful little coastal town of Nha Trang a couple of months ago. Maybe all she needed was to get away again for a few days. The thought occurred to her that it would be really nice if Rat could join her for a few days on the beach. Maybe if they spent some time together away from the Cav, they could get back to where they had been in the beginning.

It was a great idea. She decided that as soon as they were settled in Chu Lai, she'd talk to Gaines and see if he could get a few days off.

It was good to see the sprawl of the Air Cav's base when Camp Radcliff came into view. For over two years An Khe had been home to Python Flight, and Warlokk had missed it. But with two brigades of the Air Cav gone now, the place seemed almost deserted. The "Golf Course," as the big chopper airfield was called, was still busy, though. It was the world's largest helicopter landing field, and there was plenty of traffic coming in and out to keep the division supplied. In fact, it was so busy that day that the control tower had Warlokk and Alphabet go into a holding pattern for several minutes before they were given permission to land.

When he finally got the go-ahead, Warlokk dropped his Huey C-Model gunship down onto the main strip and taxied over to the division aircraft-maintenance area. Parked together in a row on the PSP runway were five shiny new AH-1G Cobra gunships. Warlokk slid his Huey Hog in beside them and shut the turbine down.

He and Alphabet climbed out of their ship and walked over to the sleek birds. These were not makeshift gunships like *Sat Cong,* the Huey C he had flown in on. They were not dumpy UHs, utility helicopters, that just had some guns and rockets bolted wherever armorers could find a place to hang them. These were real gunships — lean, ass-kicking, armored fighting machines that had been designed to get down in the dirt and slug it out with the worst that Charlie could throw back at them. The Cobra's designation said it all. The AH of AH-1G stood for "attack helicopter."

From the beginning, the Cobra had been designed to be an integrated gunship weapons system, and it looked the part. Every inch of these wicked machines had been designed to do only one thing. Kill. And they could do it well. From the 7.62mm minigun and 40mm thumper in their M-28 nose turrets past the stub wings with their rocketpods, to their sharply raked tail fin, the birds screamed "Killer." They were what the army chopper units should have been flying all along instead of jury-rigged Huey gunships.

The Bell Helicopter Company engineers had designed the Cobra around the well-proven Lycoming T-53 L-13 turbine, transmission, and broad-cord rotor blades of the Huey C Model to lessen the maintenance problems in the field. But the Cobra was over fifty miles an hour faster than the Huey C, and it could fly rings around it.

With the stub wings providing additional lift as well as being a place to hang ordnance, the Cobra's rotor head wasn't as highly stressed as it was on the Huey Hogs. It could go faster and turn faster. Best of all, from the pilot's standpoint, the Cobra's cockpit had been armored against rifle caliber ground fire. No longer would the gunship drivers be vulnerable to a stray AK round punching through the thin skin of a Huey, canceling their ticket.

All of the Cobras were painted olive drab, and on their noses by the chin turrets, they had red-and-white sharks' mouths like those worn by the P-40 Flying Tigers in World War II. On their tails were painted the big yellow-and-black

Horse Blanket patches of the First Air Cav Division. One of the machines already wore a red-and-white cavalry guide on the tail boom with a black E 1/7 stenciled over it. Echo Company, First of the 7th Cav. It was Warlokk's new bird.

Warlokk's hands were itching to get on the controls of his new machine. "Come on," he said abruptly, grabbing Schmuchatelli by the arm.

With Alphabet trailing along behind him, the pilot hurried into the maintenance office to sign for his new gunship. He was out of the building and back on the PSP in under a minute.

"Joe," he said, "I'm going to run this thing over to ordnance and have them load me up. Then maybe we can find something to fuck with on the way back to Chu Lai."

The two men quickly climbed up into the Cobra's cockpit, ran through their pre-flight, and cranked up the turbine. When the blades were spinning overhead, Warlokk keyed his throat mike and called the tower.

"Golf Course Control, this is Python Six Niner, over."

"This is Control. Is that you, Lawless?"

Warlokk chuckled to himself. "Control, be advised that Ol' Lawless is now Python Six-Niner, over."

"I always knew that you were a sixty-niner, old buddy. Whaddaya want?"

The pilot ignored the remark. "I need to taxi this machine over to the re-arm point and get her loaded up. Over."

"Roger, permission granted."

Warlokk brought the Cobra to a hover and headed over to the far end of the runway, where the ordnance men stored rockets and ammunition for the gunships. When he reached the re-arming pad, he shut down. He opened the canopy and was climbing out when the ordnance sergeant in charge of the re-arming point walked up.

"Fill her up, regular," Warlokk said. "And check the tires."

The sergeant had heard that joke many times. He yelled for his men. Two of them came out carrying a heavy metal can of 40mm thumper ammo between them. They walked to the nose of the bird, set the can down, and went back for a can of 7.62mm link-belt ammunition for the minigun. Other men brought the 2.75-inch H.E. rockets out to load into the pods under the stub wings.

Since this was not a "hot" re-arm, the ammo humpers were taking their own sweet time about it, trying hard not to work up a sweat. "Come on, come on," Warlokk muttered under his breath. He was anxious to get up into the air to try his new toy out.

"Hey, Sarge!" the impatient pilot called out. "I've got ten bucks for beer if your guys can get a hustle on and get me outta here in ten minutes."

The sergeant smiled. "No sweat, sir," he said. "Okay, boys," he yelled, "let's hump it. The beer's on Mr. Warlokk."

The idea of a cool beer to cut the dust in their throats worked like magic. Suddenly swarms of ordnance men appeared from the cool shade of the ammo bunkers to lend a hand. The Cobra was fully armed and ready to go in eight minutes.

"Thanks, Sarge." Warlokk dug into his billfold and pulled out a ten-dollar MPC note.

"Anytime, sir."

Warlokk dropped Alphabet back at their old ship. He quickly climbed on board and fired it up. When they were both ready and running, Warlokk got back on the radio to the control tower. "Golf Course Control, this is Python Six Niner. Request permission to take off."

"Six Niner, this is control. Roger, the runway is clear. Vector to the east on takeoff, over."

"This is Six Niner, Roger."

He switched his radio to the in-flight frequency to talk to Alphabet. "Python Two Seven, this is Six Niner, we are cleared. Pull pitch on my call. Over."

"This is Two Seven, Roger," came Schmuchatelli's answer. "Ready to roll."

"This is Six Niner, pull pitch now."

The Cobra and the old Huey Hog rose off the PSP. Since his new machine was so much more powerful than the old Huey, Warlokk took the lead and started down the runway in a classic gunship takeoff. When his airspeed had built up, he nudged forward on the collective. The Cobra leaped into the clear blue sky.

Alphabet did his best to keep up with Warlokk, but the old C Model just wasn't up to it. "Hey! Wait for me!" he called out over the radio. In the Cobra, Warlokk grinned and ran the throttle back down a little to give Alphabet a chance. The two choppers climbed to 8,000 feet and made a slow, graceful turn to the northeast, heading back for Chu Lai.

"What do you say we head on over to the coastline and see if we can find a place to play?" Warlokk called over to Alphabet.

"Hadn't we better get back?" the new AC protested. "I don't have a copilot, and you don't have a gunner. We shouldn't be fucking around like this, Lawless. Rat's going to shit himself."

Warlokk chuckled at that mental image. "Look, I'll take care of Rat Gaines, you just be a good little pilot and follow your flight leader."

"Okay, but it's going to be your ass if anything goes wrong."

"What could go wrong on a nice day like this?"

Alphabet didn't bother to reply. When Warlokk got a hard-on to do something, the only man who could control him was Rat Gaines. He checked his instruments again and settled back for his first flight as an aircraft commander.

CHAPTER 8

QL-1, south of Chu Lai

Second Lieutenant Tim Ratherton was not having a good day. In fact, he was up to his hip boots in dinks, and his parents were probably only a few minutes away from collecting on his GI life-insurance policy.

Unfortunately, the rest of his infantry platoon was in the shit right along with him.

Ratherton and his people had been out sweeping the road south of Bong Son when they were caught in an ambush. The lieutenant had been a bit careless. It was such a nice day up until that point. The sun was shining, but not too hot. The countryside was lush and green, and there was very little civilian traffic on the road. It was hard to believe that there were people hiding out there who were going to do their level best to waste his young ass.

Ratherton was new to the Nam. He had not yet learned that nothing and no one could be trusted, or that he should never, ever relax. This was also the lieutenant's first combat patrol. He had had his three vehicles bunched up one behind the other, just as if they were a convoy back at Fort Benning.

And Ratherton had obeyed the speed limit. The army had decided that no one should drive faster than thirty miles per hour, regardless of the reason. It cut down on traffic accidents, but it made a slow-moving vehicle a perfect target for the best anti-tank rocket in the world, the RPG-7.

The RPG, like its Chinese copy, the B-40, was a shoulder-fired, rocket-propelled, tank-killing round. It was also a great bunker-buster and general, all-around vehicle killer. It was idiotproof, had a seven-hundred-meter range and very good sights, up to a point. The problem with the RPG sights was that they were graduated only up to fifty kilometers, or thirty miles per hour. A TVA gunner just had to line the vehicle up on the sight lead and trigger the rocket off. Nine times out of ten it hit the target.

When a vehicle was traveling faster than thirty miles per hour, however, the RPG gunner would have to apply "Kentucky Windage" and try to shoot beyond the limitations of his sight. The NVA weren't too good at shooting at a target moving faster than what the sight lead could track. Those who knew this never traveled less than thirty miles an hour, MPs or speeding tickets be damned.

Ratherton was moving at a little less than thirty when the RPGs opened up on him and his little convoy.

The first round impacted low on the left front wheel of his jeep. The explosion threw the vehicle onto its side, dumping the riders onto the ground. It also crushed the A/N GRC-46 radio mounted in the back of the jeep, Ratherton's only communication with his home base.

More rounds took out both of the deuce-and-a-halves following him. Before the smoke had even cleared, RPD machine guns opened up on them from the wood line, two hundred meters away. Ratherton and his men dove for cover in the ditch by the side of the road, dragging their wounded comrades with them. Several more RPG rounds landed close to the ditch, killing or wounding even more of his people.

The young lieutenant tried to rally his men, but almost half of them had been wounded or injured. A few were trying to return fire, but the moment they poked their heads up, AK or RPD fire drove them back down. They were truly in deep *kim chee*.

At any moment, Ratherton expected the dinks to break out of the wood line and charge the ditch. When they did, they were all going to die. Without the radio, there was no way that he could call for any kind of help. No one would even know that they were in trouble until he failed to call in at their next checkpoint an hour down the road. In an hour they would all be dead.

He was frantically looking around for a way out when he spotted two black specks flying in the distant sky headed straight for them. Choppers!

Ratherton jumped to his feet, waving his arms frantically over his head and praying that the pilots would see him. A burst of AK fire drove him back to the cover of the ditch.

He cursed as the choppers flew on without heeding his plea. Without the radio, he had no way to contact them. Suddenly he had an idea.

"Hey," he yelled over the roar of the small arms fire. "Anybody got any jack-off flares?"

One of the men huddled in the ditch on the other side of the road yelled back, "I do, sir."

"Hurry, man, get 'em out!"

The troop slung his ruck in front of him and frantically dug into it. Buried under the socks, rations, and ammunition, he found three of the thin aluminum tubes. Each one contained a rocket flare. He had two illumination flares and a red star-cluster signal.

"Fire one! Quick!"

The soldier took the cap off of the top end, placed it over the bottom of the tube and slammed the end against the ground to ignite the rocket inside. With a *whoosh,* the rocket left the tube and flew into the sky.

The first one was the red star cluster. It burst several hundred feet above them with a bang. Glowing red balls shot out and slowly floated to earth. It was like the Fourth of July. The GI followed it with the two parachute flares. Even in the harsh tropical sun, the bright magnesium flares could be seen for miles.

The choppers flew on. In a few seconds, they would be gone.

"Smoke grenades," the ell tee yelled. "Everybody! Pop smoke! Pop everything you've got!"

Most infantry troops carried at least one smoke grenade with their gear and no one cared what color they had. The air was soon filled with billowing, multicolored clouds.

From an altitude of six thousand feet, Alphabet glanced down to his left and saw the ground covered with red, purple, green, and yellow smoke. It looked like the circus had come to town.

"Warlokk," he called over to the Cobra. "Check that out down there at ten o'clock."

"What the fuck's going on?" Warlokk banked the Cobra around for a closer look. Through the clouds of thinning smoke, the antlike figures of men were huddled in a ditch along both sides of the road.

"Dinks!" he called out to Alphabet. "Rolling in now."

Warlokk flicked on his arming switches and twisted his throttle all the way up against the stop. Since he didn't have a gunner sitting in front of him to control the weapons, he switched all of the firing circuits to pilot control and locked the Cobra's nose turret in the straight-ahead position.

In the Huey Hog, Alphabet armed his weapons, too, and took up a position slightly behind and to the right of the Cobra. From that position he could cover Warlokk when the Cobra swept past the enemy position. The problem was, of course, that he had no one to cover him.

Somehow, that had escaped his mind.

On the ground, Ratherton and his men cheered as the Cobra swept down low over them. The red-and-white painted

56

shark's mouth on her nose blossomed flame as Warlokk triggered the minigun and thumper in the turret. The air was filled with the sound of ripping canvas when the mini spat out 7.62mm rounds at the rate of 4,000 rounds per minute. Hot shell cases rained down on the grunts.

As Warlokk swept in closer, the dinks fired everything they had at the diving gunship. The wood line came ablaze with AK and RPD machine-gun fire. A storm of green tracer fire flashed into the Cobra's path.

The pilot kicked down on his rudder pedals, snapping the ship's tail from side to side to spread his fire over a wider area. Since he could not use the turret controls to aim the weapons, he had to point the nose of the ship directly at his intended target.

In the Huey, Alphabet started triggering his 2.75-inch rockets off in pairs from a thousand meters out. They trailed dirty white smoke as they raced down for the tree line.

Right ahead of him, Warlokk pulled out of his gun run. Now the gooks could concentrate all their fire on him. Alphabet hunched down lower in the armored pilot's seat. He was glad that he was wearing his chickenplate armored vest.

He peered through the swing-out gunsight and fired the grenade launcher in the nose. The rockets impacted with bright red-and-black bursts when the warheads exploded. Smaller puffs of black smoke appeared in between the rocket bursts as 40mm thumper grenades went off.

It was a seemingly endless hail of fire, but it didn't make the dinks slack off. Lines of green tracer fire still clawed at Warlokk's gunship. The ship took hits.

Suddenly, Alphabet was past the wood line and in the clear. He stomped down on the right rudder pedal and slammed the cyclic over to the side to bring his chopper around again as fast as he could.

The heavily laden Huey gunship shuddered in the air as it skidded into the turn. He knew better than to try that kind of turn so low to the ground, but he had no choice; he had to cover Warlokk when he made his second run.

The Cobra was already at it again. This time Warlokk was triggering the stub-wing-mounted minigun pods. Even with the burst limiters holding down the amount of ammunition going through the six-barreled weapons, the rain of fire they put out was impressive.

The combined impact of so many bullets at once shredded the jungle. Anything smaller than a tree was instantly pounded to pulp. This included the dinks. Enemy fire began to slacken.

By this time, Alphabet had his Hog turned around and was rolling in on his second run. His C-Model gunship didn't have the miniguns of the Cobra, but four M-60s mounted on his side pylons were firing straight ahead.

He bore into the target, flying even lower over the trees. The explosions from his rockets threw dirt and debris into his path. He was two hundred meters out when Warlokk broke away from his run and the dinks picked themselves up from the jungle floor. The first thing they did was shoot Alphabet's bird full of holes.

Lines of green tracer fire converged on the Huey. The grunts in the ditch saw the machine take hits. Smoke poured from the turbine exhaust, and brief fingers of fire broke from the engine compartment. In the cockpit, Alphabet knew that he was in trouble when he heard the turbine scream. The fire light was blinking on the instrument panel, and the tachometer needle was pegged against stop. The turbine was running away with itself. In seconds the transmission would freeze up, the rotor blades would snap to a halt, and he would fall from the sky like a rock.

He banked away, trying to get back over the road. He didn't want to crash in the jungle. He flipped the governor control over to decrease to slow the speeding turbine, but it didn't work. The scream in his ears reached an even higher note.

On the ground, the grunts watched as Alphabet fought to bring his wounded ship under control, and cheered when he cleared the trees. It looked to Ratherton that the burning chopper was going to fall right on top of him, but it passed over his head and hit the roadbed with a wrenching crash.

The impact snapped the tail boom off, and the body of the ship rolled onto its side. The still-spinning rotor slammed into the ground and disintegrated, throwing pieces of the blades into the air.

The lieutenant saw the pilot struggling to free himself from the burning wreckage. Without a thought about the burning fuel cells, he leaped to his feet and dashed over to help.

The door on the pilot's side was jammed, and it took a moment for him to rip it open. Inside the cockpit, Alphabet was struggling to free himself from his seat. The crash had jammed the side armor and he couldn't slide it out of the way. He also couldn't climb over it because the cyclic control had been bent back, trapping his left leg against the edge of the seat.

Ratherton wrenched the side armor out of the way. Reaching in, he grabbed the pilot by his armored vest. With a sharp jerk, he freed Alphabet's leg and had him halfway out of the open door. Alphabet gave a kick and propelled himself the rest of the way, landing in a heap on the ground.

Ratherton grabbed the pilot, pulled him to his feet and they ran as fast as they could. They had gone ten meters when the fuel cells exploded with a dull crump, driving both of them flat onto their faces. Burning JP-4 jet fuel showered over the area.

Shielding his face from the flames, Alphabet looked back at the burning chopper. Billowing, greasy black smoke and angry orange flames leaped into the sky. The fire reached toward the ammunition storage and weapons pods. Machine-gun rounds and rockets started cooking off.

The chopper pilot staggered to his feet. "Run for it!" he shouted.

The two men dashed the last fifty feet for the ditch and dove for cover.

"Thanks," Alphabet panted.

Ratherton was still stunned. More stunned, in fact, than Alphabet. In the space of less than an hour, he had been ambushed, pinned down, and then saved by two passing choppers. Then he had saved one of the pilots from a burning wreck. It had been a dramatic introduction to combat.

"You're welcome," he said simply.

Overhead, Warlokk's Cobra was adding the finishing touches to the dinks in the wood line. Those that were not blasted to pieces were on their feet, getting out of the area as fast as they could. When it looked like they were gone, Warlokk brought his Cobra down on the road next to the infantry.

Leaving his turbine turning over, he opened the side of his canopy and called over to Ratherton. "I've called for a Dustoff," he shouted. "They should be here in ten or fifteen minutes."

Alphabet got to his feet and staggered over to the Cobra. "How 'bout a ride?" he asked.

"I should leave you here for fucking up a perfectly good gunship," Warlokk snapped, glancing at the burning wreckage of his old gunship. "Your first time out and you get yourself shot down. Rat's going to have your ass for this."

CHAPTER 9

Chu Lai

Rat Gaines wasn't happy about losing one of his gunships, particularly when he had so many of them down for maintenance. But he'd rather lose a ship than a pilot.

This didn't save Alphabet from being chewed out. Rat had a strict policy. When a man deserved having his ass reamed for something, he got it. Even if he was Rat's own gunner.

"I've got half a mind to send you two fucking clowns down to a transportation company and let you drive slicks for the rest of the war," Gaines snapped at Warlokk and Alphabet.

The two pilots stood at a rigid position of attention in front of his desk. Both of them knew better than to mouth off. When Gaines was in this frame of mind, it was best to shut up and take it like a man.

Rat slammed both hands down on his desk top. "Just how in the hell am I going to explain to the colonel that I had two pilots ferrying choppers and on the way home they just happened to run into a firefight and lose one of the ships? He's going to take a strip off my ass for this, and I can't say that I blame him one bit. We're so short of choppers as it is we can barely make our missions."

"And you." The company commander stared hard at Alphabet. "You were on your first flight as an aircraft commander. It's true that the paper work hasn't been signed yet, but nonetheless, you were an AC. And I might add, you were flying without a copilot, which, as you know, is a big fucking no-no. Then you go get yourself into a pissing contest that results in one less Huey for Uncle Sam."

"But, sir," Alphabet carefully reminded him, "there were troops in contact down there. They'd have been killed if we hadn't helped them."

"I know, I know." Gaines threw up his hands in disgust. "And that's the only thing that's keeping you two from making ash²n-trash runs for the rest of your life. Now get the hell out of my office and do something useful for a change."

The pilots faced about and started out the door.

"Alphabet," Gaines called out after them.

"Yes, sir?"

"See that you're in the club at eighteen hundred hours tonight."

"Yes, sir."

Outside the hut, Alphabet turned to the older pilot. "I wonder what in the hell that was all about? If he's so pissed off, why does he want to see me at the club tonight?"

Warlokk grinned to himself. "Beats the shit outta me, old buddy. Maybe he's going to have a pilots' meeting or something."

"I guess."

Gaines sat back down at his desk and dove into a pile of paper work awaiting his attention. Lisa was due to arrive later that day and he wanted some free time. He suddenly wanted to see her very much. It had really been a long time since they had had a chance to be together more than a couple of hours at a time.

Part of it had been because the division was on the move, spread out in so many different locations. She was back at

An Khe, and he was with the Third Brigade at Chu Lai. But much of it had been simply because he had been so damned busy lately. Things had been a lot easier when they had all been together back at An Khe. Life had not been so hectic there, and it had been easy for them to spend their evenings together.

Lately, it seemed that every time he thought he was going to have a night off, he had been called out to work again. Not for the first time, Gaines realized how difficult it was when a man got emotionally involved during a war.

Even the last couple of times that they had gone to bed together had not been too good. Their lovemaking had been short and to the point, lacking the closeness they had once had. He was going to have to find a way to recapture that, and to do it he had to tear himself away from the responsibilities of commanding Echo Company and fighting a war long enough to completely relax and lose himself in her again.

"Fuck this paper work," he growled. Without even reading the document in front of him, he scrawled his name above the signature block and threw it in his out-box.

On the other side of the Chu Lai basecamp, Lieutenant Colonel Maxwell T. Jordan, the battalion commander of the First of the 7th Cav was fighting his own paper-work battles. Ever since the battalion had moved to Chu Lai, it seemed to him that the paper-work load had doubled. He had his companies spread out all over the map from hell to breakfast. Just keeping all of them supplied with beans and bullets was a major headache. And the division kept coming up with these off-the-wall missions, trying to keep a lid on things in their old AO as well as the southern half of I Corps.

Jordan felt in his bones that the tempo of the war was changing, and it was probably not going to get any better in the near future. He was going to have to light a fire under his staff officers to make sure they stayed on top of the rapidly changing situation. They had all been spoiled by their long stay in Camp Radcliff, himself included. Life had been much too simple there. Now the party was over.

The new war called for more independent action on the part of the individual Cav battalions, but Jordan had no problem with that. He prided himself on being very good at independent operations and knew that he could handle it. On his first tour in the Nam, he had been a major advising an ARVN Ranger company down in the Delta. And he was proud to say that his Ranger company had been one of the best in all of the IV Corps area.

They had specialized in night patrolling and ambushing, something that not every South Vietnamese army unit wanted to do. Jordan had figured that if the VC could work at night, then the ARVNs could do it as well. All they really needed was decent leadership and someone who could set the right example for them.

Back in the good old days, Jordan had been known as "Mack the Knife" for the Randall fighting knife he always wore. He had trained his ARVNs in silent knife kills for their night raids. Those were the good old days. One of the worst things about his promotion to lieutenant colonel was that the closest he got to field duty these days was orbiting overhead in his C-and-C ship directing battle.

Commanding a battalion was the goal of every "regular Army" officer, but it really wasn't that much fun. He reached for his ever-present pack of Marlboros, fished out his last smoke, and lit it. Taking a drag, he looked in his desk drawer and found that it had been his last pack. He started to yell for his adjutant but remembered that his S-1, Lieutenant Muller, was off taking care of business at Brigade Headquarters.

Getting to his feet, he grabbed his hat. He needed a break and decided to get his own cigarettes for a change. And while he was at the PX he needed some shaving cream. He had run out days ago and had been dry-shaving since. As he walked out of his office, Jordan mentally counted the days he had been in-country on his current tour. He was just a little short of the halfway mark. It was about time that he started thinking of putting in for an R and R. Even battalion commanders needed to get drunk and laid every now and then.

Rat Gaines was waiting at the chopper pad when Lisa stepped out of the rear ramp of the twin-rotor CH-47 Chinook cargo helicopter that had brought the last of the doctors and nurses from An Khe.

"Lisa!" he called out, waving his arm.

The nurse looked tired. Quickly he took her duffel bag and steered her over to his jeep. "Do you know where you're staying yet?"

"Just take me over to the hospital," she replied, brushing her hair away from her face. "They're supposed to have quarters ready for us."

"You can always stay with me," he offered, smiling warmly.

She shot him a dirty look that completely surprised him.

"Just for the night, I mean," he quickly amended his offer. She seemed to relax a little.

"And also," he added, "the boys're having a little get-together at the club tonight. Maybe you'd like to come?"

"No, thanks, Rat," she answered quietly. "I don't think that I'm in the mood tonight for an evening of drunken, hairy-chested pilots making complete assholes out of themselves."

Gaines felt the dig at him, but he ignored it. He really wanted to spend the night with her.

"Yeah, I'm sure you're tired. Look," he said brightly, "I've got it. Why don't we stop off at my place and you can get cleaned up. Then we can find a place to eat and come back. I have to make an appearance at the club, but I won't stay very long. I promise."

Lisa looked over at him. "Roger," she said, "I don't think so. Not tonight. Just take me to the hospital. Please."

Gaines studied her face. Lisa had not called him by his first name since their first date. He saw nothing in her eyes, and he didn't question her. Something was wrong, but it wasn't the right time to get into it.

"Sure," he said casually, trying to keep the disappointment out of his voice. "We can catch it some other time."

"Yes, maybe another time."

For the remainder of the short ride, neither of them said a word. When he braked to a halt in the parking lot, he jumped out and grabbed her duffel bag. "I'll get this for you," he said.

She reached out her hand for the heavy bag. "No, that's okay. I can handle it."

Gaines surrendered it and she threw it over her shoulder without a word.

"I'll call you tomorrow," he said hopefully. "And see how you're settling in."

She locked eyes with him. "I'll probably be real busy, so don't worry. I'll be okay."

Gaines was stunned. He hadn't been turned down so abruptly since the time he had tried to sneak into a strip joint when he was fifteen years old.

"Well . . ." he said. "Take care, Lisa."

"You, too."

She turned and headed for the hospital. He got back into his jeep and watched her walk up the steps. What in the fuck had gone wrong? He had been so sure that their relationship had been solid, something that would last beyond the war. He had even given quite a bit of thought to asking her to marry him. But she was acting like she hardly knew who he was, and he didn't have the slightest idea what he had done to deserve it.

An empty feeling chilled him like a cold monsoon rain at ten thousand feet.

He started the jeep, jammed the gear shift lever into reverse, and backed away from the nurses' building. Slam-shifting into first, he drove off with his tires spraying gravel.

Lisa stopped inside the door of the nurses' quarters. Dropping her heavy duffel bag, she leaned against the wall, exhausted. She really didn't know why she had treated Rat that way. He hadn't done anything to deserve her childish behavior. In fact, he had been sweeter and more attentive to her than he had been in weeks.

Maybe it had been his invitation to go to the club that had set her off. It seemed that they spent so much of their precious time together around the chopper pilots of Python Flight.

Tears came to the corners of her eyes. She had wanted to spend the night with him, she really had. Why in God's name had she done that to him? Wiping her eyes on the back of her hand, she shouldered her duffel bag and went down the hall, looking for someone who could tell her where she could bed down.

CHAPTER 10

Chu Lai Basecamp

The pilots and crew of Python Flight had taken over the small officers' club in Chu Lai for their party. Anyone else wanting to get a drink had to sneak around to the back door to get the attention of the bartender. If they tried to come through the front door they were unceremoniously thrown out.

Rat Gaines was a firm believer in parties, especially after one of their choppers had been shot down or crash-landed. If someone had been killed, the party was a wake for their fallen comrade. Otherwise, the party was a celebration of victory over the Grim Reaper. The pressures of combat flying, the brutal hours aircrews kept, and the ever-present knowledge that a few cents' worth of copper-jacketed lead in the wrong place could send them crashing to their deaths made the parties absolutely necessary to let off steam.

Python Flight was really letting it loose, and Alphabet was on the receiving end of it. Not only had he been promoted to aircraft commander, he had been shot down for the first time while piloting a helicopter. They were two of the most memorable moments in a pilot's life.

Gaines started the ceremonies. He called Alphabet up, made a little speech, and gave him one of his thin cigars for the promotion. He helped a grinning Alphabet light it up. As soon as the cigar was going strongly, Gaines poured a pitcher of beer over his head, completely soaking the cigar.

The men roared at the startled expression on Alphabet's face and the beer dripping off of the soggy cigar in his mouth. Then, one by one, they came up to add their congratulations. For the promotion, the men bought him beer. For having gotten shot down, they poured the beer over his head. After everyone had finished congratulating him, the new AC looked like a drowned rat.

Once the ceremony was well under way, Rat backed off to the end of the bar and started knocking back gin and tonics.

Leaning back against the wall in a chair, Lance Warlokk watched his commander. Usually, Gaines went easy on the booze before a mission, but lately, he had been drinking more. A lot more. Gaines and Warlokk didn't like it. Python Flight was one of the best Air Cav units in the entire division, but it hadn't always been that way. The sole reason that the pilots worked so well together now was because they had Rat Gaines for their commander.

In the months since Gaines had taken command of Echo Company, he had transformed the unit from a bunch of drunks into a crack fighting outfit. In the air and on the ground, Gaines demanded and received the best from all of his people.

Warlokk almost hated to admit it, but Rat Gaines was the best pilot and officer he had ever known. In the beginning, though, the tough, scar-faced chopper pilot hadn't felt that way.

Lance Lawless Warlokk was a hard drinking, hard-living warrant officer-chopper pilot of the old school. His scarred face reflected the life he led, and not all of the scars were from chopper crashes. Some had come from drunken brawls. His reputation as a bad-ass had been well known and people had wisely given him wide berth. Everyone, that was, until he had run into Captain Rat Gaines.

Warlokk had resented Gaines and the procedures the new officer had implemented to improve the unit. He had challenged Gaines, but the soft-talking southerner didn't move out of the way for anyone. Gaines had not been impressed with Warlokk's attitude. Rat used his fists, hammering Lawless Warlokk into the ground to make him see the error of his ways.

There was one thing about a professional bad-ass when he discovered that there was someone who could whip his tail ten times out of ten; he quickly made friends. It was a law of the jungle. After their brutal encounter, Rat Gaines had no stauncher supporter than Lance Lawless Warlokk.

Warlokk considered himself one of Gaines's best friends in the company and he didn't like to see his boss drinking that way. Something was wrong, and Warlokk decided that he'd better find out what it was.

When everyone had properly anointed Alphabet, the party got into full swing. The unofficial company glee club was singing off key again, a rendition of a little aviator's ditty dating back to World War I. Known by many names, the tune was one that no one had ever heard before.

"I'll be flying the clouds in the morning,
No wingman beside me to course,
So give my dog tags to the colonel
And give my regards to the force."

Now it was time for the solo performance. A man with a surprisingly good voice stood up and sang,

"Forgot by the land that bore us,
Betrayed by the ones we hold dear,
The good men have all gone before us
And only the evil are here.

70

"So stand to your glasses steady,
This world is a world full of lies.
Here's a drink to those dead already,
And here's to the next man to die."

The singer took a bow to a spattering of applause and a shower of empty beer cans. Another impromptu group started singing a more recently written song that recounted a GI's adventures with the local talent. The song went on for several explicitly graphic verses describing the sexual joys of a short time; Vietnamese streetwalker style.

Gaines downed the last of his drink and ordered another. He was not in the mood to listen to songs about getting laid, long time or short time. But the singer had a good point. When in Vietnam, a man should confine his pleasures to sampling the local talent. It was far easier and much less complicated than trying to get involved with one of the few American women in-country.

Warlokk plopped down on the barstool beside him. "Hey, Captain," he said. "Why don't you and me take a little trip down to the ville."

"No, thanks, Lance, I don't feel up to it tonight."

Warlokk leaned closer. "Rat," he said quietly, "you look like shit and you're getting drunk, and that ain't like you at all, boss."

Gaines flared up. "So fucking what?"

Warlokk put his hands up. "Hey, wait a minute now. All I'm saying is that you look like a man who could use a little relaxation right now, and I know the greatest little steam-and-cream palace in all of Southeast Asia."

Gaines ran his hand down the back of his neck. "I don't know, Lance."

"Come on, Captain. You've got a mission to fly in the morning and could probably use a steam bath and a long session under the magic fingers."

Gaines glanced down at his watch. It was only a little after eight, so he had plenty of time. "Sure." He slid off the barstool and grabbed his hat. "Why not?"

Outside the club, Warlokk climbed into the driver's side of Rat's jeep and fired it up. "I'll drive 'cause I know where we're going."

"Makes sense to me." Gaines replied, settling back for the ride.

Outside the main gate of Chu Lai basecamp, Warlokk turned off the main road and headed down a side street. Rat looked around at the small Vietnamese shops clustered along the narrow street. Suddenly he realized that they were unarmed. "You got a piece?" he asked nervously.

Warlokk patted his left side right above the belt line. "Yep, my backup gun. I never leave home without it."

Gaines relaxed.

Their destination was a small, walled French villa at the outskirts of town. A man met them at the iron gate to the driveway. He recognized Warlokk and opened the gate for them. When they passed, Gaines saw that the gatekeeper carried an old American M-1 carbine.

"Shit, that guy's armed!"

Warlokk grinned. "The mama san here doesn't want anyone bothering her customers," He braked to a halt under a tree and shut the motor off. "Welcome to paradise, Captain."

Gaines looked around the compound. Several spotlights illuminated the well-kept grounds. Gaines saw barbed wire and broken glass on top of the wall. The villa was freshly painted and looked well maintained. "Who runs this place?" he asked as they walked to the front door.

"Well, the mama san's name is Helen. She's half-French, half-Chinese and well connected. This place used to be a pleasure palace before the GIs came. Now it's an invitation-only whorehouse."

"How'd you get invited?"

Warlokk grinned as he knocked on the door. "Well, I did a little favor for Helen once."

The door was opened by a young Chinese man. From the bulge under his shirt, Gaines realized that he, too, was armed. The servant saw Warlokk and smiled. "You are welcome, Mr. Lance."

"Tell Helen that I have someone here who would like to meet her."

The man bowed slightly and left them.

Just a moment later, an older Chinese woman entered the room. It was impossible for Gaines to guess her age. She could have been thirty or sixty. Gaines figured she was about halfway between the two extremes. Her silk *ao dai* was worth a month's pay, and the solid gold jewelry obviously cost more than his annual salary, flight pay included.

She smiled. "How nice to meet you, Captain. Mr. Warlokk has told me so much about you."

Gaines took her small hand. "My pleasure, ma'am."

Helen clapped her hands and two lovely young girls stepped out. "The captain is tired," she said. "See that he relaxes."

With no further ado, Gaines was led to a room down the hall. A few minutes later, the pilot was sure he had died and gone to heaven. Had it not been for the incredible sensations of the girl's fingers on his body, he would have thought he was dreaming.

He rested his head in the lap of the second girl, who kept stuffing small grilled shrimp and bits of tangy barbecued pork into his mouth every time he stopped chewing. When he held up his hand to say that he was full, the girl brought a glass of bourbon and ice to his lips. He drank deeply.

He looked up at the two girls trying to make up his mind which one he was going to take to bed. Both were true Asian beauties and it was a hard call. He had just about decided on the one with the magic fingers, when the door opened and in walked the most beautiful girl he had ever seen.

Gaines's mouth dropped open. This girl made the two with him look like dogs. She could be Miss Universe anytime she wanted to, no contest. She was all the Asian beauties he had ever seen rolled into one, and doubled.

"My name is Andrea," she said in a musical voice. "I am here to see that you enjoy yourself this evening."

Gaines recovered his senses. He sat up and stuck out his hand. "I'm Rat Gaines, I'm very glad to meet you."

"That is a very unusual name," she said, taking his hand.

"My real name's Roger."

"I like that better. May I call you Roger?"

As far as Rat was concerned, she could call him Shit for Brains.

"Sure."

Andrea said something to the two girls in Chinese and they scampered out of the way. They had just been the warm-up act. The main event was about to start. The girl slipped out of her dress. She was wearing nothing underneath. Her breasts were perfectly shaped. "Let me finish your massage," she purred.

Rat gulped. "Sure."

She removed the small cloth covering his private parts. "Oh," she exclaimed.

Rat grinned. Her long, glossy hair cascaded over his hips and he lost the grin. His eyes closed and his head fell back. Now he really knew that he had died and gone to heaven.

In the back of the villa, Warlokk and Helen sat, drinking more of her good bourbon. "Your captain looks like a good man," the woman said.

"He is, one of the best."

"He has many problems, no?"

Warlokk shrugged. "Just the usual. Running a company is vary hard on a man sometimes."

"I just pray that it doesn't get any harder," the woman said.

Warlokk caught her tone of voice. "What do you mean?"

"I hear many things in my business, no?"

Warlokk nodded, Helen's sources rivaled the CIA's. "And I hear that much trouble is coming soon to you Americans."

"Oh?"

"There is much talk about a big attack."

"Where?"

"All over. All of the cities are to be attacked by the *cong*."

"Do the voices say when?"

"No, just that it will be soon."

"I wouldn't worry about it too much, Helen. We hear this sort of thing all the time."

"This time it is different."

"They'd be crazy to hit the cities," Warlokk said. "They know they can't get away with that."

"But they will try," Helen said, her face serious.

Warlokk helped himself to a little more bourbon and swirled it around in the glass. "Well, I guess we'll just have to kick their asses, then."

"I certainly hope so."

Warlokk knocked back the whiskey and stood up. "I guess that I'd better go check on my captain. I've got to get him back to camp."

"Remember my words, Lance."

He reached down and patted her shoulder. "I always do, Helen, you know that."

Gaines was more than ready to go. In fact, if he stayed any longer, he would have to be carried back in a trash can. Warlokk found him half dressed, struggling with his jungle boots. The two giggling Chinese girls were trying to help him lace them up, but they were only getting in the way. Warlokk shooed them out.

"We got to get going."

Gaines looked up with a dazed expression on his face. "Yeah, just let me get dressed."

"You look like you could use a quart of blood."

Gaines grinned. "Yep." He tied off the boot laces and slipped into his fatigue jacket. "Let's go."

On the ride back, Gaines rested his head against the back of the seat and slept. Warlokk didn't even try to talk to him. What Helen had said about an offensive would have to wait.

CHAPTER 11

The Mouth of the Song Boung River

Navy Lieutenant James Miller looked down from the bridge of his PBR, "patrol boat, river." A small collection of ratty huts and ragged buildings straddled both sides of the coastal highway, making up the dusty little town of Hoi An. His small flotilla of four PBRs were tied up along the bank, where the river's dirty brown water poured into the clear blue South China Sea.

He glanced at his watch. The Air Cav wasn't due for another fifteen minutes, but Miller was in a hurry to get his operation under way. He felt vulnerable and exposed in unknown territory. A collection of Vietnamese children had assembled on the riverbank and were trying to sell his men Cokes and beer. One or two of the more enterprising boys were trying to sell their sisters as well.

Miller wasn't having any of it, however. He was running a PBR unit, not a floating bar and whorehouse. He didn't really care what his men did on their time off when they were away from the boats, but as long as they were on board his vessels, they were going to act like real sailors.

The young lieutenant looked around at his small command. The PBRs weren't World War II PT boats, but they were the closest thing to it that he was going to find. Miller had been raised on tales of the PT boats in the Pacific theater. His father had been a gunner's mate on one that had made the run from the Philippines to Australia carrying General MacArthur and his family to safety. Later, he had fought in the Solomon Islands campaigns and many of the other legendary "mosquito boat" battles.

As a young boy, James Miller had mourned for the old torpedo boats that had been taken out of service after the war. When he graduated from high school, he went into Naval ROTC. After he was commissioned and while serving on an aircraft carrier, he had been delighted to hear that a "Brown Water Navy" was being formed to fight on the rivers and canals in Vietnam.

The swift boats and PBRs of the Brown Water Navy weren't PT boats, but they were as close to them in spirit as anything in the Navy in 1967. Miller applied for an immediate transfer to the Brown Water Navy and was accepted.

His first six months in-country had been spent working in the Mekong Delta with Task Force 116, code-named Game Warden, patrolling the hundreds of small waterways to stem the never-ending flow of VC troops and supplies brought in on sampans and small boats.

The Mark I Power Boat, River, that he commanded had thirty-one-foot fiberglass hulls and were capable of making over twenty-eight knots while drawing barely two feet of water. Powered by a 220-horsepower General Motors diesel motor driving a Jacuzzi water-jet propulsion system, not only were the boats fast, they were also extremely maneuverable.

The PBRs were heavily armed as well. Most of them carried a twin .50-caliber machine-gun turret on the bow, a single fifty in the stern, an M-60 machinegun, and a Mark 18 hand-cranked 40mm grenade launcher amidships. The crew all carried individual weapons to complement this as well. Two of Miller's boats had been modified to mount the over-and-under 81mm mortar and .50-caliber combination weapon carried on the bigger Swift boats for additional long-range heavy firepower.

Each boat carried a crew of four men. A first-class petty officer was the boat captain, a gunner's mate manned the forward turret, the engine man and the seaman took care of the power plants, the radios, and manned the other weapons when it came to a fight.

The PBRs usually worked in a two-boat section with a patrol officer on board one of the boats, and much of their patrolling had been done at night. Miller had done well in the Delta. His unit's tally of junks and sampans captured or destroyed was respectable. But Miller had not had the chance to get into the one big battle that he was looking for, where he could use his four boats to their best advantage; a battle of speed and maneuverability, where the PBR's quickness and firepower could be demonstrated.

When he had been offered the chance to take his PBRs into a new AO, Miller had jumped at the chance. Maybe there, in a new AO where the enemy wasn't used to dealing with the boats, he would find what he was looking for.

Since the small craft were not suitable for open sea travel, the PBR mother ship, the U.S.S. *Lincoln County,* a converted World War II LST, picked the four small boats up out of the Mekong River and carried them up the coastline of Vietnam to Hoi An. The boats were lowered over the side and made the short trip through the surf to the mouth of the river.

Miller and his exec, Lieutenant Rodney Powers, were waiting for the Cav air cover that was going to escort them upriver to a place code-named Zulu, where a team of Sea Bees had spent the last week building a patrol base. Miller and his men had worked with the army before, occasionally carrying grunts of the 9th Division into battle in the Delta. And they had often used army helicopter gunships and artillery for fire support. This was the first time, however, that he had to rely on the army to guard his patrol base. He didn't anticipate any problems. The Brown Water Navy men were a lot more like grunts than the sailors of the traditional Blue Water Navy.

Miller glanced at his watch again. It was time for the rendezvous, but where was the Air Cav? Miller still had enough "Old Navy" in him that he expected everything to take place exactly on time. A moment later, he heard the crackle of the radio.

"Barn Door, Barn Door, this is Python Lead on your push, over."

Miller reached for the microphone. "Python Lead, this is Barn Door Six, over. "

"This is Lead. Echo Tango Alpha on your location zero two, over. "

"This is Barn Door, we're waiting for you. Out."

Miller whistled over to the next boat where Rod Powers was lounging on the foredeck. "Get them cranked up, Mr. Powers."

Powers sketched a brief salute and yelled up to the boat's cockpit. "Chief! Let's do it!"

Miller made another mental note to have a talk with Powers about his carefree attitude. He didn't think he was setting a good example for the enlisted men. Powers had come to him highly recommended. He had already spent one tour on the PBRs in the Delta and the Rung Sat River, and he knew his way around the small boats. But as far as Miller was concerned, the young sailor's attitude left a great deal to be desired.

Puffs of black smoke shot out of the boat's exhausts as the big diesel motors were fired up. Miller wanted to be ready to get under way as soon as the Air Cav grunts were on board. In less than a minute, black specks in the sky rapidly approached. One chopper left the formation and came in for a landing on the riverbank. With the rotor blades still spinning, nine men jumped out. Crouched over to clear the blades, they ran to the edge of the river.

When they were close enough, Miller saw that one of the grunts had officer's rank sewn on the collar of his fatigues, the single black bar of an army first lieutenant. Had he not seen the rank badges, Miller would have never known that the man was an officer. Except for the .45-caliber pistol on his field belt, he carried the same pack and weapons as his men.

The navy officer shook his head. He had heard that the Air Cav did things a little differently than the rest of the Army, but he didn't expect this. The officer climbed on board the PBR, his right arm extended.

"Mike Alexander, sir, Echo Company, First of the Seventh Cav. We'll be your extra guns today."

Miller shook his hand. "I'm Lieutenant Jim Miller, the unit commander. How many men do you have?"

"Nine, including myself, sir."

"Put two of your men on each PBR and you can stay on my boat."

"Yes, sir."

Alexander quickly gave Brody his instructions and the grunts scrambled on board. Alexander kept Bunny and one of the new men, Lindberry, with him. Brody and Two-Step took the lead boat, Corky and Farmer another, and Gardner and York boarded the fourth.

Before they were even settled in, Miller gave the order to cast off, and the four PBRs started down the river.

Overhead, Rat Gaines orbited with his flight of three gunships and the two slicks carrying the other squads of the Blues until the PBRs were under way. Leaving Warlokk and the slicks overhead, he swooped low over the river to scout for the PBRs. He flew ahead for about a mile, turned around, and came back, skimming right over the masts on the boats.

Miller looked up at the low-flying Cobra and grabbed for the radio. "Python Lead, this is Barn Door Six, over."

"This is Lead, go ahead."

"This is Barn Door Six, do not fly so low over my boats, I say again, do not fly so low. Do you roger? Over."

There was silence on the radio for a long moment and Alexander held his breath. Obviously, the Navy officer had no idea whom he was talking to.

"Six, this is Captain Rat Gaines, the leader of Python Flight. I advise you to keep your mind on your end of the operation and let me go about doing what I do best, which is driving my gunship. I was told to provide air cover for you people and that I will. But it will be provided my way. Do you roger? Over."

Now it was Miller's turn to be stunned. "Python Lead, this is Barn Door Six. I remind you that I am in command of this operation. I say again, keep your gunship out of the way. Over."

"This is Python Lead . . ." Rat's voice was cold. "Obviously you are not familiar with army regulations pertaining to flight operations. I command my unit and no one, I say again, no one is going to tell me or my pilots how or where to fly. You got that, mister?"

Miller was stunned. Alexander was doing his level best to hide the grin pulling at his face, but he was not successful.

"Python Lead, this is Barn Door Six, what's your date of rank? Over."

"Sonny boy," came Rat's southern drawl, "I was wearing captain's bars when you were still pushing toy boats around in the bathtub. You just see to your little boats and leave the flying to me. If you've got a problem with that, I'll be glad to discuss it with you as soon as I get you to where you're going. Over."

"This is Barn Door Six. I am warning you, I will file an official report with my higher about this incident, over."

"This is Lead. File away. Y'all just make sure that you send me a copy now, you hear? I'll put it in my scrapbook. Out."

That was too much for Alexander. A snicker escaped his lips. Miller spun around and glared at him. "I don't think that's funny, mister."

Alexander wiped the smile off of his face. "Sorry, sir. It's just that I've been around Captain Gaines for a long time now, and I've learned that it's best to let him have things his way. Actually, sir, he's probably the best gunship commander in the Air Cav, if not the entire U.S. Army."

"His military courtesy leaves a lot to be desired," Miller snapped back.

"Well, sir," Alexander stood his ground, "Captain Gaines feels that this is not a courteous war."

Miller turned back to his radio and started talking to his boat captains, totally ignoring Alexander.

The platoon leader made his way forward to take a look at the twin-fifty mount on the foredeck. The Browning M-2 .50-caliber machine gun dated all the way back to World War I, but there had never been a weapon as well loved as the old Ma Deuce. And, despite several attempts to design a new heavy machine gun to replace it, she was still in the inventory doing what she did best, spitting out heavy caliber slugs at a rate of 750 rounds a minute.

The fifty cal had seen use in aircraft, on tanks, as an antiaircraft gun on ships, and as a just-plain infantry support weapon. In Korea, they had even been mounted with telescopic sights and used as sniper rifles. For over fifty years on battlefields all over the world, when Ma Deuce talked, it was best to listen up and carefully.

The twin-fifty turret on the PBR was sunk down into the hull so that only the gunner's head and the guns themselves showed above the deck for minimum exposure to enemy fire. A heavy-duty searchlight was mounted co-axially with the guns so they could pick up targets at night.

Since Alexander had been trained as a Mech Infantry officer, he was well acquainted with the .50-caliber and had fired one from the command hatch of his M-113 armored personnel carrier many times. A single fifty was nice, but he would have really liked to have had one of these Navy twin-fifty mounts on his track. He shot the shit with the gunner for a while about his weapons before he made his way to the back of the boat to check on his people.

Bunny Rabdo was sitting in the stern huddled in an over-sized life jacket. He looked miserable.

"You okay?" Alexander asked.

The FO looked up. "I'm fine, sir. They gave me a life jacket."

"I don't think we'll have any trouble today," Alexander tried to reassure him. "Not with the captain flying top cover for us. It'd be suicide for anyone to try to take us out."

Bunny looked down at the swirling, muddy water and then out at the thick jungle fifty meters on either side of them. An army could be hiding in there and no one would see them until they popped up and started shooting the small boats full of holes.

He realized he had something a lot more frightening than the water to worry about.

CHAPTER 12

On the Song Boung River

Skimming the water above the small flotilla, Rat Gaines nursed a raging hangover. He realized that he had been a little sharp with the PBR commander, but the man had asked for it. No one told Rat Gaines how to fly his gunship *Sudden Discomfort,* particularly not some navy type who didn't know shit from apple butter about gunship operations.

In the front cockpit, Alphabet's gloved fingers were wrapped around the firing controls for the gunship's armament. Since he had crashed the company's only spare gunship, he was back flying the front seat for Gaines. He didn't mind. He liked firing the guns. He swung the turret from side to side, searching the thickly covered riverbanks for any sign of the enemy.

"Captain," the gunner called back on the intercom. "It's real thick down there and I'm afraid that I might miss something. What do you think about getting Warlokk down here with us? Maybe we could run a race-track pattern."

"Yeah, you're right. I'll give him a call."

Gaines keyed the throat mike for the tactical radio. "Python Six Niner, this is Lead. How about dropping down here and helping me keep an eye on things? Over."

"Lead, this is Six Niner," came Warlokk's voice in the headphones. "Roger. Rolling in now."

The second Cobra swooped down and took up position a quarter-mile behind the lead. That way, Rat could fly ahead of the boats, circle back to do it again, and Warlokk could still keep an eye on the river while he was turning around. Then, when it was Warlokk's turn to go around, Gaines would cover for him.

Down on the river, Brody sat in front of the wheel-house on the lead PRB and watched the jungle roll by on each side of him. To the veteran door-gunner, it was a little like taking a low-level flight down the river. The main difference was that he didn't have his doorgun to keep him company, and that made him a little nervous.

Having the two Cobras overhead was good insurance, though. It would take a real crazy bunch of dinks to try anything while they were up there keeping an eye on things. Lately, the division G-2, the intelligence section, had reported that the North Vietnamese were terrified of the new Cobras and had warned their troops not to fire at the "skinny" helicopters.

But, as Brody knew well, there was always that 5 percent who never got the word, or didn't care.

He looked back toward the rear of the boat and saw Two-Step talking to the sailor who was manning the over-and-under, fifty cal, and 81mm mortar combination weapon. Like the twin-fifty mount in front of him, none of the grunts had ever seen these weapons before, and they were fascinated.

The Indian was trying to convince the sailor to let him take a turn at the gun. "Sorry." The sailor shook his head. "I can't do that. Mr. Miller, our CO, has a shitfit if we let anyone mess around with our weapons."

"No sweat. Maybe when we get where we're going, I can get you to check me out on it."

"Be glad to. Just as long as the Old Man isn't around."

Two-Step laughed. "I've been there," he said in sympathy. "Have you guys heard how long you're going to be up the river?"

"Naw."The sailor shook his head. "Mr. Miller doesn't say much to us about things like that. We just go where he tells us." He thought for a moment. "But Mr. Powers said something about our being part of a move to bring a couple of PBR units up north."

"Who's Powers?"

"Mr. Powers? He's our exec. He's a lot more laid back than the Old Man. This is his second tour in the Brown Water Navy. Anyway, he said that a task force is being set up in Da Nang to patrol the Perfume and Cau Viet rivers. You know, around Da Nang, Hue, and Dong Ha."

Those places were just names to Two-Step, but he nodded.

"He said we're being sent up this river to intercept traffic coming down from the border as part of the operation." Having found an audience, the sailor got into his subject. "Chief Stevenson, though, he thinks that we're just being sent here for bait. He says we're going to be floating targets. Four boats without the support we had in the Delta ain't diddly."

"You've got the Air Cav to support you now."

"Well, no offense to you doggies, but our chief doesn't think too much of the Army."

Two-Step laughed. "Sometimes we don't, either. But as long as you're with us, you'll be treated right. We've got a good CO."

The sailor wasn't convinced, but Two-Step knew that if the shit did hit the fan, the Navy boys would see how Echo Company did their job. The Indian settled back against the stern of the PBR. Cradling his pump gun in his arms, he went back to watching the jungle and the brown water roll by.

Several hundred meters ahead of the slow-moving boats, Gaines's Cobra was flat down on the deck scanning the banks of the river at a hundred miles an hour.

"Captain!" Alphabet called out, swinging the turret over to the portside. "On the left!"

Gaines glanced down and saw fresh red mud staining the light brown water of the river close to the bank. Someone had just been in the water there and had climbed onto the bank.

He kicked down on the right rudder pedal and slammed the cyclic over into the upper right-hand corner. The Cobra banked onto her right side as the tail came around in a sharp turn. They were in a free fire zone, but Rat wanted a better look at what they were dealing with before he expended ordnance.

"Six Niner," he called to Warlokk, as the nose of his Cobra came around, lining up on the bank, "this is Lead. I'm going in, cover my ass."

"Roger."

"Alphabet, hose 'em down."

In the front cockpit, Alphabet's gloved fingers tightened on the triggers to his nose turret. Swinging it from side to side, he sprayed short bursts of 7.62mm minigun interspaced with a few thumper rounds. If anyone was hiding in there, they'd run for their lives or shoot back. Either way was okay with him.

This time, the dinks didn't feel like running. Fingers of glowing green AK-47 tracer fire reached out from the jungle, followed by the black smoke trail of an RPG round.

"Break! Break!" Gaines screamed into his throat mike, slamming the Cobra out of the way. Those bastards were serious!

In the lead PBR, the sound of the Cobra's firing sent everyone diving for their weapons. The twin-fifty mount swung over to the portside, searching for a target. Brody dropped down behind the gunwales along the side of the craft and waited. In the stern, the sailor on the over-and-under trained his piece as well. The gunfire was ahead of them around a bend in the river. The boat's captain throttled down to make a slower approach.

88

In the second boat, Miller heard the shooting and saw the Cobras dive down for their target. "Python Lead, this is Barn Door Six, what's your situation up there? Over."

There was no answer. He saw the green tracer fire reach up for the lead Cobra and the pilot throw his machine out of the way. The second Cobra sped up and bore in, her rocketpods and guns blazing.

"Python Lead, this is Barn Door, what is your situation? Answer me! Over."

"Barn Door, this is Python Four Seven," answered the third gunship in the light-fire team. "Lead is a little busy right now. What do you want? Over."

"This is Barn Door Six, I want to speak to your flight commander. Over."

"Six, this is Lead," came Rat's southern drawl. In the background, Miller heard the ripping sound of the mini-gun and the cough of the thumper in the nose turret. "Keep out of this area and keep the fuck off the air. Out."

Miller let the microphone fall from his hand. With a roar, a Huey Hog gunship flashed overhead, just a few feet above the radar mast of the PBR. It banked slightly to the left and volleyed off a dozen rockets.

The lead PBR was just around the bend in the river, dead in the water and staying clear of the area where the gunships were working. Miller ordered his captain to swing around it and take up the lead position.

"I wouldn't do that, sir," Alexander advised him. "You'll get in the way of the gunships."

Miller shot him an angry glance. "Take her up, Chief," he repeated.

The boatswain glanced over to Alexander and turned the wheel, maneuvering around the other PBR. Now they could see what the Python gunships were doing. A section of the riverbank at least a hundred meters long was ablaze. A shower of 2.75-inch rockets and 40mm shells tore into the trees. The explosions sent limbs and pieces of tree trunks flying into the river.

With a final pass, Gaines climbed back into a low orbit over the PBRs and Warlokk took up his station to the rear. The third gunship climbed into the sky with the slicks.

"Barn Door Six, this is Python Lead. The enemy position has been destroyed. You are cleared to proceed. When we reach your destination, mister, you and I are going to have a little chat. Out."

Miller was pissed beyond belief, but he held his tongue. He called to his boats and the lead PBR took up its position again. The sailor on the over-and-under in the stern of the lead PBR stared in wide-eyed amazement at the destruction that the Python gunships had wrought on a hundred meters of the riverbank.

"Jesus Christ!" he swore softly.

Two-Step laughed. "See, I told you we'd take care of you."

The rest of the trip was uneventful, and the boats soon reached their destination, a wide spot in the river. A detachment of Sea Bees, the famed Navy Construction Battalion, were building the patrol base for the boats on the southern bank of the river. As the gunships circled overhead, the slicks flared out for a landing on the small chopper pad outside the wire, to off-load the grunts and supplies they had been carrying.

As soon as the slicks lifted off, Gaines dropped his Cobra down onto the pad and shut the turbine down. When the rotors came to a halt, he took off his flight helmet, opened his canopy, and stepped out onto the raw red earth. He fished into the pocket of his flight suit and came out with a thin cigar. Snapping open his Zippo, he fired it up and took a deep drag. Then he leaned back against the portside stub wing of his ship.

He had promised the Navy commander a little chat, and Rat Gaines always kept his promises.

Miller saw the green-and-tan Cobra come in for a landing. Before his PBR had even tied up to the dock, he jumped out and marched over to the gunship.

Gaines waited where he was and let Miller come to him. He really didn't know what the man's problem was, but the Navy man was going to get his ass kicked up between his ears if he wasn't real careful.

Gaines stuck his hand out when the Navy officer approached. "I'm Rat Gaines, Python Lead."

Miller ignored the pilot's hand. "Captain," he said shrilly. "I am going to file a full report on your conduct today."

Gaines tipped his head back and blew out a lungful of smoke. He leveled his eyes on Miller. "My conduct, mister?" he said softly. "My conduct? Just what the fuck do you think this is? Some fucking dress-white garden party?"

Miller flushed at the reference to the Navy officers' full-dress uniform, but before he could answer, Gaines's voice lashed out again.

"Obviously you have not conducted operations with Army gunships before. If you had, or had bothered to look into it, you would have learned that when I'm in the air covering your ass" — he jabbed his finger at his chest — "I am in sole command of my aircraft and crews. No one, and I mean no one, mister, is going to tell me how to fly."

The pilot took a deep breath. "Your job today was to get your little boats up the river. My job was to see that no one messed with you while you did it."

Gaines was wound up tight. Alphabet stepped out of his cockpit in case his boss really got out of hand.

"I have holes in my ship" — Gaines pointed to his Cobra — "because I was doing my job, which was protecting you. If we hadn't spotted that ambush, you'd have gotten your young ass kicked."

"Now, wait a minute," Miller started.

"No, goddamnit," Gaines cut him off. "You wait a minute, mister. I'm not done with you. I don't know just who in the hell you think you are, MacArthur or something? You're on my turf now. My grunts are defending your ass up here and my pilots are flying air cover for you. We didn't ask for this job, but as long as we're doing it, you're playing my game by my rules."

Gaines took another deep breath. "Now for your report, you're going to need my full name, rank, and serial number. You'll also need the name of my battalion commander so you can go through proper channels. But be advised that I am also going to file a report and I am going to request that my unit be relieved from this assignment."

He looked the PBR commander up and down. "You see, mister, we're the Air Cav. We're the baddest motherfuckers in town, and we don't work with no second-raters. If you ever get your shit together and learn how to act, let me know."

Gaines turned to go.

"You wait a minute!" Miller said, and grabbed the pilot's arm to turn him around.

Gaines turned back, the thin cigar clamped tightly in his teeth. He looked down at Miller's hand and then back to Miller. "Get your hands off me, boy," he said softly.

Miller flushed and dropped his hand. "Look, Captain . . ." he started.

Gaines took the cigar from his mouth and leaned closer to the navy officer. "I've heard just about all I'm willing to hear from you right now, Miller. And if you ever make the mistake of laying a hand on me again, I'm going to kick your lily-white Navy ass right up between your ears. You got that!" he roared.

Miller flinched.

"Captain Gaines," Alphabet quickly cut in. "We've got an Echo Tango Alpha back at Chu Lai, sir. We'd better get going."

Gaines looked at Miller for a moment longer, his eyes boring into him. He turned his head slightly and spat a piece of his cigar out. The Navy officer could not hold his gaze and looked away.

Without another word, Gaines turned on his heels and walked back to his ship. Miller watched him crank up, not quite sure what he was going to do about the wildman.

CHAPTER 13

Patrol Base Zulu

Lieutenant Mike Alexander gingerly stepped out of the PBR. After hours on the boat, dry land made his legs feel wobbly. He looked around at the small clearing that had been hacked out of the jungle along the riverbank. Though the docks were built and the perimeter wire was in place, the PBR base was still not finished. The Sea Bees were frantically trying to get the defensive bunkers and guard towers finished so that the grunts could occupy them that night.

With the slicks landed and the other two squads of the Blues off-loaded, along with their ammunition and supplies, Alexander decided it was time to get his people organized. Miller still had a real case of the red-ass and was ignoring Alexander, so the platoon leader walked over to a sailor who was refueling his small bulldozer from a fifty-five-gallon drum.

"Who's in charge of the construction around here?" Alexander asked.

The Sea Bee pointed over to the perimeter. "See that guy with the shaved head, sir? That's the Kaz. Talk to him."

The Kaz was well over six feet tall. He was stripped to the waist, and his muscles glistened with sweat as he lifted a heavy six-by-six beam into position on top of a half-built machine-gun bunker. A dirty Navy soft cap was pushed onto the back of his shaved head. As Alexander got closer, he saw the gleam of a gold ring in his earlobe that matched his one gold front tooth.

"I understand you're the man in charge here," Alexander said.

The big man lowered the timber into place on the bunker roof. Wiping his hands on his pants, he stuck out a big paw. "Yes, sir," he replied. "Petty Officer First Class Kasnowski. But everybody just calls me the Kaz."

Alexander took his hand. "I met another Kasnowski down in Nha Trang a couple months ago. He any relation of yours?"

The Kaz grinned like a pirate. "As a matter of fact, sir, he's my brother. He's not a bad guy, considering that he's a dogface and an officer at that."

Alexander smiled. "Well, he did me a real favor, so if there's anything I can do for you or your men, just let me know."

"Thanks, sir." Kaz grinned.

Alexander looked around at the perimeter. "Is there anything my men can do to help you with this?"

"Well, sir, right now all we need is a hand with getting these bunkers finished, so your men will have a place to stay tonight. We still need to get the sandbags filled. Everything else is pretty well under control."

"No sweat. I'll have my platoon sergeant put together a work detail for you right away."

"Thanks, sir." The Kaz reached down, grabbed onto another one of the roof beams, and lifted it off the ground.

"Gardner!" Alexander yelled out.

"Yes, sir."

"How 'bout giving this man a hand over here."

JJ dropped his ruck and grabbed onto the other end of the heavy timber. Between the two of them, they wrestled it into place.

Within minutes they had the rest of the timbers in position on the bunker roof. "Thanks, man," the Sea Bee said, wiping his forehead.

"No sweat," Gardner replied. "You got any more of those?"

The Kaz looked around the small perimeter. "Nope, it looks like this was the last one. All we have to do now is get the sandbags filled to put on top."

Leo Zack walked up with Strawberry and Harvard in tow. "Chief," he said, honorifically promoting Kasnowski one rank to that of a chief petty officer. "Here's your sandbag team. Where do you want 'em to get started?"

The Kaz pointed over to where the small bulldozer had started scooping out a hole for a command-post bunker. "Right over there, Sarge. Tell 'em to stack the filled bags at the back of each bunker and I'll have my men put 'em in place on top."

"Can do."

Brody and Two-Step took the boxes of trip flares and claymore mines from the helipad and headed out past the concertina wire to put them in place around the perimeter. The only way that they were ever going to defend this place was if they had everything they could possibly get out in front of them to provide early warning for oncoming dinks. But even then, things were going to be real tight if the shit really hit the fan.

The patrol base was too small and it was stuck way out in the middle of nowhere. It was true that they had artillery support, and the guns and mortars on the PBRs could help if they got attacked. The gunships were going to be close by, but it was still going to get real hairy if the dinks ever got too serious about taking them out. Light probing attacks they could deal with, but an out-and-out assault, no.

While Brody and Two-Step put out the claymores and trip flares, Corky, Gardner, and Farmer were building a machine-gun emplacement in their sector of the perimeter and the two cherries were filling sandbags. One of the new men was not at all happy about his assignment.

"This is just like the Army," York said caustically, tying off a filled bag. "Using manpower when they could have a machine doing this."

Lindberry was taking his turn on the shovel and didn't bother to respond to York's bitching. He was from Pittsburgh, the son of a steel worker, and he had expected to go to work in the steel mills when the draft board caught up with him after high school. He didn't really mind being drafted. His father had served in the Army in World War II, and he figured that he owed it to his country. But he also knew that as soon as he started working in the steel mills, he would never have another chance like this to travel and see a different part of the world.

Lindberry was one of those guys who never had much to say about anything. He had kept his mouth shut in basic training, he had kept his mouth shut in Camp Alpha, the in-country replacement center. He was keeping his mouth shut now. As long as he was in Vietnam, he intended to listen to his sergeants, do what he was told, and go home in a year. Long ago he had learned that not much ever came from bitching about things that couldn't be changed. Filling sandbags was one of those things.

York, on the other hand, always had something to say about everything, and it was rarely ever complimentary. He felt that he had a God-given right to point out other people's errors and failures of judgment.

Running his mouth off about school policy was the reason he had been kicked out of Harvard. But even that had not taught him to shut up. York was perfect material to become a politician or, better yet, a Fundamentalist preacher. Neither profession, however, would have ever occurred to the young elitist as being suitable to his perceived station in life.

He was still bitching about filling sandbags when Brody came back from putting out the claymores.

"Harvard, I need you to help get the rest of the squad's ammunition off the chopper pad."

York laid the shovel down and looked up from the bottom of the small hole he had dug in the ground. "I think that I've done my share for the day, Brody. Why don't you have some of the other guys do that?" He looked over to where Corky and Farmer were sitting on guard behind their machine gun.

"Your share?" Brody looked at him like he had two heads. "Just what the fuck do you think this is, man, the fucking Boy Scouts? You'd better get your ass down there, troop. Now!"

York flushed and for a moment Brody thought he was going to try to make an issue of it.

"I can take care of that for you, Sergeant," Lindberry hurriedly spoke up.

Brody turned to him. "You just keep on doing what you're doing, Strawberry."

Leo Zack had been watching the exchange between the two men and walked over to mediate the situation. Sometimes Brody could be a little rough on FNGs, particularly if he didn't take a liking to them right away. He also had a feeling that York was going to be a very hard man to like, no matter how long he stayed around.

"Brody, I need you to get that ammo moved right away." The black NCO pointed over to the chopper pad.

"Harvard was just getting on that," Brody answered with a grin. "Weren't you?"

Without saying a word, York climbed out of the hole and headed over to the pile of ammo crates.

"I'll get someone else over here to give you a hand with those bags," Brody told Lindberry as he watched York walk off.

Zack took Brody off to the side for a little NCO-to-NCO-type chat. "Just what the fuck was that all about?" he asked.

"Oh, nothin'. Harvard's just got a smart mouth, and he thinks that he's too fucking good for us."

"I can put him in one of the other squads if you'd like."

"Naw, Leo, I can handle him." Brody grinned like a cat eating a canary.

Zack looked at his squad leader for a moment. "Just don't let it get out of hand, boy."

"Leo! Would I do anything like that?"

The platoon sergeant didn't comment. He had the rest of the platoon to get squared away for the night.

Alexander had put his platoon command post, his CP, down at the end of the boat docks so he would be closer to the navy people. Since he was in charge of defending the base, if they got hit, all the sailors were automatically under his command. He wasn't looking forward to dealing with Miller on that topic, but if things got too bad, he could always have Gaines or the colonel straighten things out for him.

With his two squads from the Blues, the fifteen Sea Bees, and the men of the PBR crews, he had enough bodies to do a creditable job of defending the place once they got the bunkers finished. He prayed, though, that his plans would never have to be put to the test.

While Alexander worked on his defense plans, Bunny was busy on his radio, calling in preplanned artillery concentrations to the firing battery that had been assigned to support the PBR base. By preplanning the targets for the big guns, if they were attacked at night he wouldn't have to waste precious time registering the guns. The artillery could just shoot on the coordinates they already had plotted.

"Sir, I'm done here," the FO told the platoon leader. "I've got eight preplanned concentrations including a Firecracker-in-the-wire shot."

Firecracker artillery rounds were shells that contained many small, round bomblets instead of just one big explosive charge. The shells exploded in the air above the target and rained the bomblets down on the enemy. This was particularly useful in a defensive situation where the friendlies were in bunkers and the gooks were in the wire. It was the sort of situation they could expect if they got hit.

"Thanks, Bunny," Alexander said, looking over the artillery fire plan. "From now on, I want you to stick with me in the platoon CP. There's no telling when we might get hit and I want you close at hand to shoot for us."

"Yes, sir." Bunny grinned. Alexander's order just might keep him off the work details if he played it right. Digging holes in the ground and filling sandbags was not high on his list of favorite things.

In his jungle headquarters, Nguyen Van Tran looked up from his desk when the radio operator came into the room. "Comrade Colonel," the young man said, holding out a message form, "we have just received a message from the company watching the Song Boung River. They report that an enemy riverboat unit has occupied that base."

Tran took the report and scanned it. He should have taken action against the men building that base on the river when they first got started. He let them proceed because he had not wanted to bring attention to the NVA presence in that area. Now, however, he had to act. Once the boats started patrolling farther up the river, they were sure to discover his operations.

He stood up and went over to the situation map tacked up on the wall and checked the coordinates of the Yankee base. He had two units within striking range of them — the infantry company that had sent in the report and another platoon that was patrolling in the vicinity. That gave him five platoons against a reported single platoon of American infantry and their construction troops. That should be sufficient to do the job.

His troops were not carrying heavy weapons, they had no mortars, but they had their RPGs with them, and the deadly rocket-propelled grenades should be sufficient to do the job. The reports indicated that the base's defenses were not completed.

100

He hated to divert troop strength when every man was needed to move supplies into the staging areas for the Tet attack, little more than a week away. But the Yankee riverboat base had to be taken out. And the sooner the better. Noting a map coordinate, Tran returned to his desk and quickly wrote up an attack order.

The order was simple, the two units would rendezvous in the jungle this afternoon, scout out the enemy base, and attack during the night. Their mission was no less than the total annihilation of the enemy.

He handed the paper to the radio operator. "Send this order to Captain Nguyen and Master Sergeant Khanh immediately."

The radio operator took the message form and saluted. "Yes, Comrade Colonel."

That taken care of, the operations officer returned to writing movement orders that would send the last of the men and supplies into the staging areas for the general offensive. The problem of the Yankee riverboats was gone from his mind.

CHAPTER 14

The jungle along the Song Boung

Captain Nguyen, the NVA company commander, knelt over the crude model he had hastily constructed of the Yankee riverboat base. One of the most sacred doctrines of the People's Liberation Army of North Vietnam was that every attack was to be rehearsed as many times as possible. Preferably, the unit was taken to a secure, secluded area that resembled the objective and the attack was practiced until each man knew every movement that he had to make. If a rehearsal was not possible, a model of the objective was built and the troops studied it in minute detail.

Nguyen's model was drawn in the dirt of the cleared jungle floor. The bunkers were represented by mounds of dirt and the perimeter wire simulated by strands of grass. The shapes of the boats and the docks had been cut out of the leaves of a banana tree and placed in their proper positions. It was crude, but it served his purposes well enough.

"Remember," Nguyen told the infantrymen crowded around him, his finger stabbing the boatlike shapes on the ground, "no matter what else happens, the Yankee patrol boats must be destroyed."

He looked around the circle, his dark, hawkish eyes falling for a moment on each and every man. The men, both his own and those of the platoon that had reinforced his company for the operation, looked properly alert and attentive. It was an important mission and Nguyen tolerated no sloppiness. He had no fears about his own men. The bad soldiers in his company had all died a long time ago. Only the toughened, jungle-wise, battle-tested veterans were left. But Sergeant Khanh's platoon was a cause for uncertainty.

"Comrade Khanh," Nguyen addressed him. "Do you have any questions about any of this?"

"No, Comrade Captain," the sergeant answered stiffly, coming to a position of attention.

Khanh had heard rumors that Captain Nguyen was a fanatic, a leftover from the days of fighting the French. It was said that he had even executed his own men if they failed to perform their mission.

It was bad luck that had put Nguyen and his people on the same strike as a madman. It was good luck, though, that their mission was easy; a small, half-built base manned by a single platoon of infantry. He didn't have to worry about the boat crews or the construction troops in a nighttime firefight. They were sure to be wiped out.

"My men and I are ready, Comrade Captain."

Nguyen's eyes bored into his. "You had better be."

The sun was setting over the jungle when the grunts finished laying the last of the sandbags in place on the bunkers they were going to occupy that night. Although Kasnowski had said that he and his Bees could take care of it, Sergeant Zack put his people to work right alongside the sailors. With the friendly rivalry that appeared whenever soldiers and sailors worked side by side, each group tried to outdo the other, and the bunkers were soon finished.

It was a tired bunch of grunts that moved into their night defensive positions. Each squad was to man two bunkers. Zack, the ell tee, and Bunny would spend the night in the uncompleted platoon CP in the middle of the small base. Second Squad got the two bunkers on the far left-hand side of the semi-circular perimeter. Brody, Corky, and Strawberry took the machine-gun bunker at the end of the wire. Two-Step, Gardner, Farmer, and the other new man, Harvard, manned the other one.

As soon as they settled in, the grunts dug into their rucks for a meal of cold C rations. As always, Farmer was the hungriest of them all.

"Goddamn!" he said in disgust, kicking his ruck. "I ain't got no fucking ham and motherfuckers."

Of all the C-ration meals, the most universally disliked was the one that the Army called ham and limas, globs of fatty pork floating on top of mashed, soggy butter beans. The troops usually called this culinary delight ham and motherfuckers. Only a few brave men ever ate H and MFs if there was anything else available. Most grunts preferred to go hungry rather than touch them.

Farmer, however, thrived on ham and motherfuckers. And by making them his main meal, he always had more than enough to eat. The other guys in the Blues were glad to give him theirs or trade for other meals. A can of C-rat beanie wienies was worth three or four cans of H and MFs. Since he was always hungry, Farmer made out like a fat rabbit on the deal.

"How can you eat that shit?" Harvard asked with undisguised contempt.

"It's easy, man," Farmer grinned, snapping his fingers for emphasis. "All you do is open the can and get down." He leaned closer to the new man. "You don't happen to have any by any chance, do you?"

York reached into his ruck and came up with two cans. Since he was an FNG, he had gotten to the ration cartons a little too late to get any of the top choices like turkey loaf,

104

beanie wienies, pork and beans, or spaghetti and meatballs. Instead, he ended up with ham and motherfuckers and scrambled eggs.

Farmer was a world-class munch mouth, but he had his pride. He wouldn't touch scrambled eggs even if he were starving. It looked too much like dog puke. Many grunts agreed with him.

Farmer held up a can of pork slices. "I'll tell you what I'll do, my man," he said, sounding a lot like a used-car salesman. "Since you're in the squad now and all that, I'll give you this here pork slices for only two of those ham and limas."

Harvard made the trade. Pork slices resembled thick, round pieces of cardboard that had been soaked in lard, but they were better than ham and lima beans.

Gardner and Two-Step ate their meals in silence. The Indian looked out the aperture of the bunker into the dark woods beyond the wire. He really didn't like being in a small firebase like this. He felt trapped. In the jungle, he could run and hide. He could use the terrain and vegetation for his benefit as well as any guerilla soldier. But stuck behind barbed wire, there was no place to run, no way to maneuver or get away. If they got hit here, they were in a world of hurt.

He checked the load in the magazine of his pump gun and made sure that the claymore wires were hooked up to the clacker firing devices properly. Taking the hand grenades from his pack, he placed them right below the aperture within easy reach.

York watched the veteran grunt get ready. "What do you think's going to happen tonight?" he asked. "Are we going to get attacked?"

"Hard telling," Two-Step replied. "But they know we're here, you can count on that. Whether they decide to fuck with us or not is up to them, and there's no way to tell what a gook's going to do."

"Isn't this just a little stupid?" Harvard sneered. "I mean sticking us out here all by ourselves like this with no support."

"This ain't shit, man," Farmer spoke up. "You think this is out in the woods? You shoulda been with us when we went into Cambodia the last time. Now that was really out in the fucking woods."

Harvard hated feeling like a new guy. He particularly hated having these uneducated, smart-mouth grunts talk down to him as if he weren't good enough to be a member of their idiotic, exclusive little club. In Harvard's book, it didn't take any brains to get shot at, so he didn't understand what they all felt so superior about. That stupid little badge they wore above their left pocket, the wreathed musket of the Combat Infantryman's Badge, didn't mean shit to him.

"It seems to me," York continued, "that this is a big tactical mistake."

Gardner snorted. "What the hell are you talking about anyway? Tactics?" He slowly looked Harvard up and down. "You don't look like a fucking general to me, boy. You look like a fucking cherry who ought to be keeping his mouth shut and trying to learn how to survive this shit."

Harvard flushed. "You don't have to be a veteran to see that somebody made a mistake putting us out here," he answered angrily.

Gardner leaned closer to the new man. "Harvard, you've been running your mouth all day, bitching about everything you can find to bitch about. You know" — he stabbed his finger in his chest — "I'm getting tired of listening to your shit. My advice to you is to shut the fuck up before someone does it for you." JJ shook his head in disgust. "Christ, man, all you fucking college boys are the same, running off at the fucking mouth."

Farmer finished polishing off his dinner and leaned back on his ruck. "Hey, JJ, you just call when you need me to stand guard. I'm due to cut me a few zee's here."

Gardner chuckled. When Farmer wasn't eating, he could usually be found sacked out somewhere. Either that or poking his nose into someplace where it didn't belong.

York moved to the front of the bunker where Two-Step was staring out of the aperture at the dark forest beyond the wire. He looked out, too, but he didn't see anything interesting.

"What are you looking at out there?" he asked.

"Oh, nothing." Two-Step's voice was low. "I'm just smelling it, trying to get a feel for it."

York didn't smell anything but Vietnam. Rotting vegetation in the jungle, fresh earth, unwashed grunts. He leaned back against the side of the bunker and wished that he had been able to get himself a cushy job as a clerk-typist somewhere instead of having to do this infantry shit.

"How long do you think they're going to make us stay out here?" he asked Two-Step.

"Hard telling," the Indian answered. "Probably quite a while, though." The Indian paused, "I sure as hell hope not."

"Why?"

"I don't like the smell of this place."

"How long have you been here?"

"In the Nam? A little over two years."

York looked at him. How anyone could spend two years out of their life doing this was beyond him. "You're an Indian, right?"

"Right. Comanche."

"I guess you're used to this then, aren't you?"

"What d' you mean?"

"I mean living like this. This kind of primitive existence."

Two-Step didn't know whether he should get pissed at a typical white-man remark or take it as a compliment. He finally decided to laugh it off. "Well, the hills of Montana were never like this. But, yes, this redskin's gotten used to living like this."

Now it was Harvard's turn to answer some questions.

"What's a college man like you doing here? I heard you guys were exempt from the draft."

"We are," York said with bitterness. "But the dean threw me out of school and turned my name over to the draft board."

"That's the shits."

"Yes, it is," York said softly. "Yes, it is."

"Well, don't worry," Two-Step tried to reassure him. "In a couple of weeks you'll be used to this shit and it won't bother you anymore."

York shook his head. "That's what I'm afraid of."

CHAPTER 15

Patrol Base Zulu

Lieutenant Mike Alexander couldn't get to sleep. Usually, like a seasoned grunt, he could drop off anytime he stopped moving long enough. Tonight, for some reason, he couldn't. Maybe it was because the patrol base was unfamiliar to him or because he was in charge of its defense. Whatever the reason, it was keeping him awake.

Finally, the platoon leader sat up on his air mattress and glanced down at his Army-issue, plastic Timex watch. The luminous hands on the dial told him that it was half past midnight. He reached for his rifle and stood up, wrapping the warm poncho liner tightly around him. The night air was chilly and damp from the river. Alexander was still amazed at how cold it could get at night in Nam.

He slung a bandolier of M-16 magazines around his neck and headed for the bunkers on the perimeter. The night was velvety black. The only visible light came from the stars, and a faint glow came from the bridge of one of the PBRs where someone kept radio watch. He quickly looked away from the boat so as not to ruin his night vision.

He could hear the water gently lapping against the sides of the boat hulls and the dock. It was a soothing sound, one that his mind was not accustomed to hearing. It effectively blocked out the fact that the jungle around him was quiet. Far too quiet.

Captain Nguyen was no fool. The sappers in Sergeant Khanh's unit had been given the honor of leading the attack while his own men were positioned as the second wave. Six of Khanh's demolition experts dressed in black pajamas and head scarves crept forward on their bellies toward the three machine-gun bunkers.

Each man carried a pair of ten-pound satchel charges of high explosive. The first charge was to be put in the wire to blow gaps for the infantry to charge through. The second was for the front aperture of the bunkers. The sappers' only other weapons were Tokarov pistols stuck in the waistbands of their pants. If even one of them survived their suicide mission, it would be a miracle.

Fifty meters behind the sappers, two platoons of the North Vietnamese infantry waited in the damp grass. They carried bamboo assault ladders with them to throw on top of the barbed wire barriers, so they could scramble over the obstacle.

Two hundred meters beyond them, back in the wood line, the last two NVA platoons with the RPG launchers and the machine gunners were poised to give supporting fire and to reinforce the assault group if they got hung up.

The enemy sappers were good. On their way forward, they found and deactivated several of the trip flares and claymores that Brody and Two-Step had emplaced. They had just cleared the tanglefoot and were entering the outer ring of concertina wire when Alexander started his inspection of the perimeter.

The sapper in front of the machine-gun bunker in the Second Squad sector froze in place when he heard the American officer talking quietly to the men in the bunker twenty feet away. Unfortunately, the young North Vietnamese soldier understood English. He started listening to the low voices, trying to follow the conversation. Curiosity overcame caution and he started crawling forward. He was so intent on trying to hear what was being said that he let his attention wander. The bulky satchel charge in his hand brushed against a thin, dark wire set close to the ground. The wire was affixed to a mousetrap trigger for a claymore mine. It was a light touch, but it was enough to do the job.

The blinding flash of the exploding claymore lit up the darkened perimeter. The mine had been set to fire at a forty-five-degree angle to the wire and was only a few feet away from the sapper. Most of the 900 steel balls in the mine tore through his body. The blast also detonated the satchel charges he was carrying. The sapper was dead before he had a chance to know what he had done.

"Dinks in the wire!" Brody screamed. Grabbing the claymore clackers in both hands, he slammed down on the firing handles of the detonators, once, twice, three times. Two more claymore blasts launched steel balls across the perimeter. Two more sappers died.

Corky laid down on the trigger of his sixty, rapping out quick, short bursts through the aperture of the bunker into the wire.

The first satchel charge explosion was supposed to have been the signal for the attack. Now it didn't matter. In front of the perimeter, NVA signal whistles shrilled in the darkness. Nguyen's two assault platoons leaped to their feet and raced for the wire, firing their AK-47s from the hip.

Alexander dashed out of the bunker, racing for his CP as the men around the perimeter opened up. Lines of red tracer fire shot into the dark.

"Bunny!" the lieutenant screamed. "Bunny! Give me some light!"

On the PBRs, sailors bailed out of their bunks and raced for their weapons. The fifty gunner on the 836 boat was the first man to reach his guns. He dropped into the turret and swung his twin fifties around. Reaching down, he flipped the switch to the co-ax mounted searchlight and brought it to bear on the area beyond the perimeter.

The blinding beam of light illuminated dark, screaming figures racing for the wire. He pressed his thumbs down on the firing handles of the big guns, and Ma Deuce began to speak.

In the wood line, the RPG gunners took aim at the searchlight and fired. Three rocket-propelled grenades left their launchers. A few meters out of the muzzles, the secondary propellant charges ignited and sped the deadly antitank rounds to their target.

One RPG round hit low against the hull of the boat. The thin fiberglass did not detonate the rocket. The missile continued inside, where it impacted against the diesel motor. Then it exploded.

The second round slammed into the base of the boat's superstructure and detonated. The white-hot jet of explosive gases from the shaped warhead cut through the boat and the man standing inside the cabin. His upper body vaporized.

The third RPG hit the twin-fifty mount low on the turret ring. The blast shattered the upper body of the gunner and silenced his weapons.

PBR 836 was dead. Flames shot into the sky when her fuel tanks and ammunition exploded and burned.

Bunny ducked even lower in his hole when he saw the RPGs fire. "Red Leg Five Niner," he screamed. "This is Python Blue Six Tango. Fire concentrations Alpha, Charlie, and Delta. Give me ilium on Bravo. How copy, over?"

"Blue Six Tango," came the calm voice from the artillery fire-direction center miles away. "This is Red Leg Five Niner. Roger, fire Alpha, Charlie, and Delta. Ilium on Bravo. Over."

"This is Six Tango, get it coming, goddammit! We got dinks in the fucking wire!"

"Roger, Blue Six Tango, keep it in your pants, man. It's coming as fast as it can. Out."

112

Bunny hugged the ground, cursing the calm voice of Red Leg Five Niner. Not for the first time, he hated all the cannon cockers back at their nice secure little firebases. Five Niner wouldn't have been so fucking calm if he were the one getting overrun by screaming gooks.

"Blue Six Tango, this is Red Leg Five Niner. Shot over. Ilium on the way."

"Where's my fucking H.E.!" Bunny screamed.

"This is Red Leg Five Niner. H.E.'s coming up. Out."

The first of the 105mm howitzer illumination rounds burst over the patrol base with a faint pop. The flickering yellow-white flare descending on its parachute illuminated a scene straight out of hell.

Dark figures, their AKs blazing green tracers, scrambled over the ladders they had thrown on top of the rolls of concertina wire. Claymores exploded with bright flashes and the dark figures screamed when the steel balls ripped through their ranks.

Chi-Com grenades arched through the air in return and exploded against the bunkers with dull red thumps. Steady streams of red M-60 tracer fire blazed from the machine-gun bunkers. The thumper gunners fired their 40mm grenades point blank into the faces of the NVA.

Just as the first artillery flare flickered and died, two more popped into life above the camp, and the hellish scene came to life again.

Exploding RPG rounds added to the carnage as the NVA support element fired their rocket launchers at the bunkers. One bunker in the Third Squad sector took an RPG round through the aperture and exploded with a bone-shaking crump. The bunker's machine gun fell silent.

At the docks, the raging fires on the 836 boat illuminated the other PBRs, making them perfect targets for more enemy rockets.

"Cast off!" Miller yelled from the bridge of his boat. He hit the starter buttons to the two big diesel engines below.

With a cough of black smoke, the diesels caught. He slammed the throttles forward. The cold motors sputtered, coughed, and died. With a curse, he punched the starters again. The diesels sputtered to life and ran clean this time.

Whipping the wheel around sharply, Miller pulled his boat away from the dock and raced for open water. "Get on the guns!" he shouted down to his crew.

His men were already at their posts. In the bow of the boat, the twin-fifty turret was speaking. The gunner had his thumbs locked down on the triggers, and over fifteen hundred rounds of .50-caliber ammunition blazed out of the barrels each minute.

In the stern, the sailor on the belt-fed thumper was cranking the handle like an organ-grinder monkey gone crazy. A steady stream of 40mm grenades arched out over the bunkers and into the wire.

The other two PBRs had gotten away from the docks. One of the boats, 859, had one of the over-and-under combination .50-caliber and 81mm mortar weapons mounted on her stern. The fifty couldn't be fired while the gunner was using the mortar, but it looked like the grunts needed H.E. fire more than they did another .50-caliber.

The gunner slammed the first 81mm mortar round into the breech of the weapon, aimed it, and jerked sharply on the firing lanyard. The mortar fired with a hollow cough. The first round landed off to the side and long. He quickly reloaded and tried to make sight corrections, but the boat was bouncing around so much that he couldn't bring his weapon to bear.

"Stop the boat," the gunner yelled up to the bridge. "I can't fire!"

The man behind the wheel, Boatswain Mate First Class Johnson, chopped his throttles. The screaming engines cut to an idle, and the boat went dead in the water. It made them a sitting target again, but the men in the bunkers needed the fire support.

Johnson zipped up his flak jacket and settled his steel pot down lower on his forehead. Mentally he kicked himself in the ass for ever having left the Blue Water Navy.

The hollow cough of the eighty-one sounded again. This time, the round landed in the outer wire. The blast swept several NVA off their feet, but it also opened another hole in the wire. More screaming NVA dashed through the break.

The NVA in the wood line saw the muzzle flash of the eighty-one and brought their rocket launchers to bear on it. The trees lit up with the back blast as the RPGs fired.

On the bridge, Johnson saw the flashes of the RPG launchers and hit his throttles. With the water jets screaming, the boat shot forward. The rockets hit behind them, throwing geysers of dirty water into the air. He whipped the wheel around and the boat skidded. The bow came around to face the shore, he chopped the throttles, and the PBR settled in the water.

The eighty-one gunner brought his weapon to bear again, but the dinks were in too close to the perimeter for him to fire. The 81mm mortar was an area-defense weapon, not a point-target weapon. That close to the grunts' bunkers, he would probably land the round on top of the friendlies instead of the gooks. He raised the muzzle and aimed at the wood line to try for the RPG gunners. The mortar coughed again.

Back at his CP in the wood line, Captain Nguyen watched the progress of the battle. The Yankees were putting up a stronger defense than he had expected. He decided to commit one of his reserve platoons.

With the three sharp blasts from his whistle, the NVA surged forward. Screaming as they ran, they headed straight for the gaping holes in the basecamp's wire perimeter.

CHAPTER 16

Patrol Base Zulu

The Air Cav's grunts were fighting for their lives. Several well-placed RPG rounds had blasted one of the bunkers in 3rd Squad's sector to rubble, killing or wounding all of the men in it. North Vietnamese infantry swarmed through the hole in the defenses and fanned out inside the patrol base.

Kasnowski's Sea Bees crouched behind the bare bones of the commo bunker where they had been sleeping, their M-14s adding to the defensive fire.

"Kaz!" one of the men shouted. "Look out!"

On their left flank, screaming NVA in dark uniforms came out of nowhere. In the flickering light of the artillery ilium and the fires, they looked like something out of a nightmare. Kaz brought his rifle up to his shoulder and started firing quick, well-aimed shots. Each time he pulled the trigger, an NVA went down with a 7.62mm bullet in him. On either side of Kasnowski, the other Sea Bees blasted away. The line of NVA staggered and stopped. A sailor rose to his feet and tossed a grenade into the middle of the remaining enemy. The explosion scattered what was left.

116

"Let's get 'em!" Kaz screamed.

Jumping up out of their makeshift trench, the Sea Bees charged. One of the men jumped into the driver's seat of a bulldozer and cranked it up. The cold diesel motor snapped, popped, and caught. Raising the dozer blade for a shield, the Sea Bee drove it into the NVA like a tank, crushing their bodies under its tracks.

Faced with howling crazy men and the clanking metal monster, the NVA faltered and fell back against the perimeter wire. Concentrated fire from the back doors of the bunkers cut into their rear while the M-14s of the sailors blazed in their faces. They broke and scattered for cover inside the base.

Back in the wood line, Captain Nguyen saw his carefully prepared attack break down under the Sea Bee's counter-attack. Turning around, he shouted to his last platoon leader, "Now! Attack now!"

Over fifty NVA leaped to their feet and charged across the open ground, screaming as they ran. Not even the artillery shells falling in their path were able to slow one of Nguyen's own assault platoons.

In the bunkers, the Blues concentrated their fire on the new threat. "Ammo!" Corky screamed. He flipped up the feed tray on his pig, ready to reload.

Brody scrambled to the rear of the bunker and ripped open the lids on the 7.62mm ammo cans. The scattered cans were empty.

"We're all out!" he yelled.

"*Tu madre!*" Corky dropped the smoking pig and drew the .45 pistol from his holster. He jacked the slide back to chamber a round. Pulling the long Mexican-style Bowie knife from the sheath on the other side of his field belt, he stuck it point down in a sandbag. He had twenty-one rounds of .45 ammo in three magazines. When that was gone, he'd start using his knife.

In the other 2nd Squad bunker, Two-Step was also running low on ammo. The barrel of his sawed-off pump gun smoked as he kept stuffing shells into the magazine. Gardner was completely out of thumper grenades and had switched to shooting his sixteen. Since he didn't carry as many magazines for it as the other men did, he, too, was running low.

Farmer was doing what he always did in a firefight. Back when he had first joined the Blues, he had been so scared in his first real firefight that he thought he was going to pass out. Sergeant Zack had stopped by his foxhole and told him to pretend that he was back on the firing range in basic training.

"Just pick a target and shoot at it, son," the Black NCO had said calmly. "It'll go down."

Farmer followed that advice and it always worked. This time, however, he was on a night range and the targets were harder to spot in the flickering light of artillery flares and the flash of explosions.

A dark figure appeared in front of him. The dink was pushing something toward the opening of their bunker. Farmer fired a quick burst at him. The darkness inside the bunker was shattered when the NVA pole charge detonated with a blinding flash.

The concussion slammed Farmer back against the sandbags. He slumped down to the floor unconscious.

Gardner dropped to his side. "Farmer," he yelled above the fire storm, shaking the unconscious man. "Farmer!"

The young grunt's head lolled limply from side to side.

"Motherfuck!" Gardner screamed. He snatched the M-16 ammo bandolier from around Farmer's neck and turned back to the aperture. Slamming a fresh magazine into the well of his empty rifle, he jerked back on the charging handle and laid down on the trigger. "Motherfuck!"

Harvard huddled against the other side of the bunker whimpering in terror. So far he hadn't fired his weapon at all and the other grunts had been so busy they hadn't noticed. When the pole charge exploded, it blinded him and he cried out in fear. In a complete panic, he scrambled for the rear

118

door, but Two-Step's hand shot out and grabbed him by the belt. "Where you going!"

"I've got to get outta here!"

The Indian slammed the butt of his shotgun into his belly. Harvard bent over, retching. His virgin rifle dropped from his hands.

'Pick it up, motherfucker," Two-Step snarled. "And shoot."

He grabbed York by the back of the neck and dragged him back to the aperture, where he slammed him against the sandbags. "You fucking try to run again and I'll kill ya."

Dazed, Harvard stuck the muzzle of his sixteen out of the bunker and started shooting, not even trying to aim the weapon. He pulled the trigger until the magazine was empty. He slammed a fresh magazine into place and started shooting again.

When the Sea Bees charged, the NVA fell back to covered positions. Then they turned and fought back. Their return fire struck hard into the sailors' ranks. Green AK tracer fire flickered and bit at the Sea Bees. The man running next to Kaz took a round in the head and went over onto his face.

"Take cover!" the Kaz yelled. But there was very little cover out in the open.

The men dropped flat on the ground and tried to pick the NVA off from behind stacks of supplies and construction material. More were hit.

Kaz turned around and looked for the bulldozer. AK rounds kicked dirt into his face. "Over here!" he shouted, waving his arm at the dozer driver.

The Sea Bee saw him. AK fire ricocheted off the raised dozer blade, sparking on the hardened steel. The driver crashed the machine into a stack of bunker timbers, toppling them onto the NVA hiding behind them.

The Sea Bees ran for the dozer and took cover behind it as it inched toward another pile of construction materials. The NVA broke and ran from the armored assault.

Alexander knelt on the ground behind the center of the perimeter, trying to make it up to the bunkers. Every time he got to his feet, a burst of fire drove him back down to cover again. Through the blinding flashes, the platoon leader saw a big man running between the bunkers. From the flickering light reflected off a sweaty shaved head, he knew it was Sergeant Zack.

The black NCO had ammo cans in his hands and was trying to resupply the men. As Alexander watched, a dink ran out from behind a bunker right in front of Zack, his AK held out in front of him.

Zack didn't even break stride. He swung a heavy can of machine gun linked belt ammunition in one hand like a club. The can connected with the dink's face, and he went down heavily, his skull smashed. Zack ran two more steps and darted into one of the bunkers.

Alexander realized he was never going to make it to the bunkers. There were too many dinks inside the camp and more poured in every second. He raced back to his CP.

Bunny was still on the radio to the artillery, trying to walk the fire in closer to the outer perimeter. The 105 shells were bursting less than fifty meters in front of the bunkers, but it didn't stop the gooks storming the wire or those who were already inside.

The platoon leader dropped down into the hole. "Bunny!" he yelled over the storm of fire. "Tell 'em to shoot the Firecrackers on top of us!"

"On top of us?" Bunny squeaked.

"Yes, goddammit! Do it now!"

Red Leg Five Niner, the artillery FDC, was reluctant, with good reason, to fire Firecrackers on the base. The Firecracker artillery shells were thin-walled casings loaded with small bomblets. The shells burst in the air over the target, raining the bomblets down. Each bomblet, just slightly larger than a golf ball, contained an explosive charge that had a wire coil wrapped around it. When it hit the ground and detonated, the fragments of wire killed out to five meters. Since each shell carried dozens of bomblets, it was like being caught in a rainstorm. You could run, but you still got wet. Anyone caught in the open was going to be killed.

"Six Tango, this is Five Niner," answered the FDC. This time the voice was tense. Lives were on the line, American lives. "Give authority for Firecracker mission on those coordinates, over."

Alexander snatched the radio handset from the FO. "This is Blue Six, First Lieutenant Michael Alexander," he shouted. "I am authorizing the fire mission. Shoot it, goddamnit, shoot it!"

"This is Five Niner. Roger, sir. On the way. Good luck. Out."

Alexander took a deep breath. "Take cover!" he screamed. "Firecracker! Take cover!"

Over the roar of small-arms fire, he heard a speeding freight train, the sound of incoming artillery rounds. The platoon leader and his RTO curled into little balls in the bottom of their hole and put their hands up over their heads.

The world exploded around them.

It sounded like a Fourth of July celebration, except these firecrackers were louder. Each pop sent hundreds of deadly, razor-sharp shards of steel whizzing through the air. When they met flesh, they struck deep.

Most of the flesh they met was North Vietnamese. The dinks died by the dozens. One gook had a bomblet explode when it hit his head. His head vanished. Most of the rest of them simply died from dozens of slashed wounds that bled them to death in seconds.

In some cases, however, the flesh was American. The surviving Sea Bees were huddled under their bulldozer, but one man had his leg sticking out. He took a dozen wounds in the lower leg with one shot. Other grunts took single hits as some of the small frag found their way into the bunkers. A man in First Squad, deafened by a grenade explosion, had not heard the call to get under cover.

On the river, Miller couldn't believe what he was seeing. He had not heard the call for the Firecracker rounds and thought that the world had gone mad when the first one burst over the camp. Then he saw the NVA going down like puppets with their strings cut. He realized that Alexander had called the nightmare in on top of his own men. The Navy officer shuddered.

When the last of the six Firecracker rounds had detonated, a strange silence fell over the camp, a lull in the storm of fire. All that could be heard were the screams and moans of the wounded and the dying. Slowly, one by one, the grunts opened up on the surviving NVA.

It was a slaughter.

Slightly wounded NVA, stunned by the sudden artillery attack, were gunned down where they stood. Bodies hanging in the wire were shot again and again until they were torn apart. One wounded NVA lay out of the line of fire, screaming something in Vietnamese over and over again. It took three thumper grenades to silence him.

On the river, Miller maneuvered his boats in closer to the shore to add more weapons fire to the carnage. The three surviving PBRs went on line side by side, combining their six .50-caliber machine guns to do the talking.

The few NVA left alive scrambled over the wire, frantically trying to escape, oblivious to the razor-sharp points on the concertina wire, wounding their bodies even more. Deadly fire from the bunkers cut into their backs. They stayed where they were, hanging lifelessly on the wire.

Above the racket of firing, the voices of the American wounded cried out for medics. The NVA were in full retreat, but the victory had come with a heavy cost.

Bunny kept the artillery ilium going and chased the NVA back into the woods with H.E.. The medics, both the Navy's and the Blues', scrambled inside the base, locating and treating the casualties. Alexander got on the radio to Chu Lai and requested priority Dustoffs for the seriously wounded.

Several of the men, mostly Sea Bees and the surviving crewman from the sunken PBR wouldn't last until dawn.

Miller had his boats tie up at the docks, but kept his men at their guns. Stepping onto the dock, he slowly started through the burning wreckage of his base. Alexander recognized him and ran up. "I've got a Dustoff coming," he reported.

The Navy officer seemed to be in a daze and didn't answer him. "Sir," Alexander repeated. "I've got a medevac on the way."

Miller snapped out of it. "Good," he said softly. "How many men were killed?"

"I don't know yet. The Sea Bees got hit pretty hard and we're still trying to locate all of 'em."

In Two-Step's bunker, Gardner knelt over Farmer, gently patting him down to see where he had been hit. "Grab his legs," he told Harvard. "I want to take him outside for the medics."

Farmer groaned and moved his head.

"Farmer," Gardner shouted. "Farmer, you okay?"

The young grunt tried to sit up. His head was killing him. He reached around to the back of his head and felt a big bump. "What happened?" he asked.

"You hit a sapper and his satchel charge blew up. I think you hit your head."

"Jesus," he muttered. "At least I got the fucker who was trying to kill me."

CHAPTER 17

PBR Base Zulu

As the first light of a damp, cold dawn broke over the Song Boung River, bleary-eyed, smoke-stained men stumbled out of their bunkers and looked around at the smoking ruins of their base.

The fog from the river drifted low in the air, holding the acrid smoke close to the ground. Small fires still flickered in piles of building timbers and ammo crates. Bodies littered the entire camp, both inside and outside the perimeter. North Vietnamese and American bodies, slack limbed and bloody, were sprawled in the postures they held when death struck them down.

There were no wounded there. The serious American casualties had been dusted off and the rest had been taken to a makeshift aid station behind the half-finished commo bunker, where they were treated. The NVA wounded had all been killed.

While Bunny and Zack were busy on the radio calling in the Dustoffs, Alexander led a small patrol to police up the enemy weapons from the dozens of bodies in the wire. Brody and the veteran grunts weren't impressed by what modern weaponry could do to the human body. They had seen burned, blasted, shattered, and shredded Vietnamese bodies often enough. For Harvard and Strawberry, however, it was their first look at death. When Harvard caught sight of an NVA with half of his head sliced off by a piece of 105 frag, he dropped to his knees, turned his head away, and puked.

Farmer laughed, but Gardner felt a twinge of sympathy. He remembered how he had reacted the first time he had seen dead bodies, children who had been shot in the head at close range. He didn't think he'd ever forget.

The enemy had been dealt such a staggering blow that they had not even tried to haul off their dead. The grunts moved among the corpses, stripping them of weapons and magazine carriers and taking the arms back inside the base. Later, the arms would be evacuated back to Chu Lai.

While the men policed up the battlefield, Alexander went into the wood line to see what he could find. There were more bodies, but few weapons. He was just about to turn back when he saw an RPG in the tall grass. He stepped closer to it. A pair of hands were wrapped around the weapon. One hand was around the pistol grip, a finger on the trigger.

Alexander froze. The RPG was pointed right at the camp. If it fired, it was bound to kill someone. He brought his sixteen up, but he was afraid that a reflex action on the part of the dying NVA would trigger off the rocket.

"*Lai dai,*" he said softly in Vietnamese. "Come here."

The RPG didn't move.

"*Lai dai!*" He spoke a little louder this time.

The hands came off of the rocket launcher and went up in the air. The frightened face of a teenage boy looked out of the tall grass. Alexander grabbed one arm and dragged him away from the RPG. It was hard to tell who was the most frightened, the teenage NVA or Alexander. The lieutenant waved the muzzle of his sixteen toward the camp. "*Di di,*" he said. "Go." The NVA slowly started walking.

125

Pandemonium broke out when the grunts looked up and saw Alexander's prisoner. Their eyes flicked to the wood line, and they wondered how many of them were still hiding out there. Brody, Corky, and Two-Step headed for the trees while Alexander walked his captive back through the wire.

The patrol base was still smoking when Rat Gaines brought his Cobra in for a landing later that morning. Right next to him on the chopper pad a Dustoff was taking the last of the wounded on board for the flight back to the hospital at Chu Lai. The dead in their body bags were still waiting to be flown out.

Gaines shut down and climbed out of his gunship. He pulled his flight helmet off, laid it on the seat, and looked around at the nearly destroyed base. The ruined NVA bodies still hung in the concertina wire. The sickly sweet smell of blood and the acrid residue of explosives were thick in the air. A Sea Bee sat behind the controls of the little bulldozer digging a makeshift grave outside the wire for the dinks.

A filthy, smoke-stained Alexander walked up to Gaines, favoring one leg. The platoon leader was still wearing his flak vest and carrying his M-16 in his right hand.

Gaines reached into his pocket and, pulling out a cigar, handed it to him. "Your boys did good, Mike."

Alexander took the smoke and lit up. He seemed like he was still in a daze. He was not new to combat, but it was the first time that he had even been almost overrun.

Alexander looked down toward the dock. An oil slick from the 836 boat was still burning on the brown water. What was left of her fiberglass hull had sunk into the river, and only part of her bridge was showing. "Those Swabbies did real good, too," he added. "They made the difference, them and the Sea Bees."

Of the dozen dead, and many more wounded, over half had been sailors.

"Yeah. I've got to talk to Miller about that. You know where he is?"

"Last I saw of him, sir, he was down by the boats."

Gaines laid his hand on Alexander's shoulder. "You'd better get some rest. Let Zack take care of things for a while."

Alexander looked at him and shook his head slightly. "There's a couple of things I've got to get taken care of first, sir."

"Okay, but don't push it too hard."

"Yes, sir."

Gaines walked down to the dock. "You seen Mr. Miller?" he asked the first sailor he found.

The young man looked up at him with glazed eyes. "Mr. Miller?" he said softly. "No, sir, I don't think so."

Gaines went on past him and found the Navy officer on one of the other boats. "Lieutenant Miller?" he called out.

Miller looked up and climbed out of the boat.

"I just got word from Division," Gaines said. "A sky crane will be bringing you a replacement boat sometime around noon today. They're bringing it down from Da Nang."

"Thanks." Miller's voice was hoarse. The officer looked rough. It wasn't easy, having a quarter of his command shot to hell at one time.

"My lieutenant tells me that your men fought well last night," Gaines said, offering an olive branch.

Miller glanced over to the burned-out hulk of the 836. "It was so sudden," he said quietly. "The Three Six boat hardly even had a chance to shoot back."

"I know," Gaines offered. "That's the way it usually is. But I hear that the rest of your boats did real well for themselves. Is there anything we can do for you? Do you need us to fly anything in for you?"

"No, I think we're okay. You might want to ask the Sea Bee petty officer, though. His people lost some equipment last night."

"Can do." Gaines turned to walk away.

"Captain Gaines?"

Rat turned back. "Yes?"

"Tell your platoon leader that his men saved our base last night and that we really appreciate it."

"I'll be glad do that," Gaines responded.

"And also, " Miller stuck out his hand. "Why don't you call me Jim. Since we'll be working together, there's no need for all this military formality."

Gaines smiled and took his hand. "Glad to. And call me Rat. Everybody else does, even my own troops."

Miller smiled back. "Okay. Rat it is."

Gaines found the Sea Bee NCO, Kasnowski, talking with Alexander. The two men were making up a list.

"Sir," Alexander said when his company commander walked up, "there's a few things that the Sea Bees need if we're going to get this place rebuilt."

Gaines looked over the list of construction materials; sandbags, bunker timbers, concertina wire, and the like. "No sweat. When I get back, I'll get the S-four on it right away. He should be able to get this out to you today."

"And, sir, when you bring in the beer, how 'bout bringing enough for the Bees too?"

Gaines laughed. "Don't worry, I'll bring enough for everybody. Also, I'll need an ammo resupply list."

"Tell 'em to bring a full basic load and all the claymores and trip flares they can find. They really saved our asses last night." Alexander paused. A slight shudder ran through him with the memory. "That, the fifties on the boats, and Bunny's artillery shoot."

"You had quite a party," Gaines understated the situation.

Alexander grinned. "We sure did, sir. But I don't want to go through it anytime again soon."

"Considering your body count, I don't think you'll have to. At least for a little while."

"God, I sure as hell hope not."

"You put a pretty good dent in them and they'll have to back off for a while."

Gaines walked back to his gunship. Alphabet was standing in front of the Cobra, talking to Sergeant Zack.

"Captain," Zack spoke up. "We're going to need replacements ASAP. I've got seven men either KIA or in the hospital."

"Yeah, I know." Gaines had a copy of the casualty list in one of his pockets. "I'll see what I can do as soon as I get back. Is there anything else?"

Zack shook his shaved head. "I can't think of a thing, sir. Other than getting us all the hell out of here, that is."

" 'Fraid I can't do that, but I'll see what I can do about getting you some more men."

"Every little bit helps, sir."

Back at Chu Lai, Gaines turned the supply requests in to the S-4, the battalion supply officer, and went to the battalion commander's office. Colonel Jordan was waiting for a firsthand report. As he breezed past the adjutant's desk, Gaines came to a halt. Lieutenant Muller had finally stopped jumping to his feet every time a superior officer passed him. Now he came to a position of attention while sitting in his chair.

"Good morning, sir," he sang out.

"Good morning, Ell tee." Gaines placed the casualty report on the S-1s desk. "How 'bout getting on the horn to Brigade and see if you can get me some people. Nothing fancy this time, just One One Bravo boonie rats."

"Yes, sir! Right away, sir!"

"And, Muller? Don't shout."

"Yes, sir!" Muller shouted.

Shaking his head, Gaines knocked on the door of the colonel's office. Jordan was on the phone, but he waved Gaines in and pointed to the chair beside his desk.

"Captain Gaines just walked into my office, sir," the colonel said into the telephone. "I'll talk to him and get right back to you."

Jordan laid the phone down. "That was Brigade," he said, lighting a smoke. "They want to know if your people can continue their mission."

"Yes, sir. As soon as they're resupplied and get some replacement bodies, they'll be okay. Alexander's got things pretty well in hand."

"Glad to hear that. How'd it go out there last night?"

Gaines lit up one of his cigars. "Not too bad, considering. The Navy actually took the worst of it. I'm going to put Alexander in for a Silver Star for calling that artillery in on top of himself, and I'm sure that there'll be other recommendations as well. The Blues did a hell of a job, sir. I'm real proud of 'em."

Jordan leaned over the desk. "I'll forward a Silver Star for Alexander, but I'm going to kick his ass at the same time. He's been reading too many fucking comic books. He's lucky that he didn't get them all killed."

"Colonel, he really didn't have any choice. I haven't seen so many gooks in one place in a long time. They must have hit him with a reinforced company."

"I know, but that 'Carpenter Fire' shit can be a little hazardous to your health." Jordan shook his head and stubbed out his cigarette butt.

Early in the war, an Army captain named Carpenter had called down an artillery barrage on top of his own position when it was being overran by a horde of screaming VC. The desperate tactic had worked. The captain and most of his men had survived. From that time on, the technique had borne his name. Every infantry officer knew about it and prayed that he'd never have to use it.

"Anyway," Jordan said, "let me know if there's anything I can help with out there and let's get them back on their feet ASAP."

Rat got to his feet. "Yes, sir."

"And, Gaines."

"Sir?"

"Tell 'em that I'm proud of them, too."

130

"Yes, sir."

After stopping off at the S-2's office to take a look at the latest intell reports, Gaines drove back to his flight-operations office, where a message was waiting for him. Another Cobra was ready to be picked up at at An Khe.

"Outfuckingstanding!" he exclaimed. That was the ship that Alphabet would take over. Now Gaines could form a three-Cobra light-fire team. The remaining Huey Hogs in the company would make up the heavy-fire team, but he planned to use the Cobras by themselves. Their superior speed and maneuverability would give them an edge when he needed to respond to a problem fast. In Vietnam, an edge like that was worth more than gold.

The company commander stuck his head into the operations room. "Round up Alphabet for me and tell him to get his ass over here ASAP."

"Yes, sir."

Gaines decided to fly back to An Khe with Schmuchatelli to get the new chopper. That way, he was sure to get it back to Chu Lai in one piece this time.

CHAPTER 18

Chu Lai

Early the next morning, Rat Gaines got a phone call to attend a briefing at ten hundred hours. There were few people in the small briefing room when Gaines walked in, and most of them were staff rats from Brigade Headquarters. Navy Lieutenant Miller was sitting stiffly in one of the folding metal chairs. He barely answered when Rat said hello.

Rat grinned. It looked like the battlefield camaraderie of the day before had only been temporary. Miller was acting like he was bent out of shape about their little difference of opinion during their joint operation again. Rat plopped down in a chair and lit up a smoke.

A few minutes later, the door opened and a tall Special Forces major wearing starched ARVN camouflage fatigues walked to the front of the room.

"Good morning, gentlemen."

The major was thin with close-cropped blond, almost white, hair and faded blue eyes. He carried himself stiffly, with just a hint of aristocratic bearing.

"I'm Major Snow from Special Forces Command and Control Central," he began with a faint European accent. "I'm here to brief you on the parts that you will play in the upcoming Operation Blackjack."

The Green Beret officer, once a refugee from the Hungarian revolution in 1956, handled Roadrunner and unconventional operation-support activities for Command and Control North. Snow's only reason to be in Vietnam was to kill Asian communists until he could return to his homeland and kill communists back there. His hatred for the followers of Marx and Lenin ran deep. During the street fighting in the revolution in Budapest, a 122mm cannon shell from a Russian JS III tank had taken out a second-story flat in an apartment building. Snow's young wife of two years and their baby daughter had been there when the shell hit.

When the Hungarian revolution failed, he escaped to Austria and made his way to the United States, where he immediately enlisted in the Army. Snow was a nom de guerre he had taken upon enlistment because his Hungarian name was too difficult for Americans to pronounce. Like many of his fellow countrymen, Snow was recruited into the newly formed Army Special Forces. After further training, he was commissioned an officer. He had been in and out of Vietnam since the earliest days of American involvement, and all of his work had been in some area of covert operations.

The name on his paycheck read Snow, but the men he worked with all called him the "Ice Man," and with good reason. When he planned and executed an operation, he was as cold and as hard as ice.

Gaines had worked with him before. He sat up a little straighter in his chair. This was bound to be interesting.

"First off," Snow said, looking around the room, "let me remind you all that this briefing is classified top secret and is on a strict 'need to know' basis. Anyone here who is not cleared to that level will please leave now."

Nobody moved. The major launched into his briefing. He pulled a chrome, collapsible pointer from his breast pocket and extended it. Tapping the pointer against an area on the map, he began.

"Several days ago, CCC launched RT Sleeper, one of our Roadrunner teams, into this area for an extended look around. On the third day of their mission, they were ambushed right here." The pointer tapped the map again.

"Half of the team was wiped out and the other three men ran. Later that day, the remaining American on the team, a young staff sergeant, was able to break contact with the enemy and evade to the west, carrying a wounded man on his back. To make a long story short, he reached a CIA airfield in western Laos and was flown back to Kontum."

"Of itself, this is not unusual. Our RT teams get their asses kicked every now and then. What was of interest, though, was what this team saw right before they were ambushed. A new and very extensive supply complex in this area." The pointer's tip inscribed a small circle on the map. "A massive supply dump being serviced by a new branch of the Ho Chi Minh Trail."

"Now, because MACV wants more detailed intelligence on this area, we are sending in another recon unit. But this time, we are sending in the Recon Platoon from a Mobile Guerrilla Force unit. You people have been chosen to support this operation in various ways. Mr. Miller?"

"Yes, sir," the PBR commander answered.

"Your boats will take this team up the Song Boung River to their launch point here." Again the pointer hit the map. "When you have dropped them off, you will return to your patrol base and stand by there to extract them, should that become necessary."

"Yes, sir," Miller answered.

"Captain Gaines?"

"Yes, sir," Rat sang out.

"I asked for your unit specifically for this mission. We had so much fun the last time we were together that I thought we might do it again."

Rat snorted. The last time had been a Cambodian cross-border, hush-hush number against NVA-manned Russian gunships; a real giant rat-fuck if there had ever been one. He wasn't anxious to go through anything like that again soon.

"Anyway," the major continued, "you'll be pleased to know that Captain Ringer is also with us again this time. His Mike Force Company has been reorganized as a Mobile Guerilla Force, and they are the unit that you will be providing top cover for."

Gaines smiled broadly. He had learned a long time ago that anything Larry Ringer got involved in was bound to get complicated sooner or later. He and the Special Forces officer went back a long ways. They had started out together in an infantry officer's basic course back at Fort Benning, Georgia as two brand-new second lieutenants. Since that time, their paths had crossed more than once. Most recently it had been during that Cambodian mission, when both of them had almost gotten themselves killed.

"Your gunships will be on call in the air should the PBRs need assistance on the way in. Then they are to be on ramp alert during the mission along with enough slicks to carry your Aero Rifle Platoon into the AO should the Blackjack team run into trouble. Any questions?"

Gaines shook his head. "No, sir."

The major went on to brief each commander in detail. At the end of the briefing, he handed out thick packets of maps, lists, and orders. Rat glanced over the contents but decided to wait to study them in detail. The mission wasn't going to kick off until the day after tomorrow, so there was plenty of time to get his people and choppers ready.

On the way out of the briefing room, he ran into Miller again. This time, however, the Navy officer acknowledged him. "It looks like we're going to be working together again, Rat."

"Yep, but this time, we'll have the added enjoyment of dealing with a real bunch of maniacs — Larry Ringer's people."

Miller had a puzzled look on his face.

"Yeah," Gaines explained. "They're the Nung Mike Force, and they're far crazier than my guys."

Miller smiled. That was saying a lot. "I'm sure that we can work out something."

Gaines laughed. "Just wait 'til you meet Ringer."

Rat hurried back to his operations to alert his pilots for the mission. Since he didn't want to discuss the operation on the radio, he would fly out to the PBR base later to brief Alexander and Zack in person.

As he went over his aircraft availability list, he totally forgot that he had asked Lisa if he could see her that evening. Since his little trip to Helen's pleasure palace the other night, Rat was feeling a little more relaxed. He also realized that he had not been very attentive to Lisa lately. He had been letting the problems of commanding the company get in the way of his relationship with her. He had vowed that he was going to take time off to see her, but in the rush to get ready for the mission, he forgot.

He briefed his pilots, talked to the maintenance chief to make sure that they had enough choppers to fulfill the mission requirements, and was just getting ready to fly out to the PBR base to talk to Alexander when Lisa showed up at Python Flight Operations.

"Oh, hi," he said, surprised when she stuck her blond head around the side of the door. "Come on in."

"Are we still going to dinner tonight?" she asked.

"Aw, shit!" Rat exclaimed, rubbing the back of his neck. "I forgot all about that. Brigade's got another big mission going down, and I was just getting ready to fly out to that riverboat outfit to talk to Mike Alexander about it."

Lisa was instantly angry. It was the third time in the last couple of weeks that he had broken a date. "Well, don't worry about it, Roger," she said icily. "I'm sure that I can find someone who wants to have dinner with me."

Gaines tried frantically for a save. "I won't be long, Lisa," he said, getting up out of his chair. "Maybe we can have a late dinner."

"I really don't think so." Lisa turned to go. "Good-bye, Roger."

Gaines watched her stomp out of the room. He shook his head. Lisa asked one of the pilots in the ready room to give her a ride back to the hospital, and a few moments later, a jeep roared out of the parking lot.

Gaines walked over to his locker and got out his flight helmet. As he walked out to the flight line, he wished life wasn't so complicated. He missed the good old days back in An Khe when he had enjoyed life a whole lot more.

Back at the hospital, Lisa thanked the pilot who had given her a lift and turned to go inside when she heard the sound of a Cobra taking off. She looked up, saw Gaines's green-and-tan gunship pass overhead, and was angry at him again. She wanted to be as important in his life as the war was. She stormed inside and ran into the hospital commander, Colonel Hardell.

"Lisa," he said, stopping abruptly in midstride, "I've been looking for you."

"Yes, sir?" Lisa liked the gray-haired, fatherly colonel. In fact, he was an old friend of her parents and she had known him since she had been a baby. He was kind of an Army Dutch uncle to her and had helped her several times in her career.

"I need you to go to Nha Trang and pick up some supplies from the Eighth Field Hospital for us."

"Me, sir?"

"Yes." He laid a fatherly hand on her shoulder. "And while you're there, you might as well take a couple of days off and soak up the sun. Maybe even get a decent meal."

"Thank you, sir, I'd really like that." The thought of getting away excited her. Getting away from Gaines, her work, and the whole damned war.

"You know," the colonel continued, "I can even give you the names of a couple of places that still have cooks left over from the days of the French. Did you know that Nha Trang was a resort town back then?"

Colonel Hardell steered the nurse into his office and offered her a chair while he wrote down the names of a couple of restaurants. At his age, a good meal was one of life's finest pleasures, and he knew every chef from Saigon to Hue.

"Here you go," he said, handing her two pieces of paper. "The first slip is a list of places to eat in town and the second one is a three-day pass. I want you to leave on the morning admin flight, and don't come back for three days."

"I think I can handle that, sir," she laughed.

"You've been working very hard lately, what with the move and all." The colonel's tone became more serious. "And you look like you could use a rest."

"I'm fine, sir, but I don't mind a couple of days on the beach."

"Lisa, it's been what? Two years that you've been with the Air Cav?"

"Almost, sir."

"That's a long time, Lisa. Too long for my money. I know how you feel about these men, but you should give some thought to yourself as well. It might be time for you to transfer to one of the field hospitals. Something to take you away from the day-to-day grind you've been through here."

Colonel Hardell held up his hand. "I know what you're going to say before you say it," he said with a smile. "I just want you to consider it while you're working on your tan."

"Thank you, Colonel, I will. I really will."

CHAPTER 19

Dong Pek Special Forces Camp

Sergeant Jack Wilburn was in the back of the teamhouse getting his personal gear ready for the mission. Wilburn and his Nungs were going in "sterile." All of them would be armed and outfitted with foreign equipment so that they wouldn't look like U.S. troops. They wore specially made black NVA-style uniforms, carried NVA rucksacks, and carried enemy weapons. Just about the only thing that would identify them as American were the small rolls of U.S. C-ration toilet paper they all carried.

If the NVA spotted them at a distance, their outlines would be familiar and they would be taken for a NVA or VC unit, on the march. And even at close range, the Nungs could easily pass themselves off as being VC or NVA. In fact, on many sterile Blackjack operations, the Nungs had walked right into enemy camps, told the North Vietnamese they were a lost VC unit, and had gotten directions to the locations of other nearby enemy units. Then they went to those locations and blew the shit out of them.

This meant that Wilburn had to choose new weapons. It was usual practice to use sterile weapons only in areas where U.S. forces were not operating. When Americans heard the distinctive, familiar sound of AKs firing in the distance, they were likely to call artillery or an air strike down on the location. Since they were going into an AO that was clean of American troops, the Nungs' AK-47s and Swedish K submachine guns would work out just fine. Nobody would be around to hear them except the dinks.

In the team's arms room, Wilburn chose a Swedish K, the 9mm M-45 Karl Gustav submachine gun, as his primary weapon. The K was a simple, blow-back-type submachine gun, rugged and reliable. With a cyclic rate of six hundred rounds a minute, it was also quite effective. The K's 9mm round wasn't as hard-hitting as the 5.56mm round of the M-16, but it worked well in the typical short-range combat they faced in the thick jungle.

He took his old Canadian Browning Hi-Power pistol as his backup piece. Since it used 9mm ammunition as did the K, he wouldn't have to worry about ammo supply. Last, he drew a silenced .22-caliber Ruger Mark 1, semi-automatic pistol along with the four-power telescopic sight designed for it.

The Ruger would be his ace in the hole. The silenced weapon gave them a quiet kill capability that they might need where they were going. With the scope fitted to the pistol, it could take out enemy sentries from as far as a hundred meters away, and it was perfect for hunting small game if they ran short on rations.

The sergeant took his new pieces out to the small firing range on the edge of the camp behind the teamhouse to run a few rounds through them. Wilburn never took a weapon on a mission that he had not test-fired first. He wasn't crazy. Captain Larry Ringer found Wilburn plinking beer cans with the Ruger. Each time the silenced weapon fired, all he heard was a faint pop.

"Jack," Ringer said as he walked up. "You about squared away?"

Wilburn blasted one last can with a .22-caliber long-rifle round, hitting it low on the bottom. The can flew into the air.

"Just about, sir," he said, dropping the empty magazine out of the butt of the pistol. "I just need to draw my ammo load and pack the old rucksack."

"Good, come on inside then. There's something I need to talk to you about."

"What's up?"

"Wait'll we get inside."

Silently, Wilburn followed Ringer into the command bunker. Ringer took a quick look around to make sure that they were alone.

"I just got word that we may have a little problem with the Strikers here in the camp," he said quietly. "A VC problem."

"You're shitting me!"

Ringer looked worried. "I wish the fuck I was. CCC seems to think that they ran one in on us with that last bunch of replacements."

"But they were Nungs!" Jack protested.

Of all the local peoples who were involved in the Vietnamese war, none were more fiercely anti-communist and loyal than the Nung Chinese. Unlike the Vietnamese, who often played both sides, or the Yards who sometimes just got tired of the war and went home, the Nungs were the Americans' most faithful and trusted allies. Their loyalty was so well respected that almost all high-ranking South Vietnamese officials had Nung bodyguards instead of Vietnamese troops. Their own people could not be trusted, but the hated Nung Chinese could. Special Forces camps all had a Nung detachment to guard the American cadre, and the elite SF Mobile Strike Force units like Ringer's company were all Nung.

It was unheard of for a Nung to go bad. If Ringer's camp had been infiltrated by the communists, it was very serious.

"I know it seems impossible." Ringer took a deep breath. "I've worked with these people for years now and I didn't want to believe it, either, but CCC has been picking up hard intell indicating that someone in this camp is leaking our missions."

Wilburn's face grew hard. "You mean like the last one?"

Ringer met his eyes. "Yes."

"I'm going to kill somebody."

"That's no problem," Ringer stated flatly. "But first you've got to find out who to kill."

"I will. Believe me, I will." Wilburn got to his feet. "I'm going to have a talk with Bao. If anyone knows what's going on around this fucking place, he does."

"You think that's a good idea?" Ringer frowned. "That old fart will blab it all over the camp."

"Not if I tell him that this threatens all of them and that it's a matter of family honor."

Ringer thought for a moment. "You may be right. But for Christ's sake, take it easy until we find out something a little more concrete."

"Yes, sir. But I have to get this settled before we move out tomorrow. I can't have that shit happening out there again."

"Do what you can and get back to me."

"Yes, sir."

Wilburn left the teamhouse and went looking for the old Nung. Bao had been brought back to the camp to finish recuperating from his wound with his friends and family around him. More than likely, Wilburn thought, he was drinking whiskey and cheating at cards right now.

Jack headed for the big bunker that served as the Nung day room. Sure enough, Bao was sitting at the wooden table, an empty glass and an overflowing ashtray in front of him. The old warrior cackled in Chinese and slammed down his hand of cards.

"*Co ba,*" Wilburn greeted Bao, using the Nung word for brother. "Come with me. I need to talk to you."

Without a word, the Nung got up and followed. Outside the bunker, they walked in silence over to the edge of the perimeter wire.

"I have sad news, elder brother," Jack said formally. "We have heard that there is an enemy in the camp. A brother who has sold out to the cong."

Bao's dark, weathered face was hard. "That cannot be so, *Trung si,*" he hissed. "It cannot be so."

"I thought that at first, old friend. But it has been learned that Charlie knew where we were going on our last mission."

"This is truth?"

"It is the truth."

The old Chinese was silent for a moment. He looked back at the camp. He finally turned and faced the American, his hands clasped together in front of his face. "I am shamed, *Trung si.*" He bowed his head.

"What do you mean?"

"The son of my sister's oldest daughter. He is no good, but she begged I would speak for him in the camp. I do this because he is family."

"You mean Whiskey? The interpreter?"

"That is the one." Bao lowered his head. "I go now to kill him."

"Wait!" Wilburn grabbed his arm. "No, wait! How do you know he's the one?"

"I know. The bones tell me."

Wilburn thought fast. At the Nung shrine, their priest foretold the future by casting ancient knuckle bones on the ground and reading the patterns that they made on the earth. It was a ritual out of prehistoric times, dating back to when men used sharpened stones to kill one another. But Wilburn had been around the Nungs long enough to pay heed to what the bones foretold. Some of his best combat intell had come from what the Nung priest had seen in the cracked, brown bones that were ancient and worn shiny with use.

"What did he say?"

"The priest say my house fall under a dark moon. He say I must make sacrifices. I do this, but the shadow not go away. The priest say he see a snake in my house. Now I know who is snake."

Bao's face was expressionless, his eyes slitted. "I kill this snake in my house."

"Wait, Bao," Wilburn said. "Listen to me. I saved your life."

Bao bowed his head.

"And you are obligated to me."

"That is true, *Trung si*. This also shames me."

"Let there be no shame between us," Wilburn said, trying to relieve the obligation. "But since I saved your worthless old hide, you must listen to me. You can kill your nephew, but you must do it my way."

"I hear, *Trung si*. What is your way and when can I do this thing?"

"When we are on the mission. Not until then."

Bao looked up at him. "I do not understand."

"To kill him now is nothing. It may even make the problem worse. First we must find out who he is passing the information to."

"You are wise for one so young, *Trung si*."

"Promise me that you won't kill him until then."

Bao grinned a terrible grin. "I will not kill him. I will invite him to eat with me tonight. You will give me a bottle of your whiskey. He will get drunk on your good whiskey and he will brag to me of his accomplishments. Maybe I will hear something of value coming from his worthless mouth."

"Good. But don't kill him."

Bao looked up at the American and smiled. "As the gods will, *Trung si*."

Wilburn watched the old Nung warrior walk away. He wouldn't have wanted to get that old man pissed off at him. He almost felt sorry for Whiskey.

Lieutenant Colonel Tran was furious. He stood behind his desk, his fists clenched with suppressed rage. "I expected better of you, Nguyen."

Tran was so angry that he used the familiar Vietnamese pronoun on the captain, a word that was used to speak to children and animals. "You have disgraced yourself and the People's Revolution."

"But, Comrade Colonel . . ."

"Don't call me 'comrade,'" Tran snapped. "You have lost that right."

Nguyen was stunned. No one ever spoke to him that way. "I did not know that they had artillery support. You did not tell me that."

Tran hesitated. The disgraced captain had a good point. As the operations officer, he should have known that the Air Cav had flown a battery of 105mm howitzers into a firebase close enough to support the Yankee patrol boats. It would have made a big difference to how the attack was planned and executed.

"That is true," Tran admitted. "But the attack failed and you lost a hundred men."

"Eighty-nine, counting the wounded, and most of them were killed when the Yankees brought the artillery fire down on top of themselves."

Tran shook his head. He had heard of the Americans doing that before. It was foolishly brave, but it had worked. "Regardless, the patrol boats are still there and they can still intercept our river traffic. We must have free access to the river."

"Give me a heavy-weapons platoon, Colonel, and I can destroy them with mortars."

"No, they will be ready for that. And something more important has just come to my attention. I will deal with the patrol boats later."

Nguyen's ears pricked up.

"I have been informed that the Yankee boats are to bring a large reconnaissance force up the river into our staging area tomorrow."

Tran turned and pointed at the map. "I do not know exactly where the Yankees will be dropped off, but they must be stopped at all costs. We cannot have them reporting the location of our supplies and troop-staging areas to the B-52s. Not now, when we are so close to launching the general offensive."

Tran's voice still held a harsh tone. "I am giving you one last chance to redeem yourself, Nguyen. You will be in charge of locating this Yankee unit when it lands. Your orders are to destroy it completely. Not one man is to be left alive."

Nguyen came to a rigid position of attention. "Yes, Comrade Colonel!" he snapped back. "I will not fail this time."

Tran stared intently. "You had better not."

CHAPTER 20

PBR Base Zulu

The twin-rotor CH-47 Chinook heavy-transport chopper came to a landing on the bare-earth chopper pad outside the patrol base. The "shithook's" rotors blew a stinging storm of fine red dust up into the air as the Nungs of the Mike Force Recon Platoon hurriedly ran down the rear ramp. Panama Jack Wilburn followed them off and sprinted for the wire.

"Hey, PJ!" Brody called out from his bunker.

Wilburn walked over to him and stuck out his hand. "What's happening, man?"

Brody took his hand and slapped him on the shoulder. "SOS, same old shit. How's the leg?"

Wilburn pounded his fist against his right thigh. "It'll do for now."

"Great." Brody looked the Special Forces sergeant up and down, his eyes stopping on the Swedish K. "That's quite some outfit you're wearing there. You guys look like a bunch of dinks."

"That's the general idea. We're trying to blend in with the local scenery."

Wilburn and his men were all wearing black uniforms like a main-force VC unit. Their heads were covered with scarves and their Bata boots had been dyed black as well. Their ammunition magazines were carried in NVA-style chest pouches and they all wore bulging NVA rucksacks. Most of their canteens, however, were U.S. issue and hung on Army pistol belts. But many VC and NVA units wore captured American equipment, particularly canteens and field belts.

"I understand that you're going to be our ready reaction force," Wilburn said.

"Yeah," Brody grinned. "So you better make sure that you don't step in the shit again. We like it here and we don't want to have to go out in the fucking woods and bail your asses out of some firefight."

Wilburn laughed. "If I remember it right, Brody, I was the guy who had to save your ass the last time."

"Something like that. Anyway, how about a cold one? The Old Man flew us out a resupply. With ice, too."

"No, thanks," Wilburn declined, shaking his head. "But I'll have a Coke if you've got one."

There was a lone can left hidden under the ice in the Styrofoam rocket-box cooler. Brody fished it out and handed it to Wilburn.

"Thanks, man," he said, punching two holes on the top with the P-38 can opener on his dog tag chain.

"Just remember, man, you owe me," Brody laughed. "That's our last Coke."

Brody noticed that one of the Nungs, a young man without a weapon or any field gear, had his arms bound behind his back with commo wire. "It looks like you got a prisoner."

"A traitor," Jack spat. "He's one of ours, but he's gone bad."

"Why you taking him with you then?"

148

Wilburn smiled tightly. "Insurance," he said. "Insurance. The little fucker's been passing information to Charlie and I want him where I can keep a close eye on him."

"What're you going to do to him?"

"Oh," Wilburn said casually, "he's going to have a little accident, I think."

"Something fatal?"

"Why, of course." Wilburn chuckled. "What else?"

The Special Forces sergeant drained the last of the Coke. "Well, I've got to go see about our transportation. Where can I find that Navy officer?"

"He's probably down by the boats," Brody grinned. "He doesn't like us grunts very much."

"He's going to love my people then."

Brody laughed.

A half hour later, the three choppers of Rat Gaines's light-fire team showed up and the four PBRs cast off for their run up the river. The gunships were to orbit out of sight so as not to draw attention to the riverboats' mission, but they would be available in minutes if anything happened. Brody and his squad watched from the shore as the boats, packed to the gunwales with grinning Nungs, passed out of sight beyond the bend in the river.

"Hope Wilburn makes it this time," Two-Step said.

"Man, I don't know about that guy," Brody answered. "It seems that every time he goes out, he steps in some deep shit."

"I know I wouldn't want his fucking job," Gardner said.

"You got that shit right." Brody looked around at his men. His eyes stopped on Harvard. "Well, gang, we still got a few sandbags to fill today, so let's get on it before ol' Leo comes looking for us."

"Fuck a bunch of sandbags," Farmer muttered.

"You got that shit right." said York.

In the command PBR, Wilburn checked over his map as the riverbanks flowed slowly past them. He had not chosen their drop-off point yet because he wanted to get a feel for the terrain first. Also, with the traitor on the loose, it hadn't been safe to do that back at the camp. But now that they were on the move, it was time to decide where they were going.

Wilburn thought about what Bao had told him when they had met earlier that morning.

The old Nung's face had been expressionless, but his manner had been grim. "I was right, *Trung si,*" he stated flatly. "The one called Whiskey is a *cong.*"

"What'd he say?"

"He say that he will start a bar when he is *fini* with the camp here." Bao looked properly disgusted.

Most of the Nungs served on six-month contracts with the Special Forces, but it was rare for one of them to quit. Especially to go into business for himself. Business was for the city Chinese, the Cantonese, not for the Nungs. The Nungs were warrior bred, and once they signed on with the Special Forces units, they stayed.

"Did he say anything else?"

"No. But some of the other men say that he talk a lot with the pig Mama San."

There was a small farming village not too far from Dong Pek and the camp garbage was picked up by an old Vietnamese woman who fed it to her pigs. The Nungs bought pigs from her to eat during their feast-day celebrations so the arrangement worked well for everyone. Or so everyone had thought.

Bao spat. "I think she is *cong,* too, *Trung si.*"

Old Mama San didn't look like a typical VC agent, but it was entirely possible. It was not unheard of for one of them to work for both sides. Wilburn would pass that information on to Ringer so that the captain could check her out as soon as they were safely away.

"What do you want me to do?" Bao asked. "Can I kill him now?"

"How is your health, old man?" Wilburn asked. "Can you go on the mission with us?"

Bao drew himself up to his full height. He thumped himself on the chest and squared his shoulders. "Yes. I can go. I am not dead yet."

Wilburn grinned. "Good. I want you to bring Whiskey with you. I don't want to leave him here behind us. Just tell him to get suited up, but don't do anything until we get him on the chopper. If that Mama San's watching, I don't want her to get suspicious. But once he's on that bird, take his weapons away and tie him up."

Bao's eyes glittered. "You are very wise, *Trung si.*"

"I wish you'd stop saying that."

"Ah, but it is true."

On the Song Boung now, hours later, Wilburn wasn't so sure how wise he was. The PBRs were moving slowly up the center of the river. Every weapon on board was sweeping the banks looking for the slightest sign of trouble.

The Special Forces sergeant really didn't like the idea of a naval insertion at all. He felt too vulnerable in the middle of the river where everybody and their dog could see and hear them coming for miles away. He would have preferred a night parachute drop or the standard heliborne eagle flight insertion. Floating around in little boats just wasn't cutting it.

He studied his map again, folded it, and went back to the bridge. "Sir," he addressed Lieutenant Miller. "I think I've got a spot picked out."

The PBR commander studied the map for a moment. "I thought that you wanted to go a little farther upstream."

"Yes, sir, but on second thought, I've decided to stop short of the objective area and walk the rest of the way in."

"You don't like our taxi service?"

"No, sir, it's not that," Wilburn replied. "It's just that I feel a little conspicuous out here on the water. I'd rather be in the jungle where we can duck back and hide if we have to."

"That's no problem, I'll drop you off anywhere you want."
Miller looked at the map again. "That looks to be just a little over two klicks up the river. I'll tell my lead boat."

"Thanks, sir, I'll alert my people."

With their diesel motors at an idle and their gunners nervously scanning the dense foliage in front of them, two of the PBRs ran their bows up on the red mud of the riverbank. The other two boats circled protectively in midstream to provide instant fire support if anything went wrong.

Dropping down from the deck into the red mud, Wilburn was the first man off of the boat. He was glad to have his feet on solid ground again. Behind him, the Nungs clambered off and fanned into the jungle along the bank.

As soon as the first two PBRs were off-loaded, the other two boats came in. When the last man was on shore, the four boats quickly turned around and headed back downriver, out of Indian country.

From the tiny bridge on the lead PBR, Miller waved goodbye. Wilburn didn't see him. He was already heading deeper into the jungle. If they were going to reach their operational area by nightfall, they had to get humping.

In the middle of the formation, Bao held the end of a rope noose. The other end was around Whiskey's neck. The traitor's arms were still bound behind his back and a neck scarf had been tied over his mouth so he couldn't cry out. The young Nung was having a rough time keeping up. Bao tugged on the rope every now and then, painfully forcing him to move faster, and grinning every time he did it.

Rat Gaines put the finishing touches to his day's work and leaned back in his chair. For once, things seemed to be pretty well under control. There wasn't anything that was screaming for his personal attention. Maybe he could pay a little attention to Lisa tonight instead of worrying about business.

He rang through to the hospital and asked if she was still on the ward. The duty nurse told him that Lisa had left for Nha Trang the day before and that she wouldn't be back for a couple of days. Gaines frowned. Lisa hadn't said anything to him about that.

He grabbed his hat and headed out the door. Finally he had the whole night off and Lisa was running around in Nha Trang. Somehow it didn't seem fair. On impulse, he drove down past the flight line and found Alphabet busy working on his new Cobra gunship.

"What's the matter?" he asked. "That thing crap out on you already?"

"No, sir," the new AC replied. "I'm just doing a little fine-tuning here. I wanted to go over the firing-control circuits myself before I take her up tomorrow."

"You found me a gunner yet?"

"Yes, sir, I've got you a real winner this time. Sean O'Leary. He just transferred in on a second tour."

"Where's he at now?"

"Probably at the pub. He's Irish."

'That's a good recommendation,' Gaines laughed. "Well, if I don't catch up with him tonight, tell him to report to me first thing in the morning."

CHAPTER 21

Nha Trang

Lisa Maddox leaned against the well-worn oak bar at La Frigate and sipped her Remy Martin cognac. She looked out over the silvery, moonlit beach and the peaceful waves that broke softly on the sand. It looked more like the shore of a lake than the South China Sea. After spending the afternoon in the sun and eating the best meal she had had in years, the nurse was more content than she had been in a long time.

Colonel Hardell had been right. La Frigate was a true French restaurant in the old tradition, and the food had been fantastic. Even the waiters still spoke French. The fine silver and china on starched linen tablecloths brought back fond memories of her childhood, when her father had taken her to restaurants in Europe. The meal was excellent, and for the first time in weeks, she had a hearty appetite.

She looked up when a party of five walked into the dining room, an American officer and four Vietnamese. The Vietnamese were armed with M-1 carbines, and the weapons looked out of place in such peaceful surroundings. She looked closer and noticed that the young American officer was also wearing a pistol in a shoulder holster.

The officer and one of the Vietnamese, a heavyset man, sat down at one of the tables close to her, and the head waiter hurried over to them. The three remaining Vietnamese took up places in the corners of the room, watching the doors and patio.

Lisa's curiosity was sparked by the presence of bodyguards. Trying not to be too obvious, Lisa watched as the important Vietnamese man spoke to the head waiter in rapid-fire French. The head waiter motioned to one of the serving boys, who hurried over to the table with a liter bottle of Algerian rose.

As soon as the waiter left, the American and the Vietnamese started talking as if they were equals. The American captain — Lisa had finally noticed the bars on his cap — was a good-looking man in an intense way, tall and slim with his hair cropped short. He looked boyish except for the Air Cav-style mustache he wore. She couldn't read his subdued black-and-olive-drab shoulder patch, but he had some kind of Vietnamese-style insignia on his pocket and wore the three-rosette rank badge of a Vietnamese *dai uy,* a captain, on his jungle fatigue jacket. They were speaking English, but the captain used many foreign words. They seemed to be in an Asian language, but certainly not Vietnamese.

The Vietnamese glanced over at her and said something to the captain. He looked up and gave her a not so quick once-over. He smiled and said something to the Vietnamese in a different language. To her surprise, she recognized the language as German.

Their meal came and the two men started eating. Lisa finished her brandy and ordered another. She didn't feel like leaving immediately. The American laughed about something and she looked over at him again. This time, she caught his eye and he smiled at her. An open confident smile. She flushed and looked away.

Whoever he was, he had a wicked smile. When their meal was over, the captain stood up and said something to the Vietnamese. The Asian grinned and glanced her way before walking out of the room with one of the bodyguards. The other two men stayed where they were, their eyes never leaving the captain.

He walked to the bar and ordered a gin and tonic. He took the drink and turned to her.

"You must be new in town," he said, holding out his hand. "My name's Rick Kasnowski, but my friends call me the Kaz."

Lisa took his hand. "I'm Lisa Maddox. Glad to meet you, sir."

"Sir?" he said, looking around the room in mock horror. "Sir? My God, is there an officer in here?"

Lisa laughed.

"Can I buy you a drink?" he asked with a big grin.

"I really should be getting back," she said halfheartedly. "Why?"

The nurse stopped and thought about his question. Why did she need to go? Why did she feel that she had to run from this man?

"Okay," she said and settled back. "But only if you'll tell me why you have a bodyguard."

"Well" — Kaz grinned — "it's a long story. But if you have the time, I'll be glad to."

He called the bartender over and ordered another round. "It's real simple. I'm their commander and they have orders to make sure that I behave myself when I'm out in public."

"But who are they?"

Kaz leaned closer to her and whispered, "I'm not supposed to let this out, but they're the real power behind the throne here in Vietnam. They're the Nungs."

"The who?"

"They're Nung Chinese. They're the best damned troops in all of Southeast Asia and they guard the American base here, Camp John F. McDermott."

156

"You mean they're not Vietnamese?"

"Oh, God, no!"

"And who are you?"

"Like I said," Kaz answered with a grin, "I'm their glorious leader. The bodyguard is their idea. Somebody tried to bump me off one night and since then, I can't go out of the camp without them trailing along."

He leaned closer again and spoke softly. "You know, I tried to run away once, but they came after me and dragged me back to the camp kicking and screaming."

He looked around the room. "Did you see that guy I was having dinner with? He's the worst one of them all. He's Dan, my chief interpreter, and he follows me around everywhere I go. It's terrible. I can't even sneak off for a beer without finding him lurking around behind the potted plants."

Lisa was confused. "But why don't you put in for a transfer?"

Kasnowski looked shocked. "Transfer? My God! If I got transferred, I'd have to go to work! Please don't talk about transfers, someone might hear you."

Lisa laughed. "I get the feeling that you're pulling my leg."

Kaz glanced down at her legs. Even though she was wearing shapeless jungle fatigues, Lisa felt that he could see all the way through thcm.

"No," he said slowly, "but that's not a bad idea." He quickly changed the subject. "I noticed that you're wearing a Cav patch. What're you doing down here in this tropical paradise?"

Lisa would have rather had him talk about her legs, but she answered his question anyway. "I've been taking a little break for the last couple of days. I'm heading back up to Chu Lai in the morning."

He glanced down at his watch. "Say, I've got an idea. Since you're new in town, have you seen all the sights yet?"

Before she could answer, he added, "It's perfectly safe. My bodyguards also have strict orders to make sure that I act like a perfect officer and a gentleman at all times."

She laughed.

"Since I have to earn my pay for the next thirty minutes or so, I thought that you might like to take a ride on up to the top of Hawk Hill and look down on the bright lights of town. You can see all the way to the big Buddha from there."

She studied his face for a moment and came to a snap decision. "Sure, why not?"

"Great," he said, draining his glass with one gulp. "Let's go."

He nodded to the two Nung guards, and they followed them to the restaurant's parking lot.

Back in Chu Lai, Rat Gaines decided to stop off at the officers' club to see if he could find his new gunner. At least he could grab a quick sandwich and wouldn't have to risk ptomaine poisoning by eating in the mess hall.

The club was in its usual state of shambles. A cloud of cigarette smoke hung at about shoulder height. He looked through the fog and saw several of his pilots over at a table in the corner. They were singing again, something about " . . . your son's coming home in a body bag, do da, do da. Your son's coming home in a body bag, all the do da day."

Rat got as far from the drunken mob as he could and took a seat at the bar.

"What ya got to eat tonight?" he asked the bartender.

"Sorry, sir, we only have cold cuts. The cook's sick."

Rat sighed. He probably had the clap again. He still wasn't up to trying the mess hall, so it looked like it was going to be sliced pony peter again. "Okay, give me a bologna-and-cheese, please."

"Sorry, sir, we're all out of horse cock. How about salami?"

"Sure," Rat sighed. "Make it two. And bring me a beer, please."

Gaines wolfed down his sandwiches and looked around the smoky club, trying to see if he could find his new gunner.

Sitting by himself at a table against the back wall was a slim warrant officer wearing brand-new jungle fatigues with aviator's wings above the left pocket and an emerald green ascot at the throat. That might be him. Gaines picked up his beer and walked over to the table.

"Are you O'Leary, by any chance?"

The WO/2 put his beer down and stood up. "Yes, Captain, I am. Sean O'Leary."

Rat stuck out his hand. "I'm Rat Gaines, Python Flight CO. I understand that you've been assigned to be my new gunner."

O'Leary shook his hand. "Yes, I believe that I have. I was talking to your old gunner. What's his name? Something Italian?"

"Schmuchatelli," Gaines laughed. "But we all call him Alphabet."

"Anyway," O'Leary continued, "he said that you wanted someone with experience and I've done eighteen months in the left-hand seat of a gunship."

"Who were you with the last time?"

"The Two Eighty-first out of Nha Trang."

Gaines looked at O'Leary in a new light. The 281st Assault Helicopter Company was one bad-assed gunship outfit. They did all the Sneaky Pete stuff for the 5th Group Special Forces, a lot of cross-border time. If O'Leary had lived through eighteen months with that bunch of maniacs, he had to be damned good.

"Why didn't you go back to them?"

O'Leary's eyes were hooded. "I got tired of being shot down."

That made sense. The 281st usually didn't fly places where the Air Rescue people could go in. Most of the time when they got shot down, they had to walk out, usually by heading in a southerly direction and following the sun.

Gaines laughed. "You're probably going to find the Cav rather dull after working with the Two Eighty-first."

"I think I can live with it."

"Are you looking for an AC slot?"

"Nope."

"Why not?" Gaines was puzzled. Most veteran copilots sooner or later wanted a chopper of their own.

"Well, Captain," O'Leary said, his brown eyes locked on Gaines, "if it's all the same to you, all I want to worry about are my guns. I don't mind flying, but I find that it tends to distract me from what I'm supposed to be doing over here."

"And what's that?"

"Killing dinks."

There was a certain tenseness visible behind O'Leary's calm mannerisms that suddenly made Gaines be cautious.

"You ever worked with Cobras?"

"Not much. I got a little transition time on them back at Wolters, but I'm looking forward to a chance to try one out full time."

"Tell you what," Gaines said. "You come on down to Python Operations in the morning and I'll give you a chance at it."

"Sounds fine with me, Captain. I'll be there."

"Good. Now how about a drink?"

"Thank you, Captain, but I still need to get caught up on my sleep."

"No sweat," Gaines said. "I'll see you in the morning."

When O'Leary left, Rat returned to the bar and ordered one last drink. A Red Cross girl at the other end of the bar giggled as she tried to fend off the gropings of a grunt lieutenant. Gaines casually wondered what Lisa was doing in Nha Trang. He forced his thoughts back to his new warrant officer. He wasn't sure about O'Leary, but he'd give him a try in the morning. He made a note to himself to take a look at the man's 201 file, too.

CHAPTER 22

Nha Trang

When Lisa got out to the parking lot outside the restaurant, she found a highly polished M-151 jeep waiting, a command jeep with two radios mounted in the back. Kasnowski led the nurse around to the passenger side before climbing in behind the wheel. The Nung interpreter and the three guards crowded into the backseat.

Kaz started the jeep up and pulled out of the walled parking lot onto Beach Road. He took the microphone from the clip mounting on the dash and pressed the push-to-talk switch on the side. "Broad Tenant Base," he said. "This is Two, over."

"This is Base," came the voice from the loudspeakers mounted in the back. "Go ahead."

"This is Two, I am leaving La Frigate, en route to your location, Echo Tango Alpha five mikes. Over."

"Base, Roger."

After a short trip down past the moonlit beach, the jeep turned in on a road running next to the Air Force base and passed under a sign over the road reading, Camp John F.

McDermott. Two guards at the main gate sharply came to present arms as the jeep passed.

"Two of my people," Kaz explained.

The huge American logistical base was spread out along both sides of the road. Dozens of large prefab metal buildings and hundreds of smaller wooden tropical huts littered the area. Motor pools and supply dumps were everywhere. Well over five thousand Americans called the camp home.

Kasnowski drove through the camp and stopped the jeep in front of a small compound built off the side of the road. The three bodyguards jumped out, but Dan, the interpreter, remained in the back. Kaz pulled the jeep onto the road again. After passing a small Vietnamese village of tin shacks, the road turned and climbed up a small hill. On the way, Lisa saw several guard towers along the lighted perimeter fence of the American camp. At the crest of the hill there was a large wooden watchtower with a heavy machine-gun bunker and a searchlight mounted on top. Beyond the tower was a small perimeter surrounding a Hank antiaircraft missile battery that protected the camp from enemy air attack. The hill took its name from the missiles.

The officer pulled the jeep up at the base of the tower and stopped. As he had promised, the lights of the city below were spectacular. And the moon reflecting off the calm sea looked like a picture postcard.

"It's beautiful," Lisa said.

"Would I lie to you?"

The nurse knew that Kasnowski was observing her as she looked down at the bay. She reached up and undid her long blond hair and shook it out. A slight breeze had come up and it gently ruffled her hair.

In a war zone full of dirt and shapeless uniforms, Lisa's long blond mane was her single vanity, a reminder to herself of her femininity. And tonight, with the brandy sitting warm in her stomach, the moonlight reflecting on the calm sea, and this mysterious young officer sitting next to her, she was very much aware of it. The war was far from her mind.

Kasnowski was also very much aware of Lisa's femininity. He sat quietly on his side of the jeep and let the natural, moonlit beauty of the bay of Nha Trang work its magic on the nurse.

"I know this nice, quiet little beach," he said. "If you'd like, we could take a swim later."

Lisa looked over at him. "Why, Captain, I think you're trying to seduce me," she said with a sly smile.

His eyes locked on hers. "The idea had occurred to me," he admitted. "Do you mind?"

Lisa stopped to think for a moment. Did she mind? No, she admitted to herself, not really. Under the circumstances, it seemed like the right thing to do.

"Maybe," she answered with a laugh. "We'll see."

Kasnowski switched back to playing tour guide, pointing out the areas of interest in the city below. He was telling her about the huge statue of the Buddha on the northwest edge of town when the blare of a radio message broke in.

"Broad Tenant Two, this is Base, over."

He snatched up the mike. Instantly, he was all business. "Two, go."

"This is Base, we just got a call from India Delta Charlie. They've got a report of a problem in Cao Dai and want you to take a look at it. Over."

The Kaz's voice was intense. "What kind of problem, over?"

"They've got a report of a small boat making a landing close to Francious, over."

"Roger, get the alert platoon on it. I'll be there in zero five. Out."

"Sorry 'bout this," he said, starting up the jeep and heading back down the hill. "I've got to get back to work. I'll have my duty NCO take you to wherever you're staying tonight."

Lisa was disappointed. She had just about talked herself into that midnight swim. She could see that Kasnowski was just like Rat Gaines. When duty called, he came running.

163

Tonight, though, Lisa was not going to let the war get in the way.

"Could I go with you?" she asked boldly. "And wait until you're done?"

The Kaz glanced at her. If the gods were good to him, this would only be a fifteen-minute job. "Sure, why not? This shouldn't take a minute."

It turned out that the alarm was only an errant fisherman returning to shore. The man claimed that he had been caught out at sea with a broken motor and had had to row back. The Nungs thoroughly searched both him and his boat, but found nothing except his day's catch of fish.

When the troops were climbing back into the deuce-and-a-half truck, Kasnowski turned to Dan and told him to go back to camp with them. The Nung grinned broadly and climbed into the cab of the truck with the driver.

"Tell Jimbo that I'll be checking the guards on the beach," Kaz called after him. Dan grinned even more.

It was only a short trip from the fishing village to the Special Forces beach at the end of the Air Force base runway. A Nung guard was at his post guarding the entrance and two more were on either end of the expanse of shining sand. Kasnowski returned the man's salute and called out a greeting in Chinese as he passed.

He drove the jeep down to the edge of the water and stopped. The waves breaking on the sand rippled in the moonlight like molten silver. In the distance, the shadowy shapes of Hon Tri and Hon Moi Island broke the shimmer of the water.

"All we need to have right now is a loaf of bread and a jug of wine," Lisa said, surprising herself with her boldness.

"I can't do much about the chow, but I've got a bottle of brandy," Kasnowski replied. He opened up the ammo box welded between the front seats of the jeep and pulled out a bottle.

"I like to come down here and watch the sun rise with a little brandy in my coffee," he explained. He opened the bottle and handed it to her. "I don't have any glasses, so we'll just have to rough it."

Lisa laughed. "People would spend thousands of dollars to have it this rough."

"Yes, it is nice, isn't it. I'm thinking of coming back here when the war's over, building me a little house right on the beach and writing my memoirs. Maybe I'll even write the great American novel if I can sober up long enough."

Lisa took a long drink and passed the bottle over to him. "How about that swim you offered me?"

"Sounds good to me."

Turning around behind the driver's seat, he pulled an Army-issue wool blanket out of the pouch behind the seat cover, tucked the bottle under his arm, and stepped onto the sand. Lisa followed him, unbuttoning her fatigue jacket as she walked. The warm breeze on her skin felt as gentle as a lover's caress. By the time Kasnowski had spread their blanket and turned around, Lisa was naked from the waist up and stepping out of her fatigue pants.

He didn't say a word. He just took his clothes off as fast as he could.

She beat him to the water, dove into the surf, and started swimming through the warm, gentle waves with strong, sure strokes. Kasnowski followed her in and caught up fifty feet from the shore. She stopped swimming when he pulled up next to her and started treading water. He turned to face her. The moonlight on her wet body made it glow. She looked like an ancient sea goddess. He moved closer to her and folded her into his arms, treading water for both of them.

"You're going to drown us," she laughed. A wave broke over their heads.

"What a way to die." He ducked his head to take one of her hard nipples into his mouth.

She moaned and threw her head back. Another wave broke over them, and when they emerged from it he rolled onto his side, taking her with him. Holding her close, her breasts pressed tightly against him, he started swimming back to the shore.

She let him carry her in that strange embrace. She felt the hard muscles of his legs as he kicked and wanted to wrap her own legs around him. A few feet from shore, her feet brushed the sand and she stood up in the waist-deep water. Kneeling in front of her, Kasnowski enfolded her in his arms and pressed his face against her warm, slick belly. She wrapped her arms around his head and pulled him closer. His hand came up between her legs and she opened them for him, moaning when he touched her. She sank to her knees in the surf.

"I think we'd better get outta here," he suggested softly. "Before we both drown."

She laughed. Hand in hand they ran for the blanket.

She was so anxious to feel him inside her that she was reaching for him before they had even stopped moving. She locked her legs around his hips and held on as he rode her, plunging furiously into her.

It was over in a short minute, but the night was not. When they caught their breath, he reached over for the bottle of brandy and offered it to her. She took a short drink and handed it back.

"You're beautiful," he said simply.

She looked up at him. "So are you."

For the first time in what seemed like ages, Lisa was far from the war. She was simply a woman reveling in being young on a moonlit beach. The Air Cav and everything back at Chu Lai were far behind her. She might as well have been on another planet for all that her old life mattered.

Kasnowski lowered his head and took her nipple into his mouth again. She reached over and pulled him on top of her and guided him back inside her. This time, their lovemaking went slowly. Her first orgasm came, quickly followed by another and yet a third before he climaxed. When he rolled off her, he took her chin in his hand and lifted her eyes to his.

"They always told me that if I was a real good little boy, when I died I would go to heaven. Well, I must have died sometime recently and was too damned busy to even know that it happened."

Lisa brushed his cheek with her hand. "No," she said softly. "I'm the one who's in heaven. I haven't had such a good time in longer than I can remember."

"Well," he said, "maybe we can do this again sometime."

"No, I don't think so," she said sadly. "Nights like this don't happen twice."

He studied her for a moment. "You're probably right," he finally said with a sigh. "But the night's not over yet."

She reached for him again. "You're right," she said. "It isn't."

CHAPTER 23

Deep in the jungle

Panama Jack Wilburn crouched in the deep night shadows beside a stand of bamboo and watched. A long column of North Vietnamese porters made their way down the trail. Since getting off the boats, Wilburn had marched the Nungs all day, moving as fast as possible through the dense jungle. They had reached a major trail through the jungle just as night fell.

He split his unit into small recon teams and left his headquarters element in a night defensive position on a ridgeline a klick away. Then he led one of the five-man recon teams in close to watch the trail.

Every third soldier in the NVA column carried a hooded lantern to light the way. The lantern's glow was so faint, they couldn't be seen more than a few meters away. In the dim light, Wilburn couldn't tell what the North Vietnamese were carrying, but it was bad news no matter what. This was the third such string of porters that he had observed that night. Something big was going down, there was no question about it. Exactly what it was, however, he had yet to find out. He backed away from his observation point and returned to the rest of his small recon team. The skinny young Nung that they all called Cowboy was anxiously waiting for him.

"What you see, *Trung si*?" he asked.

"Boo koo VC. They're packing supplies down the trail."

"What we do now, *Trung si*?"

Wilburn thought for a moment. "Cowboy, why don't you go down there and play VC for me. Try to hook up with one of the supply parties. Talk to them, find out what they're doing. But make sure you get back to our camp by early morning, eight o'clock."

Cowboy grinned in the dark. Infiltrating enemy formations and learning what they were doing was his favorite game. He was good at it.

"Sure, *Trung si*," he said confidently, proud to have been chosen for the mission. "No sweat."

The young Nung grabbed his AK-47 and moved down the hill to the trail. Wilburn took the rest of his team back up the mountain to their patrol base.

So far, they had not found where the supplies were coming from or where the NVA were taking them. But a great deal of war material was on the move, much more than usual, and it was being sent into government-controlled areas of southern I Corps. Somebody was in for a hard time real soon.

Back at the patrol base on top of the ridgeline, Wilburn talked quietly to Bao, getting reports from other teams before sending his nightly radio report to Major Snow at the Special Forces CCC headquarters in Kontum.

"It is the same, *Trung si*," the old Nung said. "All teams report boo koo VC."

Wilburn got out his map. Hiding under his poncho liner, he shined his red-filtered penlight on it, plotting the trail he and the other teams had found. All of them led back to an area of dense jungle and rough terrain on the edge of the Vietnamese-Laotian border, the same area that his last team had been in when they had been hit. He did not like the way this was shaping up at all.

He called for the radio. Speaking softly, he made his report. CCC rogered his message and ordered him to move closer to the border. They also wanted him to snatch a prisoner.

Wilburn gave the radio handset back to the Nung on radio watch. Prisoner snatches were always tricky, not only taking the man alive, but getting him extracted for interrogation later. There was too great a chance of the mission being blown when the chopper came in. Softly he called Bao over.

"They want us to get them a prisoner."

The Nung was silent for a moment. "That is not good, *Trung si.*"

"I know. But we have to do it."

"Can we not say that it is impossible?"

Wilburn grinned. "No, Bao. We have to try."

The Nung shrugged his shoulders in the dark. "Okay, we try."

Wilburn wrapped himself up in his poncho liner and tried to find a soft place to sleep next to the radio operator. With the soft hiss of radio squelch in his ears, he dropped right off to sleep.

On the bank above the trail, Cowboy watched as a party of two dozen NVA troops slowly made their way downhill by the dim glow of the lanterns. When the last man had passed him, he dropped onto the trail and started following.

Twenty minutes later the NVA stopped along the side of the path for a rest break. Cowboy stopped short of the NVA, just around the bend in the trail. Shrugging out of his rucksack, he reached in and dug out a cold rice ball wrapped in a banana leaf. With his AK slung over his shoulder, he slowly walked up to the end of the column, munching on the rice ball.

The NVA on trail watch was startled when he saw the Nung approach.

"Peace, comrade," Cowboy said when the NVA went for his weapon. He squatted on his heels beside the man. The NVA soldier eyed his big rice ball.

"You have no food, comrade?" Cowboy asked. He broke his rice ball in two and gave half of it to the guard. "Here. You need to eat."

The guard took the food and happily stuffed the sticky rice and cold pork fat mixture into his mouth. He removed the NVA canteen from his belt and took a deep drink. Then he offered the canteen to Cowboy.

"Here, try some of this," he said. "It will rinse the taste of the trail from your mouth."

Cowboy drank. The canteen was full of rice wine.

"Thank you," he said, handing it back.

The guard looked closely at him. "I have not seen you before," he said.

Before Cowboy could answer, however, the NVA went on. "But, there are many new fighters now that I have not seen. So many that it is no wonder that the cook runs out of rice. Maybe in the cities, there will be enough rice."

Cowboy almost jumped at the reference to the cities, but he made no comment. He was more than happy to listen.

The NVA soldier continued. "I have heard that the southerners always have enough rice. I also hear that they have Imperialist whiskey and good French beer. The beer I can use. I do not know about the whiskey. I have not tried that, have you?"

"No," Cowboy answered carefully. "That will be a new thing for me, too."

"I also hear that all of their women are eager to sleep with the brave fighters for the People's Liberation Army. That, too, is something I will have to try for myself when we get to the cities next week."

Cowboy had to keep himself from jumping up and running away with what he had just learned. They were planning an attack next week!

"Say," the North Vietnamese asked curiously. "What is your name, comrade?"

"Minh," Cowboy answered calmly. His heart was pounding. "Tran Cao Minh."

"We had a Major Minh once. A real demon."

"I have not heard of him."

"That is a good thing. He was not a man you wanted to know."

"I must sleep now," Cowboy said. He didn't want the NVA to get too curious about his family or his village. He could not afford to answer a lot of detailed questions. He leaned back against the side of the trail and closed his eyes. He woke suddenly with the muzzle of an AK-47 stabbed into his throat. He looked around in panic. It was almost dawn and several men were standing in front of him. One of them shined a lantern into his eyes.

"Who are you?" came a voice outside the circle of light. It was Captain Nguyen's chilling voice.

"I am fighter Minh," he responded automatically.

"What unit?"

Cowboy thought fast. "The Eight Hundred Twelfth Regiment of the People's Liberation Army."

"You lie."

"No, comrades." He brought his hands in front of him, clasped in a gesture of mercy. "I am a new replacement."

"Tie him up," the cold voice said.

"Yes, Comrade Captain."

Hands dragged Cowboy roughly to his feet, stripping his pack and rifle from him. He submitted to having his arms bound behind him. With the muzzle of the AK stuck in his throat, he had no choice. "Why do you do this to me?" he asked.

A fist smashed against the side of his face. "Silence," the cold voice barked.

The lantern's light was held over his rucksack which was dumped out on the trail. Everything in the pack was Vietnamese, Chinese, or French. Except for the hand grenades.

172

The Captain picked one of them up and bounced it in his hand. "Where did you get this?" he asked.

"It was issued to me, comrade."

"Where?"

"At the supply point."

Suddenly, a hand spun him around and his shirt sleeve was ripped from his right arm. Fingers unbuckled the U.S.-issue o.d. plastic Timex watch from his wrist.

"And this?" the captain asked.

"I took it from a dead Yankee," Cowboy said defiantly.

The NVA captain studied the Nung for several moments. "Bring him along," Nguyen said.

A rope noose was slipped down over his head and tightened around his neck. With a tug on the rope, Cowboy followed after the NVA.

As they walked back up the trail, Cowboy frantically tried to think of a way out of this. He cursed his stupidity and his bad luck.

All the Nung could do was tough it out and keep trying to make the captain believe he was a new replacement who had just come down the Ho Chi Minh Trail. He would keep his eyes open and try to escape if he got a chance. He had to get back to Bao and the *trung si* with what he had learned.

Early the next morning, Wilburn looked at his watch again. The sun was climbing high in the sky and Cowboy had still not returned. "Bao," he called.

"Yes, *Trung si?*" the old Nung also seemed worried. Cowboy was another one of his nephews, his brother's son. The old Chinese was fond of the boy.

"We can't wait any longer," Wilburn said. "We've got to get moving."

"I understand, *Trung si.*"

Bao felt the dark shadow hanging over his house more than ever as each hour had passed without any sign of Cowboy. He had found the snake in his house, but the gods had not relented. Maybe he should have disobeyed the *trung si* and sacrificed his worthless nephew Whiskey as soon as he had learned about his treachery. Maybe then, the gods would have been satisfied. They were still angry with him and had taken his other nephew instead.

"Tell the men to saddle up," Wilburn ordered.

"Can I leave one man behind?" Bao's voice showed signs of rare emotion.

Wilburn thought for a moment. "I'm sorry, Bao. It's too dangerous."

The vigorous old Nung suddenly seemed to look his true age. Wilburn remembered carrying him out on his back just a few weeks ago. He reconsidered.

"Okay," he said. "Leave one of the teams behind. But only for one day. They must join up with the rest of us tonight."

Bao's face was expressionless, but he bowed his head slightly. "I thank you, *Trung si.*"

"Cowboy's a good man. I don't want to lose him, either."

One team of six Nungs was left behind in an ambush position overlooking the campsite. Before he left, Wilburn gave them the map coordinates to their next overnight campsite several klicks closer to the Laotian border. He also gave them specific orders. When night fell, they were to move out. If Cowboy had not returned by then, they were to consider him dead.

In minutes, the rest of the Recon Platoon loaded up and moved out.

CHAPTER 24

Chu Lai

Rat Gaines went down to the flight line early that morning and found Sean O'Leary already there. The cover for *Sudden Discomfort's* chin turret had been pulled off, and the new warrant officer was working on the Cobra's minigun.

"Good morning, Mr. O'Leary." Gaines greeted him with a smile.

"Good morning, Captain." O'Leary's hello was more formal.

"Is there something wrong with the weapons?" Gaines asked, a little taken aback by the gunner's stiffness.

"No, sir, I just wanted a chance to go over the guns before I had to use them."

"We've got an excellent ordnance sergeant and he does a real good job of keeping track of them for me," Gaines said.

"No offense, sir" — O'Leary wiped his hands on a rag — "but nobody works on my guns but me."

Rat didn't mind his men being dedicated to their work, but O'Leary seemed to be taking it just a little too seriously. Then again, everyone had their own way of doing business.

Gaines didn't mind as long as it didn't get in the way of the mission.

"How long before you're going to be finished?"

"Just give me another five minutes or so, Captain."

Gaines opened the pilot's canopy on his ship and dumped his helmet on the seat. He walked down the flight line to where Warlokk and Alphabet were pre-flighting their gunships.

"Good morning, sir," both men said in unison when they saw him walk up.

"Mornin', boys." Gaines looked up at the sky. Thick, high clouds were rolling in from the mountains to the east. "I don't know how much flying we're going to get in this morning before it gets socked in solid."

The three Cobras were scheduled to practice light-fire-team tactics for an hour or so. The session was primarily for Alphabet's benefit, but it never hurt for all of them to rehearse the motions when no one was shooting back at them.

Warlokk spat on the ground. "No big deal, sir. It ain't going to get that bad."

"We'll see."

O'Leary walked up to the group, his helmet in his hand. "I'm done, Captain."

"Great," Gaines said. "By the way, have you met Lance Warlokk and Joe Schmuchatelli?"

"I've met Joe." The Irishman nodded to Alphabet. He stuck out his hand to Warlokk. "Sean O'Leary," he said.

Warlokk took his hand, a puzzled look on his face. "Say, aren't you the guy from the Two Eighty-First?"

"I flew with them for a while," O'Leary said, a cautious expression on his face.

"Back in Sixty-six?"

"Yes."

"I met you once before, I think, down in Nha Trang. You had just come back from a cross-border op with your bird shot all to hell. You flew it back in from the left-hand seat."

O'Leary's eyes were wary. "Yes, that was me."

176

"Good to see you again," Warlokk said enthusiastically. "That was one of the greatest pieces of flying I've ever seen."

O'Leary was obviously embarrassed by Warlokk's praise. "Captain," he said to Gaines, "hadn't we better get going before the weather moves in?"

Gaines agreed and the three pilots went to their machines. Strapping himself into the rear seat of *Sudden Discomfort*, Gaines started over the checklist. When that was done, he keyed his throat mike. "Python, Python, this is Lead. Crank 'em. Over."

Rat's left hand twisted the throttle on the collective to the flight-idle position and squeezed the starting trigger. The starter energized, spinning the Lycoming turbine over. The burners lit with a *whoosh* and the smell of burning kerosene. Overhead, the forty-four-foot main rotor slowly started spinning as the Cobra came to life.

"Six Niner, Roger," came the call as Warlokk started up.

"Three Seven, go," Alphabet radioed.

When the rotors of the three gunships were up to speed, Gaines called the tower. "Chu Lai Control, this is Python Lead, request permission to take off."

"Roger, Python Lead," the tower answered. "You are clear for main runway."

"Python, this is Lead. We are cleared for takeoff, follow me."

The three Cobras rose a few feet off the PSP taxiway in a hover and started forward. A slight pressure on the rudder pedals brought the tails around and they were lined up for takeoff. The turbines screamed as the pilots ran them up past 6,600 RPM.

"Python, this is Lead. On my command, pull pitch . . . now!"

The tail booms on the three heavily laden gunships lifted, and they started down the runway in a classic gunship takeoff. Rat Gaines was in the lead slot, Warlokk in the number-two position, and Alphabet brought up the trail.

A hundred meters down the runway the Cobra pilots hauled up on their collective controls, pulled back on their cyclics, and the three gunships rose gracefully up into the air. The formation was so tight that they looked like they were tied together with string. As soon as they cleared the outer wire of Chu Lai basecamp, Gaines banked away to the east and climbed for altitude, the other two machines playing "follow the leader" right behind him.

Lisa Maddox stepped off the morning ash-'n-trash flight from Nha Trang with a bright smile on her face. Three days in the sun, to say nothing of her night on the beach with Kasnowski, had done wonders for her morale. She felt charged up and ready to get back to work.

She was also eager to see Rat Gaines again. There was something about having strayed from him for one night that made her feel closer to him. She knew that she had been a little hard on him lately and realized that he was consumed by the war because he was trying to do the very best he could at a very difficult job. She had a little better perspective and was more understanding about his obsession with his unit and his work.

Lisa halfway expected to see the pilot waiting for her when she stepped off the chopper, but he was nowhere in sight. She hadn't even told him that she was going to Nha Trang, much less when she'd be coming back.

She picked up her AWOL bag and headed around the end of the airstrip to the hospital, thankful for the cloud cover overhead. Usually by midmorning the heat radiating off of the tarmac was blistering. About halfway to the hospital, someone drove by in a jeep and gave her a ride the rest of the way.

When she walked into the hospital, she saw that everything was just as she had left it — barely controlled chaos. Hardly anyone had even noticed that she had been gone. She changed into her work uniform and got right back at it.

As she checked over the charts for the new patients on her ward, she made a mental note to give Gaines a call around lunch time. Lisa found herself whistling softly as she went about her business. Sometimes all it took to put things in their proper perspective was to spend a little time with another man. A little strange stuff, as Gaines himself would have put it in his colorful Southern idiom. She giggled.

Later in the morning, the hospital commander, Colonel Hardell, caught the nurse smiling as she made her rounds. "I take it you had a nice time?" he asked.

"Yes, sir. I really did."

While Lisa was making her rounds in the ward, Gaines decided that his group had had enough practice working together as a light-fire-team. It was old hat to him, and War-lokk and Alphabet had picked up the finer points very quickly.

"Python, this is Lead. I think that's about enough for the day. You two head back for the barn. I'm going to drop in on the Blues and see how they're doing. Over."

Two rogers quickly followed. The Cobras broke away from formation and headed east. Gaines put his machine into a banking turn for the PBR Base Zulu on the Song Boung River. It had been awhile since Rat had seen the base, and he was amazed. In the few days since the attack, the whole place had been completely transformed.

There was twice as much barbed wire in front of the perimeter now, more mines, more bunkers, and more machine guns. Even a section of two 105mm howitzers had been airlifted in for instant fire support. Outside the wire, Kasnowski's Sea Bees were busily shoving back the wood line so the NVA couldn't get so close to them again.

Gaines flared out for a landing on the small heliport and shut down. Alexander was there to meet him by the time he unbuckled and climbed out of the cockpit.

"Have you heard anything from Ringer's people yet, sir?" Alexander asked his company commander after greeting him.

179

"Nothing yet," Gaines answered. "And no news is good news, as far as I'm concerned. We're still standing by in case they step on their foreskins. So far it looks like it's going okay."

"How's Lieutenant Miller treating you now?" Gaines asked.

"Just fine, sir," Alexander laughed. "I think he's finally figured out that things work a lot better if he lightens up on that "by the book" horseshit. You won't believe this, but he dragged poor Farmer over to me and wanted me to give him an article fifteen because he didn't salute."

Gaines shook his head and smiled. "Oh, Christ. What did you do?"

"First I had Farmer get back to work. Then I took the lieutenant aside and explained to him why grunts don't salute officers on firebases. Once he understood the point about officers making good targets for the snipers lurking out there in the woods, he finally calmed down."

Gaines laughed. "If he sticks around you guys long enough, the Navy probably won't take him back."

"Those Sea Bees, though, they're okay," Alexander said with open admiration. "Kasnowski's the biggest scrounger I've ever seen. He came back the other day with a fifty-kilowatt generator and a refrigerator loaded in a sling under a slick. He said that if we were supplying the beer, the least he could do was to keep it cold."

"Where'd he get it?"

Alexander shrugged. "I didn't want to know, sir."

"That's probably wise." Gaines laughed. "The adjutant tells me that he's got some warm bodies coming in tomorrow, one one bush-type bodies. I'll send them out here as soon as they show up."

"Good. I really need the replacements, sir. First and Third squads are in pretty bad shape, and if we had to move out, we'd be in a hurt."

"You'd better use Brody's squad for your ready reaction force until the new men get a chance to settle in."

"That's what I was thinking, too, sir. I've got them standing by."

Gaines took one last look around the base. "I've got to get back to Chu Lai while I still can. I need to make sure the animals haven't torn the place up while I was gone. If anything goes down around here, be sure to give me a call."

"You can count on that, sir."

Shortly after Gaines took off, Lieutenant Miller came looking for Alexander. "We have a mission," he said. "A routine two-boat patrol back down the river. I'll need some of your men for extra guns."

"No sweat, sir. I've got Brody's squad standing by."

"Good. We'll be moving out in fifteen minutes."

"Yes, sir."

Alexander found Brody at the back of the bunker taking a break from filling sandbags. "Sergeant Brody."

"Yes, sir."

"The Navy's moving out in fifteen minutes and they want some extra guns on their patrol. Get your people saddled up and down to the dock."

"How long're we going to be out, sir?"

"He said just a couple hours."

"I'll get 'em moving, sir."

Brody butted his smoke and buttoned up his fatigue jacket. It was about time that they had something to do other than fill sandbags.

He walked around to the back of the bunker. "JJ, tell everybody to get their shit together and down to the dock in ten minutes."

"Where we going?"

"Beats me. Down the river, I guess."

"You got it."

Gardner gladly dropped his entrenching tool and went to round up the rest of the squad. He, too, was sick and tired of filling sandbags. A little midday cruise on the river sounded good to him.

CHAPTER 25

Deep in the jungle

North Vietnamese Captain Nguyen looked down at Cowboy and smiled. The defiant young mercenary was not as defiant now. He was too close to death for that.

Had the prisoner been one of the older Nungs who had worn the uniform of the Imperialists for many years, he might have gone to his death without speaking a word. But this one was younger, and now he babbled through broken teeth and smashed lips about a rendezvous point where he had been instructed to meet up with the rest of his mercenary recon team.

Much of what the tortured captive said was sheer nonsense about barbarous Chinese gods and the spirits of his ancestors. To the Vietnamese, the Nungs were primitive people. They worshiped as they had done long before the compassionate Buddha brought his message of enlightenment. Finally, Nguyen had heard enough. "You will take me to your rendezvous point now." It was a command, not a question.

Cowboy painfully nodded his bloody head. The young Nung was not afraid to die any more than his warrior brothers were. He was, however, afraid of being slowly beaten to death. The North Vietnamese officer was a master at inflicting pain on prisoners, ensuring that they did not die too quickly.

The only thing Cowboy could think of to end the pain was to take the NVA officer to where the other Nungs were hiding. His own brothers would kill him then and the pain would end.

Captain Nguyen smiled at the prospect of locating the Yankee recon team.

Cowboy was abruptly jerked to his feet. "Water," he gasped.

A canteen was slammed into his face. He sought the mouth of it like a baby seeking its mother's nipple and drank long and deeply. The pain of the water against his split lips and the stubs of his broken teeth made him more alert. He shook his head to get the clotted blood out of his eyes.

With an AK jammed painfully into his sore kidneys, Cowboy started through the jungle in front of the NVA point man. He planned to lead them to the camp along the steepest part of the hill that *Trung si* Jack had camped on. Hopefully the Nung flank guards would be able to see the enemy coming in time to spring an ambush. Also, he told the NVA point man that the camp was on top of a ridge beyond the hill where it was actually located. He didn't want the point man to be too alert until he had walked into the killing zone and it was too late.

It wasn't much of a plan, but it was all that Cowboy could think of through the numbing waves of pain that swept through his body. He had totally forgotten that the Nung platoon had been scheduled to move out of that location earlier that morning.

With his arms tied behind his back, it was hard going. He had to break brush with his battered face and broken shoulders. A branch whipped back against the ruined left side of his face and he cried out. Most of the skin had been sliced away from around his eyes and cheekbones, leaving raw flesh and nerves exposed. The light touch of a leaf was sheer agony. At least the NVA captain had not broken his feet.

The point man jabbed the muzzle of his rifle into his ribs again. Cowboy choked off another cry of pain and continued, comforting himself with the thought that it wouldn't be too much longer before he could finally die and leave the pain behind.

The six Nungs in the ambush position heard the NVA coming through the brush up the side of the ridge, but they held their fire. From their location on the other side of the small clearing, they had plenty of time to let the enemy get closer.

Cowboy was surprised when he broke out of the brush into the clearing and saw that it was empty. Then he remembered that the unit had moved out that morning. They were gone and *Trung si* Jack had not waited for him. His mind raced. What was he to do now? He continued across the clearing, edging to the right and away from the campsite. As he approached the brush on the other side, he heard a jungle bird cry out and recognized it as a signal.

Cowboy lashed out with his right foot, catching the point man off guard. The North Vietnamese went down and the Nung raced for the tree line.

"Brothers!" he shouted in the Nung dialect. "They attack the cities next week! Next week! Tell *Trung si*! Tell Bao! Next . . ."

A shot rang out. Cowboy fell to his knees and then pitched forward face first onto the ground. The grass felt cool against his battered face as he died.

The tree line erupted in a blaze of small-arms fire as the Nungs sprang their ambush. The NVA point man and several others following him were hit in the first burst of fire. At the rear of the NVA patrol, Nguyen yelled for his men to move forward, eager for victory.

Twice the North Vietnamese troops charged across the clearing for the tree line. Both times, the Nungs easily beat them back. From safety behind the crest of the ridge, Nguyen screamed at his men, cursing them and threatening to execute them all if they didn't close with the mercenaries and destroy them.

Sending a fire-support team around on the left, the most covered flank, the NVA tried again. They crawled into the clearing under the covering fire of their RPD machine gun. Fifty meters from the tree line, they jumped to their feet and charged, their AKs blazing.

There was no return fire. When they reached the tree line, they found it empty. The Nungs had vanished into the dense jungle.

Nguyen cursed with rage when he walked out into the clearing. He stood over the body of his late captive and delivered a savage kick to Cowboy's battered head. The skull caved in with a sickening crunch. It made him feel better.

He called his platoon sergeant over. "Track them," he ordered furiously. "Track them and find where they have gone or I will have you shot."

"Yes, Captain," the NVA sergeant said nervously. He spun around and shouted to his men. "After them!"

As the NVA ran into the trees, Nguyen called for his radio operator and had him contact Colonel Tran's headquarters.

A klick and a half away, Wilburn heard the firing in the distance. "Hold it up," he ordered, raising his hand.

The Nungs immediately fanned out in the jungle, facing back along the way they had come, and melting into the thick vegetation. When the firing stopped, Wilburn ordered one of the recon teams to go back and investigate.

After a long wait, the recon team returned with the flee-ing ambush team. The leader of the ambush team im-mediately reported Cowboy's death to Bao and sadly said they had been forced to abandon his body.

Old Bao was silent throughout the report. When the man was finished, he had only one question. "He was brave, my nephew?"

"Yes, honored Uncle." The Nung bowed to him. "He was very brave. His death honored your family."

Bao slowly got to his feet. The expression on his face look-ed as if it had been carved in stone.

"Where are you going?" Wilburn asked. One of the other interpreters had given him a running translation of the report, so he knew what had happened.

Bao stopped. "I am going to wipe out a disgrace to my family," he said quietly.

Wilburn knew better than to try and stop him. The affair was out of his or any other American's hands. The Nungs worked for the Special Forces on a basis of trust and mutual respect. Part of that respect was that the Americans allowed the Nungs to follow their ancient warrior customs. If Wil-burn tried to interfere with Bao's vengeance, the old Nung would lose face and the unit would probably disband on the spot.

Bao went over to where Whiskey squatted on the ground. He reached down and jerked him roughly to his feet. "My nephew is dead," he said. "And you have brought dishonor to my house."

"But I am your nephew, too!" the man pleaded.

Bao spat in his face. "Silence!"

Whiskey said no more. The look in his uncle's eyes ter-rified him.

"When your mother was born" — the old Nung's voice was barely audible — "I told my sister to kill her, but she would not. The signs at her birth said that she would bring disgrace to the family. My sister pleaded with me and, to my shame, I relented. I ordered that she be sold into a brothel as soon as she became a woman." He shook his head. "But when the time for that came, my sister did not have the heart to do it. When your mother was married, I thought that the bad luck would pass on to your father's family. I did not expect that it would come back and strike at me through your worthless person."

The old Nung pulled a K-Bar fighting knife from the sheath on his belt. "Now you will tell me what you know. If you do that, your death will be easy."

Whiskey fell to his knees, begging for his life. Bao jerked him upright again. "Dog," he spat. "My honored nephew died on his feet like a man. To honor him, you will spend the last few moments of your worthless life on your feet in an imitation of a man."

"What do you know of the *cong's* plans? What has the old pig woman relayed to you?"

Whiskey started babbling, protesting his innocence. Bao's hand flashed and struck him across the face. "Do not further dishonor yourself by lying," the old man hissed. "You are a dead man already, and the Great Grandfather General is watching you."

Whiskey saw only death in his Uncle's hard eyes. "I know nothing," he said quickly. "Only that a big attack is being planned. I do not know when it is to take place or where. Please! That is all I know."

Bao studied him for a long, silent moment.

"I swear, honored Uncle, it is the truth!" Whiskey pleaded.

"Do not swear anything. You are a dead man."

"But the old woman has told me nothing else."

Bao was silent, listening to his inner voices and the spirits of the generations of Nungs who had gone before him.

Without conscious thought, the knife flashed. The big blade buried itself to the hilt in Whiskey's throat. The point severed his cervical vertebra and came out through the back of his neck. Bao locked eyes with his nephew as he died, blood gushing from his half-opened mouth. In the younger man's eyes, there was only shocked disbelief.

With a twist of his wrist, Bao jerked the knife free. Whiskey's body slumped to the ground at Bao's feet, jerked a few times, and was still. Bao knelt briefly on the ground, wiped the blade of the knife on the dead man's shirt, and rose to his feet. He walked back to where Wilburn waited.

"He knew nothing," he said.

Wilburn nodded, but kept silent.

The old Nung spoke rapidly in Chinese. Several of the men grabbed Whiskey's body by the arms and legs and carried it into the thick brush.

"His evil spirit will remain here," Bao explained to the American. "So it cannot harm the Nung people."

When the Nungs returned, Bao spoke to them all briefly, then turned back to Wilburn. "We are ready, *Trung si*. Give us your orders."

Wilburn was relieved. The mission was still on. "Tell 'em to move out," he said, looking around the shadowy jungle. "We still have to find out what in the hell the dinks are doing out there."

CHAPTER 26

On the Song Boung River

Navy Lieutenant 'JG' Rod Powers was the patrol officer for the afternoon's mission, and that was just fine with him. He leaned back against the side rail of the bridge in Boatswain Mate Johnson's 859 boat and watched the muddy water of the river slowly roll by. His PBR and the 873 boat that followed were only making some fifteen knots, barely half the speed that they were capable of when their twin diesels were running at full throttle.

Rod Powers was in no hurry to return to the patrol base. He knew that the minute he did, Miller would find some insignificant shit detail for him to take care of. He was much happier spending a lazy afternoon cruising down the river.

Powers was a laid-back, easygoing sort of guy. He had learned long ago to take life easy in the Nam whenever he had the chance. That was the only way that he could deal with the frantic, heart-pounding chaos of sudden combat. He rested up for it whenever he could. And today, he was resting.

In the stern of the trailing PBR, Bunny Rabdo was not enjoying himself, however. The FO huddled in his oversized life jacket and watched the dirty brown wake of the boat streaming behind him.

"You don't look like you're having too much fun," Gardner said after he made his way back to join him.

Bunny looked up. "Hi, I didn't see you there, JJ," he said. "And, no, I'm not having fun."

"Why don't you ask the ell tee to let you stay behind next time?"

"I can't do that." He shook his head and glanced down over the side of the boat. "I don't want the other guys to think I'm some kind of candy-ass."

"There's nothing wrong with being afraid of the water, Bunny," Gardner tried to make the FO feel better. "Lots of guys can't swim."

"I know, I know. But I don't want to let anybody down."

"You're not letting anyone down, man. Nobody's going to get on your case about it."

"I just don't want to slack off," Bunny said firmly. "I go where you guys go. You might need my help."

"Well, you just try to take it easy today. The Navy guys said we're not going to be out here too long."

"Jesus, I hope not."

Gardner decided to leave the FO alone for a while and went back to the front of the boat.

Harvard was sitting on the deck in front of the bridge, looking pissed off. Gardner didn't bother to acknowledge his presence. He didn't like the new man's attitude and wasn't going to waste time on him until he got his act together and stopped bitching about everything. Two-Step was at the bow of the boat, scanning the riverbank on both sides of them.

"What's up?" Gardner asked.

The Indian turned to look up at him. "I don't like this riverine shit one bit. It just doesn't feel right to me."

Gardner sat on the gunwale of the boat and looked into the jungle as well. He didn't like being out in the open, either.

It was different when they were up in a slick looking for dinks. They were doing over a hundred miles an hour at a couple of thousand feet off the ground, and they usually had a gunship escort. If anyone popped up and took a shot at them, they could bring a world of hurt down real quick.

On the river, they were only moving fifteen knots an hour and the jungle was less than a hundred meters away. A dink with an RPG could ruin their whole day real fast. He had seen how vulnerable the PBRs were to rocket fire. Two hits and these tin cans were history.

He looked up the river and saw Brody sitting in the back of the lead boat. Brody waved. Gardner shot him the finger.

Ever since Brody had taken that last six-month extension on his Nam tour and had re-upped for another two years, he had developed a real lifer's attitude. He didn't seem to give a shit where he was. Usually, Gardner didn't, either. One place was just about as good as any other unless it was on the water. He could swim, but he understood how Bunny felt.

The lead boat was just rounding a bend in the river when the brush along the left bank exploded with small-arms fire. Green tracers and the smoke trails of RPGs reached out for them.

The Navy gunner manning the twin-fifty turret swung his heavy guns around to the side and opened up with a long burst of return fire.

The boat captain slammed his throttles forward and the PBR leaped through the water. With the surge of power, the deck tipped and Gardner's feet flew out from under him. He went down, his head slamming against the gunwale. With a small cry, he fell over the side of the boat. The dirty brown water closed over him.

Bunny looked up just in time to see Gardner go under.

"JJ!" Bunny jumped up and rushed to the side of the boat. Gardner had already sunk out of sight.

"Man overboard!" he shouted at the bridge, waving his arms frantically. "Stop the boat!"

Over the roar of small-arms fire, no one heard the FO. They were too busy trying to stay alive. Bunny looked back where Gardner had fallen. Without conscious thought, he held his breath and vaulted over the side, landing in the water with a big splash. No one noticed him go, either.

Sputtering and spitting in the waves of the boat's wake, the FO watched the PBR race away. He turned around in the water and started dog-paddling back to where he thought his buddy had sunk.

When Gaines brought his Cobra in for a landing in Chu Lai, he found that Lance Warlokk was still down on the flight line. When the rotors stopped turning, Sean O'Leary opened the front cockpit of the Cobra and stepped out. With a nod to his pilot, he walked over to the operations shack, leaving Gaines standing with Warlokk.

"Do you know who your new gunner is, Captain?" Warlokk asked with a big grin on his face.

"What do you mean?" Rat was puzzled.

"That's 'Tiger' O'Leary," Warlokk explained. "One of the hottest gunners ever to fly the left-hand seat in a Hog. He's got the DFC, several Silver Stars, and more Air Medals than this whole company put together. He's a fucking living legend."

"What'd he do to get the Distinguished Flying Cross?" Gaines asked.

"That mission I was asking him about," Warlokk replied. "He and his AC were on a Sneaky Pete number across the Cambode border doing a hot extract when they got the shit shot out of them. The AC bought it right away, but Tiger there took the controls. Firing the guns at the same time, he brought the bird down and got all of the SF people on board. Then, on the way back out, he ran into a real shit storm again. The bird took several hits, the people in the back were shot all to hell, and he took a couple of rounds himself. Staying on the controls, he had one of the Green Beanies patch him up, and he flew all the way back to Nha

Trang. I was there when he brought the bird in. And, man, I tell you, I've never seen a Huey that shot up that was still able to fly."

"What happened to him?"

"Well, last I'd heard, when he finally got out of the hospital, they sent him back to Fort Wolters as an instructor. The rumor was going around that the Army'd offered him a commission, too, but it looks like he turned it down."

"I wonder why he didn't take the commission?" Gaines shook his head.

"Maybe he didn't want to lose his membership in WOPA," Warlokk grinned.

WOPA, the Warrant Officer's Protective Association, didn't really exist. According to legend, the Mafia-like organization looked after brother warrant officers who had been wronged by commissioned officers. Gaines wasn't so sure, though, that WOPA was fictitious. He had heard of bad-tempered commissioned officers having their pay records scrambled, household goods being rerouted to Bumfuck, Ethiopia, and other cute little inconveniences. In all of those cases, a warrant officer had been involved. Gaines was always careful not to piss those guys off.

"You really don't believe in WOPA, do you, Captain?" Warlokk asked with a sparkle in his eyes.

"No, not at all," Gaines laughed. "That's why I always hand-carry my own records when I transfer. I don't want some crusty old WO/four transferring them to my new duty station for me."

"Well, if you ever have any trouble with any warrant officers, sir, you just talk to me. I'm the unit WOPA representative."

"That figures."

Warlokk laughed. "What you say we go get ourselves a beer, Captain?"

"Okay, but only if it's a short one. I've got to check in with Lisa tonight. She's been pissed at me for not spending more time with her, so I'm going to take her to dinner tonight."

Warlokk was surprised to hear Gaines talking so openly. Usually he kept his personal life completely to himself. At one time, Warlokk and his WO pilot buddy, Cliff Gabriel, had vied with each other for the nurse's attention. Now that Rat had staked a claim on her, Warlokk had backed off.

"A short one it is," he laughed. "I don't want you to keep her waiting."

Rat grinned, "Neither do I."

Bunny was in a complete panic. "JJ!" he yelled, frantically splashing his arms in the water. "JJ, where are you!"

He was so busy fighting the water and his fear of drowning that he almost missed Gardner. The grunt was out cold. The blow to the side of his head had knocked him out, but enough air had been trapped in the fabric of his flak vest to give him buoyancy and keep him from sinking to the bottom. He floated to the surface of the river, facedown in the water.

Bunny let out a yelp when Gardner's body surfaced right next to him. "JJ!"

The FO stopped his frantic paddling, grabbed for the unconscious man, and pulled his head out of the water. The oversized life jacket he wore was barely able to keep both of them afloat, but Bunny managed to keep the grunt's head from going back under.

The FO looked downstream for help but the PBRs were already out of sight around the bend in the river. He could still hear the snarl of their engines and the roar of weapons fire. Suddenly, Bunny realized that he and Gardner were easy targets floating around in the middle of the river.

Holding on to the epaulets of JJ's flak vast with one hand, Bunny hugged the big man to his side and started kicking his feet and dog-paddling with his free arm, trying to make it to the bank some twenty meters away.

Had the FO just relaxed and let the current take them, he would have gotten to shore sooner and with less effort. His frantic flailing and kicking only impeded their progress. Finally, Bunny's feet touched the mud of the riverbed. He grabbed Gardner under the arms, dragged him through the sticky slime, and laid him in shallow water. Fighting to catch his breath, Bunny grabbed onto a tree root and climbed out. Once his boots were on solid ground, he pulled his unconscious friend completely out of the water and onto the bank.

He heard an AK fire on full automatic. It sounded like it was close by, and he panicked. Grabbing the epaulets of Gardner's flak vest again, he scurried backward, dragging the grunt even deeper into the jungle to get him away from the dinks.

A root caught his foot and he fell heavily. Dragging Gardner wasn't going to work. He was going to have to carry him. He knelt down beside the unconscious man and pulled his upper body over his shoulder. Clasping his arms around Gardner's waist, he got to his feet. Staggering under the weight of the much bigger man, he fought his way through the dense vegetation.

He carried him several hundred meters before his strength gave out, and he laid Gardner back down behind a clump of bamboo. Exhausted, Bunny fell to the ground, his chest heaving. Gardner weighed almost twice as much as he did, and it had taken all of his strength to bring him this far. The FO took a few shuddering breaths and crawled over to tend to his friend.

Gardner was breathing easily, but he was still unconscious. Bunny opened the flak vest and laid his head against the big man's chest. His heart was beating faintly. The FO looked around the jungle. His artillery maps and compass were back in his rucksack on the PBR. Along with, he suddenly realized, his rifle. Reality hit. They were in the jungle with no food, no water, and no weapons. And he didn't have the slightest idea where they were.

CHAPTER 27

Chu Lai

The dinner in the small Chu Lai officers' club by no stretch of the imagination could have been called a culinary delight, but it was a welcome change from the crimes that were committed daily against perfectly good food in the battalion mess hall.

"That was nice," Lisa sighed contentedly. It was not La Frigate, but it had been good.

Rat leaned back in his chair and lit one of his thin cigars. "Yep, that it was. But then, you have to work real hard to screw up a ham steak and canned corn. I must admit that the french fries were a little strange. The cook must have run outta grease. They were actually crisp for a change."

Lisa sipped her coffee and listened with amusement to Gaines's witty tirade about Army food. "Have you ever thought of opening a restaurant?" she asked, a slight smile playing at the corners of her lips.

"Me? No, I just like to eat the stuff, I leave the cooking to others."

"How about that famous Captain Roger 'Rat' Gaines Stroganoff that you're always bragging about? Or your chili? I'd like an opportunity to sample your own culinary abilities."

He laughed. "That's just something I used to do when I was younger and far more foolish. It was a good excuse to entice some young thing to come over to my place for a couple of hours. I actually haven't done much cooking in years."

He leaned closer to her. "I'll tell you a secret. The only reason I ever got started is that women are crazy about guys who cook. There's something about watching a man slaving over a hot stove that makes them go wild with passion."

"Well . . ." She put her coffee down and winked at him. "Why don't you come over to my place and cook something for me. Maybe you can heat up a can of beanie wienies or something."

He drained his coffee. It was still light outside, not even seven o'clock, but what the hell? "Great idea. You got any C-four?"

Lisa laughed.

A few minutes later, Gaines sat on Lisa's narrow Army-issue bed, nursed his drink, and watched while the nurse brushed out her long blond hair. He felt a sensation in his lower body that was definitely not the booze working on him. He reached over and gently stroked her hair. She turned her head slightly and smiled at him, a smile that made his knees weak.

The brushing ritual completed, Lisa faced her lover. She slowly unbuttoned her fatigue jacket and shrugged it off of her shoulders. Reaching behind her back, she unsnapped her bra and let it fall, enjoying the look that came over Rat's face when her full breasts sprang into view. She was glad that men were so visually oriented. She liked the way that he looked at her when she was naked. It made her feel warm inside. She kicked off her jungle boots, slid her long legs out of her fatigue pants, and slipped her panties down past her hips.

198

"God, you do that nicely," Gaines said in awe as she stood before him, completely naked.

"Thank you, sir. So do you," she answered with a pleased smile.

Taking his cue, Gaines got out of his uniform in a flash and lay down beside her. The warm touch of her bare skin was electric. He reached for her breasts with both hands, reveling in the smooth, firm softness of her flesh. She opened her legs and pressed her belly against his firmly muscled thigh. Not releasing her breasts, Gaines sank into her slick, hot softness and paused, soaking up the sensation. She thrust her hips up at him, and they were off and running.

It had been quite some time since they had been together and, even though Rat had recently exhausted himself at Helen's place, he didn't last long.

Soon, they lay sweaty in each other's arms, laboring to catch their breath.

"Rat," she murmured in his ear. "You can come and play at my house anytime you want."

"How long can I stay tonight?"

She pretended to look at her watch. "Oh, I don't know. At least another fifteen minutes."

"That ought to be good for a couple more rounds."

"It'd better be."

Gaines chuckled and reached for his glass. "You haven't told me about your R and R," he said, sipping at his warm drink.

"Oh, it wasn't too exciting." She was careful to keep her voice neutral. "I mostly just laid around on the beach and got tanned."

As careful as she was, however, Rat caught a note in her voice, a hint of something exciting. He didn't question her about it. Whatever it was, it had made her one hell of a lot easier to live with. He reached for her again and she came to him, curling her soft body around his.

"How'd you like to do that again?" he asked with a big grin. "It's been so long. I'm not a hundred-percent sure that I did it right."

"Oh, Rat," she said with a mocking southern-belle accent. "I thought you'd never ask."

Bunny carefully parted the leaves in front of him and peered out into the darkening jungle. Everything was still clear. He checked on Gardner again for the tenth time. The nasty purple bruise on the side of his head seemed to have grown even larger, but the big man was still breathing easily.

Bunny shook him gently. "JJ," he whispered as loudly as he dared. "JJ." He got no response from the unconscious man.

Bunny was really scared. He had no idea where they were. He had even less of an idea about what he should do next. He frantically tried to remember his combat first-aid training back in Basic and AIT. The only thing he could remember was how to treat gunshot wounds.

He knew what to do for a sucking chest wound. The drill instructor in basic training told them that "a sucking chest wound is nature's way of letting you know that you've been in a firefight." He had remembered that real well, but that kind of Army joke wasn't going to help Gardner.

Suddenly, he remembered watching a television program where a man had a concussion. The doctor had made a real big deal out of looking into the patient's eyes. He leaned over and raised Gardner's eyelids. It was so dark now that he couldn't have seen anything even if he knew what he should have been looking for. At his touch, Gardner groaned and moved his head slightly.

"JJ!" Bunny gently patted the side of his face. "Wake up!"

Gardner moved his head again and his eyes fluttered open. They were glazed with pain. He tried to speak, but it came out as a moan.

"It's okay, JJ." Bunny smiled in the dark. "We're safe."

Gardner opened his eyes fully. "Where are we?" he croaked.

"You fell off the boat. I jumped in and got you to shore. We're in the jungle now."

Gardner tried to move. Bunny put his arm around the big man and helped him into a sitting position.

"Oh, Jesus Christ," Gardner moaned, carefully feeling the side of his head. "What the fuck happened? Did I get hit?"

"No. The boat made a sudden turn and you slipped. I think you hit your head on the railing when you fell overboard."

Gardner tried to stand, but his head was spinning and he sat back down abruptly.

"Don't move yet." Bunny tried to sound calm.

"Man, you got that shit right."

Suddenly, what the little FO had said registered in Gardner's mind. "Jesus, Bunny, you jumped into the river to save me?"

Bunny was embarrassed. "When I saw you go over the side, I didn't think about the water. I just went after you."

"But you're afraid of water."

Bunny laughed. "I didn't remember that until I was in the river."

"Christ, man," Gardner said softly, "you could have drowned. I really owe you one."

"No sweat, man," Bunny replied, as if it were something that he did every day. "What are we going to do now?"

Now that Gardner was awake, Bunny was ready to turn the whole operation over to him. He wasn't a real boonie rat, practiced in finding his way through the jungle. He was just the artillery FO who went along with the grunts for the ride and brought smoke down on the bad guys. When he was in the jungle, he always had grunts to tell him where he was going.

"We got any water?" Gardner asked. His mouth felt like it was coated with mud.

"Sorry, JJ, it's all back on the boat. Our weapons, too."

"Oh, fuck," Gardner said softly. Now he knew they were in real deep shit. "Have you heard any movement?" he asked quietly, looking around at the darkening jungle.

"No."

Gardner checked out their area again. It was almost dark now and the clouds blocked any light from the stars. Part of him wanted to stay right where they were, the part with the throbbing head. But he knew that they should try to get back to the river. The Navy would probably be looking for them and a riverboat ride beat walking back to the base.

"Look, Bunny," he said. "I want to get back to the river. Do you know where it is?"

"Sure," the FO replied confidently. "No sweat. It's right over that way." He pointed into the darkness.

CHAPTER 28

Patrol Base Zulu

Lieutenant Mike Alexander was shaking with rage, his fists clenched tightly at his side. "You did what, mister!" he screamed. "You did what?"

Rod Powers didn't know what to say or do next to get Alexander to back off. The grunt officer looked like he was going to eat him alive.

"I already told you," he repeated, a note of fear creeping into his voice. "The boats were under fire and we couldn't turn back right then. When we're ambushed, our standing orders are to try to break out of it. And when we did go back, we couldn't find them."

Alexander snarled. "I don't know how you do things in the fucking Navy, mister. But in the infantry we never, and I mean fucking never, leave one of our troops behind. We never even leave our dead behind, for Christ's sake. We'll die before we leave our buddies like that." Alexander looked up at the sky and closed his eyes. "Jesus fucking Christ, I don't believe you fucking people. What in God's name is wrong with you?"

"Now, Lieutenant," Miller cut in, "aren't you overreacting a little here?"

Alexander spun around to face him squarely. So far, the PBR commander had kept pretty much out of it, but Alexander was more than ready to get into it with him.

"Sir," he said sharply, "I hold you equally responsible for this rat-fuck. What do you guys teach your officers in the Navy anyway? It's no wonder that you won't even eat with your enlisted men. You don't give a flying fuck for 'em."

Miller was incensed. "You can't talk to me that way, Lieutenant."

"I just fucking did," Alexander shot back. He paused and looked Miller up and down slowly. "Sir."

Miller stiffened. "I'll see about that, mister. I'm reporting this to your commanding officer."

Alexander laughed. "You just do that. And while you're at it, tell him that your XO here let two of his people fall into the water and ran away and left them sitting there." The grunt officer stuck his nose right into the Navy officer's face. "Rat Gaines is going to tear your fucking ass off for this, Lieutenant. Nobody messes with his troops."

While this was going on, the grunts of the Blues and the sailors were standing around in two separate groups. They didn't like to see their officers arguing, but nevertheless the conflict quickly spread to them as well. They started yelling insults back and forth and were quickly threatening each other with their fists.

Sergeant Zack could see that things were getting out of hand. The Navy chief petty officer was already moving among his men to get them calmed down. There was going to be one hell of a fistfight unless Zack got Alexander cooled down. He walked up to the lieutenant.

"Lieutenant Alexander, sir," he said politely. "I think you should make a report to the company commander about this incident. While you're doing that, sir, I'll get a patrol together and see if we can find the men."

The ell tee spun around to face Zack. "Find them?" he yelled at the sergeant. "Just how in hell are we going to fucking find them? It's night and the woods are full of dinks."

"Sir," Zack said patiently. Alexander wasn't the first officer who had ever yelled at him, and he wasn't going to be the last. "We can search the banks of the river."

Miller and Powers stepped out of the way. They were more than willing to have Alexander's rage directed at someone else for a change. As far as they were concerned, he was completely out of control. Zack leaned closer to his platoon leader and took him by the arm.

"Sir, this shit isn't good for the troops," he whispered in his ear. "You're going to have to stop this shit right now, sir."

The old NCO was right.

"Okay, Sarge," Alexander said, shrugging Zack's hand off. He turned back and fixed his eyes intently on Powers. "Right now I have two men to find. You'd better hope to Christ they're still alive 'cause if they're not, I'm going to tear your fucking head off."

Powers stood stock-still, a shocked expression on his face. Still muttering to himself, Alexander executed a snappy about-face and walked back to the bunkers. Brody and three of his men were already suited up and waiting for the word to go.

"We're ready, Ell tee," Brody said softly. "I figure we can reach the ambush site in just a little over two hours."

"Isn't that pushing it a little?"

"We plan to run, sir."

Alexander saw the tight look on Brody's face. These were his men and they had been in his squad for quite some time now. Long enough to have become blood brothers through shared danger.

"Okay," the platoon leader said. "Remember to stay on the horn and keep me updated."

Just then, Kasnowski, the Sea Bee NCO, walked up to the bunker with one of his men. "Lieutenant, me and my buddy here would like to go with you if we can. We want to help."

205

Alexander paused. Both Sea Bees were armed and carrying heavy ammo loads. "I don't know, Chief. It's pretty rough out there at night."

Kasnowski laughed. "Sir, I'm an old deer poacher from the hills of Oregon. I've been stumbling around out in the woods at night for as long as I can remember. And old Peanut here, he's a Georgia possum hunter. Let us give your guys a hand, sir. Dodging game wardens like we've done is good practice for shit like this."

"It's okay with me," Brody spoke up. "I'm real short-handed and I can sure as hell use them, sir."

With Bunny and Gardner gone, he only had five men left. Two of them were the FNGs, who were being left behind. This was no kind of mission for two cherries.

"I think you should let 'em go along, sir," Zack broke in.

"Okay, okay. Just get moving."

The six men ran for the wire and quickly made their way through the perimeter concertina and the mine fields. In seconds, they were out of sight in the darkness of the woods surrounding the base.

Alexander ran his hand down the back of his neck. Now he had to get on the horn and tell Gaines about this. Rat was going to have a hemorrhage. Alexander shuddered. At least the CO wasn't going to be pissed off at him — he hoped.

A light knock on the door of Lisa's room instantly awakened Gaines. He shook Lisa. "What is it?" she called out.

"Lisa, it's Lance Warlokk. Sorry to bother you, ma'am, but is Captain Gaines with you?"

"Yeah, Lance." Gaines sat up on the edge of the bed. "What is it?"

"Really sorry to bother you, sir, but we've got a real problem. The Navy lost two of Alexander's people. They fell off a boat."

Rat put his head in his hands. "Oh, fuck." He swung his legs over the side of the bed and reached for his clothes. "Just a second!"

"Yes, sir."

Gaines turned back to Lisa. She smiled as he reached out and stroked her cheek. "I'm sure as hell sorry about this."

"I know, Rat," she sighed. "It's not your fault. Maybe next time."

"Yeah, next time."

Gaines was still buttoning up his fatigue jacket when he opened the door and stepped into the hall. Warlokk caught a glimpse of Lisa under the thin sheet. It was almost like seeing her naked, and he turned his eyes away.

"I'm really sorry, sir," he continued to apologize. "But Alexander's about to shit himself, and the colonel's been looking for you."

"Okay," he said as they hurried down the hall. "What happened this time?"

By the time they reached the parking lot, Warlokk had managed to fill Gaines in on what details he knew.

Gaines swung into the driver's seat of his jeep and fired it up. "I'm going over to the TOC to see the Colonel." The TOC, the tactical operations center, was the brains and pulse of an infantry battalion. Any rescue mission he planned would have to start there. "While I'm getting him calmed down, you alert Gabe and his crew along with my new gunner. I'm going in after them."

"I'm going with you." Warlokk's tone left no room for argument.

"Okay" — Rat jammed the gearshift into reverse — "but get 'em going. We're lifting off in ten minutes."

"Right, sir."

The TOC was in a mild uproar when Rat walked in. Colonel Jordan looked up and motioned him over to the big topo map on the wall. "Just what the fuck's going on out there, Gaines?"

"I don't know, sir," Rat shook his head. "I just found out about this myself."

"Christ." Jordan angrily butted his cigarette out on the concrete floor and reached for another. "I can't believe that two of your clowns fell out of a fucking boat."

"If I might remind you, Colonel, my people don't have much experience working with boats. We're an Air Cav company, not a bunch of fucking Marines. If the Navy had wanted Marines to ride around in their little boats, then they should've asked for jarheads instead of us, sir."

Jordan slowly took the cigarette from his mouth and looked Gaines square in the eye. "I don't need that kind of shit from you right now, Captain. I've got enough problems without listening to your smart mouth."

"Sorry, sir." Gaines quickly backed down. Jordan was in an even worse mood than he was. "I've got a slick and two guns standing by, sir. So why don't you just let me go out there and see what the situation really is. I'll get back to you right away."

"You'd better do something useful," Jordan growled. "The brigade commander's hot on my ass about this thing already."

"I'm gone, sir." Gaines did an abrupt about-face and hurried out the steel door.

Down at the chopper pad, Gabe's slick and the two Cobras were already fired up, their rotors spinning. Rat jumped out of his jeep and sprinted for his ship. Snatching his helmet off the seat, he jammed it on his head and keyed the throat mike.

"Python, this is Lead," he radioed, buckling his shoulder harness. "Send status, over."

"Six Niner, ready."

"Three Five, go."

Gaines switched over to the tower frequency. "Control, this is Python Lead, over."

"This is Chu Lai tower, go."

"This is Python Lead, I have an emergency flight leaving now, over."

"This is Control, I don't have you logged for a mission, over."

Gaines ignored the tower. "Python, Python. This is Lead, follow me."

The pilot twisted the throttle up to takeoff RPMs and eased up on the collective. The rotor blades bit into the cool night air and the Cobra rose off the PSP. A kick down on the rudder pedal swung the tail boom around, and she was lined up with the main runway.

"Python," the panicked voice of the control tower radioman squawked in Gaines's ears. "You are not cleared for takeoff."

"No shit," Gaines radioed back. "What're you going to do about it? Send me to Vietnam?"

By now, *Sudden Discomfort* was moving down the runway, her tail high. Rat ignored the frantic calls from the tower and hauled up sharply on the collective. The Cobra leaped up into the black sky.

He looked back over his shoulder and saw the running lights of Warlokk's bird right behind him. Gabe was following him closely.

"Keep it tight," Gaines warned. Rogers from the two other choppers followed.

Flying a helicopter at night was never easy. They were not equipped for it, but it could be done, and it often was in Vietnam. Flying choppers in formation at night, however, was usually a quick way to die in a midair collision. Only the very good or the very foolish ever tried it.

Gaines wasn't too sure which category he fitted into. He banked to the north and headed for Patrol Base Zulu.

CHAPTER 29

Deep in the jungle

In dragging Gardner to safety, Bunny had gotten completely turned around. Instead of leading Gardner to the bank of the river, the two men walked straight into the jungle. Bunny and Gardner were thoroughly lost. They had marched for almost an hour and they still hadn't reached the river.

"Oh, Jesus, JJ," Bunny said quietly, looking around in the dark. "I think I've really fucked up. We should've been there by now."

"No sweat," Gardner said, trying to sound confident through a blinding headache. "It's got to be around here somewhere."

The big man stopped cold and looked up. If the stars had been out, he could at least have gotten a rough bearing to the North Pole, but there was not a single break in the solid cloud cover. The way things were going tonight, it might be best if they just stopped and tried to sleep until the sun came up.

Gardner was just about to tell Bunny that they were halting for the night when he heard a faint, metallic noise. He grabbed Bunny by the arm and pulled him down to the ground. Both men froze in place, listening intently.

They heard it again.

Gardner tapped the FO on the shoulder. Laying his finger over his lips, he pulled him off the narrow trail they had been following and into the brush. They heard more noise, the sounds of a troop unit on a night march, faint, metallic clinks from weapons, the creaking of packs and equipment belts, and the dull, rhythmic slap of sandaled feet against the soft earth.

A minute later, an NVA point man walked right past the grunts' hiding place. A few meters behind him came a complete column of men, at least a full company of well-equipped NVA Regulars.

Gardner and Bunny held their breath, afraid that the North Vietnamese could somehow hear them. Bunny closed his eyes tightly in fear and, putting a finger between his teeth, bit down hard. Anything to make this waking nightmare go away. When the column had finally passed, Gardner got to his feet.

"We'd better get the fuck outta here," he whispered.

Bunny croaked his agreement.

The two men turned and chose a new direction at random, hoping that this time it would lead them back to the river.

"Hold it up," Brody said, gasping for breath. The panting grunts and Sea Bees halted. The men had been running for the last half hour. Most of them dropped to the ground to catch their breath. Only Brody, Two-Step, and Kasnowski remained standing.

"Why d'ya stop?" the Kaz panted.

"Gotta take a short break," Brody answered. "We're no good if we're this beat."

"Fuck that," Kaz growled. Turning to Two-Step, he asked, "Indian, you want to scout on ahead with me for a little while?"

Two-Step didn't mind the Sea Bee's calling him an Indian. He knew that the man meant it as a compliment. And at the moment, there was no time to waste on social niceties."Sure," he said. "Let's go."

The two men moved up the trail that paralleled the riverbank. Two-Step believed that his Indian background gave him an edge when it came to moving through the jungle like a shadow, but the Sea Bee followed behind him as silently as any VC. Two-Step was impressed. He wondered if this big Polack was half-Indian.

He heard a noise ahead of him and froze in place. An errant breeze brought him the faint smell of rotten fish. It was *nuoc-nam* fish sauce that Vietnamese soldiers ate with their rice. The Kaz slipped up beside silently. Two-Step touched him on the nose. The big man breathed deeply and nodded his head. Two-Step quietly handed his shotgun to the Sea Bee. Reaching to his boot top, he came up with his razor-sharp K-Bar fighting knife. The Sea Bee nodded again, and the Indian slipped into the brush.

Gaines and Warlokk flew cover over the PBR base while Gabe put his slick down on the small helipad outside the wire. Then Gaines landed his Cobra beside him while Warlokk remained in the air, orbiting the patrol base. Night was a bad time to put down anywhere outside the wire. Sergeant Zack met his company commander at the entrance to the small base.

"Sir, I've got Brody out looking for Rabdo and Gardner."

"Any luck yet?"

"No, sir. They checked in about five minutes ago and nothing yet."

"Where's Miller?"

"Probably down by the boats." Zack paused. "Sir, before you talk to him, Lieutenant Alexander really tore into him. The Navy people are going to be a little touchy right now."

"Good for the ell tee," Gaines replied. "If he hadn't said something to those clowns, I'd have torn a strip off his ass. Where is he anyway?"

"He's coming now, sir."

"Captain," Alexander reported. "I've got a search team out looking for them now."

"Sergeant Zack told me."

"It doesn't look good, sir. The Navy found blood on the boat they were on. They don't know if they were hit or what. All they know is that one of them yelled 'man overboard.' They think it was Bunny and that he jumped in to save Gardner."

"Christ, I thought Rabdo couldn't swim." Gaines looked astonished.

"He can't, sir," Alexander shook his head. "Not a stroke. But he was wearing a life jacket."

"I understand that you got a little rough with our Swabbie friends?"

Alexander stiffened. "Captain, they left two of my men behind. I just wanted them to know that we're the Air Cav, sir, and that we don't do that kind of shit in this outfit."

Gaines slapped him on the shoulder. "Good man. You saved me the trouble. Now, you go check the perimeter while I talk to Mr. Miller."

"Yes, sir."

Miller met Gaines halfway to the docks. "Captain Gaines," he said formally. "I'd like to lodge a complaint about your lieutenant."

Gaines reached into the breast pocket of his flying suit and pulled out a cigar. He lit it up and drew in a lungful of smoke.

"Mr. Miller . . ." The pilot's voice was soft, and his southern accent was very pronounced now. People who had been around Rat Gaines for a long time knew that as a danger sign. Unfortunately Miller wasn't aware of that characteristic. "You and I need to have us a little talk here." The pilot looked around the base. "Is there somewhere we can have a little privacy?"

The Navy officer led him to the far side of the commo bunker. "Now, about Lieutenant Alexander . . .," Miller started.

"Just shut the fuck up and listen to me, Miller!" Rat growled.

Miller's mouth fell open.

"I understand that your XO left two of my men behind on an operation. Is that right?"

"Yes, but . . ."

"No fucking buts, mister. In my army, we officers don't make excuses. Now what have you done to find my men?"

"Mr. Powers . . ."

Rat jabbed Miller in the chest. "I asked you what you've done to locate them, Miller. Not your fucking XO."

Miller was silent.

Gaines got instantly pissed. "I'll tell you what you're going to do, and you're going to do it 'rat' now. You're going to get those boats of yours moving and they're going to use those searchlights up and down the river until you find Gardner and Rabdo, dead or alive."

"But . . ." Miller tried to speak.

Gaines grabbed the Navy officer by the front of his shirt and slammed him back against the bunker. "If you're not moving in thirty seconds, Miller, I'm pulling my troops out of here and I'm going to leave your sorry ass hanging. Of course, that's after I stomp your ass into a mud hole and then stomp the mud dry. You got that?"

Miller nodded. He was afraid that the wild southerner would go for his throat if he didn't. By now, Gaines realized that he had gotten a little out of control and that he was unfairly taking his frustrations out on Miller. He released the PBR commander and stepped back.

"Lieutenant Miller," he tried to explain. "Look, I'm really sorry about all this. I've had my colonel on my ass this evening and now I'm taking it out on you. I know that working

214

with the Cav is a new experience for you and I like to think that we have done our best to cooperate with you. But I think there's a real basic misunderstanding here that is getting in the way of our having a smooth-running operation."

Miller nodded.

"I don't think that you realize the strength of the bonds between me, Alexander, and those men," Gaines continued. "Those grunts out there are my sole reason for existence. They are mine to command and mine to protect. And I take both of these responsibilities equally seriously. The reason that I feel this way is that I have shared those men's lives so closely. I have eaten what they ate, I have slept where they slept, we all shit in the same holes, and we drink out of the same bomb craters. We're Army grunts. We live together and we die together. Now, I know that you care for your men, you wouldn't be here if you didn't. But I'm not sure that you have the closeness with your people that Alexander and I have with ours."

"No, I guess we don't," Miller admitted reluctantly.

"Anyway, that's the reason that Alexander got so excited with you and your XO. I guess that I owe you an apology for threatening you."

"That's all right." Miller was more than ready to make peace to get the Air Cav officer off his case.

"Then can I ask you to get your boats moving and maybe we can still find Bunny and JJ."

"We can do that, Captain."

"Thanks a lot." Gaines turned to go. "By the way, I'll be overhead with both of my gunships in case anything comes up and you need fire support."

Two-Step returned to Kasnowski's position as silently as he had left. He took his shotgun back from the Sea Bee and leaned over to whisper in his ear.

"He was a road guard watching a trail," the Indian said. "Something's going on tonight. Why don't you go on back and bring Brody up here. I'll keep watch while you're gone."

The Sea Bee nodded and slipped back into the jungle.

Brody and his people joined him in just a few minutes.

"Treat," Two-Step briefed him. "They had a guard on a trail junction, so they must be moving troops tonight. You want to call it in?"

Brody thought for a moment. They were out there to look for Gardner and Bunny, not get into a pissing contest with an NVA unit of unknown size. But on the other hand, it was too good a chance to pass up. "I'll call it in," he said. "Maybe I can get some artillery on it."

Bunny was gone, but the ell tee or Sergeant Zack could just as easily get the guns zeroed in on the trail. Then all he'd have to do was wait till they caught the NVA moving and bring a little smoke down on their asses.

He took Two-Step by the arm and moved back to the end of the formation. Getting out his poncho liner, he made a tent over the two of them and took out his map. In the red filtered light of his flashlight, the two grunts pinpointed the trail junction and wrote down its coordinates. Brody took the radio handset from his harness and keyed it.

"Blue Six, Blue Six, this is Blue Two."

"Two, this is Five," came Zack's voice. "Go."

"This is Two, we have found a trail junction and a road guard. I think the November Victor Alpha will be moving down it tonight. Request to call arty on the location, over."

"This is Five, send it."

"This is Two, nine-two-four three-eight-six. Azimuth two-seven-three H.E. Will call, will adjust, over."

"This is Five, Roger, copy. I'll get it set up. Anything on our two Mike India Alphas? Over."

"This is Two, negative. We'll be moving out again in zero five, over."

"This is Five. Be advised that the Swabbies will be on the water and Python is here. Be on the lookout for them. Over."

"This is Two, Roger. Anything further? Over."

"Five, negative. Out."

Brody put his map away and stuffed his poncho liner back into his pack. "Gaines is back there and Zack says that the boats are moving out, too."

" 'Bout fucking time," Two-Step whispered. "Now maybe we can get this shit wrapped up."

CHAPTER 30

Patrol Base Zulu

The PBRs were just pulling away from the docks when Gaines and Gabe got their choppers back in the air. They turned east down the river. Gaines sent Gabe into a high orbit and called Warlokk down on the river with him. He wanted Gabe and his slick well out of the way of ground fire until they had located Bunny and Gardner.

Miller was leading the two-boat PBR section. They made their way back to where they had been ambushed earlier that day. He was still fuming at Gaines's abusive remarks and determined to show the loudmouthed redneck that he and his men were just as concerned about the two grunts.

Running up and down the river at night with the searchlights on was the craziest thing that Miller had ever done. Every Charlie in the neighborhood was going to see them and it was an open invitation to get their asses blown out of the water. But the PBR commander had to do it. If he didn't, Gaines would probably blow him out of the water.

He ordered his boatswain to throttle back so the gunners on the searchlights wouldn't miss anything. Overhead, Rat and Warlokk swooped low over the boats, flying their gunships parallel to the riverbank. Rat turned the landing light in the belly of his Cobra on. The powerful beam turned night into day along his flight path. Every leaf and tree root at the edge of the bank was clearly visible.

If Bunny and Gardner's bodies were there, he'd see them. If they were alive somewhere, when they saw the lights they'd make their way to the river so the Navy could pick them up. But Gaines was also aware that flying low and slow with the landing light on made him a prime target, too.

Back at Zulu, Lieutenant Alexander was trying to coordinate the whole giant rat-fuck. Between Miller's boats, Gaines and Warlokk in the air, and Brody's men stumbling around somewhere in the dark, it was not an easy task.

"Blue Two," he radioed. "This is Six."

"Two, go," Brody's low voice came in over his headphones.

"This is Six. Be advised that Python and Barn Door are on the move now. Vector into position at least five hundred meters away from the river. I don't want them to fire you up by mistake, over."

Brody rogered and reported that he had left two men covering the trail junction they had discovered in case the NVA tried to move down it. Alexander wrote down their new location on his map — one more goddamned thing that he had to keep track of. He drained the last of his cold coffee.

The platoon leader wanted to get Bunny and Gardner back, but with the way things were going, he was beginning to think that the rescue effort should have waited until morning. It was just a little too complicated to coordinate at night. Sergeant Zack walked up to the CP and took a seat on the sandbag wall.

"Anything happening, Lieutenant?"

"No, nothing, yet." Alexander answered wearily. "You got the perimeter covered?"

"Yes, sir. We're spread a little thin right now, but I got some Sea Bees to fill in on the Second Squad bunkers. They wanted to help out, and I figured that it was a good idea. At least if anything happens, the captain and Mr. Warlokk are close by."

Somehow this was not very comforting news to Alexander. This place was beginning to have real bad vibes for him. He wanted very much to get back to playing Aero Rifles and not goddamned Marines stuck way the hell out in the fucking woods.

"Okay, you keep track of that end of it, and I'll try to hold it down here. Who's in charge of the other two PBRs?"

"Lieutenant Powers is, sir."

"Well, make sure that he's tied in with you and knows what they're supposed to do if we get hit again."

"I've talked to the Navy chief, sir. He's got everything under control," Zack said in a reassuring tone. He knew the ell tee was still furious about the men being lost in the first place.

"I'm glad somebody does. This place is starting to look like a Chinese fire drill."

"Yes, sir. I got to agree with you on that."

Zack put his helmet back on. "If you don't have anything else for me right now, sir, I'm going back out on the perimeter."

"Right, Sarge, I'll yell if I need you."

Zack turned to go.

"Sarge?" Alexander said.

"Yes, sir?"

"Thanks."

"No sweat, sir." He smiled. "That's what the Army pays us NCOs for."

In the jungle, Bunny and Gardner were trying to make their way through the dense vegetation as silently as they could. It was slow going in the dark. Bunny wanted to take one of the trails they had passed, but Gardner quickly vetoed the idea. There was no way of telling who they would meet up with on an established trail. He didn't want to risk it without any weapons. It was safer to stick to the cover of the jungle.

They still hadn't reached the river, and Gardner was just about to suggest that they stop for the night, when he saw a faint glow in front him.

"Look!" he whispered.

Bunny's heart leaped. The light had to be coming from the direction of the river.

"Let's go!" The FO tugged on Gardner's arm. "They're looking for us!"

"Wait," Gardner cautioned. He had noticed that the light was moving too fast for it to be one of the riverboat searchlights. A faint whop-whopping sound reached his ears. It was a chopper. Captain Gaines.

"We've got to be real careful," Gardner cautioned. "The dinks can see those lights, too."

"Hurry," Bunny said, his voice rising. "They're moving away."

"They'll be back," Gardner said confidently, trying to calm Bunny down a little. "But you're right, we've got to get going."

From where they were, the light looked almost half a mile away. It would take them at least half an hour to cover that distance at the rate they were traveling.

The NVA platoon leader was surprised to see the lights of the helicopters in the sky. He debated whether or not he should investigate or just continue his patrol.

Colonel Tran had assigned him and his thirty men the mission of keeping an eye on the Yankee riverboat base until a new attack against it could be planned. He knew that it was his duty to report this activity, but when he did, the colonel would want to know more.

He called a halt and watched the light for a moment. It seemed to be moving upriver, as if the Americans were searching for something. Just then, he saw another set of lights behind the first one, moving slower. Suddenly he realized that the first light was from a low-flying helicopter. The second set had to be from the riverboats.

Now the North Vietnamese officer had no choice but to investigate. The Yankees rarely moved at night, so whatever this was, it had to be important.

He ordered his men to move out again, this time turning them toward the river as fast as they could go.

Brody, Two-Step, and Kasnowski crouched in the shadows behind a clump of bushes. Peanut was behind them, looking the other way, guarding their rear. Ahead of them there was a break in the underbrush and they could see a trail running through the middle of a clearing. The searchlights reflecting from the low-hanging clouds gave a dull glow to the jungle, almost as good as starlight.

"Listen!" Two-Step hissed. "Someone's coming."

Silently, the Indian moved out to the edge of the clearing to get a better look. He wished that he had a Starlight sniper scope. With the night scope, he would have almost been able to see the faces of whoever was coming down the trail. He moved deeper into the shadows.

A single figure, darker among the shadowy trees, trotted out into the clearing. Thinking that it was Bunny or Gardner, Two-Step was just about to shout when several more men ran out behind him.

The Indian silently ducked back into the brush. "Dinks!" he whispered. "At least a platoon of 'em."

Brody, Kasnowski, and the other Sea Bee readied their weapons as the clearing quickly filled with NVA.

"Let 'em get closer," Brody whispered. "Wait . . . Wait . . . Now!"

The sudden eruption of fire took the NVA completely by surprise. The chatter of Brody's M-16 on full automatic, the single shots of the Sea Bee's heavier M-14, and the coughing roar of Two-Step's sawed-off pump gun broke the night's silence. Several dark figures dropped to the ground and they heard the screams of wounded men.

222

Though they had been caught by surprise, the North Vietnamese platoon reacted well. They instantly deployed and returned a withering blast of automatic weapons fire. Green AK tracers cut into the brush around the four Americans. They heard someone shouting commands in Vietnamese. The dinks were trying to get around their flanks.

With their muzzle blasts giving their locations away, there was no way the firefight was going to end well. There were too many dinks for four men to handle.

"Pull back!" Brody yelled, hurling a grenade into the clearing.

The four men jumped to their feet. Firing behind them as they ran, they raced into the safety of the jungle. The NVA fired after them, but didn't pursue.

"Better call this in, Treat," Two-Step panted, stuffing shotgun shells into the magazine of his pump gun. "The Old Man'll want to know about those guys."

"Yeah, you're right." Brody took the radio handset from his assault harness and keyed the mike. "Python, Python," he said as quietly as he could. "This is Blue Two, Over."

"Python Lead, go," came Rat's terse answer.

"This is Two, we just ran into a bunch of gooks heading for the river. I'd say about a platoon of 'em. Over."

"Roger," Gaines answered. "I saw the firing. Where are you now? Over."

"We moved upstream a couple hundred meters, over."

"Roger, keep well away from those guys. I'm going to shoot 'em up if I can spot 'em again. Out."

"Now what?" Kasnowski asked.

"Fucked if I know," Brody replied. "But we'd better stay away from there for now. I don't want that Cobra on my ass."

"That's affirm," Peanut agreed.

"Why don't we head for the river ourselves?" Two-Step suggested.

"That makes as much sense as anything else right now," Brody admitted. "Let's go."

A little farther downstream, Gardner and Bunny heard the firefight and dropped to the ground. When the firing ended, faint yells and commands pierced the darkness. The voices didn't sound like they were speaking English.

"Come on!" Bunny tugged at Gardner's arm.

"Wait a minute," the grunt replied roughly, shaking his hand loose. Gardner listened carefully, straining his ears for any noise. The jungle was quiet again. Whoever and whatever that brief fight had been about, it was over for the time being.

"Okay, let's go."

The two men carefully got to their feet and continued in the direction of the lights.

Not far behind the two Americans, the NVA platoon leader hurried his men along. Whatever that small Yankee patrol had been doing, they were gone now and he could not waste time following them. He still had to investigate the lights along the river.

Unknown to the three groups of men on the ground, the NVA were closing in fast on the two lost grunts. It had become a race to the river — one that Gardner and Bunny couldn't possibly win.

CHAPTER 31

On the Song Boung

Leaving Warlokk to search the riverbank, Gaines brought his Cobra in over the jungle parallel to the river, looking for any sign of the NVA unit that Brody had ambushed.

In the jungle, the NVA platoon leader heard Gaines pass overhead. There was very little chance that the helicopter pilot would spot them, but he ordered his men to take cover regardless. He wasn't taking any chances.

One of the NVA troops, however, didn't trust the cover of darkness and jungle canopy. Nervous from the gunship prowling overhead, he made the mistake of taking a shot at Gaines with his AK.

"Rat!" Warlokk broke in suddenly. "Behind you! You're taking fire!"

Gaines stomped down on the rudder pedal and slammed the cyclic over to the side, making the Cobra bank sharply away. "Go get 'em!" he snapped.

Warlokk zeroed in on the brief muzzle flash of the AK. In the front cockpit, his gunner tightened his fingers around the triggers of the firing controls. The minigun and the automatic thumper in the nose spat flame. Lines of red tracer lashed the darkness and brief pinpoints of light marked the explosions of 40mm grenades.

The North Vietnamese scattered under the gunship attack. "Run for the river!" their platoon leader shouted, sprinting through the jungle. "Cease fire and run!" He guessed correctly that the closer they got to the boats, the less likely it was that the helicopters would shoot at them.

Bunny and Gardner saw Warlokk's Cobra's flash overhead and unload its ordnance in the jungle right behind them.

"Oh, shit! There's gooks back there!" Bunny screamed.

The two grunts took off running. If the NVA were right behind them, they had to get to the river first. Behind them, Bunny and Gardner heard the NVA yelling as they ran from the Cobra's attack. The grunts ran even faster. The jungle canopy came to an abrupt end and the two grunts found themselves at the edge of the muddy riverbank. The dim lights of the patrol boats were far to their left, heading on downstream. They had gotten there just a little too late.

"Hey!" Bunny yelled as loud as he could, waving his arms in the dark. "We're back here! Hey! Goddamnit, turn around!"

The sailors on the PBR didn't hear Bunny shouting, but the NVA did. Short bursts of AK fire erupted from the jungle behind them. The men dove into the water while green tracer fire swept past them. They hugged the muddy bank of the river. AK rounds slapped into the shallows, raising little geysers of muddy water. "Oh, shit!" Bunny moaned. "Oh, shit!"

Downstream, the last PBR in formation heard the gooks firing. Instantly, the boatswain spun the wheel around and headed back at full speed. The searchlight beam swept the edge of the river, passing over Bunny and Gardner. For a moment both men thought they had not been spotted. Then it came back and stopped, fully illuminating them — for the benefit of the NVA.

Gardner lifted his head out of the mud. "Cut the fucking light!" he yelled.

The fifty gunner in Johnson's boat switched off his searchlight. "There they are!" he yelled up to the small bridge.

"Hold on!" Johnson shouted. "We're going in!"

The fifty-gunner squeezed his triggers and Johnson spun the wheel around, chopping his throttles at the same time. The NVA were firing at them and he winced each time he heard a round hit the boat.

Overhead, Gaines saw the muzzle flashes of the enemy fire, but there was nothing he could do to help. The NVA and the PBR were too close to each other. He watched helplessly as the patrol boat made its run in. Green tracers sparked and bullets ricocheted off the .50-caliber turret's armor plating. PBR 859 ran her bow into the mud of the riverbank at an idle, all her weapons blazing.

"Run for it!" the sailors on deck shouted to the two lost grunts.

Gardner and Bunny jumped to their feet and splashed through muddy water to reach the side of the PBR. The twin fifties in the forward turret hammered their deep-throated roar, and red .50-caliber tracers flew past their heads in a steady stream. Hands reached over the side to pull them on board. Before they even had their boots on the deck, the boatswain slammed his gear box into reverse and the throttles forward. The big diesels bellowed and the water jets drove the PBR backward into the open river. With a spin of the wheel, the captain slammed the gearbox lever forward. The boat's nose came up out of the water and they were moving.

The two grunts fell flat on their faces and hugged the deck until the boat was around the bend, out of range of enemy fire.

As soon as the riverboat was clear of the bank, Gaines brought his Cobra in for a gun run. A burst of 2.75-inch H.E. rockets blazed from the stub-wing pods. Trailing orange fire in the night, they slammed into the jungle. The blinding flashes of their exploding warheads lit the darkness.

227

The chopper's nose was aflame with O'Leary triggering the minigun in the chin turret. The ripping sound of four thousand rounds of 7.62mm firing every minute sounded like a chain saw gone berserk. A solid finger of flame reached from the gunship's nose to the dark trees, shredding the foliage and any gooks who were hiding in it.

When Rat pulled away from his gun run, Warlokk swept in right behind him, his thumper and minigun punching even more jungle into confetti.

The PBRs had the cover they needed to get out safely.

A sailor helped Gardner and Bunny to their feet.

"You okay?" the Navy man asked.

"Yeah, we're fine now. You don't happen to have anything to drink, do you?"

"Water." The sailor reached for the canteen on his belt. "Mr. Miller don't allow no booze on shipboard."

"Water's just fine," Bunny said. "It'll hold us 'til we can get to a cold one."

With Bunny and Gardner safe, Gaines called Gabe with orders to drop back down and pick up Brody's people. Brody had his people ready on the riverbank when Gabe brought his slick to a hover as close to the trees as he could. With Gaines and Warlokk circling overhead in case there were any more dinks who wanted to play games, the grunts splashed through the water and clambered on board. Gabe pulled pitch and they were gone in seconds.

Brody got on his radio to Corky and Farmer and had them get ready for a fast pickup, too. They had not seen any more NVA moving down the trail they were watching, and it was to dangerous for them to stay in the woods till morning.

Gabe swooped down and they scrambled on board. "Jesus, man," Farmer said when he saw his squad leader. "I thought you'd forgotten about us."

"Quit bitching, Farmer," Treat grinned. "It's good training for you."

"Your ass, too, Brody."

By the time the PBRs reached Zulu, Gaines had already set his Cobra down on the helipad and was waiting on the dock along with the rest of the Blues to welcome the two men back.

"Hey, Bunny," Farmer shouted as the FO stepped off the boat. "You learn how to swim yet?"

With a big grin on his face, Bunny shot him the finger. Everybody roared.

When Miller stepped onto the dock, Gaines walked up to him with his hand out. "Thanks, Miller. Your people did a damned fine job out there."

The Navy officer was taken aback. Just an hour ago Gaines had been ready to tear his head off. Warily, he took Rat's offered hand. "Well, thanks. So did you and your men."

"It was no big deal," Gaines said modestly. "We do that kind of shit all the time. Tell you what. Why don't me and my lieutenant buy you and Mr. Powers a beer. I understand my boys have a couple of cold ones stashed away somewhere, courtesy of the Sea Bees."

"Well . . ." Miller hesitated. He still didn't know what to make of this man.

"Aw, come on," Rat grinned. "It's our way of saying thanks."

"All right." The Navy man caved in. "But only if you'll accept a little bourbon chaser with it."

Rat grinned. "Right on. Now you're talking like a real grunt."

Miller shook his head. "God help me."

"But I can only have one," the pilot was quick to add. "I'm driving tonight."

As it turned out, the Blues had more than a few cool ones available. Gaines quickly authorized two cans per man for the celebration and invited all of the sailors to join them. The animosity between the two groups was gone after the PBRs had rescued Bunny and Gardner. The men were safe and, most importantly, they had worked jointly on a successful mission. It was time to forget about how the two grunts had gotten lost and better to party.

"Hey, man," Brody called over to Corky. The Chicano machine gunner was leaning against a sandbag talking to Gardner.

"Hey, what?"

"I thought you were short." Brody grinned. "But it looks like you're getting ready to take another burst of six."

"What are you talking about, man? What is this extension shit?"

"Well, you've been out running around in the bush like some fucking FNG. Short-timers ain't supposed to be outside of their basecamp. Looks like the re-up sergeant's been fucking with your DEROS."

"Brody" — Corky stepped up to him — "I'm gonna tell you somethin'. You're the one who's short, lifer. Short in the brains department for sending me out in the fucking woods. I've got thirty-three days and a fucking wake-up, my man, and then I'm history. So you can pucker up and get ready to kiss my Chicano ass good-bye."

"You're not going to take a burst of six?" Brody asked in mock horror.

"Fuck you, Brody."

York sat apart from the party. His eyes were narrow tense slits as he watched the men drinking, laughing, and winding down from the tension of battle. Vietnam was worse than a nightmare. Even the beer tasted flat. He had to get out, and he told himself that there had to be a way.

Kasnowski made his way to the center of the group and stood on a bale of sandbags. "Hey, guys!" he called out, hands in the air to call for silence. No one paid too much attention to him until he hollered over the raucous noise of true party animals. "Shut the fuck up!"

The men quieted down suddenly and turned their attention to the Sea Bee.

"Tonight we are here to honor two of our Army buddies." Boos and catcalls rang out in the night air. Kasnowski ignored them, calling over to Gardner and Bunny. "Men, I would like you two to come over here for a moment."

The two grunts obliged and walked up to the Kaz.

"Gentlemen, today you qualified to join a very special fraternity. There are very few members of this group, and you should feel honored to be counted as two of their newest members."

Bunny and Gardner looked blankly at each other, wondering what in hell he was talking about.

"Very few men have ever mastered the skill of falling overboard from a naval vessel as thoroughly as you two did today. As a matter of fact, I've never seen anyone do it quite as well."

Laughter broke out. Gardner looked sheepish and Bunny just grinned.

"I now initiate you into the International Brotherhood of Flotsam and Jetsam."

The Sea Bee had two cans of beer in his hands and before the startled grunts could react, he poured them over their heads. The crowd roared as the other Sea Bees marched up one by one and added a symbolic sprinkle. They didn't give them the whole can because there wasn't enough to waste. Even the grunts got into the act. Soon Bunny and Gardner were soaked.

Gaines and Alexander stood back with Miller and Powers and watched their men celebrate. Gaines held his canteen cup out for another short shot of Miller's bourbon. "You know, Jim," he said as he watched the Sea Bees drench the two grunts, "this base is likely to set Army-Navy cooperation back twenty years."

"More like fifty," Powers muttered.

Gaines let out a hearty laugh.

CHAPTER 32

CCC Kontum

Special Forces Major Snow walked into the FOB commander's office at CCC headquarters, a slip of paper in his hand. "Colonel," he said, "I think we may have a little problem with the Blackjack operation."

"Aw, shit! What is it this time?" LTC Grimes shook his head.

"I'm afraid they've been blown. Even with the precautions they took after they found out about the traitor in their camp, Wilburn thinks that he's had an NVA unit tracking them since they left the boats."

"What do you think?"

"He's not the kind to panic unless there's something to panic about."

"I didn't like that idea of a PBR insertion anyway. Where is he now?"

Snow walked over to a small-scale map mounted on an easel. He checked the coordinates on the paper and stabbed his finger at it. "Right about here and heading east into the suspected buildup area."

"Has he called for an extract?"

"No, sir, not yet. But I'd like your permission to alert the pickup unit anyway."

"Who's doing that for us this time?"

"The Air Cav again, sir. Python Flight from the First of the Seventh. I know them. They're good people."

"How about sending the rest of Ringer's Mike Force in to reinforce him?"

"I don't want to do that yet, sir. We still don't really know what's going on in there. I'm afraid that if we enlarge the op, it'll tip the NVA off and they'll come down on us like a ton of shit. The terrain is in our favor and there's still a chance that Wilburn can evade and get back to work."

"Okay. Keep me posted."

"Yes, sir."

Major Snow went back into his office and stood in front of his own big-scale topo map on the wall. There was something big going down. He still didn't have the hard-core proof he needed, but he could sense it nonetheless.

The Hungarian refugee placed the tips of his fingers on the map and slowly moved his hand across the printed lines indicating the rugged hills and valleys along the Laotian border. He could almost feel the topography of the land and danger there. He shook his head and sat at his desk. He couldn't send a hunch back to Saigon. He was a professional soldier, a plans and operations officer for the Special Forces, not a Gypsy on some street corner in Budapest telling fortunes for pocket change. But in the past, his hunches had often proved more accurate than studied intelligence estimates.

He quickly wrote out a message and took it to the radio room for transmission to Wilburn when he called in later that night. He stuck the carbon copy into the mission file. That done, he returned to his office and poured himself another cup of coffee. It was going to be another long night, cat-napping on the cot in his office until Wilburn got back.

Lieutenant Colonel Tran worked late at his desk in his hidden jungle headquarters. Sweat rolled unnoticed down his face. With the blackout curtains pulled over the windows, the air in the small room was stifling and heat from the sputtering kerosene lamp only added to his discomfort.

In the flickering lamplight, the North Vietnamese officer put the finishing touches to the movement orders for the next day and read them over. Preparations for the offensive were almost finished, and soon he would be able to relax. The next two days would see the last movements of troops and supplies into staging areas for the upcoming offensive.

He mopped the sweat from his forehead with a khaki handkerchief. It had taken a great deal of work to coordinate everything and to keep it all hidden from the Yankee spy planes and their recon teams. But it was worth it. If everything went well, in a month the foreign invaders would be gone. The southern half of his homeland would be reunited with the north under the leadership of the glorious People's Liberation Army.

It had been a long, hard struggle for the Vietnamese people to gain unity. Soon, with crushing blows, it was finally going to come to pass. The American Marines were about to face a second Dien Bien Phu at their Khe San base and a massive offensive was set to be launched against the cities of the south. The weak-willed American people would never recover from two such stunning defeats at the same time. Their politicians would surrender and the war would finally be over.

He smiled, remembering the once-proud French Foreign Legion officers bowing their heads as they passed the glorious flags of the People's Republic of Vietnam on their way to captivity after the fall of Dien Bien Phu in 1954. That was a sight he would remember all the days of his life. Soon thousands of arrogant Americans were going to be humiliated the same way.

Before turning in for the night, Tran decided to check with the radio room for the latest report from Captain Nguyen.

The last thing he needed was for the Yankee recon team Nguyen was tracking to stumble onto the big troop movement scheduled for the next morning.

Until all of the NVA troop units were safely in their staging areas, the offensive could still fail. A B-52 bombing attack would shatter his careful planning. Nguyen had to find those Yankees.

The small radio bunker off to the side of the headquarters building was almost empty. Only the radio operator and his sergeant were there. Both men jumped to their feet and assumed a rigid position of attention when Tran entered.

"Do you have a report from Captain Nguyen?" the lieutenant colonel asked the NCO.

"No, Comrade Colonel," the sergeant answered. "We have heard nothing yet."

Tran frowned. "When was the last time he checked in?"

The sergeant shuffled through a stack of message forms. "At eight o'clock, Comrade Colonel."

Tran glanced at the clock. It was almost twelve. "Let me know as soon as he reports in."

"Yes, Comrade Colonel."

Tran ducked his head and pulled aside the blackout curtain over the door to climb the steps out of the radio bunker. Through the breaks in the canopy of the trees overhead he observed a starless sky. Heavy cloud cover had been moving in all day. It meant there was even less of a chance that a spy plane would spot his troop movements.

Heartened by the change in the weather, the North Vietnamese officer made his way through the darkness to his sleeping bunker. If he was lucky, he could get a few hours' sleep before dawn.

Sergeant Jack Wilburn halted the Nungs for his midnight radio transmission back to CCC in Kontum. One team of Nungs went back down along their trail and one team was sent ahead. With two more groups out to both flanks, he was isolated and could make the radio call without being interrupted.

At 0015 hours, the small loudspeaker on the radio cackled. "Dry Rock, this is Black Angel, over."

"Dry Rock," Wilburn answered. Then he sent a sequence of eleven three-digit code groups. Each of them stood for a word or phrase, and the code was impossible to break without using the code book. It was a hassle to have to encode his message and to decode CCC's return message, but he would only transmit in the clear when he had made contact with the enemy and all need for secrecy would be gone. Until then, he had to maintain commo security.

The radio was silent for a moment before CCC's answer was received. "This is Black Angel. Copy eleven groups. Break. The CCC riddled off thirteen groups of numbers. How copy? Over."

As they were sent, Wilburn wrote the code groups down on the acetate covering of his map. "Dry Rock, copy thirteen. Out," he answered briefly. Keeping the length of transmissions short was vital to radio security.

Under the dull glow of his red-filtered penlight, the Special Forces sergeant took the SOI code book from the cord around his neck and started breaking down the three-digit code groups to see what the Ice Man had to say.

When he was done, he called Bao over. "They want us to continue," he told the old Nung. "But they're worried about our contact this morning. They're going to alert our pickup unit in case we get our asses in a bind tomorrow and have to get out in a hurry."

The Nung nodded. "Good. I think we find bookoo VC here, *Trung si.*"

"So do I," Wilburn agreed. "I can smell 'em."

He looked up at the cloud-covered sky. It was solid, no stars were showing through at all. If they did need an extract, that might cause a problem. The weather was getting worse and he knew that in the morning, the clouds would

236

be right down on the tops of the hills. The monsoon season had come a little early this year.

"While we're stopped here," Wilburn continued, "tell the people to take a half-hour break. We'll move out again at zero two hundred."

"Yes, *Trung si*."

If they pushed on through the night, they would be in the middle of their target area before dawn. Then he could put his teams in place while it was still dark.

Wilburn closed his eyes for a little rest. Old Bao would awaken him when it was time to move out again. On a night move like this, even fifteen minutes' sleep counted. There was no sense in tiring himself out any more than necessary.

Captain Nguyen cursed the night. His scouts had lost the trail of the Yankee recon team in the dark. Whoever they were, they were good at covering their trail. He had no choice but to stop and make camp until first light in the morning. At dawn, they would move out once more and try to make contact with the intruders.

As Nguyen gave orders for his exhausted troops to halt for the night, he was confident that he would catch up with the Yankees in the morning. They seemed to be moving directly for the staging area inside the Laotian border. If they reached there and reported what was going on, it would be a disaster.

Several North Vietnamese battalions were leaving the staging area in the morning to move into their attack positions for the big offensive. If the Yankees spotted them, the essential element of surprise could be lost. He had to catch up with the Yankees and eliminate them once and for all. Tran would have his head on a pole if he didn't.

CHAPTER 33

Deep in the jungle

"Holy shit!" Wilburn whispered to himself as he peered through his binoculars. "Will you look at that!"

His team was halfway up the side of a ridge overlooking the narrow valley below. Hidden in the trees across the valley was the biggest enemy supply dump that Wilburn had ever seen. And, it had been so carefully constructed that it would never be spotted from the air.

The NVA had cut the underbrush under the closely packed trees to open up the ground underneath. Enough of the trees had been left standing for their branches to effectively form a solid overhead canopy that hid the supplies of material.

From certain angles, Wilburn saw past the screen of brush left along the wood line. From where Sergeant Wilburn was, he watched dozens of NVA troops going about their business. It looked as if they were issuing the supplies piled around them rather than stockpiling them for future use. Men took long crates from a pile and headed deeper under the trees with them. Troops were being outfitted.

He put the field glasses down and charted the location of the dump on his map. Reaching into his rucksack, he brought out a small Minolta camera. The Minolta was fitted with a special lens for long-range shots. He quickly took several photographs of the area, overlapping each picture so that when they were printed, they would form a continuous mosaic of the entire area. The Ice Man would want pictures of this.

It was still two hours before the scheduled time for his next communication with CCC, so Wilburn decided to spend the time observing the dinks. Suddenly Bao nudged him. "*Trung si!*" the Nung hissed softly, pointing to the far left. "Look! The *cong* come!"

Moving into the wood line at the far end of the valley was a long line of NVA infantry in dark olive green uniforms. Wilburn snapped his field glasses up to his eyes. Through the binoculars, he saw that they all had full packs and combat equipment, and wore NVA pith helmets. These weren't local VC people or NVA that had been hiding in the hills. They were NVA regulars, fresh troops from the north! At least two companies of troops were moving into the supply area where ammunition and other supplies were being distributed. In half an hour, they were on the move again, heading east, away from the mountains and deeper into South Vietnam.

Wilburn finally had the goods Major Snow wanted; not only the supply site to report, but also the route that the enemy battalion was taking.

"Bao," he said. "I want to follow them and see where they're going." The Nung ran to alert the rest of the team.

They trailed the NVA unit long enough to see that it was headed deep into the heart of South Vietnam. Wilburn called a halt and gathered his men. The other Nung teams also reported seeing large units of NVA moving toward the east. The enemy was engaged in large-scale infiltration into the south for a big offensive. There was just no other possible explanation for this level of activity. Wilburn ordered his men to move out in one group toward their PZ, their chopper pickup zone.

Wilburn and his command group were on the point as they moved down the ridgeline into the small valley below. The terrain offered very few good PZs. The far end of the valley was the closest area suitable to bringing the choppers in. As soon as they secured the PZ, he would make his call.

As messed up as the mission had been at the start, it looked like a success — quick in to look around and a quick out. Just the way he liked it.

Captain Nguyen was not pleased with his trackers. For the second time that morning, they had lost the trail of the Yankees. He checked the load in his 7.62mm Tokarov pistol and was just about to critique the tracker's performance when the man rushed up to him.

"Comrade Captain," the scout said breathlessly, nervously eyeing the Tokarov. "I have found their trail again."

Nguyen holstered his pistol. "Where did they go?"

"They went northwest, comrade," he pointed. "Toward the supply point."

Nguyen brought out his map. "Show me."

The scout studied the map for a moment. "Here, comrade." His finger traced a line. "The tracks were moving this way." He paused and looked up at his company commander. "And I think that there are more of them than we thought."

"What do you mean?" Nguyen snapped.

"I found where they stopped last night. The signs show that there are at least two teams, maybe even three. I would say maybe eighteen men."

Nguyen thought for a moment. If this were true, then it was even more imperative that he get back on their trail. The longer they stayed alive, the more time they would have to spot something that they should not see and radio a report back to their headquarters. Nguyen called for his company sergeant, who quickly appeared.

"Yes, Comrade Captain." Sergeant Khanh was obviously nervous. After the disastrous attack on the riverboat base, Khanh had been the senior surviving sergeant in Nguyen's company. He was acting as the company sergeant until Nguyen could get a better, more experienced man. Khanh did not care for his new assignment and prayed to go back to his old unit.

"The tracker thinks that the Yankees have more than one recon unit in the area. I want you to form four teams. We will spread out and look for them. I will take one team, you will take the second. Make sure that you pick good men for the last two."

Khanh hurried away and Nguyen went back to his map. If he ran his teams in toward the supply point, they should make contact with the Yankees. And they would be able to block the enemy from leaving the area if they were already there. One way or the other, he would finally make contact and wipe them out. Coming or going, it didn't matter to him, as long as they were ultimately dead.

Khanh was back in minutes. "We are ready, Comrade Captain."

"Give the order to move out toward the supply site. I will take the team in the middle, you take the right flank."

Wilburn had almost reached his destination, a small valley in between two ridgelines, when the drag team following half a klick behind radioed that they had spotted a small group of NVA tracking them. Wilburn told them to double-time to rejoin the main body.

Taking Bao and his six Nungs off to the side, Wilburn ordered the main body ahead to the PZ with orders to wait for them there. As soon as they were moving again, he hurried back with his small team to see what they were up against. He didn't need to have someone dogging their tails while they were trying to extract. If he couldn't resolve this quickly, he'd have to call it off and hide in the jungle.

When the drag team passed them, the Nung team leader reported a dozen of the enemy half a klick behind them. Wilburn sent the team ahead and prepared an ambush.

The path they were following widened at a bend. He took two claymores from the Nung's rucks and set them with their backs to big tree trunks. He aimed them by having one of the Nungs step onto the trail as if he was approaching enemy. Lying behind the anti-personnel mines, Wilburn used the built-in sight and aimed both claymore's at the grinning Nung's blackened belt buckle. When each mine was detonated, its 900 steel balls would blast a swath fifty meters wide down the trail. Anyone alive after that would be taken out with small-arms fire.

After sighting the mines, Wilburn camouflaged them with brush and hid behind a neighboring tree. The Nungs spread out on his right side back in the brush. If everything went as planned, it would all be over in thirty seconds or so.

He pulled the bolt handle on his Swedish K out of the safety notch, let it go down into the firing position, and took an extra magazine out of his ammo pouch. Laying the submachine gun within easy reach, he took one of the claymore clackers in each hand and settled down to wait.

He was barely under cover when an NVA point man wearing an olive-colored uniform slowly walked into view. His uniform and equipment were brand-new, as was his AK-47 assault rifle. He was fresh, not an experienced jungle fighter. That would make it a lot easier.

The point man walked into the killing zone and stopped for a moment. Since the NVA could see quite a ways down the trail, which was clear, he turned and waved his comrades forward. Wilburn could tell that the soldier didn't like being out on point. His eyes darted from side to side without really seeing anything.

The NVA point man waited until his buddies were only a couple of meters behind him before he moved out again. Wilburn let him go past. The rest of the NVA patrol were rookies, too, crowded together in a nice little bunch. Wil-

242

burn waited patiently until they were in the middle of the killing zone, right where the Nung had stood when he had sighted the claymores a few minutes earlier.

The two mines detonated as one. Eighteen hundred .25-caliber steel balls swept the jungle trail at waist height. Seven of the eight NVA were blown off their feet. The eighth went down to a burst from one of the Nungs.

Wilburn dropped the claymore clackers, snatched up his submachine gun, and spun to his left. The NVA point man had turned halfway around, a look of horror frozen on his face. Wilburn didn't give him time to recover. He dumped half a magazine of 9mm into him.

Spinning the other way, he unloaded the remaining rounds into the tangled pile of bodies on the trail. The K's bolt locked back on an empty magazine.

Silence filled the jungle. Nothing moved for a few moments. Wilburn dropped the empty mag from his K and slapped a new one into place. He pulled the bolt back into firing position and slowly got to his feet. The Nungs followed him out into the killing zone. All nine of the NVA were dead. The Nungs quickly checked the bodies for documents. Taking them by the arms and legs, they dragged the bloody corpses into the thick brush and dumped them out of sight. Their weapons followed. Wilburn tried to scuff dirt over the bloodstains on the trail, but there were just too many of them. Anyone passing by that way would know in an instant that there had been a firefight.

"*Trung si*," Bao came up beside him. "You *di-di mau*. I take these Nungs and we stay behind to kill *cong*."

"No, goddammit," Wilburn said hotly. "I didn't leave you the last time, and I'm not going to leave you now."

The old Nung laid his hand on Wilburn's arm. "It is different this time, *Trung si*. This time it is my honor to stay. The *cong* are looking for us because they were warned by my worthless nephew."

Wilburn was silent.

"You have to go back to Kontum," the Nung reasoned. "Take the film and show them what we find here. This is bookoo important, *Trung si*, old Bao is not. I can stay and kill *cong* so you can get away."

"I'm calling for an extract. And I'm going to get all of our asses out of here." Wilburn locked eyes with the Nung. "And that means you, too, you old fuck."

"Ah, *Trung si*," Bao said quietly. "You do not understand. But maybe it is not the right time yet." The old Chinese looked up. A gentle rain had begun to fall. "You call the chopper. Maybe he come in and get you. Maybe I go, too. We see."

"Come on," Wilburn growled. "We've got to get to that PZ."

CHAPTER 34

Deep in the jungle

Major Stone was in the operations room in Kontum monitoring radio traffic when Wilburn's request for an emergency extract came in. He rushed to the radio room and put the call in to Python Flight at Chu Lai.

Rat Gaines was on the flight line checking the Jesus nut on his Cobra's rotor head with the maintenance sergeant. It was called the Jesus nut because if it failed, a pilot had barely enough time to say, "Oh, Jesus!" before he crashed. They were just finishing the inspection when the operations sergeant raced up to them in his jeep.

"Captain," the sergeant shouted before the jeep had even come to a stop. "Got a call from Special Forces. You've got to go get that recon team."

"Oh, shit!" Gaines jumped down from the engine housing and ran over to the jeep. "Where're they at?"

"Here, sir." The sergeant laid his map out on the hood of the jeep and pointed.

The PZ location was not far from the Laotian border in steep, mountainous terrain with narrow valleys. Even on a good day, it was a bitch of a place to pull an extract.

"What's the weather like up there?" Gaines sounded concerned.

"That may be a real problem, sir," the sergeant said, looking up at the lead gray, overcast sky. "The weather people say that it's worse up there than it is here."

"That's just what we fucking need."

Gaines quickly copied the grid coordinates and radio frequency of Wilburn's team and stuffed the notepad back into the leg pocket of his flight suit.

"Get 'em going," he snapped. 'Rat' now!"

"Yes, sir." The sergeant reached into the passenger side of the jeep and handed Rat his flight helmet. "You'll be needing this, sir."

"Thanks, Sergeant."

Python's chopper pilots and crew came storming out of the operations shack and raced for their birds. Gaines climbed into his Cobra, buckled the harness, and slipped the helmet over his head. As he ran over his pre-start checks, he radioed the tower for flight clearance. He didn't want any bullshit from those people today.

In seconds, the air was filled with the smell of burning kerosene and the sound of whining turbines as the rotors started turning over.

Gaines had almost everything that could fly scheduled for the mission — four slicks for the extract, his Cobra light-fireteam, and a heavy-fireteam of Huey Hogs. It was enough to deal with almost anything they might run into. The men of Python Flight lived up to their motto, You Call, We Maul. No one ever said that when Python Flight was needed, they didn't take their work seriously.

"Python, Python, this is Lead. As soon as you are go, get airborne. Take a heading of three-ten and assemble on the way. How copy? Over."

A chorus of rogers followed as each pilot finished his pre-flights and taxied onto the PSP.

Gaines fired up his turbine and ran the RPMs up. He was ready to go, but his gunner still hadn't shown up. The pilot was just about to leave without him when he saw a three-quarter-ton truck charging across the field. O'Leary jumped out of the back and scrambled into his cockpit.

As soon the gunner locked his canopy down, Gaines eased into a hover and nosed his ship onto the main runway. *Sudden Discomfort's* tail came up as she started down the strip. Within seconds, Gaines hauled up on the collective, and they were airborne.

"Glad you could make the party," Gaines called up in the intercom.

"Sorry 'bout that, Captain," O'Leary answered. "I was in the arms room helping the ordnance guys work over a minigun."

"You get it fixed?"

"Yes, Captain."

Gaines still hadn't figured O'Leary out, but he had to admit that the man loved his weapons. The fact that he was a loner was not a big problem in Echo Company. In war, many men were loners. It kept them from having to suffer the loss of a friend. But O'Leary seemed to be a man who had completely cut himself off from what was going on around him. As long as it didn't interfere with company business, however, Gaines could live with it.

Gaines concentrated on overtaking the choppers that had taken off ahead of him. With the Cobra's superior speed, it was only a matter of minutes until he was leading the formation. "Python," he radioed "this is Lead, let's police up this formation."

He cut his throttle, dropping his airspeed so the slicks and the even slower C Model Huey Hogs could keep up with him. He would welcome the day when all his gunships were AH-1 Cobras and the underpowered, overburdened Huey Hogs could finally be retired.

247

As soon as the entire flight was in formation, Gaines flipped open his map and started navigating to the location he had been given. He looked out through the canopy toward the mountains to the west. The clouds seemed to be hanging low in the sky, much lower than they were along the coastal plains around Chu Lai.

He decided to call Wilburn to get an on-the-spot weather report, and switched the frequency on the AN/ARC-131 FM tactical radio. He keyed the throat mike on his flight helmet. "Dry Rock, this is Python Lead. Over."

"This is Dry Rock," came the reply. "Send your traffic. Over."

"This is Python Lead, I am about four zero mikes out from your location. I need to get a local weather report. Over."

"This is Dry Rock. We're socked in here. Visibility is about a quarter of a mile and it seems to be getting worse. The cloud cover is dropping. Over."

It looked grim. Getting in there at all, to say nothing of being able to pull off an extract, was going to be tight.

Wilburn huddled in the brush with a gentle, misty rain falling. Along with the rain, the clouds had lowered. Now they hugged the earth. Over the last couple of hours, the weather had steadily deteriorated, and it was getting worse by the minute.

Usually Wilburn didn't mind the rain. It was good for his kind of work; cool, with a background noise that masked the sound of his movements from enemy ears. But he didn't see how Gaines's choppers were ever going to get to them through it. Even the tops of the ridgelines were shrouded in fog. He glanced down at his watch: Gaines had said forty minutes. He would leave the ambush teams out till the last minute. The extract was going to be difficult enough without having to bother with unexpected visitors.

As Wilburn waited, the wind picked up as well. Before long, it was uncomfortably cold. Combined with the cloud cover, it was going to be even more difficult for the pickup.

At the altitude that Gaines and his flight were flying, the clouds weren't so thick, but it was impossible for him to see the ground. He had to guess how far they had come. He brought the formation down a little lower and keyed his throat mike. "Dry Rock, this is Python Lead," he called. "Can you hear us yet? Over."

"This is Rock, that's a negative. I'll call you when I do."

Gaines was worried. He was usually a good instrument navigator, but with the winds, it was easy to get blown off course. He flew on.

"Python," Wilburn radioed. "I've got you now. You're to the north and heading away from me."

"Roger."

Gaines brought his Cobra around, bringing the whole formation with him.

"You're passing overhead now."

"Python, this is Lead. Go into an orbit now."

Without any landmarks to guide them, it was going to be very difficult for the pilots to hold their orbit over Wilburn's location. Gaines peered down through the thin clouds and saw nothing but a solid mass of dirty gray-white below him. It looked like he was flying over water, not a jungle.

"Lead, this is Three Five," came a voice in his earphones. Three Five was Cliff Gabriel, and if any pilot in Vietnam could get in there, it was he. "Why don't you let me have a crack at it?"

"This is Lead. Roger, Three Five, see what you can do."

Gabe switched to Wilburn's frequency so the men on the ground could try to talk him down. "Dry Rock, this is Python Three Five, I'm going to try to make it down to you. Tell me when you hear me directly overhead."

"Roger. You are to the north of us now."

Gabe turned the slick south. Cutting his airspeed as much as he dared, he gently came off the collective and gradually decreased his altitude. As his speed and altitude dropped, the thick, dark clouds enveloped the slick and visibility dropped to absolute zero. The cold rain started blowing inside the chopper, soaking everyone in it.

Gabe's eyes were locked on his instrument panel. With all his visual reference gone, his instruments were all that he had to tell him where and how he was flying. Hueys were not designed for instrument flying, but Hueys were called upon to do a lot of things in Vietnam that the designers had never intended.

"You're getting closer," Wilburn's voice sounded in his headphones.

"Roger," Gabe answered tensely.

With his airspeed down, the gusts of wind blowing across the ridgelines and through the valleys buffeted the ship. Gabe's hands and feet were in constant, expertly coordinated motion, trying to hold his craft steady as he continued his descent.

"It sounds like you're right overhead now."

"Roger."

Gabe ran his throttle up, but dropped his collective. If he had to abort his descent, he wanted all the power he had instantly on hand to climb back out. He could pull pitch faster than he could run his turbine up. A sharp gust of wind rocked the slick, sending it onto her side. Gabe righted her. With his eyes fixed on the altimeter, he continued his descent.

"You're moving away from me," Wilburn called. "To the east now."

Gabe cursed as he eased down on the rudder pedals to swing the nose back. "Gabe! Look out!" the door gunner shouted.

With the turbine screaming, Gabe hauled up sharply on the collective. The rotor blades bit into the air, and the slick soared upward.

"Jesus, Gabe," the door gunner called up. "What the fuck're you trying to do, man? You almost crashed us into a hill!"

Gabe leveled out and keyed his throat mike. "Lead," he called. "This is Three Five, I'm afraid that this is a no-go.

The winds are throwing me all over the sky. There's just no way I can get in. Over."

"This is Lead. Roger. Climb out and head on back."

"Three Five. Roger."

"Dry Rock, this is Python Lead, I'm really sorry 'bout this, PJ," Gaines radioed, "but it's a no-go. We just can't get in. It's instruments all the way, and the wind's too strong for that. We'll stay on standby, and if the weather breaks, give us a call. Over."

"This is Dry Rock. No sweat, Python. Thanks for trying. I'm going to try for a PBR extract. Over."

"This is Python Lead. Good luck. Out."

Captain Nguyen also heard the helicopters circling overhead in the clouds. He knew that they were there for only one thing. The machines were trying to extract the Yankee recon unit.

"Hurry!" he shouted to his men. "Hurry before they get away!"

The North Vietnamese had no need to hurry, though. Jack Wilburn and his Nungs weren't going anywhere.

CHAPTER 35

Deep in the jungle

Wilburn listened to the rain-muffled sound of the beating rotors of Python Flight fade into the distance. He looked at the jungle at the end of the valley. The chopper extract had been worth a try, but now it was time for them to get the hell out. Any dinks in the neighborhood were sure to have heard the choppers and would be on their way to investigate.

He gave the radio handset back to his RTO and got to his feet. "Bao," he said, turning to the Nung. "Let's get 'em moving. I want to make it to the river before dark."

"Yes, *Trung si.*"

Once the headquarters element started moving out, Wilburn got on the radio to CCC to tell them his backup plan to go downriver to meet up with the PBRs. Major Snow was worried. He told Wilburn that he would get the Navy moving in time to join them as soon as he reached the river. Snow also decided to schedule a B-52 bomber raid on the enemy supply point they had reported.

It sounded so simple on the radio. All Wilburn had to do was to make his way undetected through some twenty klicks of dink-infested jungle and get on the PBRs for a leisurely cruise back up the river. He had thirty-six people, including himself, to keep hidden. NVA units were hot on their tail, and the enemy was not about to give up. Possibly Major Snow's planned air strike would create enough confusion that they could get away. Somehow, though, Wilburn doubted it was going to be that simple.

Captain Nguyen examined the wet ground in front of him. The tracker was right. A large group of men had halted there very recently. He reached down and picked up a filter-tip cigarette butt and sniffed at it. He could still smell the tobacco.

He looked around for any sign of the wet grass having been blown down in a circular pattern, proof that the helicopters had actually landed and taken the Yankees away, but there was no such sign. He was certain that the helicopters had not been able to come down because of the rain and low-hanging clouds.

Since the weather gave no signs of clearing, it was unlikely that the helicopters would be coming back. The Americans would head back to the Song Boung River. They would never get away. There were too many units along the river that Nguyen could call upon to join the chase.

The NVA captain turned to his radioman. "Tell the other teams to converge on this location," he ordered. "We have them now."

"Yes, comrade." The radioman bent over his microphone to keep it out of the rain and transmitted his message. "They are coming as fast as they can, Captain," he reported.

"Good. Now raise the regimental headquarters, I want to talk to Colonel Tran."

When Tran came on the air, Nguyen quickly told him what he had found. Tran gave him orders to pursue them immediately. By the time the call was completed, only one of the NVA tracking teams had made it back to his location.

254

Nguyen decided not to wait for the others. He proceeded immediately with the twelve men he had with him. He was in a hurry to close with the intruders as quickly as he could before the rain washed out their trail and he lost them again.

Alexander was sitting on a cot in his newly bunkered platoon CP when he heard Miller shouting for him. He poked his head out the door and saw the sailors scrambling for the boats.

"Lieutenant Alexander!" Miller shouted. "Get your men ready! We have to extract the Special Forces!"

After telling Bunny to round up Zack and Brody, Alexander grabbed his gear and headed for the docks. When he got to Miller's boat, he found the PBR commander and his exec leaning over a map spread out on the bridge.

"I just got a call from the Special Forces in Kontum," Miller explained. "Sergeant Wilburn's recon unit couldn't be extracted by air and they want us to go up and get them out."

Alexander checked out the map. "When are we leaving, sir?" he asked.

"I don't really have a pickup time yet," Miller answered. "They said that they'd get back to me as soon as they get an ETA for the sergeant and his people."

"How many of my people do you want, sir?"

"Since there's so many of them I can only take two of your men per boat. That'll make us pretty overloaded on the way back, but I want your guns for the run in."

"Yes sir. I'll get them standing by and we'll be ready to move out as soon as you are."

Alexander left the Navy to their preparations and went back to his CP. There was no real hurry, but he wanted to give Brody the warning order. By Air Cav Blue Team standards, there was still all the time in the world to wait before they had to push off for the run down the river. But when the Navy called, he didn't want his people to waste a second.

Brody and his squad were suited up and ready to go in under five minutes. One good thing about being a grunt was that there was not too much that an infantryman had to keep track of, and it all fit in the ruck on his back. They gathered on the riverbank and watched while the sailors made last-minute checks of the motors and weapons on the PBRs.

Gardner sat on a bale of sandbags and stared across the brown water to the brush on the opposite bank. "JJ," Bunny said. "You think we're going to have any trouble this time?"

The big grunt turned toward the little FO. Ever since Bunny had rescued Gardner from the water, he had followed him around everywhere, like a younger brother constantly underfoot. Gardner was starting to get a little annoyed by his constant company, but he put up with it. Bunny had saved his life.

"I don't know, man," he answered honestly. "It's hard telling what the dinks will do. But I imagine we'll make some kind of contact." He glanced down at the patrol boats. "There's enough of them along this river, and it's kind of hard to hide a PBR in the water."

Bunny followed his eyes. "When do you think they'll let us go back to our choppers?"

"Beats the shit outta me, but I'm ready for it. This river-ine shit just isn't cutting it at all."

"That's a big rodg."

York was sitting off by himself listening to the other men speculate about their chances on the long trip up the river. He didn't add to the conversation. The more he was around these men, the more he despised them. He was sick and tired of living the life of a grunt in Vietnam.

He racked his brain trying to figure out a way to miss the mission, but he couldn't think of a good enough excuse to be left behind. No matter what he said to Brody, the squad leader would laugh in his face. He put his mind into high gear, desperately trying to think of a way out.

"Harvard!"

York looked up at the sound of Brody's voice.

"I'm putting you with Two-Step."

York nodded silently. That was just what he needed, to be teamed up with a savage. He had seen the way the Indian looked at him the morning after the attack on the camp, his dark eyes hooded and secretive. He had read the disgust on the Indian's face for his momentary panic. He'd been scared, he admitted it, but he didn't think that it was a criminal offense. The way he saw it, the intelligent reaction to danger was to run. No man with even an ounce of brains would have wanted to stick around with what had been going on that night.

Coming from an established, affluent family, Richard York had never needed to learn the value of teamwork. He had never needed to depend on anything other than his family's wealth. Money had bought him everything that he had ever wanted, including friendship. And because of that, he had never trusted another man. Nor had he ever trusted himself.

Trust implied equality. To Harvard, men who had not enjoyed a privileged life could never be his equals. But combat was the world's ultimate democracy. It was a lesson York had yet to learn.

Wilburn and his Nung command element were in the middle of a diamond patrol formation when the NVA hit his drag team some five hundred meters to his rear. At the first sound of firing, he wheeled around and grabbed for the radio.

While the sergeant frantically tried to get a situation report, Bao quickly took another team of Nungs and headed down their trail on the double. The rest of the mercenaries deployed, waiting to see if more NVA were coming.

There were a few tense moments before Wilburn could get the drag team leader on the radio. The Nung had been hit by a small patrol, probably not more than five men. The Nung had fought back, though. One of the NVA might have gotten away. The rest were dead.

257

Wilburn took out his map and spread it on the ground. Now that the NVA knew where he was, he had to break the trail. He decided to detour over the ridgeline to his right and head for a pickup point a little farther down-stream. It would add an hour or so to the march, but it might throw them off his trail.

He got back on the radio to the drag and talked to Bao. He wanted the Nung to leave a couple of booby-trapped claymore mines at the contact site. They wouldn't slow the NVA up for too long, but they might inflict a few casualties and make them a little more cautious. It was worth a try.

As soon as Bao returned, Wilburn issued his orders and the Nungs started up the steep ridge. Halfway up the hill, Wilburn heard the muzzled sound of a claymore explosion to their rear. The NVA were closer than he thought.

At the top of the ridge, Wilburn took out his field glasses and scanned the valleys on each side of him. The brush was thick in most places, but through the rain and breaks in the vegetation, he saw dark figures of men slowly moving up both of the valleys. They were only a half an hour behind. Less, if they decided to pick up the pace.

Now it turned into a footrace. Wilburn and his men had to keep their distance from the enemy, and the Navy had to be waiting for them when they got to the river. Fifteen minutes' delay could be fatal. The Special Forces soldier quickly made a decision to take the valley to their right, the upstream side. It was closer to the boats and it seemed to have fewer NVA crawling around in it. His people had been on the move since early morning without a break.

As they headed down the other side of the ridge, Wilburn got on the radio to the Navy. They were critical to their survival. He prayed that nothing delayed them on their run up the river.

Nguyen smiled when he got the report that the Yankees had been spotted dropping over the ridge into the neighboring valley, and quickly consulted his map. There were other units he could call in from the south to pick up their trail.

He made a quick radio call back to Colonel Tran requesting assistance. Tran assured him that all available units in the vicinity would be ordered to report to him and would be under his command for the operation.

After his call to Tran was completed, Nguyen ordered his small group forward. He wanted to be first to make contact with the intruders.

CHAPTER 36

On the Song Boung River

The diesel engines of the four PBRs purred like powerful jungle cats as they propelled the boats up the muddy river. With the recent rain, the water level was higher up the banks than usual and muddier than ever. The grunts and Navy gunners scrutinized the dense brush along the banks as it passed by them, their fingers ready on their triggers.

Miller's plan was to take the boats almost to the pickup point and then pull into cover along the bank and wait until Wilburn got there. With the weather holding the gunships on the ground, the Navy officer wanted to be as close as he could before he made the last mad dash upstream to get the stranded recon team. He felt naked without his air cover overhead. He had finally come to fully appreciate Rat's gunships.

The PBRs were about halfway to their destination when Miller received Wilburn's call. "Barn Door, this is Dry Rock. Over."

"This is Barn Door Six. Over."

"This is Dry Rock, what's your position? Over."

Miller quickly consulted his map. "Dry Rock, Barn Door. We are at eight-two-three, four-six-seven. Over."

"This is Rock, copy eight-two-three, four-six-seven. We will be at one-oh-two, six-three-five in about an hour. We are being pursued and will need a quick pickup. Over."

"Barn Door, Roger, good copy. We'll be there. Out"

Alexander leaned over Miller's shoulder while the Navy officer plotted Wilburn's pickup point. "Will we make it there in time, sir?" he asked.

Miller looked at his watch. "We should."

Just then Bunny, who had been marking the coordinates on his map, spoke up. "Uh . . . Ell tee, sir, I hate to tell you this, but that's way out of the artillery fan. There's no way the guns can shoot for us if we get in trouble up there."

"Are you sure about that?" Alexander asked with a frown.

Bunny was offended that the lieutenant would doubt his word as a seasoned professional forward observer. "Of course I'm sure, Ell tee," he said indignantly. "I plotted those guns myself."

The lieutenant glanced up at the leaden sky. With the weather holding the gunships on the ground and no artillery support available if they needed it, this operation was going to be a little hairier than he liked. It had every potential of becoming a full-blown disaster.

He looked over the side of the boat at the brown water rushing by, cursing the riverine operation and the weather. Like Miller, he, too, felt naked without the comforting sound of rotors beating overhead.

Lieutenant Powers was riding on Petty Officer Johnson's boat, 859, and they were in the lead as the small flotilla made its way upriver at only fifteen miles per hour. Miller had the boats hold their speed down to lessen the chance that their motors would be heard by nearby NVA. Also, at the slower speed, the gunners could carefully search the riverbanks for any signs of an ambush as they passed.

The 859 boat had just passed a bend where the river narrowed when the dense brush on both sides erupted with fire.

The patrol boat pilots slammed their throttles forward, and the gunners opened up with all their weapons.

Under the cover of heavy automatic-weapons fire, motorized sampans full of NVA sprang out of branches overhanging the banks and tried to close in with the PBRs.

The trail boat, 848, was slow in winding her engines up, and the sampans were able to block her way upstream. With a puff of dirty black smoke, an RPG rocket leaped from its launcher. A few feet out of the muzzle, the secondary propellant charge kicked in and the anti-tank rocket slammed into the PBRs wheelhouse.

The round penetrated the thin fiberglass and detonated against the steering box. The boatswain took the full force of the blast, but thin fragments of the rocket's body sliced into the radioman who stood at his hand-cranked thumper. He fell, seriously wounded. The blast damaged the boat's engine controls. PBR 848 stopped dead in the water.

The NVA in the sampans shouted victoriously and closed with the stricken PBR. The sailor in the fifty turret tried to bring his guns to bear, but he couldn't depress the muzzles far enough to zero in on the small boats when they were in that close. He reached behind him and grabbed his M-16. Jacking a round into the chamber, he started shooting at the sampans.

In the stern of the boat, Corky and Farmer had their sixty up over the gunwale, adding its fire to the remaining weapons on the boat. Corky laid down on the trigger, hammering out long bursts. His rounds tore into the sampans, but it didn't slow them down. There were just too many of them, packed with gooks, their AKs blazing. Return fire hit all around him, splintering the fiberglass hull.

"Behind you!" Farmer screamed, swinging his M-16 around. A quick burst sent an NVA soldier over backward. More gooks swarmed up from a sampan that had snuck up on their far side. Farmer snapped off two more bursts before his bolt locked to the rear on an empty magazine. "Sonofabitch!" he screamed in frustration.

Corky spun around. Laying down on the trigger again, he sprayed a long burst of 7.62mm into the borders. Farmer snatched a grenade from his ammo pouch and pulled the pin. Letting the spoon fly off, he counted to two and dropped it over the side. The instantaneous blast splintered the sampan and it sunk out of sight.

Farmer ducked back down for cover and slammed a fresh magazine into his sixteen. "Up front," he yelled, hitting the bolt release and bringing the weapon back up to his shoulder.

NVA were swarming over the bow of the boat. The fifty gunner picked them off with his rifle as soon as they stuck their heads up until a concussion grenade sailed through the air and landed in the turret with him. The blast threw him against the armored side of the turret, knocking him unconscious.

The lead boat broke out of the ambush, but Brody whirled around when he heard the distinctive sound of an RPG rocket detonating. He saw the wheelhouse of the 848 boat enveloped in the blast, and when it went dead in the water, the sampans moved in for the kill. Brody raced for the bridge.

"Powers!" he yelled, pointing back down the river. "We got to go back and help them!"

Powers turned around to look and hesitated for a split second. Brody was going after Corky and Farmer if he had to drive the PBR himself. He started into the wheelhouse.

"Fuck it," Powers shouted to the boatswain. "Let's do it!"

Johnson slammed his throttles forward and spun the big wheel all the way over. The PBR danced sideways as the powerful water jets kicked her stern around and pushed the bow back downstream.

Miller saw the lead boat spin around and head back. He snatched up the radio just as 859 blasted past him, her diesels bellowing as she raced to help 848. He dropped the handset when he realized what Powers was doing. It was suicidal, but it was the only hope for the men on PBR 848.

Though all his instincts and training told him to run for it and save his last two boats, Miller ordered his boatswain to turn about and radioed for the remaining PBR to follow. They sped after Powers, back into the ambush.

The dinks tried to block 859 with their sampans, but Johnson didn't give an inch. "Hang on!" he shouted. He drove straight for them. An RPG round was launched from the bank. Johnson whipped the wheel around, skidding the boat to the side. The rocket exploded in the river, throwing a geyser of muddy water into the air.

The twin fifties in the forward turret opened up again, blasting the NVA in the small boats and clearing a path through the sampans. Johnson drove the shallow draft hull right over the wreckage and the floating bodies. Not all of them were dead. He ignored their screams. The boat plowed through.

Suddenly, the PBR shuddered and slowed to half its speed. "It's the water jets, sir," Johnson shouted to Powers. "We sucked something in!"

"Keep going!" Powers yelled. He didn't even want to think about what might be lodged in them.

Ahead, gooks swarmed over the decks of 848. As fast as the few remaining men cleared them off, more appeared. PBR 836, the number-three boat in the column, had been close enough for her guns to help, but her gunners were forced to hold their fire for fear of hitting the crew by mistake. Finally, it no longer mattered.

"Get in closer," Brody yelled.

Powers pulled 859 along the starboard side of the stricken boat. His blazing deck guns cleared a path in front of them, but most of the sampans were hiding on the other side of the PBR. When the boats were still a few feet apart, Brody slammed a fresh magazine into his sixteen and jumped for the deck. Gardner was right behind him.

"Corky!" Brody yelled. "Farmer!"

Just then, an NVA lunged for him. Gardner smashed the butt of his sixteen into his face, slamming him back. The last sailor still on his feet fired his .45-caliber pistol, hitting the dink in the throat.

NVA still swarmed up the sides of the boat and onto the deck. The grunts took what little cover there was in the wheelhouse and fired into them at point-blank range. The return AK fire splintered fiberglass and tore through the thin hull.

Another RPG round flew out of the jungle. This one hit low on the 848's hull and penetrated the engine compartment before it detonated. Sheets of flame shot from below deck when the fuel exploded. An NVA crouching at the front of the wheelhouse was caught in the flames. Screaming, his uniform caught fire and he dove into the water, a living torch.

"Get outta there!" Powers shouted to the grunts from the bridge. "Abandon ship!"

The last sailor jumped for the 859 boat.

Grabbing the wounded Navy fifty gunner under the arms, Gardner dragged him to the side of the stricken boat. Hands reached out and pulled him across to safety. He dashed back into the flaming wheelhouse or the 848 and scooped up the body of the boatswain. Throwing his dead weight up over his shoulder, he jumped for the deck of 859.

Brody dragged the body of the radioman over to the side of the sinking 848. A sailor leaped across and helped carry him on board. Brody glanced back; Corky was still in the stern, his M-60 blazing at the bank. "Corky!" he yelled. "Let's go!"

The Chicano machine gunner draped his ammo belt over his shoulder. Ripping off one last burst, he ran for the side. He cleared the gunwales with a leap and smashed into the deck of 859.

Johnson slammed his throttles forward, and the PBR pushed through the water. The flames were hot enough to blister the paint on 859's hull as she pulled away from the burning wreckage of 848.

By this time, Miller and the number-three boat had blasted their way through the packed sampans blocking their way. Bodies and debris littered the water behind them. Bringing their bows around again, they took up positions in front and in back of 859 as she pulled out and turned back upstream. Her water jets clogged with debris, the 859 boat could only make half speed as the two other remaining boats ran back through the ambush site.

The enemy fire was not as intense. The PBRs had taken their toll of the attackers. With their guns blazing, the boats pushed through the kill zone and made for free water.

In Miller's boat, Alexander and Bunny crouched against the PBRs hull. The thin fiberglass was no protection at all, even from AK fire, but it made them feel better.

"Gimme the radio!" Alexander shouted over the heavy roar of the .50-calibers in the forward turret.

Bunny handed him the microphone.

"Switch it over to the company push!"

The FO turned the tuning knobs on the face of the Prick-25 radio. "It's set, sir!"

Alexander keyed the handset, praying that the small radio would reach all the way back to Python Flight at Chu Lai. He gave another prayer that Rat Gaines could somehow get through the weather to help them. If not, they were finished.

CHAPTER 37

Chu Lai

At Python Operations back at Chu Lai, bad weather had grounded the choppers. The rain was coming down in torrents, and a gusting wind rattled the buildings. Rat Gaines was in the radio room drinking coffee when Alexander's frantic call came in.

"Python, Python, this is Python Blue Six. Over."

Over the hiss of the radio carrier wave, Gaines heard the roar of gunfire in the background. He grabbed for the microphone.

"This is Python Lead, go ahead."

"This is Blue Six, Captain, we need help bad," Alexander shouted. "We ran into one hell of a big ambush. We fought our way out of it, but we lost one of the boats. We still got dinks crawling all over us and we've got wounded on board. We're outside the artillery fan, and if we don't get some air support real soon, we're finished."

"This is Python," Gaines said calmly. "Send your location. Over."

"We're at nine-two-five, two-eight-one. Over."

"Roger, copy." Gaines paused and shot a quick glance out the window. What he saw was discouraging, but he kept his voice even.

"Listen, Mike, you just hang on now, you hear? I'll get something to you as fast as I can. Just hold on now. Over."

A burst of static cut Alexander's answer off. Gaines put the microphone back down. Outside, the rain was coming down in sheets. He turned to the operations sergeant. "Get Warlokk, Gabe, and Alphabet in here ASAP." he ordered.

"Yes, sir."

Gaines hurried to his locker and quickly got out a clean flight suit. Stripping off his jungle fatigues, he dressed as fast as he could. With the weather, there was no way he could fly a gun team straight to the ambushed men. He would never be able to find them through the clouds. There was, however, the slight possibility that he could get to them by flying down the river. When it was cold and overcast, as it was today, the heat rising off the water usually cleared the air directly above the course of a river. Hopefully, once they found the Song Boung River, they could drop down and fly up it until they reached the boats.

It wasn't much of a plan, Gaines had to admit. It was dangerous to fly a chopper at all in this kind of weather, but it was all that he could think of at the moment and it was going to have to work. Any other pilot would call him insane for even considering the mission, but Alexander and his men had completely run out of options. Rat Gaines was their last chance.

He zipped up the legs of his flying suit and pulled on his gloves. He pulled out one of his thin cigars and fired it up. A condemned man, he thought, always has a last smoke.

In the jungle, Wilburn was pushing his Nungs as fast as they could go. They had only half an hour until they were to meet up with the PBRs. And about four klicks of jungle. They would make it with time to spare if they didn't run into any more trouble and stayed in front of the NVA. He decided to send his point element and one of the recon teams ahead to secure the pickup site. He and Bao would keep the last two teams with them and bring up the rear.

He halted his men and they took cover in a brush-covered draw leading into a ravine that went the rest of the way down to the Song Boung River. He wanted to give the point element at least a five-minute head start, so he and Bao could protect their rear. That way, no matter what happened, at least half of the recon team would make it out.

The intermittent rain had stopped again, but it was still cloudy. Now that he had stopped moving, Wilburn felt the slight chill of the wind. The temperature was low, not even eighty degrees, and the cold made him uncomfortably aware of his full bladder. He reached down, unbuttoned his fly, and relieved himself. As always when he was urinating, he felt extremely vulnerable. His eyes quickly scanned from one clump of bushes to the next all along his front.

A flash of movement some hundred meters away at the head of the draw caught his eye, and he focused in on it. He lost it, but he knew that was the NVA. The trackers had found them again.

The point teams had been gone for only a couple of minutes and if he got into a firefight now, they might not get away at all. He low-crawled over to Bao and whispered in his ear. The old Nung grinned and nodded his head in assent. Quickly, Bao passed the word for the Nungs to start pulling out. They would go on halfway down to the river and wait while Bao and Wilburn stayed behind to hold up the NVA trackers.

Wilburn got the silenced Ruger from his ruck and mounted the scope on it. If he was going hunting, he wanted his hunting piece. He and the old Nung shrugged off their rucks and gave them to one of the Nungs to take back. He slung his Swedish K submachine gun over his back. Motioning for Bao to follow him, he faded silently into the jungle like a shadow.

Bao moved out to cover his left flank, his K-Bar fighting knife in his hand. For this to work at all, their kills had to be silent.

From a perch halfway up a banyan tree, Wilburn carefully rested the barrel of the Ruger against the trunk and sighted in on the NVA kneeling on the ground in front of him. He was looking at footprints on the jungle floor. As Wilburn had expected, the man looked down the trail. When he raised his head, his face came into focus in Wilburn's scope. He gently squeezed the trigger and the silenced Ruger made a barely audible pop.

The .22-caliber hollow-point round entered the NVA's right eye, mushroomed as it plowed through his brain, and came to rest against the back of his skull. The man pitched forward on his face without a sound.

Wilburn climbed down from his tree and walked over to him. The gook lay in a kneeling position, his face in the dirt. The sergeant pulled a grenade from his ammo pouch and wedged it under his chest. Making sure that the spoon was held firmly in place, he pulled the pin and put it in his pocket. Now, when the body was moved, the grenade spoon would fly off and the grenade would explode.

Motioning for Bao to follow, Wilburn moved out again. There were still plenty of targets to hunt and very little time left in which to do it.

The next kill was Bao's. He waited silently, pressed against a tree trunk along the trail while another tracker walked past him. The NVA must have sensed the Nung's presence. He stopped an instant before Bao slapped his hand over the man's mouth and pulled his head back. One swipe of the K-Bar left the NVA's throat gaping. His feet kicked as the blood pumped from his jugular.

When the kicking stopped, Bao let him fall slowly to the ground. Rolling him onto his belly so his slit throat wouldn't show, the Nung put a booby-trapped grenade under his body as well.

The third kill went to Wilburn. It was another shot with the silenced Ruger pistol, but at a range of almost a hundred meters this time. The dink went down. But unknown to Wilburn, he had a buddy walking just a few feet behind him.

This second dink knew what the score was. He shouted a warning, ducked back into cover, and sprayed AK fire all over the jungle in front of him in one long, full magazine burst.

The party was over.

Bringing his submachine gun around, Wilburn sent half a magazine after the dink and jumped down from his tree. "Bao," he yelled. "*Di-di!*"

More AK fire followed. The two men ran flat out through the jungle, heedless of the wet branches slapping against their faces. Just as they reached the Nung defensive positions along the riverbank, Wilburn heard one of the booby-trapped grenades explode behind them. Now he knew right where the dinks were. Too goddamned close.

Bao shouted for the Nungs to get ready, and Wilburn snatched the handset from the radio operator. If the boats were more than fifteen minutes away from the pickup now, they would be too late.

"Barn Door, Barn Door," he radioed, "This is Dry Rock, over."

"This is Barn Door Six," Miller answered from his command boat. "Go."

"This is Dry Rock, what's your ETA to our location? Over."

"This is Barn Door, I've run into a lot of trouble here. I've got Python coming in to clear the way for us, but it doesn't look like I can get there for at least another twenty, thirty minutes. I'm really sorry 'bout that. Over."

"Dry Rock, Roger, out," Wilburn answered in a calm tone.

There was no use in him getting on Miller's case about the delay. Fortunes of war, he thought. He laid the microphone back down and looked back up the small valley, cursing.

Now it was time for them to get serious about the situation. Sneaky Pete recon troops or not, when they got done with the dinks today, the bastards would know that they'd been in a fight.

"Bao," he yelled. "The boats will be late. We have to hold on for another half hour."

The old Nung nodded and immediately shouted orders to the Nung troops. They moved out into a bigger perimeter and found well-covered firing positions in the trees. They were Nungs, they knew how to fight and, once again, they would teach the *cong* that it was not a wise thing to tangle with them.

They didn't have long to wait. The first NVA appeared in just a few minutes. Approaching on line, the NVA went by bounds, one squad moving while another covered. Then the first dropped into cover and the second moved out. It was good tactics for the terrain, but the Nungs didn't bite at the bait.

The Nungs waited silently without moving until the first of the NVA were less than fifty meters away. At Bao's command, they opened up all at once with everything they had.

The initial barrage of fire tore into the NVA squad in the open. Most of them went down at once. A few tried for cover but were cut down before they could make it. The Nungs had drawn first blood, but now the NVA knew where they were. Now they would deploy and start whittling Wilburn's people down with their superior numbers. It was a game that the Special Forces sergeant couldn't win.

At the rear of the NVA, Captain Nguyen ordered his men to probe the Yankee's flanks while they kept the center pinned down under heavy fire. Now he had them. He knew from his radio reports that the boats were under heavy attack all along the route and that one of them had already been sunk.

There would be no boats coming up the river today and the Yankee recon unit was doomed to die where they were. He put in a quick call back to Colonel Tran's headquarters.

When the volume of fire to his front increased, Wilburn quickly realized what the dinks were up to. "Watch the flanks!" he yelled over to Bao.

The Nung waved that he had heard and quickly sent a couple of his men over to reinforce each side. The flanks were tied into the river and to get round them, the NVA would have to swim. It wasn't the flanks that Wilburn was worried about, it was his entire line.

The Nungs were equipped as light infantry recon troops and they didn't have heavy weapons with them, not even machine guns or grenade launchers. Their AK-47s and Swedish Ks were good for jungle ambushes, but not the kind of knock-down, drag-out brawl that was developing.

They needed something heavier than assault rifles to tip the scales in their favor. Either the twin fifties on the PBRs or a couple of gunships would do quite nicely.

CHAPTER 38

Chu Lai

When Warlokk and Alphabet rushed into the pilot's ready room, they found their commander standing in front of the operations map, a cigar clamped in the corner of his mouth. Gaines's face was grim.

"What's up, sir?" Warlokk asked.

"Where's Gabe?" Rat asked.

"We haven't seen him since earlier this morning when we stood down."

"Well, I guess you two'll just have to do, then. The Navy's got their asses in a real crack. They went up the river to pull Wilburn out and they ran into a shit storm."

"Oh, Jesus," Alphabet said softly.

"Also, they're way outside the artillery fan," Gaines continued. "Alexander just called, he said that one of the PBR's is gone and they're pinned down. I'm going to go in after them."

"In this weather?"

Gaines shot a quick look out the window. "Yep," he said. "Want to come along?"

"Rat," Warlokk cautioned. "You can't see a thousand feet out there."

Gaines pulled on his gloves. "More like five hundred. I'm going to fly up the river. If, of course, I can find it in this shit."

Warlokk nodded his head. "Let's do it," he said. He sprinted for his locker and grabbed his gloves and flight helmet.

"Hey," Alphabet yelped. He wouldn't miss this for anything. "Me, too."

In seconds, the three pilots were racing for their birds. Gaines had not called for the gunners to join them. It was bad enough to risk three pilots and three very expensive, brand-new helicopters without adding three more men to the suicide mission. The pilots could fire their armament from the rear cockpit without the gunners.

Much to Gaines's surprise, then, Tiger O'Leary and Alphabet's gunner were waiting for them when they reached their birds. "I heard you were going somewhere," Tiger said laconically.

"You don't need to buy into this one," Rat replied tersely.

"Why not?"

Gaines looked at him and shrugged his shoulders. "Okay, I hope to hell you've got your GI life insurance form filled out."

O'Leary gave a rare grin. "It all goes to my favorite charity, a home for broken-down old gunship pilots."

Rat grinned. "Well, we're sure as hell never going to make it to that home."

"Who wants to get old?"

In seconds, the three Cobras were heading down the rain-slicked runway, their blower systems vainly trying to keep the canopies clear. Rat was thankful that he wasn't flying a Huey. With the open side doors, a Hog's cockpit would have been full of cold water by now. He flicked on the cockpit heater switch, banked to the northwest, and headed for the Song Boung River at full speed.

278

He switched his FM radio over to Alexander's tactical frequency.

"Blue Six, Blue Six, this is Python Lead on your push. Over."

All he got was static in his earphones. He called again. "Blue Six, this is Python. What's your status, over."

Still nothing. He checked his note pad and switched the radio to the PBR frequency. "Barn Door, this is Python Lead on your push. Over."

"Python, this is Barn Door," came a faint voice. Gaines could hear gunfire in the background. "Are you en route to this location? Over."

"This is Python Lead, that's affirm. Our Echo Tango Alpha is about fifteen mikes. What's your situation down there? Over."

"This is Barn Door. We need assistance soonest. I have one boat down. I am still trying to make it upriver to the Dry Rock element, but there're gooks all over the place. Over."

"Python, Roger. We're coming as fast as we can. Over."

"This is Barn Door, copy. Out."

"Okay, boys," Rat called to the other two gunships. "Turn the wick up and follow me."

Rogers followed as the three Cobras sped through the rain.

Bao wiped the sweat from his eyes. He slammed a fresh magazine into the bottom of his AK-47 and pulled back on the bolt handle to chamber a round. Sighting carefully, he squeezed off a single shot. His target, an NVA about to throw a Chi-Com grenade, went down. The grenade exploded with a muffled bang.

Bao glanced over to the *trung si*. Wilburn was on the radio again, trying to guide the riverboats in. The PBRs were almost there, but in ten more minutes it would all be over. The *cong* were too close and there were too many of them.

The old jungle fighter smiled at the Special Forces sergeant. My young, long-nosed friend, he thought, a true warrior must die here today, but it will not be you. Bao's duty was clear. He would give Wilburn his life just as the young man had saved him in the ambush weeks earlier. Maybe when the great wheel of death and rebirth spun again, they would have a chance to fight together once more.

The Nung whipped out his razor-sharp K-Bar knife and chopped off a lock of his black hair from the front of his head. He would not be going home to Dong Pek today, but his hair would take his spirit back to the temple.

Quickly he crawled over to the tree where Wilburn had taken shelter. "*Trung si,*" he said. "It is time now. I take my team and we will cover you when the boats come."

"You'll get cut off," Wilburn protested. "I don't know if I'll be able to hold the boats long enough for you to get back."

"Do not hold the boats, *Trung si*. It will not be necessary."

He handed Wilburn the lock of hair. "Take this back to camp," he said. "Give it to the priest."

Wilburn closed his fingers over the hair. He knew what the symbolic gesture meant. "You don't have to do this, old man," he said softly.

Bao laughed. "That is why I want to do this thing, *Trung si* Jack. I am an old man. Remember, long-nose, with my people, an old man does only what pleases him. It is my pleasure to kill many *cong* here so you and the Nungs can escape."

Wilburn was silent. His throat tightened and he fought to control his emotions.

"Do not grieve for me," the Nung said. "We have killed many enemies together. In the next life we will kill many more." He touched Wilburn's arm. "Also, it is my honor to die here, *Trung si*. My worthless nephew disgraced me. Now I can wipe out that shame."

Wilburn took the Nung's hand. "Farewell, elder brother," he said in Nung Chinese.

"Farewell, younger brother," Bao replied.

The Nung turned and shouted an order. Five voices answered. He yelled his war cry and leaped to his feet. Firing the AK from his hip, he ran for the NVA positions. Five other Nungs rose and charged the enemy, too. The remaining Nungs doubled their fire to cover old Bao's last charge.

Momentarily stunned by the sudden assault, the NVA fire slackened.

"Fire!" Nguyen screamed, pulling his Tokarov pistol from his holster. "Fire!"

Bao almost reached the first of the NVA positions before they recovered. He dropped behind a tree as a burst of fire tore into the brush beside him. Changing magazines, he eased the muzzle of his assault rifle around the trunk. Fifteen meters in front of him, an NVA poked his head out of his hiding place to see if the Nung was still alive. Bao dropped him with a single shot.

By now, the other Nungs had joined him. Two of them were hit, one seriously. The badly wounded man took a grenade from his belt. Holding it firmly in his hand, he pulled the pin. Holding his submachine gun in his other hand, he got to his feet and with a shout of defiance charged straight at the NVA, firing as he ran. He took several hits, staggered and fell forward, throwing the grenade. When it exploded, NVA soldiers screamed and died.

Two more of the Nungs prepared to charge. Bao yelled for grenades. On his command, three sailed through the air. When they exploded with muffled crumps, the two Nungs leaped to their feet and charged, screaming.

AK fire cut one of them down in midstride. The other one dove into a nest of startled dinks. His AK sprayed a full thirty-round magazine into them before the bolt locked back on empty. With a savage cry, he dropped the useless weapon. He grabbed for his bayonet with one hand and a grenade with the other.

He slashed two of the NVA before they could fire at him. Spinning around, he jerked the pin out of the grenade just as he was hit in the chest. With the last of his strength, he tossed the frag at his killer. They both died instantly.

Bao increased his fire until the bolt on his AK-47 locked back on an empty magazine. He quickly checked his ammo pouches. They were empty. Dropping the rifle, he drew the K-Bar knife from the sheath on his belt. The heavy fighting knife had his name inscribed on the blade, and it had been a gift from Wilburn. He had killed many *cong* with it. It was good to die with such a weapon in his hand.

"*Cong* dogs," Bao shouted in Vietnamese. "I am Tran Van Bao, a warrior. I want to meet with your officer in honorable single combat with a blade."

"Barbarian!" Nguyen shouted from his position safely in the rear. "Imperialist lackey! What do you know of honor, mercenary? You wear the uniform of the long-nose barbarians and you fight for money."

Bao laughed. "I fight for my pleasure, *cong*, and the bones of my ancestors." He spat on the ground. "The bones of your ancestors were eaten by dogs."

"Nung dog," Nguyen screamed. "I will show you who my ancestors were."

"I know who your unhonorable ancestress was, dung eater," Bao taunted. "She took long-nose Frenchmen up her ass for a handful of rice. Then she washed them clean with her tongue. It is no wonder that you like the taste of Ho Chi Minh's shit."

"I will meet you, Nung," Nguyen screamed. "Prepare to die!"

He ripped a long-bladed machete from the pack of the man beside him and started into the open. He paused long enough to take the pistol from his holster and stuff it into the back of his belt.

"I am here, Nung," the NVA announced.

Bao stepped out from his tree, the K-Bar knife held low in his right hand. When he saw Nguyen's machete he whipped the cloth from around his neck and loosely wound it around his left forearm. With the longer reach of his opponent's weapon, he needed to get in close to use his knife. That meant that he had to stop the machete blade.

Nguyen saw Bao's smaller knife. With a cry of rage, he launched himself at the Nung, his arm sweeping the machete down in a powerful slash. Bao sidestepped the jungle knife and tried to slash the Vietnamese's arm, but he lacked the reach. He stepped back quickly, the knife held out in front of him.

"You said you wanted to fight," Nguyen sneered. "Why do you run away?"

Bao did not answer Nguyen's taunt. He circled him slowly, his eyes fixed on the eyes of his enemy.

"Come, Nung, I am waiting to kill you."

Bao saw the next attack in Nguyen's eyes and turned aside, but not in time. The long jungle knife sliced into the muscles of his upper left arm. He bit back the pain.

"You are an old man," Nguyen hissed. "This is no sport."

Bao had but one chance before the loss of blood weakened him. Shifting the knife down low, he sprang for the NVA, holding his bloodied left arm out as a shield. Nguyen recoiled, slashing the machete down in a defensive parry. The long blade bit deeply into Bao's shoulder, catching the bone. But the fighting knife in Bao's hands stabbed upward into Nguyen's lower belly and lodged in his breastbone.

Nguyen's belly opened and his wet guts poured out at his feet. He fumbled behind his back, reaching for the pistol.

Bao staggered backward, pulling at the machete in his shoulder. He tugged the blade free and swung it. Nguyen's Tokarov fired. The machete bit into the NVA's neck just as his pistol bullets hit the Nung in the chest. Both men fell to the ground.

Tran Van Bao felt life slowly leave his body. He turned his face up to the gentle rain. It had been a good life and if he was lucky, the next one would be even better. Wilburn's face remained in his mind.

"Until next time, *Trung si*," he murmured softly as he died.

CHAPTER 39

On the Song Boung

Only a few meters above the muddy brown water, the three Cobras flew flat out. They were so low and the twisting river was so narrow that their rotor tips almost touched the overhanging branches along the banks. The noise of their rotors reverberated from the jungle like the roll of a hundred kettle drums.

In the finest tradition of Custer's 7th Cav, Python Flight was coming to the rescue.

"Barn Door," Gaines radioed on ahead. "This is Lead, over."

"Barn Door, over." Miller answered over the sound of small-arms fire.

"This is Lead. You should be able to hear me now, over."

"I can't hear you yet . . .. Wait! Yes, thank God!" Miller's voice could not hide his relief.

Gaines flew around the next bend and the PBRs came into sight. "There they are, boys," he called to his gunships. "Let's do it!"

Gaines took the left bank, Warlokk the right, and Alphabet followed Gaines. With their first pass, guns, rockets, and thumpers hammered the jungle on each side of the Navy boats.When the sleek gunships wheeled around for another pass, they were more selective, choosing their targets with care.

Guided expertly by the two gunners, O'Leary and Tex, the 7.62mm minigun rounds and 40mm thumper grenades wreaked havoc among the NVA who had survived. Torn, bloodied bodies splashed into the water at the river's edge. After the second pass, hardly any of them fired at the boats anymore. Navy gunners carefully targeted and dropped the few NVA who were trying to flee into the jungle. Suddenly all was quiet.

The Cobras swooped down low over the boats, barely clearing the mastheads. Cheers broke out and the men waved their arms in victory.

"Python, this is Barn Door. Thanks, I think that's got it. But before we continue, I need to take a look at one of my boats. Can you keep an eye out for us if we stop here for a moment? Over."

"Python, Roger. You do what you have to do. Out."

While the choppers circled, Powers's engine man dove over the side of his boat. A minute later, he came to the surface with a mangled Vietnamese arm in his hand. It was the object that had been clogging the water jet.

"Python, this is Barn Door, we are getting underway again. Over."

"Python, Roger, let's do it. Dry Rock is waiting."

"Bao is dead now, *Trung si*," Salem, the Nung interpreter announced.

"I know."

"I think he kill *cong* captain." The interpreter smiled. "So he die happy."

For all his months in Nam, Wilburn still hadn't gotten used to the Nungs' cheerful view of death.

"I hope so," he said.

The NVA fire had halted for the duel. Now they wanted revenge, and the battle raged anew. Just then, the first of the PBRs rounded the last bend in the river and saw the Nungs at Wilburn's small beachhead. Its bow turret blasted the jungle on either side of them and the boat headed in for a landing.

"The boats, *Trung si*! They are here!" one of the Nungs shouted. Wilburn looked over his shoulder and saw the PBR put its bow into the bank. Gaines's' Cobra gunship flashed overhead, her nose turret blazing fire into the jungle.

"Pull back!" Wilburn shouted.

The NVA had seen the PBR, too, and immediately took it under fire. By this time, the other two boats had appeared and they stayed in midstream to cover the boat taking on men. The other two gunships flew in low, suppressing the enemy fire.

The Nungs scrambled on board, taking their wounded with them. As soon as the PBR was full to overflowing, it back-watered, and another one pulled in to take its place.

"Wilburn," someone shouted from the deck. "Get 'em moving! Hurry!"

"Go! Go! Go!" the Special Forces sergeant shouted to his men.

More Nungs scrambled on board, and the boat pulled away. Now only Wilburn and his command group were left on the shore. Even with the gunships and the PBRs firing everything they had, the NVA still tried their best to stop Wilburn from getting away.

The twin fifties hammered over their heads as the sergeant and his group dashed for the bank. The Nung next to Wilburn took a hit and stumbled. The American grabbed him and dragged him the last few feet to the water. Hands reached down and dragged them all on board. The boat began moving backward the instant the last man was hauled up over the side.

Wilburn lay on the wet deck for a moment staring up at the sky. He never thought that he would be so glad to see Swabbies in all his life.

Just as the last PBR was pulling away from the bank, Alphabet made one last run against the ridgeline to cover its withdrawal. In the front cockpit, Tex, his gunner, volleyed the last of the rockets into NVA positions. They exploded with blinding flashes.

Alphabet was so intent on bringing maximum smoke on the dinks that he forgot the cardinal rule of gunship tactics. Never overfly your target if you can help it. Always bank away from it.

As the Cobra swept down low past the ridgeline, an RPD machine gun opened up on him from his portside. He threw the gunship to the right to avoid the line of green tracer fire reaching up for them. His evasive action came too late.

He felt the airframe shudder as it took hits. In front of him, the gunner's canopy exploded in a shower of blood and plexiglass. His gunner slumped over his sight.

"Tex!" he yelled over the sudden blast of cold, wet air pouring into the cockpit. "Tex!"

There was no answer.

The pilot keyed his throat mike. "Lead, this is Alphabet. I've been hit. Tex is down and he doesn't look good. Over"

"This is Lead, can you make it back? Over."

Alphabet swept his eyes over his instruments. "I'm still in the green, Captain, so I'll try it alone."

"Roger, get on the Air Rescue net and alert them in case you go down. Head straight for the Dustoff pad. I'll call back and have the hospital standing by. Good luck, Joe. Out."

Alphabet banked gently and climbed for altitude. He didn't want to fly too high because of the cold air blowing in on his wounded gunner. He turned the cockpit heat control up to full blast. With most of the canopy gone, it wouldn't help much, but it might keep Tex from freezing to death before getting to the hospital.

Gaines watched the wounded bird fly off. After making a quick call to Chu Lai to alert the Dustoff pad, he got back to business. He and Warlokk still had to get the riverboats back through the gauntlet.

"Six Niner," he radioed. "This is Lead."

"This is Six Niner, go."

"Lead, what's your fuel and ordnance status? Over."

"Six Niner, not too good. My rockets are all gone but I've got a few thumper rounds and a little minigun left. Fuel is marginal to get back. Over."

"This is Lead, Roger. Jettison your empty pods. It'll help on your fuel, over."

Warlokk flipped the wing-stores jettison switch and the four rocketpods fell away. The Cobra instantly picked up speed, so he throttled back a little. If they didn't have to fight too much on the way back, he might have enough JP-4 to fly back to Chu Lai.

On the PBRs, Wilburn's wounded Nungs were taken below decks for safety. The medics frantically worked to stop the bleeding until they could be med-evaced. On deck, the grunts, the Nungs, and the sailors alike braced themselves for the run back down the river. This time, though, they had the Cobras overhead and the PBRs were running as fast as they could, their diesels bellowing.

The first few klicks were quiet after the beachhead, but that was to be expected. It would take a few minutes for the NVA to radio ahead to their other units that they were coming.

Powers's boat was in the lead again and he had most of Brody's people on board, as well as Wilburn and his Nung command group. The small PBR was filled to overflowing, but they had a lot of firepower on board.

Overhead, Gaines and Warlokk throttled back and flew as slowly as they could in a long, oval racetrack pattern over the boats. As soon as they searched a half a klick of riverbank ahead of the PBRs they flew back to do it over again.

"Python Lead," Miller called up to the choppers. "This is Barn Door. Over."

"Lead, go."

"Barn Door. You are approaching the ambush site, over."

"Roger, I see the sunken boat. Stay on your toes."

When the river narrowed at the site of the earlier battle, Gaines and Warlokk pulled into a tight orbit right over the boats.

The dinks hiding in the jungle had almost stopped the boats there the first time, and they were burning to try their luck with the PBRs again. They heard the choppers overhead, but they didn't pay them much attention. They had not been under fire from Cobras before and had not yet learned that they were a much different animal than the Hueys they were used to dealing with.

The boats were ready for them. The sailors were at their weapons and all the grunts were down behind the gunwales as the lead PBR rounded the bend into the killing zone. They didn't wait for the dinks to shoot first.

The fifty turret in Powers's boat started its deep-throated roar. Low on ammo, the gunner only sent short bursts into likely hiding places. Thinking that they had been spotted, the NVA opened up. It was a mistake.

Gaines and Warlokk had been waiting for muzzle flashes to zero in on, and now they had them. The two ships split up, each taking a side of the river. With the gunships hitting them from above and the fifties on the boats blasting them from head on, the NVA didn't have a chance. A few of the dinks launched sampans to cut the boats off again.They lasted all of twenty or thirty seconds before the Cobras caught them leaving their camouflaged hiding places and turned them into bloody hamburger with a couple of quick squirts of minigun fire.

In only a few seconds, the patrol boats were past the narrows and the ambush was over. Only a few bodies floating on the water gave any sign that the PBRs had even been that way again.

With Gaines and Warlokk circling protectively over-head, the three heavily laden PBRs continued down the river, making it back to Patrol Base Zulu without further interruption. When Gaines saw that they were safely within sight of the docks, he called down to Miller.

"Barn Door, this is Python Lead. Patch me through to my Blue Six element. Over."

There was a short pause before Alexander answered. "Python, this is Blue Six, go."

"This is Lead, I've got your Dustoffs on the way, but we've got to head back to the barn, we're bingo fuel. You might want to know that Alphabet and his gunner got back safely.Over."

"This is Six, glad to hear that they made it. Thanks for your assistance. Over."

"This is Lead, no sweat GI. Out."

"This is Six, have a safe trip home. Out."

The men on the boats cheered and waved as the two gunships banked away for the trip back to Chu Lai.

CHAPTER 40

Patrol Base Zulu

An anxious reception committee was waiting for the three battered PBRs when they tied up at the dock. The medics, both the Navy's and the Blues', swarmed on board to see to the wounded. Litter parties were hurriedly formed to carry them to the chopper pad to await the arrival of Dustoffs that would speed them to the hospital at Chu Lai.

After the wounded had been cleared out, the men wearily stepped onto dry land. Wilburn immediately got on the horn to Kontum with a request for transportation back to his camp.

When he had placed his call, the Special Forces sergeant sat quietly and stared out over the river. Old Bao was finally gone and he hadn't even been able to recover his body. Five other good men had gone with him, making a total of seven when he counted Cowboy. It had been an expensive mission. He hoped that it had not all been for nothing.

"PJ."

Wilburn looked up and saw Brody standing in front of him. "Yeah, man."

"You okay?"

"Yeah. I'm just tired."

"You guys got hit pretty hard out there."

A look of pain passed over Wilburn's fatigued eyes. "Yeah, we did," he admitted. "I just hope it was all worth it."

"Can I get you a beer or a Coke?"

"No, thanks, but I do think I'll make myself a cup of coffee before our ride gets here." He dug into the bottom of his ruck and came out with a packet of C-ration instant coffee.

"God! Don't drink that shit, PJ," Brody said. "The Sea Bees always have a fresh pot going. Come on, I'll get you some."

"That sounds great." Wilburn almost smiled as he got to his feet. "I could sure use a little real coffee right now."

"Actually," Brody laughed, "It's more like paint remover. But it's hot and it's so strong it'll make the hair on your head stand up."

Wilburn laughed. "Sounds like my kind of coffee, the shit that Captain Ringer makes."

While Brody and Wilburn went off in search of the Sea Bees' coffeepot, York was once again trying to figure out how he was going to get his young ass out of the grunt outfit.

The trip up the river had been the absolute last straw as far as he was concerned. Suicide missions were insane. He wasn't about to get himself killed over shit like that. There had to be something else he could do while he was serving his time in the Army. Something far away from places like this.

He decided to go have a serious talk with the lieutenant about getting a job in the rear somewhere. He knew that there was no use in his trying to talk to the platoon sergeant about it, but Alexander had to have a college degree. Coming from one college man to another, York was certain the officer would understand that the Blues just wasn't any place for a man of his skill and talents. The lieutenant didn't look like he was busy with anything, so York walked up to him.

"Do you have a minute, sir?"

"Sure, York. What's on your mind?"

"Well, sir, I was thinking about what I've been doing here and I think that I might be of more use to the unit back in the battalion headquarters."

"Oh? How's that?"

"Well, sir . . ." York immediately launched into a long recitation of his college-trained administrative talents and skills.

Alexander listened to him with a tight smile on his face.

"That's all very well and good," Alexander said when York had finally finished. "But you've got one little problem here."

"What's that, sir?"

"Your MOS. You're a One One Bush, a field grunt, not a Remington Raider."

"But, sir, surely with my college experience I'm better qualified to do clerical work than many of the people you already have doing it right now." It was not going at all the way York wanted it to.

"No doubt you are," Alexander said with a big grin. "But in its infinite wisdom, the United States Army called upon you to fulfill your obligation to your country as a grunt. And thousands of dollars have already been spent training you to do that job."

"But, sir, I thought that a person could switch his MOS."

"Yes, they can."

York's face lit up until Alexander quickly added, "In certain instances and only in certain MOS. It just so happens that in your MOS, you can become a One One Charlie or Delta, or some other combat MOS, but not a clerk-typist."

"I see," York said. It was obvious from the smile on the lieutenant's face that he wasn't interested in York's problem. The grunt decided there was no point in wasting his breath. "Thank you for your time, sir." His voice was lifeless.

"Oh, not at all. Other than that, how're you settling into the unit?"

"Just fine, sir, just fine." Without another word, York turned and walked off.

Alexander made a mental note to himself to have Zack keep a close eye on the guy. It was beginning to look like he was nothing but trouble for the platoon. Alexander knew that Zack and Brody could keep his young ass in line. He wasn't so positive, however, that they could ever make a decent grunt out of him.

Colonel Tran stood and stared at the map on his wall. It was obvious to him now that the Yankee riverboat base had to be destroyed. He should have seen to that after the first attack had failed. But he had so much on his mind that he had allowed it to take second place to the preparations for the offensive. Once again the riverboats had proved to be a real thorn in his side. They absolutely had to go.

He studied his unit movement orders carefully and consulted the map. There was an infantry battalion on the march a few kilometers to the north of the river. He could divert them, have them make a river crossing to the west of the base, and send them into the assault early the next morning. When they had eliminated the Yankees, they could be sent back to their original route and would have only lost a day's time.

Tran quickly wrote out the necessary attack orders and called for his orderly and handed him the message. "See that this is sent out immediately."

The NVA colonel need not have wasted the time and effort to bring further pressure to bear on Patrol Base Zulu. The Navy Riverine Command in Da Nang had already decided that the remote Patrol Base Zulu had become more trouble than it was worth. It had already cost them two PBRs. Several more were damaged and there were not enough spare boats available to reinforce them.

The decision was made to pull the surviving PBRs out immediately and reassign them to the Perfume River at Hue. This news was greeted with cheers by the men at Zulu. None of them, neither the grunts nor the Swabbies, had really liked being stuck so far out in the sticks. The Blues were particularly glad to be going back to what they knew best, motoring around in the sky in their choppers, looking for dinks to waste.

The PBR sailors warmed at the thought of being in a regular Navy facility with hot chow, warm showers, clean racks, and people who spoke their language. Life with the Air Cav grunts had gotten just a little too crazy, even for sailors of the Brown Water Navy. There was no doubt that they were good men, but they were just a little too *dinky-dau.*

The only people at Zulu who did not greet the decision with great enthusiasm were Kasnowski and his Sea Bees. After having busted their asses to build the patrol base, they now had to tear it down in less time than they had spent putting it up. They were philosophical about it. After all, this was the Nam.

As soon as he got the word, Kasnowski went looking for Lieutenant Alexander. If he was going to effectively dismantle this place in just two days, he needed some help from the Army. High-explosive help.

"You're going to do what?" Alexander said in complete disbelief.

"Yes, sir, the fastest way to level this place is to blow everything up. We can roll up the wire and slit all the sandbags, but it'll take too long to dismantle those bunkers, sir. We built 'em to last."

"You got a point there," Alexander agreed. "Give me a list of what you need and I'll pass it on to my supply people."

"Yes, sir, I can do that right now. "

Kasnowski sat down on the sandbagged blast wall. Taking out his demolition reference card, he started figuring how many two-and-a-half-pound blocks of military TNT and C-4 he needed to completely destroy everything. The point of the exercise was to see that nothing was left for the dinks to reuse.

"Here it is, sir," the Sea Bee said when he was finished.

Alexander looked at the long list of C-4, dynamite, det cord, blasting caps, and detonators.

"Jesus, you got enough stuff here to start a major war."

Kasnowski grinned broadly. "That's the general idea, sir. To make this place look like it's been through a B-52 raid."

"It'd be a hell of a lot easier just to call in an Arc Light strike, a few seven-hundred-fifty-pound bombs in the right places should do it quite nicely."

"I've seen that done, too," the Sea Bee said. "But, we still have to go in afterward and make sure that they did the job. It's actually quicker and much easier to do it this way."

"Okay, I'll call this in and see how fast they can get it to us."

"Well, it'll take at least four hours for my guys to rig all of the bunkers, so we'll have to have it as soon as possible if we're going to make it out of here on time tomorrow."

"I'll tell them to put a hustle on it."

"Thanks a lot, sir."

"No sweat, Kasnowski, anything to help. Also," the lieutenant added with a grin, "I like a little explosives demonstration as much as anyone else."

"Well, sir, I can promise that you'll really get your money's worth outta this one."

Harvard was at his wit's end. Emptying sandbags that he had filled just a few days ago was the most idiotic waste of time he had ever heard of.

"Why don't we just leave them here?" he asked.

"Harvard, for the last fucking time" — Brody's voice was weary — "Will you just fucking do it and quit bitching, for Christ's sake?"

"But it doesn't make any sense."

"It doesn't have to," Brody exploded. "Jesus! Can't you get that through your thick fucking head? Nothing here makes any fucking sense. You just do it and shut the fuck up about it."

CHAPTER 41

Patrol Base Zulu

The first hint that the grunts were going to have some uninvited help that morning to tear down the patrol base came when they heard the distant dull cough of NVA 82mm mortar rounds leaving their tubes.

"Incoming!" someone screamed shrilly.

The grunts raced for the bunkers on the perimeters. On the docks, the PBR sailors looked around, not realizing what was going on until the first round hit with a dull crump. Then they flew to their posts, fired up the boat engines, and cast off for the safety of open water.

The Sea Bees either raced for the shelter of the bunkers or dove under the bulldozer. Kasnowski, however, ran for the Blues' CP. "Ell tee!" he yelled. "The bunkers! They're rigged for demo!"

Alexander looked stunned. "Oh, fuck!"

He had totally forgotten the explosives. So had his men. The bunkers' timbers had been packed with TNT and C-4 so they could be blown up as the Americans withdrew from

Patrol Base Zulu. If an enemy round hit in the wrong place, the bunkers were going to blow with the men inside.

"We've got to pull the blasting caps!" Kasnowski yelled over the explosions as a second volley of 82mm rounds impacted. Alexander zipped up his flak vest and grabbed his steel pot. "Let's go," he shouted.

On his way out, he turned to Bunny. "Get the artillery going!" he yelled. "And call Gaines!"

As Alexander and Kasnowski dashed out of the CP bunker, Bunny reached for the other radio and switched it over to the Python Push while he waited for the artillery FDC to plot their targets.

"Python, Python, this is Blue Six Tango, come in."

"This is Python Control," came the voice of the radio operator back at Chu Lai. "Send it."

"This is Six Tango. We're under attack and need help ASAP. Over."

"This is Python Control, what kind of attack? Over."

"Dinks, you asshole," Bunny screamed. "Fucking dinks. Tell Rat to get his ass up here or we're fucking finished. Out."

He slammed the handset down and picked up the one to the artillery again. That was all he needed right now, some shithead RTO who didn't understand English. "Fuckin' REMFs!" he growled.

Gaines was in his office next to the radio room when Bunny's frantic call came in. Over the loudspeakers, he heard the dull crump of the NVA mortar rounds in the background. He jumped to his feet and ran into the pilots' ready room.

"Let's get it, boys!" he yelled. "All guns to Zulu! Move it!"

The pilots and gunners scrambled to their feet and raced for the door.

" 'Rat' now!" Gaines shouted after them.

There was no showy Python Flight formation takeoff that day. As soon as a gunship had her rotors turning, she lifted into the air and headed to the northwest.

With their 82mm mortars still firing over their heads, the NVA infantry came boiling out of the tree line, screaming and firing as they ran. They had a greater distance to cover because the Sea Bees had bulldozed the wood line back. But they also didn't have to worry about the mines and claymores that had been emplaced at the edge of the wire. The grunts had taken most of them up in anticipation of leaving the next morning.

RPD machine guns opened up from the flanks and RPG rocket launchers sent their deadly little rockets slamming into the bunkers and wire. The lead element of the enemy assault carried long tubes-full of explosives, bangalore torpedoes designed to slide under the concertina wire to blow clear lanes in it.

The defensive fire took its toll on the sappers with the bangalores. One NVA disappeared in a bloody spray when a burst of M-16 fire hit the explosives he was carrying. But with the claymores gone from the wire, enough of the sappers survived to emplace their deadly torpedoes. The charges exploded, throwing dirt and fragments of wire into the air. When the smoke cleared, the wire in front of the bunkers was gone. The road was wide open for them to storm the camp.

Harvard was only halfway to the bunker when the ground attack started. He slid to a halt behind a bale of unused sandbags. If the gooks were attacking the bunkers, there was no sense in him getting trapped inside with the rest of those fools.

Another man who had been caught out in the open raced for a bunker. A burst of AK fire cut one of his legs out from under him, and he went down. Dragging his bloodied leg behind him, the wounded man crawled on his belly for the bunker door and dove inside.

Suddenly Harvard had an idea that completely shut out the havoc going on around him. He had just seen one way to get out of his situation. A wound. That would get him at least into a hospital. Once he was there, he should be able to find something to do in the rear.

He knew that a bullet in the leg would hurt like hell, but he had just seen a wounded man scramble to safety, so it couldn't be all that bad. York knew that he couldn't depend on the NVA to give him the kind of wound he wanted, so he decided to shoot himself in the leg. In the heat of battle, no one would ever know.

He pulled back on the charging handle to his M-16 and placed the muzzle against the middle of his thigh, aiming for the muscles along the top of his leg. He took up the trigger slack and fired.

Unfortunately, York had never learned what his instructors had tried to teach him back in Basic. He didn't believe what they had told him about the destructive power of the small, high-velocity 5.56mm round that the M-16 fired. As far as he was concerned, all those tall tales about a sixteen bullet deflecting in the body when it hit a bone was just the Army's own version of ghost stories, told to frighten impressionable trainees. He was wrong.

And instead of squeezing the trigger slowly, as he'd been taught, he jerked it instead. Pulling the muzzle of his rifle out of line with the flesh of his leg, the round entered at an acute angle. After tearing through the muscle, it hit the thigh bone and deflected. Traveling down the length of the bone, it entered under his kneecap, blew it off, and shattered the top of his lower leg. With the storm of fire in the background, no one heard the terrible scream of agony as York destroyed his left leg.

Brody, however, had seen everything. He was just about to yell at him to get into the bunker when the man pulled the trigger. He winced when York's leg disappeared in a bloody spray. He grabbed the grenades and got back to the front of the bunker. He'd never seen anyone blow their own leg off. The stupid bastard could bleed to death, for all Brody cared.

By this time, the first of the artillery rounds had started falling. Bunny had called for a mix of airburst VT fusing and regular ground burst on the 105mm howitzer rounds. The combination was spectacular as the first volley fell in the open area in front of the perimeter. The VT airburst rounds sent hundreds of red-hot, razor-sharp steel shards slicing down into the NVA. The ground bursts blew them to screaming bloody shreds.

It didn't stop the North Vietnamese assault, though. Their orders were to take the camp at any costs.

"Red Leg Five Niner, this is Blue Six Tango," Bunny radioed to the artillery FDC. "Repeat range, right five zero, fire for effect."

"Six Tango, this is Five Niner. Roger."

In the bunkers, the grunts faced an unending horde of screaming NVA. With the claymores gone and holes blown in the wire, the gooks were swarming all over them. Corky's M-60 barrel started smoking as he laid down on the trigger. "Ammo!" he yelled to Farmer.

Two-Step's shotgun roared repeatedly, its blasts echoing in the confines of the bunker. He dropped down below the aperture to stuff more shells into the magazine and racked back on the slide to chamber a round. When he came back up, his first round blasted an NVA trying to push a bangalore torpedo into the bunker. The steel balls blew him in half.

Gardner calmly fired the last of his thumper rounds and saw a gook disappear when the 40mm round hit him in the chest. He dropped the thumper and grabbed his M-16. The gooks were so close now that the grenade launcher wasn't much use anyway.

While the battle raged, Kasnowski and Alexander ran for the bunkers to defuse the demolition charges. The Sea Bees had placed the explosives in the middle of the roof timbers. The two men clambered onto the top of the first bunker just as the NVA hit the outer wire.

Lying flat on his belly, Alexander fired at the swarming NVA while Kasnowski ripped the firing wires and detonators out of the explosive blocks. "I got this one, sir," he yelled.

The Sea Bee and Alexander dove off the backside of the roof to cover. The next bunker was twenty feet away and swarming with gooks. Alexander laid down a base of fire, ripping off short bursts from his sixteen. "Hit it!" he screamed.

The two men jumped from cover and dashed for the rear of the next bunker, firing as they ran.

They had only two more steps to go when Kasnowski stumbled and fell. Alexander reached down and grabbed him by the shirt, dragging him the last few feet to safety. "You okay?" he asked.

There was a rapidly growing wet, red patch on Kasnowski's fatigue pants. "I'm fine," he panted, feeling the wound. The bullet had passed completely through his leg. "Let's go."

Alexander gave Kaz a boost to the roof and climbed up after him. When the explosives were defused, Alexander dropped down off the back of the roof first and gave Kasnowski a hand down. "How's the leg?"

"Okay," the Sea Bee panted. "Let's go."

Alexander covered Kaz with a sustained burst of 5.56mm fire as the Sea Bee limped cross the open ground to the next bunker. When Kaz was safe, he slammed a fresh magazine into the rifle and dashed across himself. Just as he dove for cover, he felt a bullet hit, and his foot instantly went numb.

He looked down in panic, expecting to see a stump. The round had only taken off his bootheel. It was the shock that had stung his foot. "Let's go!" he yelled.

Kasnowski pulled himself onto the roof and was reaching for the detonators just as a Chi-Com grenade sailed through the air and landed on top of the bunker. Without thinking, the Sea Bee lashed out with his foot and kicked it over the side. The stick grenade had barely cleared the roof when it exploded. The concussion knocked the Kaz over the back of the bunker. He landed on the ground with a heavy thud.

Alexander rushed to his side. "You okay?"

Kaz looked up with surprise on his face. "I think I broke my fucking arm," he said just before passing out.

Gaines's *Sudden Discomfort,* along with Warlokk's and Alphabet's Cobras, had gotten well ahead of the pack by the time they reached the Song Boung River. Gaines banked sharply to the left to fly the last few klicks up to Zulu and got on the horn to the base. "Blue Six, Blue Six, this is Python Lead. Over."

"This is Six Tango, go," Bunny answered.

"This is Lead, I am on station, ready to roll. Cut off the arty so we can come in. Over."

"This is Six Tango, wait one. Out."

The FO was back on the air in just a moment. "Lead, this is Tango, Willie Peter is the last round, then you're clear, over."

Gaines rogered and waited for the burst of white smoke in the air that would signal the artillery's last round. Then it was time for him and the boys to get to work. From his low orbit to the north, he saw the gooks charging the wire. It was going to be a good day for a Cobra party.

The white phosphorus artillery shell exploded over the camp, and Rat keyed his throat mike. "Python Snakes, this is Lead. Let's go get 'em, boys."

With Gaines leading the pack, the three Cobras dropped out of the sky one right after the other. In the front cockpit of *Sudden Discomfort,* O'Leary played his firing controls like a master. The turret swung from side to side, spraying 7.62mm rounds and 40-mike-mike grenades like a garden hose spraying water. H.E. rockets shot out of the stub-wing pods in pairs as Gaines brought the ship in on a gentle curve over the perimeter. When he pulled out of his firing run, War-lokk's ship was right behind him, ready to start his.

The NVA were so stunned by the artillery that by the time the Cobras were overhead, they didn't even try to shoot back. It was a slaughter.

"Lead, this is the Hog Driver," came the call on Rat's chopper-to-chopper radio frequency. "We're on station now. Over."

"Roger, Hogs." Gaines looked over his shoulder and saw the five-ship Huey Hog heavy-fire team. They had finally caught up with the much faster Cobras. "Go to work in the wood line. Over."

"Hog driver, Roger, out."

While the Cobras concentrated on the gooks who were storming the wire, the Hogs dropped down. Flying parallel to the perimeter, they started hammering on the rest of the NVA battalion still hiding in the jungle. One of the Hog drivers saw the muzzle flash of an 82mm mortar and lined it up in his gunsight. Triggering his 2.75-inch rocketpods, he sent half a dozen H.E. rockets racing for the mortar position. One of them detonated in the mortar ammunition stockpile, and it went up with a blinding flash.

The concussion of the exploding mortar shells rocked the Huey in the air as it flew over the VC gun pits. The explosion also took out three other mortar tubes and their crews.

Another Hog spotted the NVA battalion command group and opened up on it. The rockets, 40-mike grenades and minigun rounds turned that little part of the jungle into a killing ground. When he flew past it, nothing was left but a smoking hole in the ground.

Now that the gunships were on station, turning gooks into carrion, the assaulting waves of NVA infantry faltered under the intense, unrelenting fire. The grunts in the bunkers didn't let up on the dinks, either. Everywhere the NVA turned, they were slaughtered. Two of the Cobras came down again, this time side by side less than fifty feet off of the ground, spitting death. The surviving NVA turned and bolted back for the jungle.

CHAPTER 42

Patrol Base Zulu

With the gunships chasing the remnants of the shattered NVA battalion farther back into the jungle, the Americans started crawling out of their bunkers to see how badly they had been hurt.

They had gotten away with very little damage this time. Because the first mortar rounds had given them enough warning to take cover before the infantry attacked, everyone had gotten to a bunker in time. Bunny's artillery shoot had thinned the gooks out quite a bit before they got to the wire, and Gaines's gunships had shown up in time to finish them off.

In fact, Patrol Base Zulu had gotten off very lightly, indeed. Only six men had been wounded and the worst of them was Harvard. York had nearly bled to death by the time the medics were able to get to him. His leg wound was so bad that all they could do was shoot him full of morphine and slap him on the first Dustoff chopper that came in for an emergency medevac.

Kasnowski had come to by the time the fighting ended. The medics put his broken arm in a sling and bandaged his leg while he talked to his sidekick, Peanut, giving him detailed instructions about how to rerig the explosive charges on the bunkers.

"Goddamnit, Kaz," Peanut complained. "We just got done rigging everything before you and that ell tee went and fucked it all up."

"I know, I know," Kaz agreed with him. "But we had to do it, so now you have to do it all over again."

"Okay, Okay." Peanut walked off in the direction of the bunkers muttering to himself.

The other four wounded men had suffered only minor hits and went out on a routine evac with the second Dustoff.

As soon as the Dustoffs had cleared the pad, the men got back to work preparing for their departure. The last North Vietnamese assault was the final insult for the Navy command and they requested that the Air Cav help them pull out immediately. With the recent damage to both boats and the base, there was no need to delay the planned departure of the PBRs by even another day. Zulu had proved to be a very expensive failure.

The Cav was all too willing to oblige. Zulu was tying up too many of their resources as well. They quickly dispatched a small fleet of the big twin rotor CH-47 Chinook cargo choppers to transport everything out that was salvageable.

While Peanut and his assistant rewired the demolition charges, the other Sea Bees ran their bulldozer down the length of the perimeter to tear up the wire so it couldn't be reused. While they did that, the grunts carried stockpiled construction materials and supplies out to the waiting Chinooks. As soon as one of the big choppers was loaded, it took off and another one came in to take its place.

While this was going on, the sailors rigged their boats to be lifted out on sling loads, one PBR per Chinook, for the long trip back to Hue. When the Sea Bees were done with their little bulldozer, it, too, was readied for a chopper ride out. After several hours of backbreaking work, everything was ready and the last five Chinooks came in. The first one hovered over a PBR and a heavy cargo sling was lowered down from its belly. The sailors quickly hooked the chopper's sling to their rigging and jumped off the boat.

Slowly, the Chinook pilot pulled his pitch and the patrol boat rose from the muddy river, water dripping from its hull. As soon as it was a couple of hundred feet up in the air, the chopper turned and headed away to the east. A second one took its place, hovering over the docks, ready to haul out the next PBR.

When the boats were gone, one more Chinook lifted the bulldozer, and a last one landed to take on the Navy men. Only Brody's people and two Sea Bees were left on the ground. Peanut and an assistant had stayed behind to make certain that the demo charges went off. If they didn't explode, Brody's squad would have to guard them while they tried to fix whatever had gone wrong with the fuses.

As soon as they got word that Gabe was on the final approach to pick them up, Peanut set the timer for the explosion.

"This had better fucking work," Brody said, walking out to the clearing to wait for Gabe's slick. "I don't even want to have to come back down here to fix a fuse that didn't work."

"Oh, they'll go, all right," Peanut grinned. "I double-fused everything and wired all of the charges together with det cord. If even one of them blows, the whole thing will go off."

With one of Gaines's gunships flying escort, Gabe flared out for a landing and the men scrambled into the back of the Huey. The pilot pulled pitch and was back up in the air in seconds.

Gabe flew in a tight circle a quarter-mile away from the base. If they were any closer than that, there was a real danger of their being knocked out of the sky by the explosion.

Peanut sat in the open door with the grunts, his eyes riveted on his wristwatch. "Thirty seconds," he said, almost to himself, as he counted down. "Twenty-five . . . twenty . . ."

The grunts waited in anxious anticipation. There was something about the incredible power of hundreds of pounds of explosives going off all at once that held a terrible fascination for almost everyone.

"Four . . . three . . . two . . . one!"

The ground leaped into the air, and billowing clouds of red-and-black flame erupted from the bunkers. The concussion hit the slick with a dull thump and slammed it sideways in the air. Gabe fought to control the machine.

"Jesus," Farmer said in hushed awe. "Will you look at that!"

Half of a twelve-by-twelve roof timber sailed through the air, spinning over and over before it landed in the river with a muddy splash. More debris showered down, beating the water to a foamy brown froth.

The smoke of the explosions slowly cleared, revealing a scene of complete devastation. Kasnowski had placed his charges well. Nothing was left of Patrol Base Zulu except for firewood. And the gooks were welcome to it.

On the open ground beyond the perimeter, the blasted bodies of the North Vietnamese dead lay in the mud. Their weapons had all been collected and hauled back to Chu Lai, but no attempt had been made to bury the bodies. They could rot where they lay.

"Well, that's that," Gabe called back to Brody. "Let's go home."

"You got that shit right."

As the chopper banked away from the flight back to Chu Lai, not one man on board was sorry to be leaving Riverine Patrol Base Zulu forever.

"Jesus Christ, does this place ever look good!" Farmer sighed as he looked around at the muddy, rain-soaked Echo Company area at Firebase Lasher. It didn't look like much had changed at the small firebase while they had been gone. Except, of course, that which had been dust when they had left had now been turned into well-churned, red mud that clung to their boots with every step through it.

"Man, I never thought I'd be so glad to see this fucking dump again."

Gardner laughed. "Just goes to show you, Farmer. Things aren't ever so bad that they can't get just a little bit worse."

"That's a fucking fact." Farmer took a deep breath and smelled himself. "Jesus, do I ever need a shower! I smell like I died!"

"You got that shit right, *amigo,*" Corky laughed. "But you're going to have to beat me to it."

"You troops better get your shit squared away first," Zack ordered, stepping out of the company first sergeant's tent. "Just because you're back in civilization, it don't mean that you can start lying dead on me now. Besides," he added with a big grin, "you boys got bunker guard tonight anyway."

"Aw, Sarge," Farmer moaned. "Give us a break."

"Don't bitch at me, troop." Zack pointed over to the company bulletin board. "Take it up with the company commander. He's the man who signed the guard roster, not me."

The platoon sergeant looked around. "Any of you guys seen Brody?"

"No, Sarge," Farmer said. "Not since we unassed the choppers."

"I saw him headed over to the hospital area," Two-Step said. "I think he was going to visit that Sea Bee, Kasnowski."

"Well, as soon as you see him, tell him I need to talk to him."

"Will do, Sarge."

"One last thing, boys," Zack said, looking straight at Farmer. "Nobody goes into the ville for the next couple of days."

"Hey, what's the deal, Sarge?" Farmer asked. He had been looking forward to a little mini R and R at one of the local bars, a few beers, and a little boom-boom in the back room with one of the girls.

"Sorry 'bout that, troop. MACV's called a truce for the gook New Year, Tet, as it's called."

"Truce? You mean like stop the war?"

"Yeah, a cease-fire. The dinks aren't supposed to shoot at us for two days and we aren't going to shoot at them."

"Well, I wasn't planning on nobody getting killed in no bar, Sarge." Farmer grinned. " 'Less of course the girls start fighting over who's going to have the pleasure of taking me back to her room."

"Give me a fucking break, Farmer," Corky groaned.

"And, Farmer," Zack cautioned. "I'd better not find your young ass missing when I go looking for you, boy. You're gonna stay right here with the rest of us."

"Okay, Sarge." Farmer put up his hands. "Okay, I hear you." The young grunt turned to Lindberry. "Hey, Strawberry, you don't happen to play poker, do you?" No one on the Blues played cards with Farmer anymore because he won too often. He was always on the lookout for fresh meat, and the new man seemed like a good candidate.

Strawberry slowly smiled. "I've played a couple hands now and then."

"Great!" Farmer grinned. "Since we can't go nowhere, how 'bout a little game tonight?"

"Your cards or mine?"

Farmer laughed. "Mine, of course. I'll get a couple of the Red Legs lined up for it too."

"I don't care what color their legs are, just as long as their money's green."

Farmer grinned. "It is, brother, believe me."

Brody found Kasnowski in good spirits despite the fact that his left arm was in a cast all the way from his elbow to his shoulder.

"No big deal," the Sea Bee said with a gold-toothed grin. "It's a clean break. It's going to take more than this to get me outta here."

"How's the leg?"

"Oh, that one hardly even counts." He stuck his right leg out to show a bandage around his thigh. "Bullet wound, through and through, like they wrote in my chart. All it did was eat up a little meat. I'll be outta here in a couple of days, go on up to China Beach for a little recuperation R and R. Do you know that they've got real round-eyes up there? Red Cross and USO girls."

"Sounds like rough duty."

"It is, believe me."

The Kaz looked down the ward to an empty bunk at the end. "You know that guy who was in your squad, the college boy?"

"York?"

"Yeah." Kasnowski shook his head. "They said he's going to lose his leg."

"That stupid fuck," Brody said, his face grim. "Any asshole who'd do something like that, I ain't got no sympathy for him. None at all. Nobody in their right mind shoots themselves, much less with an M-16. He deserves anything he gets."

"I guess it did a real job on his leg. Blew off the whole kneecap."

"That's the thing about a sixteen round." Brody was something of an expert on 5.56mm wounds. "It's so light that when it hits a bone, it'll bounce off it and travel, tearing up everything along the way. He probably thought that he was going to get a clean wound and get out of the field. You know, I'll bet he flinched when he pulled the trigger. It'd hard not to if you were shooting yourself. The round traveled down his thigh bone and really tore his leg up from the inside out. I could see that when we put him on the Dustoff."

Kaz shook his head in disgust. "Simple-minded bastard. It just don't make any sense for a man to do something like that."

"Only if you're a real dumb fuck."

"You going to report it?" Kaz asked.

Brody thought for a moment. "No. If I do that they'll give him a dishonorable discharge for a self-inflicted wound. He's got enough problems right now, as it is."

"Man, that is sure one fucked-up dude."

"Yeah," Brody agreed. "The Nam can do that to you sometimes."

CHAPTER 43

Chu Lai

The door to the small Chu Lai officers' club flew open with a bang. Lisa looked up and was startled to see Rick Kasnowski walk in. He stopped, looked around the smoke-filled room, spotted her standing at the bar, and sauntered over. "They told me that I might find you here," he said with a smile.

"What in the world are you doing here?" she asked, recovering from her surprise.

"My brother's in the hospital here, so I hopped a flight to come up and see him. I'm heading back tonight on the late flight."

"Is your brother okay?"

"He'll be fine," Rick said, running his eyes over her. "He just got nicked."

"I didn't know that you had a brother."

Kasnowski grinned wickedly. "There's a lot you don't know about me. But I guess that we didn't really have too much time for talking that night, did we?"

Lisa blushed and looked down at the floor. "No, I guess we didn't."

Just then, Rat Gaines came back from a short trip out back to tap a kidney. Lisa looked over at him in panic. "Oh, Rick," she said quickly, "there's someone here I want you to meet."

Kasnowski saw a short, stocky captain wearing a flight suit and a yellow ascot at the throat walk up to the bar. From the way the pilot was looking at him, Kaz knew that this was the competition. Maybe even Lisa's steady interest. It was time for Kasnowski to tuck his horns in.

"Rat," Lisa said hurriedly, "I'd like you to meet Rick Kasnowski."

Kasnowski smiled and put out his hand. "They call me the Kaz."

Gaines took it. "I'm Rat Gaines," he said.

The two men studied each other for a moment and tested their grip like two schoolboys.

"I met Rick on my last trip to Nha Trang," Lisa quickly explained. "He commands a mercenary unit down there."

Rat glanced down at the pocket patch that the Kaz wore on his fatigue jacket, a Chinese dragon in white and green with the yellow and red stripes of the Vietnamese flag superimposed on it.

"We're CIDG, actually," he explained. "Nungs. We work for Fifth Group Special Forces and guard the basecamp down there."

"What brings you all the way up here?"

"My brother got hit and I wanted to visit him."

Rat's ears perked up. "Is he a Sea Bee, by any chance?"

"Yes, he is. Do you know him?"

"As a matter of fact, I do," Gaines explained. "He was on a mission with my people when he got hit. How's he doing anyway?"

"He just got scratched. He'll be okay in a couple of days."

"I'm glad to hear that, he's a good man." Gaines turned to the bartender. "Can I buy you a drink?"

"I was just about to buy Lisa one."

"Oh, I'll take care of that." Gaines said casually, locking eyes with Kasnowski.

Kasnowski figured as much. "I'll have a gin and tonic," he told Gaines, his voice calm. You won some, and you lost some, he reminded himself. It was fun while it lasted with Lisa, and he couldn't blame himself for trying.

While Rat ordered for all of them, Lisa frantically tried to think of a way out of this mess. Running into Kasnowski in Chu Lai was absolutely the last thing in the world she had ever thought of happening. She was thrilled to see him again, but not at the expense of getting Rat pissed off about it. Especially when things were going so well between them again. Her night on the beach with Rick had been fantastic, like something out of a movie. At the time, she had really needed it. The night was etched in her mind as the most erotic one of her life. But she had been around long enough to know that one-night stands were never more than just that.

She valued her relationship with Rat Gaines and she didn't want anything to ever come between them. This was a dangerous situation. Rat was no fool. From the way Rick had looked at her, Gaines had to know that there was something between them.

Rat turned around with the drinks. They all sipped in strained silence. Kaz felt that as the interloper, it was his place to speak up first. "I see that you're a pilot," he said to Gaines.

Rat saw the olive branch and took it. "Yeah, I run an Air Cav company here. Echo Company, First of the Seventh Cav."

Kasnowski saw the big colored patch on the right breast of Rat's Nomex suit with its embroidered motto, Python Flight. You call, We Maul.

"Gunships?" he asked.

"Right. We're converting to Cobras right now, so we're running half Snakes and half Huey Hogs."

"Sounds like fun."

317

Rat grinned. "It's got its moments, but most of the time it is, believe me." Now it was Rat's turn. "What's this unit you've got?" he asked, looking at the First Logistical Command patch on the shoulder of Kasnowski's jungle fatigues.

Rick saw his glance and explained. "It's kind of a weird setup. I'm carried on the books of First Log Command, but my people are all part of the Special Forces CIDG program. Our job is to guard that big logistical camp in Nha Trang. First Log doesn't have any grunts to defend themselves, so they borrowed us from Fifth Group."

"Sounds like a fun situation."

"Not really. First Log is the biggest bunch of REMFs in-country and most of the time it's a real gold-plated bitch trying to work with 'em or to get anything out of them."

"Where'd you meet Lisa?" Gaines's tone was casual, but his eyes didn't blink as they locked on Kasnowski's.

The Kaz took a deep breath. "Well, I was in La Frigate, a French restaurant downtown, and I saw her sitting at the bar. It looked like she was by herself, so I bought her a drink."

Lisa held her breath waiting for Rat's response. Rick's answer had been very transparent. Any American male past the age of eighteen knew how that story ended. Gaines, however, seemed to accept Rick's answer at face value. He was too much of a southern gentleman to ask what had happened after the drink, but he knew full well that the evening had not ended in the bar. He had seen it on Lisa's face the moment he spotted the two of them together.

Well, at least she has good taste, Gaines thought. She hadn't gone to bed with an REMF. The Kaz seemed to be an okay kind of guy. He winced inwardly, but kept a pleasant look on his face. He didn't own Lisa, and ever since she had returned from her little R and R, they had been on much better terms. He was not about to rock the boat over anything as trivial as a little shot of strange stuff.

Gaines liked to think of himself as being a big boy. What Lisa wanted to do when she was away from him was her own

318

business. He relaxed a little more and started talking to Kasnowski about the problems of commanding companies in Vietnam.

Lisa relaxed, too. It seemed that her secret was safe. She deeply appreciated the fact that Rick was willing to let their one night together be just that. One incredible night that she would never forget.

As the two men talked, a drunken major wearing general staff brass on his collar weaved his way up to the bar and stood next to her. "Hi, baby," he slurred, leering at her. "How 'bout if I buy you a little drink?"

"No, thank you," she answered before either Rat or Kasnowski could respond.

"Aw, come on," he whined, his eyes blatantly focused on Lisa's prominent breasts. "Just a little drink. Won't hurt nothin' if you have a drink with me."

"No," she said again firmly and stepped back out of his reach.

The man recoiled at her sharp tone. "Frigid bitch," he snarled. "All you nurses are nothing but a bunch of fucking prick teasers. You're all fucking talk. You never put out."

Gaines, Rick, and Lisa all burst out laughing at the same time.

The drunk gazed at them with a puzzled expression on his face. "What's so fucking funny?" he asked.

"You want him?" Kasnowski offered, openly acknowledging Rat's prior claim to the defense of Lisa's honor.

"Thank you," Rat bowed like the southern gentleman that he was. "I appreciate the offer, but I think that she can probably handle this one on her own."

The drunk was pissed at being laughed at. He lunged out and grabbed Lisa's arm. Without even thinking, her knee came up, slamming into the man's crotch. The major went down to his knees, gasping for breath, both of his hands protectively covering his genitals. Rat and Kaz scooped him up by the arms. "Back in a flash, love," Rat said, with a big grin. "We've got to dump the garbage."

Lisa laughed and watched her men drag the major away.

CHAPTER 44

Special Forces CCC Kontum

Major Snow stood in front of the big map in his office and stared at the red grease-pencil marks showing the locations of the enemy activity that Wilburn's team had reported.

"Do you think MACV's going to act on this, Ice Man?" Colonel Grimes asked.

"I don't know, sir." Snow shrugged his shoulders. "But my feeling is that they won't, and I don't know how to make them take this thing seriously."

He tapped the map. "Wilburn's stuff looks real good to me and I think that his assessment's right in line. It ties right in with bits and pieces of information that I've been picking up for the last six months now. But there's no way to tell how those clowns down in Saigon are going to react to something that goes counter to what they've been telling everyone for months."

The Hungarian major turned and stared out the window at the lighted perimeter. "They've got a real problem down there in Saigon, Colonel. They've been feeding bullshit to the press and the American public for so long they've started believing it themselves."

Grimes chuckled. He could always count on the Hungarian major to cut through the layers and layers of bullshit. "They've been talking about this 'end of the tunnel' garbage for so long that they've completely ignored what's been happening out in the field lately. Now when Westmoreland tells President Johnson something, regardless of how often we tell them that their estimates are wrong, it becomes the gospel truth and they base their plans on it. The real problem is that Westy's been lied to or misinformed so many times by ass-kissing staff officers who don't want to rock the boat he doesn't know what the truth is anymore, and that frightens me."

"Sir," Snow asked, his voice filled with frustration. "How did it ever get to be this way? What happened to the concept of a commander making his decisions based on what he learns from the battlefield?"

"Ice Man, you're out of touch with the modern world," Grimes told him, shaking his head. "You're talking about something that's a thing of the past. This is a political war now, Snow. The White House even tells bomber crews when and where to drop their bombs. You're an anachronism here. You should have served with Rommel in North Africa. Now that was a commander who only believed what he saw with his own eyes. Shit, he even used to take his armored car out ahead of his lines and make his own recons."

Snow laughed. "I can just see that bunch of MACV lardasses in Saigon going out on a recon patrol. They'd shit themselves before they left the wire," Snow continued with a note of resignation in his voice. "I've sent Wilburn's intell forward, including the photos. Now all we can do is sit back and wait to see what they do with it."

The CCC commander studied his operations officer intently. "You really think that they're going to hit during the Tet holiday, don't you?"

Snow met his eyes squarely. "Yes, sir, I do. I can feel it. I just can't believe that MACV is so stupid as to accept this half-assed offer of a Tet truce. A blindman could see through that. Instead of a truce, we should be on a full red alert with everything we have out looking for those little bastards." He clenched his fists in frustration. "For Christ's sake! The NVA have broken every truce that they've ever signed, every last, single one. Can't those people down in Saigon even read their own files? The North Vietnamese only call for a truce when they're up to something."

Now the Ice Man was off and running on his favorite topic, the futility of ever trusting a communist.

"With this truce approved, everybody will be fucking off and no one will be minding the store. Most of the ARVNS will be gone on holiday and now the U.S. forces will be stood down as well. We might as well just invite the little bastards in for dinner. Jesus!"

"Maybe the truce will work this time."

"Well, maybe they can teach a fucking fish to fly, too, sir."

Grimes laughed.

"Colonel, mark my words. The dinks are up to something big. We've been watching it build up for months now. All along the border we've had reports of increased troop movement, to say nothing of what the Roadrunner teams have seen moving down from the north on the Ho Chi Minh Trail. It's coming, I promise you." Major Snow dug into his back pocket and brought out his wallet. "I've got a hundred dollars here that says we're going to get our dicks knocked stiff tomorrow night, January twenty-ninth, the start of the Tet truce. Shit, sir, I'll make it a thousand dollars."

Grimes held up his hand. "I know better than to bet with you, Snow. This time, though, I just hope to hell that you're wrong."

The Ice Man looked out the window. The dark shadows beyond the perimeter lights could be hiding an enemy regiment at that very moment.

"So do I, sir," he said softly. "So do I."

That evening in Saigon, Lieutenant Colonel Ron Hardy of the MACV G-2 staff had his feet propped comfortably up on his oak desk. A cup of coffee was ready at hand as he went through the last of the day's intelligence reports. Like people who save the comic section of the daily newspaper to read last, he always saved the summary of the reports that filtered down from the Special Forces units in the field so he could have a good laugh before he quit for the day.

The colonel was in a real hurry, though, so he scanned through them quickly. Madame Lin, the half-French wife of his ARVN counterpart was throwing a Tet party for the G-2 staff. Missing one of Lin's parties was unthinkable. They were the high point of the Saigon social scene, and both the ambassador and General Westmoreland would be there. A man such as himself who aspired to higher rank could not afford to miss it.

As he flipped through the pages, he came across the photos Wilburn had taken of the NVA supply dump hidden under the trees. He barely glanced at them. They were just more pictures of the goddamned jungle. He tossed them aside, scanned the summary of Wilburn's operation, and laughed when he came to the part about the pig woman being an NVA spy. It required a very active imagination to be in the Special Forces, but why did they all think they were James Bond incarnate?

Hardy scribbled a note to remind himself to contact SFOB in Nha Trang, the Special Forces headquarters. He was going to tell them to quit sending him garbage. He had better things to do. He extracted Wilburn's report from the rest of the summary and dropped the remainder in his out-box.

He drained the last of his coffee. Getting to his feet, he crumpled Wilburn's photos and reports into a tight ball and tossed the wad into the trash can. Madame Lin's Tet party was just getting started. He didn't want to be late.

GLOSSARY

ALPHA   The military phonetic for *A*

AA   Antiaircraft weapons

AC   Aircraft commander, the pilot

Acting jack   Acting NCO

Affirm   Short for affirmative, yes

AFVN   Armed Forces Vietnam Network

Agency, the   The CIA

AIT   Advanced individual training

AJ   Acting jack

AK-47   The Russian 7.62mm Kalashnikov assault rifle

AO   Area of operation

Ao dai   Traditional Vietnamese female dress

APH-5   Helicopter crewman's flight helmet

APO   Army post office

ARA   Aerial rocket artillery, armed helicopters

Arc light   B-52 bomb strike

ARCOM   Army Commendation Medal

ARP   Aero Rifle Platoon, the Blue Team

Article 15   Disciplinary action

ARVN   Army of the Republic of Vietnam, also a South Vietnamese soldier

ASAP As soon as possible
Ash and trash Clerks, jerks, and other REMFs
A-Team The basic Special Forces unit, ten men
AWOL Absent without leave

BRAVO The military phonetic for *B*
B-40 Chinese version of the RPG antitank weapon
Bac si Vietnamese for "doctor"
Bad Paper Dishonorable discharge
Ba-muoi-ba Beer "33," the local brew
Banana clip A thirty-round magazine for the M-1 carbine
Bao Chi Vietnamese for "press" or "news media"
Basic Boot camp
BCT Basic Combat Training, boot camp
BDA Bomb damage assessment
Be Nice Universal expression of the war
Biet (Bic) Vietnamese for "Do you understand?"
Bird An aircraft, usually a helicopter
Bloods Black soldiers
Blooper The M-79 40mm grenade launcher
Blues, the An aero rifle platoon
Body count Number of enemy killed
Bookoo Vietnamese slang for "many," from French *beaucoup*
Bought the farm Killed
Brown bar A second lieutenant
Brass Monkey Interagency radio call for help
Brew Usually beer, sometimes coffee
Bring smoke To cause trouble for someone, to shoot
Broken down Disassembled or nonfunctional
Bubble top The bell OH-13 observation helicopter
Buddha Zone Heaven
Bush The jungle
'Bush Short for ambush
Butter bar A second lieutenant

CHARLIE   The military phonetic for *C*

C-4   Plastic explosive

C-rats   C rations

CA   A combat assault by helicopter

Cam ong   Vietnamese for "thank you"

C&C   Command and control helicopter

Chao   (Chow) Vietnamese greeting

Charlie   Short for Victor Charlie, the enemy

Charlie tango   Control tower

Cherry   A new man in your unit

Cherry boy   A virgin

Chickenplate   Helicopter crewman's armored vest

Chi-Com   Chinese Communist

Chieu hoi   A program where VC/NVA could surrender and become scouts for the Army

Choi oi   Vietnamese exclamation

CIB   The Combat Infantryman's Badge

CID   Criminal Investigation Unit

Clip   Ammo magazine

CMOH   Congressional Medal of Honor

CO   Commanding officer

Cobra   The AH-1 attack helicopter

Cockbang   Bangkok, Thailand

Conex   A metal shipping container

Coz   Short for Cosmoline, a preservative

CP   Command post

CSM   Command sergeant major

Cunt Cap   The narrow green cap worn with the class A uniform

DELTA   The military phonetic for *D*

Dash 13   The helicopter maintenance report

Dau   Vietnamese for "pain"

Deadlined   Down for repairs

Dep   Vietnamese for "beautiful"

DEROS   Date of estimated return from overseas service

Deuce and a half   Military two-and-a-half-ton truck

DFC Distinguished Flying Cross

DI Drill instructor

Di di Vietnamese for "Go!"

Di di mau Vietnamese for "Go fast!"

Dink Short for *dinky-dau*, derogatory slang term for Vietnamese

Dinky-dau Vietnamese for "crazy!"

Disneyland East The Pentagon

Disneyland Far East The MACV or USARV headquarters

DMZ Demilitarized zone separating North and South Vietnam

Dog tags Stainless steel tags listing a man's name, serial number, blood type and religious preference

Donut Dolly A Red Cross girl

Doom-pussy Danang officers' open mess

Door gunner A soldier who mans a door gun

Drag The last man in a patrol

Dung lai Vietnamese for "Halt!"

Dustoff A medevac helicopter

ECHO The military phonetic for *E*. Also, radio code for east

Eagle flight A heliborne assault

Early out An unscheduled ETS

Eighty-one The M-29 81mm mortar

Eleven bravo An infantryman's MOS

EM Enlisted man

ER Emergency room (hospital)

ETA Estimated time of arrival

ETS Estimated time of separation from service

Extract To pull out by helicopter

FOXTROT The military phonetic for *F*

FAC Forward air controller

Fart sack sleeping bag

Field phone Hand-generated portable phone used in bunkers
Fifty The U.S. .50 caliber M-2 heavy machine gun
Fifty-one The Chi-Com 12.7mm heavy machine gun
Fini Vietnamese for "ended" or "stopped"
First Louie First lieutenant
First Shirt An Army first sergeant
First Team Motto of the First Air Cavalry Division
Flak jacket Infantry body armor
FNG Fucking new guy
FOB Fly over border mission
Forty-five The U.S. .45 caliber M-1911 automatic pistol
Fox 4 The F-4 Phantom II jet fighter
Foxtrot mike delta Fuck me dead
Foxtrot tosser A flamethrower
Frag A fragmentation grenade
FTA Fuck the army

GOLF The military phonetic for *G*
Gaggle A loose formation of choppers
Get some To fight, kill someone
GI Government issue, an American soldier
Gook A Vietnamese
Grease gun The U.S. .45 caliber M-3 Submachine Gun
Green Berets The U.S. Army's Special Forces
Green Machine The Army
Grunt An infantryman
Gunship Army attack helicopter armed with machine guns and rockets

HOTEL The military phonetic for *H*
Ham and motherfuckers The C ration meal of ham and lima beans
Hard core NVA or VC regulars
Heavy gun team Three gunships working together
Hercky Bird The Air Force C-130 Hercules Transport plane

Ho Chi Minh Trail The NVA supply line

Hog The M-60 machine gun

Horn A radio or telephone

Hot LZ A landing zone under hostile fire

House Cat An REMF

Huey The Bell UH-1 helicopter, the troop-carrying workhorse of the war.

INDIA The military phonetic for *I*

IC Installation commander

IG Inspector general

IHTFP I hate this fucking place

In-country Within Vietnam

Insert Movement into an area by helicopter

Intel Military Intelligence

IP Initial point. The place that a gunship starts its gun run

IR Infrared

JULIET The military phonetic for *J*

Jackoff flare A hand-held flare

JAG Judge advocate general

Jeep In Nam, the Ford M-151 quarter-ton truck

Jelly Donut A fat Red Cross girl

Jesus Nut The nut that holds the rotor assembly of a chopper together

Jet Ranger The Bell OH-58 helicopter

Jody A girlfriend back in the States

Jolly Green Giant The HH-3E Chinook heavy-lift helicopter

Jungle fatigues Lightweight tropical uniform

KILO The military phonetic for *K*

K-fifty The NVA 7.62mm type 50 submachine gun

Khakis The tropical class A uniform

KIA Killed in action

Kimchi Korean pickled vegetables

Klick   A kilometer
KP   Kitchen Police, mess-hall duty

LIMA   The military phonetic for *L*
Lager   A camp or to make camp
Lai dai   Vietnamese for "come here"
LAW   Light antitank weapon. The M-72 66mm rocket launcher
Lay dead   To fuck off
Lay dog   Lie low in jungle during recon patrol
LBJ   The military jail at Long Binh Junction
Leg   A nonairborne infantryman
Lifeline   The strap securing a doorgunner on a chopper
Lifer   A career soldier
Links   The metal clips holding machine gun ammo belts together
LLDB   *Luc Luong Dac Biet*, the ARVN Special Forces
Loach   The small Hughes OH-6 observation helicopter
Long Nose   Vietnamese slang for "American"
Long Tom   The M-107 175mm long-range artillery gun
LP   Listening post
LRRP   Long-range recon patrol
LSA   Lubrication, small-arms gun oil
Lurp   Freeze-dried rations carried on LRRPs
LZ   Landing zone

MIKE   The military phonetic for *M*
M-14   The U.S. 7.62mm rifle
M-16   The U.S. 5.56mm Colt-Armalite rifle
M-26   Fragmentation grenade
M-60   The U.S. 7.62mm infantry machine gun
M-79   The U.S. 40mm grenade launcher
MACV   Military Assistance Command Vietnam
Ma Deuce   The M-2 .50 caliber heavy machine gun
Magazine   Metal container that feeds bullets into weapons; holds twenty or thirty rounds per unit
Mag pouch   A magazine carrier worn on the field belt

Mama San An older Vietnamese woman

MAST Mobile Army Surgical Team

Mech Mechanized infantry

Medevac Medical Evacuation chopper

Mess hall GI dining facility

MF Motherfucker

MG Machine gun

MI Military intelligence units

MIA Missing in action

Mike Radio code for minute

Mike Force Green Beret mobile strike force

Mike-mike Millimeters

Mike papa Military police

Minigun A 7.62mm Gatling gun

Mister Zippo A flamethrower operator

Monkey House Vietnamese slang for "jail"

Monster Twelve to twenty-one claymore antipersonnel mines jury-rigged to detonate simultaneously

Montagnard Hill tribesmen of the Central Highlands

Mop Vietnamese for "fat"

Motengator Motherfucker

MPC Military payment certificate, issued to GIs in RVN in lieu of greenbacks

Muster A quick assemblage of soldiers with little or no warning

My Vietnamese for "American"

NOVEMBER The military phonetic for *N*. Also, radio code for north

NCO Noncommissioned officer

Negative Radio talk for "no"

Net A radio network

Newbie A new GI in-country

Next A GI so short that he is the next to go home

Niner The military pronunciation of the number 9

Ninety The M-67 90mm recoilless rifle

Number One Very good, the best

Number ten Bad

Number ten thousand Very bad, the worst

Nuoc nam A Vietnamese fish sauce

NVA The North Vietnamese Army, also a North Vietnamese soldier

OSCAR The military phonetic for *O*

OCS Officer candidate school

OCS Manual A comic book

OD Olive drab

Old Man, the A commander

One five one The M-151 jeep

One oh five The 105mm howitzer

One twenty-two The Russian 122mm ground-launched rocket

OR Hospital operating room

Out-country Out of Vietnam

PAPA The military phonetic for *P*

P Piaster, Vietnamese currency

P-38 C ration can opener

PA Public address system

Papa San An older Vietnamese man

Papa sierra Platoon sergeant

PAVN Peoples Army of Vietnam, the NVA

PCS Permanent change of station, a transfer

Peter pilot Copilot

PF Popular Forces, Vietnamese militia

PFC Private first class

Piece Any weapon

Pig The M-60 machine gun

Pink Team Observation helicopters teamed up with gunships

Phantom The McDonnell F-4 jet fighter

Phu Vietnamese noodle soup

Point The most dangerous position on patrol. The point

man walks ahead and to the side of the others, acting as a lookout

POL Petroleum, oil, lubricants

Police To clean up

POL point A GI gas station

Pony soldiers The First Air Cav troopers

Pop smoke To set off a smoke grenade

Prang To crash a chopper, or land roughly

Prep Artillery preparation of an LZ

PRG Provisional Revolutionary Government (the Communists)

Prick-25 The AN/PRC-25 tactical radio

Profile A medical exemption from duty

Project Phoenix CIA assassination operations

PSP Perforated steel planking used to make runways

Psy-Ops Psychological Operations

PT Physical training

Puff the Magic Dragon The heavily armed AC-47 fire support aircraft

Purple Heart, the A medal awarded for wounds received in combat

Puzzle Palace Any headquarters

PX Post exchange

PZ Pickup zone

QUEBEC The military phonetic for *Q*

QC *Quan Cahn*, Vietnamese Military Police

Quad fifty Four .50 caliber MG's mounted together

ROMEO The military phonetic for *R*

RA Regular army, a lifer

Railroad Tracks The twin-silver-bar captain's rank insignia

R&R Rest and relaxation

Ranger Specially trained infantry troops

Rat fuck A completely confused situation

Recondo Recon commando

Red Leg An artilleryman
Red Team Armed helicopters
Regular A well-equipped enemy soldier
REMF Rear echelon motherfucker
Re-up Reenlistment
RIF Recon in force
Rikky-tik Quickly or fast
Ring knocker A West Point officer
Road runner Green Beret recon teams
Rock and roll Automatic weapons fire
Roger Radio talk for ''yes'' or ''I understand''
ROK The Republic of Korea or a Korean soldier
Rotor The propellor blades of a helicopter
Round An item of ammunition
Round Eye Vietnamese slang for ''Caucasian''
RPD The Russian 7.62mm light machine gun
RPG The Russian 77mm rocket-propelled grenade anti-
   tank weapon
RTO Radio telephone operator
Ruck Racksack
RVN The Republic of Vietnam, South Vietnam

SIERRA The military phonetic for *S*. Also, radio code
   for south
Saddle up To move out
Saigon commando A REMF
SAM Surface-to-air missile
Same-same Vietnamese slang for ''the same as''
Sapper An NVA demolition/explosives expert
SAR Downed chopper rescue mission
Sau Vietnamese slang for ''a lie''
Say again Radio code to repeat the last message
Scramble An alert reaction to call for help, CA, or res-
   cue operation
Scrip *See* MPC
SEALS Navy commandos
7.62 The 7.62 ammunition for the M-14 and the M-60

SF Special Forces
Shithook The CH-47 Chinook helicopter
Short Being almost finished with your tour in Nam
Short timer Someone who is short
Shotgun An armed escort
Sierra Echo Southeast (northwest is November Whiskey, etc)
Sin City Bars and whorehouses
Single-digit midget A short timer with less then ten days left to go in The Nam
Sitrep Situation report
Six Radio code for a commander
Sixteen The M-16 rifle
Skate To fuck off
SKS The Russian 7.62mm carbine
Slack The man behind the point
Slick A Huey
Slicksleeves A private E-1
Slope A Vietnamese
Slug A bullet
Smoke Colored smoke signal grenades
SNAFU Situation normal, all fucked up
Snake The AH-1 Cobra attack chopper
SOL Shit Outta Luck
SOP Standard operating procedure
Sorry 'bout that Universal saying used in Nam
Special Forces The Army's elite counterguerrilla unit
Spiderhole A one-man foxhole
Spooky The AC-67 fire-support aircraft
Stand down A vacation
Starlite A sniper scope
Steel pot The GI steel helmet
Striker A member of a SF strike force
Sub-gunny Substitute doorgunner
Sweat hog A fat REMF

TANGO The military phonetic for *T*
TA-50 A GI's issue field gear

TAC Air Tactical Air Support

TDY Temporary duty assignment

Terr Terrorist

Tet The Vietnamese New Year

"33" Local Vietnamese beer

Thumper The M-79 40mm grenade launcher

Tiger suit A camouflage uniform

Ti ti Vietnamese slang for "little"

TOC Tactical Operations Center

TOP An Army first sergeant

Tour 365 The year-long tour of duty a GI spends in RVN

Tower rat Tower guard

Tracer Ammunition containing a chemical that burns in flight to mark its path

Track Any tracked vehicle

Triage The process in which medics determine which wounded they can best help, and which will die

Trip flare A ground illumination flare

Trooper Soldier

Tube steak Hot dogs

Tunnel rat A soldier who goes into NVA tunnels

Turtle Your replacement

201 File One's personnel records

Two-point-five Gunship rockets

Type 56 Chi-Com version of the AK-47

Type 68 Chi-Com version of the SKS

UNIFORM The military phonetic for *U*

UCMJ The Uniform Code of Military Justice

Unass To get up and move

Uncle Short for Uncle Sam

USARV United States Army Vietnam

Utilities Marine fatigues

VICTOR The military phonetic for *V*

VC The Viet Cong

Victor Charlie Viet Cong
Viet Cong South Vietnamese Communists
Ville Short for village
VNAF The South Vietnamese Air Force
VNP Vietnamese National Police
Void Vicious Final approach to a hot LZ, or the jungle when hostile
Vulcan A 20mm Gatling-gun cannon

WHISKEY The military phonetic for *W*. Also, radio code for west.
Wake-up The last day one expects to be in-country
Warrant officer Pilots
Waste To kill
Wax To kill
Web belt Utility belt GIs use to carry gear, sidearms, etc.
Web gear A GI's field equipment
Whiskey papa White phosphorus weapons
White mice Vietnamese National Police
White team Observation helicopters
WIA Wounded in action
Wilco Radio code for "will comply"
Willie Peter White phosphorus
Wire, the Defensive barbed wire
World, the The United States

X-RAY The military phonetic for *Z*
Xin loi Vietnamese for "sorry 'bout that"
XM-21 Gunship weapon package
XO Executive officer

YANKEE The military phonetic for *Y*
Yarde Short for Montagnard

ZULU The military phonetic for *Z*
Zap To kill
Zilch Less than nothing

Zip   A derogatory term for a Vietnamese
Zippo   A flamethrower
Zoomie   An Air Force pilot

Zip A derogatory term for a Vietnamese national
Zippo A flamethrower
Zoomie An Air Force pilot

ABOUT THE AUTHOR

The author served two tours of duty in Vietnam as an infantry company commander. His combat awards and decorations include the Combat Infantryman's Badge, three Bronze Star medals, the Air Medal, the Army Commendation Medal, and the Vietnamese Cross of Gallantry. He has written four novels and numerous magazine articles about the war. He and his wife make their home in Portland, Oregon.

Vietnamese "Tet" New Year, 1968. Communist forces break the cease-fire and launch a massive assault against the cities of South Vietnam. Fighting street to street, house to house, hand to hand, Treat Brody and the men of the Blues retake the ancient city of Hue in . . .

SURPRISE ATTACK!